Someone to Hold

Someone to Hold

A Novel

ANITA STANSFIELD

Covenant Communications, Inc.

Covenant.

Cover photograph © Maren Ogden Photography

Cover design copyrighted 2002 by Covenant Communications, Inc.

Published by Covenant Communications, Inc.
American Fork, Utah

Printed in the United States of America
First Printing: February 2002

09 08 07 06 05 04 03 02   10 9 8 7 6 5 4 3 2 1

ISBN 1-57734-991-1

Prologue

Salt Lake City, Utah

Christina Hardy opened the door with a key and walked into the kitchen, inhaling the sweetness of home that she felt each time she entered. Leaving the cold, January air behind only added to the coziness and security surrounding her. Just last week she had enjoyed celebrating the arrival of a new year with family and friends, and she felt extremely grateful for all she had. Life wasn't perfect, by any means. But she loved her home, she loved her husband, and she had three beautiful, healthy children. And now she'd been offered a promotion at work that made her feel on top of the world. She had no intention of taking the job. Working part-time during the middle of the day, while her children were in school, suited her just fine. The little gift shop in a downtown mall was the perfect place to work. It gave her just enough income to help with the extras that were needed in raising a family, but her job was free of pressure and stress. The offer of promotion to manager of the store held no fascination whatsoever for her. She was capable of doing the job, and flattered that it had been offered. But she liked her life just the way it was, and had no desire to change it.

Christina was shuffling through the mail when she heard the door open. She turned to see her husband, Keith, appear in the kitchen.

"This is a nice surprise," she said. "What brings you home this time of day?"

His silence brought her attention to the severity in his eyes, and her heart quickened with dread. "What's wrong?" she demanded. "Did you get laid off? Are you—"

"No, nothing like that," he said. "But I do need to talk to you . . . and it can't wait any longer."

"Any longer?" she echoed, feeling the implication settle into the pit of her stomach. Whatever was wrong had been wrong before now—without her knowledge.

While she attempted to gather the words to ask, he said firmly, "Sit down, Christy."

Christy took two careful steps backward and sank awkwardly into a chair beside the dining table. Keith sat across from her without meeting her eyes. While she expected him to reach for her hand in a common gesture of facing their challenges together, he leaned back in a way that seemed to encourage distance between them.

"What is it?" she demanded when he said nothing. He glanced at her sharply but still he didn't speak. "You're scaring me, Keith," she said with a little laugh that didn't begin to disguise her rising fear. Still he remained silent, as if the words he needed to say were far too difficult to gather. Christy tried to imagine what could possibly be so hard. They'd been married nearly fifteen years, sharing the ins and outs of everyday living. They'd brought three children into the world and worked together to raise them. They'd endured financial struggles, illness and accidents, and many disagreements. But the less-than-perfect state of their lives had always been buffered by the eternal bonds they shared. The prospect of eternity had always put the pettiness of their human frailties into perspective. But looking at her husband now, Christy felt a growing dread that she was about to be tested in a way she'd never fathomed. The anticipation began to completely unnerve her and she blurted, "Just say it and get it over with."

He cleared his throat loudly and looked away. "Okay, fine," he said. "I keep hoping I'll come up with a way to say it that won't hurt you, but I guess we just have to accept that's impossible." Christy sucked in her breath just before he added in a hard voice, "I'm leaving you, Christy. It's over."

A one-syllable noise erupted from Christy's mouth, something between a laugh and a sob. *"Leaving?"* she choked, wondering if this could possibly be a joke, or if it was the absolute horror it seemed to be.

"That's right," he said. "I've been leading a double life for quite some time now. It's time I came clean. It can't go on this way. I have to go."

Through an excruciating silence, Christy managed to assemble a reasonable thought in the midst of her fogged brain. "You can't come clean and *stay?*"

He looked abruptly away. "No," he said, "I can't."

That horrible noise came out of her mouth again, betraying the absolute shock that any human being would feel when told that life on planet earth had ceased to exist, and in fact, had perhaps never existed as it had been perceived. "I can't believe it," she said, more to herself. And then to him, "How can you just . . . just . . . throw away everything we have for . . . for what? *What?*"

"I'm sorry, Christy. The last thing I want to do is hurt you, but . . ."

"But living a lie and leaving me high and dry are meant to . . . what? What, Keith?"

He looked away and stated firmly, "I have to leave."

"And that's it?"

"Yes, that's it. You have every reason in the world to hate me, and I would never expect you to forgive me. But this is the way it has to be."

"According to whom? What say do I have in this?" He didn't answer and she continued, "What have I done to bring this on?" Still he said nothing. "I realize we had our disagreements, and our marriage wasn't perfect, but we had a lot going for us—or at least I thought we did. Has your apparent contentment here just been some kind of . . . charade?" His eyes told her it had been, and she bit her trembling lip. "Did I not love you enough, treat you good enough? Did I not give you enough to make you happy?"

"The reasons don't matter, Christy."

"Would that be because the reason is . . ." she forced herself to say it. She had to know the truth. "Are you trying to tell me there's someone else?"

He gave her a hard stare that clearly said what he obviously didn't want to say. Christy felt her insides grow cold as he said, "I know it's hard, but what we had is all in the past."

"It seems to be in the present . . . at least it is for me."

"I know I'm not being fair, but you're just going to have to accept it and move on."

"I see," she said, feeling as if she'd turned to glass, and he'd just hit her with a sledgehammer. She'd couldn't fathom ever putting the pieces back together. *Ever.*

She was startled from her thoughts when he mumbled, "That's all I have to say. I'm sorry." He jumped to his feet and rushed from the room.

Christy followed, feeling a desperation with no point of reference. Never in her life had she been so thoroughly frightened and confused. "That's all you have to say?" she echoed. "I've given you fifteen years of my life, and that's all you have to say?" She watched in horror as he tossed two pieces of luggage on the bed and haphazardly threw clothes and belongings into them. "Keith!" she shouted when he made no response. He looked up sharply but said nothing. "Talk to me, for the love of heaven! We've shared *everything!* We have three children. Does that mean nothing to you?"

"It means a great deal to me, Chris, but it doesn't change what I have to do now."

He continued packing while Christy's mind frantically searched for possible pleas to make him stay. She forced back her tears and stated in a shaky voice, "Okay, Keith, so you made a mistake. We can work it through. Forgiveness is possible. If we could just—"

"Listen to me, Christy, and listen carefully." His eyes took on an unfamiliar hardness that deepened her fear. "The mistake would be to stay. She's my eternal soul mate, Christy. I know that now. Don't make this any harder."

Christy felt as if she'd fallen from a great height to land flat on her back. The wind rushed from her lungs, leaving a tangible pain burning in her chest. She wilted onto the bedroom carpet, barely managing to remain sitting, with no will to move or speak while he finished packing. *Eternal soul mate?* A memory of kneeling with Keith at a temple altar made her suddenly nauseous. While the temptation to scream or sob or beg threatened to barge through the shock, she tightened her fists and told herself that her dignity was all she had left.

"I'll get the rest of my things next week," he said, moving toward the bedroom door with a suitcase in each hand.

Christy felt the threat and finality of his departure and forced her voice past the shock enough to say, "What will I tell the children?"

"Tell them whatever you have to."

Logic pressed her to demand, "And how will we manage? You know my income would never—"

"I'll send money," he said coldly, as if doing so would be a great inconvenience.

Their eyes met and the hovering emotion crept close to the surface. In her mind she could see herself slapping him, screaming at him, demanding to know how he could do this to her. But she only countered his gaze with eyes that she hoped would express some degree of the horror she felt too numb to express.

"Good-bye," he said. And her next awareness was the closing of the door.

Christy startled herself from staring at the carpet to glance around the room. It was the same room it had been a few minutes ago. Same curtains. Same furniture. Same house. But everything had changed. *Everything!* And she couldn't even begin to imagine how she would make it through the next hour, let alone keep herself together enough to tell her children that the man she had chosen to be their father had turned out to be deceitful and selfish.

"Help me, Father," she murmured into the emptiness surrounding her, hoping that her feeble prayer would somehow break past the wall of fear and cynicism she felt accumulating around her. "Oh, help me," she cried, feeling the shock dissipate as the pain rushed in to drown her. She pressed her face to the floor and heaved one painful sob after another. But instinctively she knew that no amount of tears could ever free her from the incomparable agony of what Keith Hardy had just done to her life.

Chapter One

Christy awoke in a familiar cold sweat and groaned to recall the content of her dream. Same old dream, week after week, month after month. Every waking minute she was preoccupied with the results of her former husband's bad choices. And even in sleep she couldn't find peace or reprieve.

Forcing her mind to the present, she sat up abruptly and glanced at the clock. She'd shut off the alarm and gone back to sleep. "Oh, garbage!" she muttered and hurried into the shower. Being late today could be disastrous. At least she didn't have to wake the children and get them going. That was *one* advantage to having them out of school for Christmas vacation. She had yet to think of another one. At this point in her life, the very idea of Christmas was like an oncoming freight train, continually reminding her that last Christmas they had been a family, and all had been well. No, not well, she had to remind herself. It had only seemed well because she'd chosen to be oblivious to the signs of an unfaithful husband. The betrayal and deceit were worse, by far, than the actual reality of being a single parent.

Christy quickly blew dry her shoulder-length, medium brown hair and brushed it through, grateful that straight hair was in style. She put barely a minute's worth of makeup onto her chiseled features, and wearing mismatched socks beneath her khaki trousers, she headed out the door, taking a detour through each of the children's rooms to wake them only enough to let them know she was leaving. With the door locked behind her, she drove the long, snowbanked winding road that led from the canyon neighborhood where she lived, onto the highway that would take her into the heart of Salt

Lake City. Once she got out of the canyon, a quick call on the cell phone guaranteed that her assistant manager would be there to see that the door to the little store she managed would be open on time to accommodate early-morning Christmas shoppers.

The Christmas decor of the city was beautiful, as it always had been. But for the first time in her life, Christy resented the oncoming holiday. How could she not think about all the years when she had spent the holidays with her husband, always believing that their marriage was good and they would be together forever? The divorce had gone through quickly, mostly because Keith had been anxious to marry his *eternal soul mate*. Christy had spent the ensuing months trying to convince herself that she was better off without a man who had deceived and betrayed her. But she missed him, she loved him, and she just couldn't seem to accept that life could go on without him. A thousand times she had asked herself if her longing for him to come back was simply force of habit or wishful thinking; or did these feelings mean that eventually they would be back together again? Was she so accustomed to believing that their marriage was the center of her life, that she couldn't accept any other idea? Or would he at some point realize he'd made a mistake and come back to her?

Just as hundreds of times before, the questions had no answers. She had prayed endlessly for the guidance she needed to press forward on the path best for her. But she could see no other path beyond wanting her life to go back to the way it was, while a cloud of confusion and discouragement hovered over her continually.

Tomorrow was Christmas Eve, and the last thing Christy wanted was to celebrate. How could she find any pleasant anticipation in knowing that Keith would be taking the children Christmas Day, and keeping them for days? The very idea of having her family divided through this holiday season hurt more deeply than she could express. But she had to put on a smile for her children and get through; they were the most important thing in all of this, and she would not see their holiday dampened by her sour mood. They had already struggled more than any children deserved to. The divorce had been hard on them, and she'd done her best to carry them through varied degrees of anger, depression, and bad behavior. Only during the last few weeks had all three of them begun to show signs of normalcy.

And she would not let her own continuing discouragement tempt them back to the struggles they'd just emerged from.

Christy parked in the multilevel garage of the mall and hurried to the store that she had managed for eleven months now. She couldn't deny being grateful for the job, and for the fact that she actually enjoyed her work. If only she didn't have to work such long hours, and be away from the children. *Keep perspective,* she reminded herself. *You have much to be grateful for.*

Christy entered the store to find only one customer, whose purchase was being rung up at the counter.

"Good morning," Rodney said to Christy while he was handing the woman her change.

"Good morning," Christy replied and walked past him to her little office just off the back storage room. She took off her coat, looked over a few papers on the desk, then went out to the counter where Rodney was replacing the tape in the cash register. Rodney Hillam had worked in this store nearly as long as she had. He was in his late twenties, married, with one small boy. He was reliable and had a great deal of integrity. They had quickly become friends via working together, and he had been supportive and kind through her divorce.

"Store looks great," she said, knowing he had closed last night and opened this morning. "You do good work."

"Of course," he said with a little chuckle.

Knowing he had things under control, Christy quickly checked over the store books, made a few phone calls to place some orders and clear up a mistake on an invoice. Then she pulled out her checkbook and quickly figured out where she stood. Since she was paid a salary, and always put in much more than forty hours a week, she felt good about using little snatches of time to keep up on her own life. She'd earned a healthy bonus for her good sales record this past year, and she had carefully used pieces of it to pay off a few little bills, and get a barely adequate Christmas for the kids. She thought of all the little extras that had become holiday traditions through the years—traditions that had been drastically altered by circumstances beyond her control. She had prayed and stewed over how to appropriately adjust their Christmas celebration in light of their new situation. And she'd felt good about letting go of some of those extras that simply didn't matter when it came down to the true meaning of the holiday. She had weighed her plans and her finances carefully, while words from a sacrament meeting talk had hovered in the back of her mind. Some time in October, a sweet sister in her ward had spoken on the blessings of tithes and offerings, quoting the scriptures from Malachi related to the Lord's promises. And a particular phrase had stuck in her head all these weeks, as if the Spirit were trying to teach her something by its repeated suggestion: *Prove me now herewith . . . if I will not open you the windows of heaven.*

Now that she'd reached this point, with her December bills paid, and a little set aside in savings, she looked at the amount she had left and wondered where to put it. The money she had wouldn't go very far in light of the nearly five-thousand-dollar debt she had, mostly consisting of legal fees and court costs related to the divorce. Each time she thought of the debt, she became angry all over again for Keith's antagonism over her wanting the house. She reminded herself that anger would get her nowhere, and she uttered a quick prayer over where she should put the few hundred dollars she had left, when she knew she'd have no more extra money for months. If these legal bills went unpaid until she got another bonus, her credit rating could be messed up for years. And deep inside she felt a keen temptation to rush out and do some last-minute Christmas shopping to get her children some of the extras they couldn't afford.

While she was still debating and weighing her options, Rodney poked his head in to say, "It's getting busy and Mazie's late. I could use your help."

"Of course," Christy said and went out to run the till while Rodney answered questions and did gift wrapping. When it began to get *really* busy, Christy glanced at the clock and growled under her breath. Mazie was nearly twenty minutes late—for the third time in two weeks. When she came in a few minutes later, Christy gave her a hard glare that she hoped would put across the message she couldn't verbalize while they were surrounded with impatient customers. Mazie dug right in and the crowd quickly thinned out as they were helped.

The crowd continued through the day. Rodney went down the hall and returned with sandwiches for himself and Christy that they took turns sneaking into the back room to eat. Mazie insisted that she needed a full lunch hour, since she had important things to do. The first half hour she was gone, Rodney and Christy barely kept the crowd from getting impatient, then all of a sudden the store was empty.

"Wow," Rodney said. "What a day. And it's barely half over."

"Yeah, and tomorrow will be about the same. Please tell me Mazie's not scheduled."

"Actually, Pam's coming in the morning, and Blake in the afternoon."

"Good," Christy said without adding her growing frustrations with Mazie. Her employment was in jeopardy, and she was going to have to let her know. There were aspects of being a manager that she really hated.

With the store quiet beyond the low hum of the radio, Rodney turned up the radio a bit, declaring, "I love this song. *Sleigh Ride* is my favorite. What do you think?"

"It is a great song," Christy had to admit, although she wasn't terribly keen on *any* Christmas music lately.

When the song ended, the news began. Christy listened with half an ear while she straightened some shelves. She felt indifferent to reports of what was happening locally and throughout the world, until she heard another account of what had become one of the hottest topics around the city lately. A man named Bruce Chandler, who apparently had more money than heart, in Christy's opinion, had set up some sort of charity game through the holiday season. This multimillionaire was publicly advertising that this was the season when we should all be doing good deeds. He was having employees of his corporation act like they were in need of assistance, and anyone lucky enough to respond as a good Samaritan would be rewarded with cash or great prizes. The grand prize was some exorbitant amount of money, and the entire thing made Christy incredibly angry.

"Oh, we have another winner," she said sarcastically to Rodney, who was dusting items on a shelf several feet away. "Who does this Chandler guy think he is? He's a vain and lofty snob, if you ask me. This whole charity game thing makes me sick."

"And angry, obviously," Rodney observed

"Yes, actually," she said.

"What's so bad about it?" he asked. "If it provokes some good will, then—"

"But it's not good will," Christy argued. "What kind of charity is it when the motive is a desire to be rewarded?"

"Well," Rodney said, "you've got a point, but I still think it's done more good than harm."

Christy grumbled under her breath and Rodney added, "Maybe you should admit that you're really angry with Keith Hardy, and accept that some millionaire's silly game isn't affecting your life one way or the other, and you should just let it slide."

Christy turned toward him, so astonished she couldn't think of a response. "Don't fly off," he said, putting up a hand. "I'm your friend and I think it's something you need to think about."

"What do I need to think about?" she retorted.

"I'm simply pointing out that I've observed the fact that you get angry over silly things lately. I'm no shrink, but I think you're getting angry over things that really don't affect you, because you can't get angry with Keith." He turned his attention back to the shelf in front of him. "It's just an observation. Take it or leave it."

Christy took a deep breath and told herself not to get angry and prove him right. "I was just grumbling a little," she said. "What Bruce Chandler does with his money is irrelevant to me."

"Is that *the* Bruce Chandler?" Mazie asked, coming close enough to hear the last sentence, without having any idea of the conversation.

"I assume," Rodney said.

"I grew up in his ward," she boasted, as if that somehow made her kin to royalty. She spouted off a monologue of gossip that was likely ancient history, considering it had been years since she'd seen any of the Chandler family. Christy paid no attention; she'd long ago trained herself to tune out Mazie's senseless prattling. She seemed to like hearing herself talk.

When the radio news ended and another Christmas song began, Christy's mind wandered to the holiday at hand. She thought of how little she had felt she could buy for the children, and resented knowing that Keith would spoil them. Overall she knew they would have more than adequate gifts, and spending more of her precious money in an attempt to compete with Keith would be ridiculous. But the very idea of spending any portion of the holiday without her children made her sick to her stomach. Feeling an angry smoldering that made her think of Rodney's *observation* of a few minutes ago, she quickly forced her thoughts elsewhere. Turning to help a new batch of customers, she steeled herself to be happy and excited for her children. They deserved to enjoy Christmas; they'd already lost so much this year. She wanted their time together to be good, and she could only pray that they wouldn't see through what an effort it was for her to appear brave and happy.

Christy was relieved when the evening shift arrived and she could finally go home. She quickly finished figuring her checkbook before she left, and found herself confronted once again with where to put her precious extra money. Then an idea occurred to her that felt right. She thought of the help she had received from the Church through the adjustment period of being without Keith's income. Without that assistance she never would have made it until now without starving or having her utilities turned off. Christy quickly wrote out some checks to put some money toward her legal bills and not get herself into credit-rating trouble, then she wrote out a check for fast offerings with what she had left. She felt good about giving something back to the Lord that might help others in the way that she had been helped. She pulled a donation slip and envelope out of her planner and got it ready to mail, then she left work feeling better than she had thus far through the Christmas season. She dropped her stamped envelopes into a public mailbox on the way out of the mall and prayed that nothing unexpected would come up during the remainder of the month.

Christy used the drive home to put herself in the proper frame of mind. She scanned radio stations, looking for something to lighten her mood. When she heard another report of "the charity game," she snapped off the radio and decided that she preferred silence. Taking advantage of the quiet time to pray, she felt better prepared to face the evening by the time she pulled in the driveway. As always, she took a long gaze at the house and sighed contentedly. She loved the house, and not simply the structure itself. She often recalled the first time she had seen the exterior of the house, its rugged wood and gray

stones looking right at home among the many pine trees in the yard
that was surrounded by a stone fence. The interior had a great deal of
woodwork, offering a frontier-like atmosphere that went well with
much of the early-American furniture they had slowly accumulated
through the years. It was a nice home, adequate for raising a family,
but not excessive. More importantly, she loved the location—the
distance from the city, the mountain setting without being too far into
the mountains. She loved the neighborhood and the many neighbors
whom she knew she could call on in need; and the ward was warm
and comfortable. Her children had good friends here, and the schools
were good. Living in this home represented many important aspects of
security, and she found fulfillment in the work she did that kept that
security intact for her children—and herself—even though that meant
working many long hours in order to pay the mortgage.

As usual, Lucy came running to the door to greet her. She'd
always needed an extra portion of mother's reassurance, and they
shared more cell phone calls each day than the other two children put
together. But that was okay. Christy was grateful she had this way of
keeping tabs on her children in spite of her many hours away.

"How was your first day of Christmas vacation?" Christy asked,
smoothing Lucy's short, dark hair that made her look so much like
her father.

"Good," Lucy said. "I got my room cleaned, like you said. And I
wrapped all my presents, and we watched the Christmas movie we
borrowed from Mellyn's family."

"Sounds good," Christy said. "Where're Tim and Charlotte?"

"Tim's at Danny's house. His mom said she'd bring him home
about eight. Charlotte's in her room, talking to Shawna on the
phone."

"Okay. I'm going to say hi to Charlotte. Would you put some
water on to boil for some macaroni, and I'll be back in a few
minutes."

"Sure," Lucy said and hurried to the kitchen. For a nine-year-old
she was resourceful and usually willing to help, which was more than
she could say for Charlotte. Still, for being thirteen, Charlotte was
relatively easy to get along with. Another point for which Christy was
grateful.

Christy went to the basement and knocked lightly at Charlotte's bedroom door. When she heard the familiar "Yeah," Christy stuck her head in to see Charlotte painting her toenails, her long, dark, permed hair hanging around her shoulders.

"I'm home. You doing okay?"

Charlotte put her hand over the phone. "Yeah, I'm fine. We're not having macaroni again for dinner, are we?"

"I'm afraid so," Christy said. "But tomorrow's Christmas Eve and we're having a *real* dinner."

"Cool," Charlotte said in a bored tone, then she returned to her phone call. Christy closed the door and reminded herself that teenagers were not supposed to be warm and considerate.

Soon after dinner was over and the house tidied, Tim came home to report his afternoon of playing with his best friend, who lived five minutes away. Tim had a stronger resemblance to his mother than his sisters did, with medium-brown hair cut short. He was barely more than a year older than Lucy, and had always been a good kid. The two of them were close in a way that made Christy hope they would always be close, no matter how old they got. She knew that their friendship as siblings had gotten them both through a tough year. Having someone close in age who understood fully how difficult it was to have a father leave the home with no warning had been a comfort to them both.

*****

Christy rose early the next morning and prepared Christmas dinner so it would be ready to go in the oven when she got home. She showered and made certain everything was as ready for Christmas as it could be, then she kissed each of the children and locked the door behind her.

The sky was dark with heavy clouds, but she saw no sign of precipitation before she arrived at the mall to begin a day that she knew would be crazy. By the time she left work mid-afternoon, she felt exhausted from constant crowds of frenzied shoppers. And she felt just plain weary from nearly a year of trying to pretend that everything was okay. All she could do was pray that she could get through the rest of the holiday season without falling apart.

Chapter Two

Waiting through three light changes just to make a left turn, Christy played with the radio buttons, hoping to find a song or some senseless babble to distract her thoughts. She paused on a station that seemed to offer the right frame of mind, but two minutes later she was listening to a discussion on this charity game spurred by multi-millionaire Bruce Chandler.

"Oh, help," she muttered and frantically switched stations until she heard the strains of a Christmas song that made her want to honestly examine her feelings, rather than hide them away for fear of crumbling all over again. She drove while tears flowed silently and without restraint. It was the first time she'd allowed herself to cry at all in months, and she reminded herself not to get carried away. She had to show a bright countenance to her children when she arrived home. The snow that had lightly dusted the windshield when she'd first emerged onto South Temple was now coming down hard and heavy. She felt a pang of concern for the countless drivers who had destinations of celebration in the coming hours, and uttered a quick prayer on behalf of the safety of all travelers this Christmas Eve. She wiped some fresh tears as she reminded herself that in spite of her crusted emotions and cynicism, she still cared very much about her fellow men. The thought brought on fresh tears as she felt a fleeting glimpse of the love her Father in Heaven had for her. Perhaps she wasn't a lost cause, after all. Perhaps she had found some hope that she would be able to get through Christmas, yet.

Winding up the canyon road, Christy focused more intently on the road, and her knuckles tightened around the steering wheel.

Snowy weather was the only disadvantage she could find in living out here, and this particular storm was getting nasty. She was startled when flashing lights appeared too suddenly and she got some idea of the poor visibility. She quickly determined they were the emergency blinkers on a car pulled off to the side of the road. She wondered how long it had been there, and couldn't help thinking how dreadful it would be to be stranded on this little-traveled canyon road in such weather. It was miles to a phone in either direction, and the storm was worsening steadily.

Unconsciously she slowed the car, scanning the roadside as she drove. Christy gasped when she saw a lone figure walking by the side of the road, not fifty yards ahead of the car she'd passed. The instinctive need to be a good Samaritan outweighed her fear of picking up a stranger. She quickly tallied the times in her life when she had been helped out of car trouble by kind strangers, and figured this was a good time to put some payback into the cycle of giving. She uttered a quick prayer and tried to search her feelings as she decided to pull over. Carefully she applied the brakes and pushed the button to roll down the window on the other side of the car.

As the stranger came closer and bent to look in the window, a gust of wind blew snow into the car, making it clear that even conversing with him in such weather was practically impossible. At the same moment when she got a quick glimpse of his face, she began eliminating her options for helping him. She knew her cell phone wouldn't work out here, and the storm could leave him in serious trouble without shelter. Uttering another quick prayer that she wouldn't end up in trouble, she felt good about her decision to reach over and open the passenger door.

"Get in!" she called. The man hunched into his coat and hesitated only slightly, as if he was weighing the same feelings she'd considered only moments ago. Another gust of wind accompanied him into the car before the door closed again. Christy steered back onto the road while he brushed the snow out of his brown curly hair, and a quick glance told her he was near her own age. His hooded eyes were framed with dark lashes she could easily envy, and his strong jawline merged high cheekbones with a firm chin. It only took a second to assess that he wasn't half bad to look at. The thought surprised her—

she hadn't encountered any such thought since before her marriage to Keith. In spite of her minimal efforts at dating, she'd never gotten past simply feeling that it was good to get out. But now she was looking at brown eyes that peered almost shyly toward her with an expression of surprised gratitude.

"Thank you," he said, rubbing his hands together.

"I assume that was your car back there."

"Quite," he stated with disgust. "I just had it serviced yesterday; apparently they missed something."

"It happens."

"And I couldn't get a signal on the cell phone, or I would have—"

"No, they don't work through this stretch. It's a little like the Bermuda Triangle."

He chuckled and an uncomfortable silence ensued until she asked, "Where you headed?"

"Windwood Park," he answered.

Christy smiled toward him. "You're in luck. I live there."

He nodded, seeming pleased. "I have an aunt there. She invited me to spend Christmas with her." He sighed as he took off his gloves and held his hands in front of the tiny heater vent as if it were a blazing fire. She sensed something distasteful in his brief response.

"Is that a positive prospect then, or—"

"What?" he asked.

"Spending Christmas with your aunt? Or am I being too nosy?"

"No, of course not. I'm delighted to spend Christmas with her; I always have, in fact. She's a wonderful lady."

"But . . ." she pressed, deciding trivial conversation would be far better than an uncomfortable silence.

He looked surprised but didn't hesitate to say, "But . . . my father passed away a couple of months ago. This is my first Christmas without him there, so . . ."

"I see," Christy said, hating the way she related so completely to his feelings. However, she felt sure that having Keith die would have been preferable; at least her memories would have been safe and untarnished.

Following more silence, he said, "My aunt will be truly grateful to you."

"Why is that?" she asked glancing toward him. Startled by his good looks, she quickly returned her eyes to the road, grateful for the need to concentrate on the falling snow. He was almost too handsome to be true, a fact that made her leery. Keith had been the most handsome man she'd ever met, but his good looks had drawn another woman to him and . . . Christy stopped her thoughts abruptly. She had to learn to keep every thought pattern from running into Keith.

"Well," he said, "my aunt claims that Christmas wouldn't be Christmas without me there. For that and many more reasons, I'm grateful to you, as well. You are a true good Samaritan."

Christy cast him a quick smile and remained focused on the road. Her mind sifted through the thoughts that had preceded her picking him up, and with no premeditation she blurted, "You don't work for Bruce Chandler, do you?" The accusation in her tone was brought home to her when he turned startled eyes toward her.

When she glanced toward him again, his confusion was evident. She was about to explain when he chuckled carelessly. "No," he said easily, "I don't." Christy felt him watching her before he added, "You sound as if you dislike the man."

"I don't know him, obviously. But I'm not impressed with this game he's playing. Surely there are people with real needs that—"

"Like me," he interrupted, "just now."

"Yes, like you."

"But you didn't stop because you were hoping to be rewarded," he stated rather than asked.

"No, of course not."

"Personally," he said, "I think what Mr. Chandler is doing has some merit, in spite of its possible flaws." Christy tossed him a dubious glance. "His *game* has actually provoked many people into being charitable for a change, and crime has gone down twelve percent during the month of December."

"You're kidding," she said with a little laugh.

"I'm not," he chuckled.

"Where did you hear that?"

"Uh . . . there was an article in the *Deseret News* a few days ago."

"I suppose I should make myself more informed," she said, unable to recall the last time she'd opened a newspaper. There simply wasn't time for such things since . . . She forced her thoughts elsewhere and asked, "Do you want me to take you to your aunt's home or—"

"It's quite a ways up," he said. "I could just call once we get out of the Bermuda Triangle and—"

"Actually, my cell phone never works up here at all. But you're welcome to come to my home and call, or I can take you up . . . really." After being with him for several minutes, she certainly felt no need for alarm in taking him to her home. Being more concerned with the increasingly slick roads, she hoped he would go for the first option.

"Thank you," he said. "If it's all right, I'll just use your phone and the chauffeur can come for me."

"Oh," she said lightly, "your aunt must live on the *other* side of Windwood Park."

He chuckled, albeit tensely. "Actually," he said, "my aunt is terribly conservative, in spite of being rather well off. The chauffeur thing is more of a joke. He's more of an assistant who takes care of a number of things, and he's a dear friend of the family."

"I see," she said, then it occurred to her that *all* of Windwood Park was in her ward, and she asked, "What's your aunt's name? Maybe I know her."

"Beatrice Hammond," he said.

"Beatrice? No kidding?"

"No kidding," he said.

"She's my Relief Society president."

"Really?" he said and chuckled.

"And a fine one, at that."

"Of course," he said. "She's as fine as they come."

"I didn't know she had an *assistant,* though."

"She's pretty quiet about it, I believe," he said gazing out the window. "And your name would be?" he asked.

Christy didn't even glance toward him now as the visibility worsened and she slowed the car to a crawl. "Christina," she said.

"Just Christina?" he asked.

"Well, I share the surname with my children, but I'm not terribly fond of the man who gave the name to *me.*"

"Divorced?" he said with a ring of compassion.

"Yes," she stated, trying not to sound bitter.

But she feared that he'd picked up on it when he added, "It hasn't been long, I'd wager."

"Well, nearly a year since he left, and the divorce went through rather quickly. But . . . this is . . . my first Christmas . . ." She couldn't bring herself to finish without tempting the emotions she'd trifled with earlier.

"Well," he said with a deep sigh, "it does get easier . . . with time."

Christy glanced toward him quickly, then shot her eyes back to the road. "You're divorced?"

"Yes," he said, his voice tinted with sadness.

"Wow," she said, "I was beginning to think I was the only one on this half of the globe." He laughed at the ridiculousness of the statement and she added, "I mean . . . I know it's prevalent, but . . . all of *my* friends and associates are either still single or happily married."

"You should get out more," he said and they both laughed.

She wanted to ask him a thousand questions, but settled for, "And your name would be?"

"Cameron," he said.

"Just Cameron?"

He chuckled and said, "I thought we were on a first-name basis . . . Christina."

She laughed softly. "So we are . . . Cameron. It's nice to meet you. If your aunt is a Relief Society president, I guess it's not totally awkward for me to ask if you're a member of the Church."

"I should hope not," he said. "Yes, I am. Born and bred Latter-day Saint. And so you don't have to feel awkward about asking the other questions that pop into your head, I am a returned missionary and was married in the temple."

Christy smiled briefly toward him. "Yeah, me too." He smiled back and she wanted to comment that they had a great deal in common. Instead she pulled into her driveway, relieved to leave the treacherous roads behind. She pushed the button on the garage door opener and slid the car safely into its little haven. Putting the car into park, she heaved a deep sigh.

"Very good," he said. "I'm impressed."

"With what?" she asked.

"You stayed calm and cool for such nasty conditions."

She smiled. "I think the conversation helped."

Christy led him through the door into the kitchen where Tim and Lucy came running, full of excited giggles. She'd barely greeted them with hugs before they looked beyond her to see the man that had followed her in the door.

"This is Sister Hammond's nephew," she explained. "His car broke down and he's going to call for a ride to his aunt's home."

"Hi," Lucy said to him.

"Hello," he said with a warm smile.

"This is Lucy," Christy said. "She's nine, and Timothy is ten."

"Hello, Timothy," he said, shaking the boy's hand as if they were peers.

"Hello," Tim replied, then to his mother, "Come and see what we've been doing."

"I'll be right in," she said. "The phone is there." She motioned toward it with her hand, taking note of the total disarray of the kitchen. She could tell they'd eaten Ramen noodles and hot dogs for lunch, and they'd been decorating cookies again. "Go ahead and make your call," she said. "I'll just be in here."

"Thank you," he said just as Charlotte appeared in the doorway, obviously drawn by the sound of a strange voice.

At her inquisitive glance, Christy repeated her explanation, then she said to Cameron, "This is Charlotte. She's thirteen."

"It's nice to meet you, Charlotte," he said.

"Hi," she replied with teenage succinctness.

Christy waved him toward the phone and followed the children into the family room to see the Christmas artwork they'd been busily engaged in. Even Charlotte seemed to have enjoyed drawing and cutting out Christmas pictures to hang in the windows. She was grateful they'd found a positive activity, and they'd been getting along, but the room was a disaster. After giving their artwork some worthy attention, she attempted to pick up a bit, but Cameron was already standing in the doorway. She couldn't help but smile as she barely heard Charlotte whisper, "He's cute, Mom."

"Did you get through?" Christy asked him.

"Yes, thank you. My ride should be here soon."

"It could take a while with those roads," Christy said. "You might as well sit down," she offered, brushing the cat from the sofa. She added to the children, "Go get your things together for tomorrow and see that your rooms are straightened." They reluctantly left the room, each showing their own brand of curiosity toward their visitor. "Have a seat," she offered when he was still standing.

"Thank you," he said and pushed a hand through his still-damp hair as he sat down. She tossed a dirty pair of socks and a dish towel out of his sight range while he glanced the other direction and added, "Your home is nice."

"Thank you," Christy said, moving a stack of unread newspapers in order to sit in the rocker across from him. "It's the one thing I got away with in the divorce settlement. The home, the neighborhood, the ward, the school; it's all part of the children's security, so I fought for it. Unfortunately, a healthy mortgage came with the bargain, but it's worth it."

"Well, it's very nice," he concluded firmly.

"Thank you. And I'm glad to know you can appreciate it through all the clutter. You must excuse the mess. Leaving three children all day with the oldest in charge doesn't make for organization."

"Feels homey," he said as if he sincerely meant it.

Christy looked at him longer than she'd dared while she'd been driving the car, then she glanced abruptly away when he glanced toward her. While she was tempted to admit that she felt more comfortable with him than she'd felt with any man since Keith had left her, she simply asked, "So, where did you serve your mission, Cameron?"

"Texas," he said.

"Really?" she laughed. "I went to Florida."

"Y'all went to the south, too, I reckon," he said with a perfect Texas accent and she laughed.

They exchanged mission stories as comfortably as old friends until Lucy came in to report, "Okay, Mom, I have my pajamas, and snow clothes, and hair stuff and two changes of clothes, and my toothbrush."

"That should do it," she said. "Now just make certain your room is picked up."

"It's almost done," she said and hurried away.

"Going out of town?" Cameron asked.

"No," Christy said, forcing her voice past the hurt in her answer. "The children will be going with their father. He's picking them up about noon tomorrow."

"I see," he said and she responded to the sincere compassion in his eyes.

Without hardly thinking, she added, "I can't even fathom spending most of Christmas Day without my children. It's all so . . . ludicrous."

"Yes, it is," he said gently.

She glanced sharply toward him, marveling at how open she'd become. "Forgive me," she said. "I'm afraid you've hit upon a sore point."

"Your feelings are understandable. The first everything is hard, I think."

Christy nodded. "Do you have children?"

"I have a son," he stated. "But he died several years ago."

"Oh, I'm so sorry," Christy said, feeling immediately grateful to have her children alive and healthy. She wanted to ask how a person could survive divorce *and* losing a child, but she couldn't bring herself to delve any deeper into the conversation.

"Hey," he said brightly, "this thing at my aunt's is well . . . it's nice and all, but . . . you see, she didn't have any children, so tomorrow she'll be having a lot of friends and siblings over who don't have any of their children close by, and I'm always a bit out of my element, if you know what I mean, and . . . what I'm trying to say is . . . since we're both having one of those tough first Christmases—why don't you join me tomorrow after your children leave, and . . . my aunt would be thrilled, I'm sure. And . . . well, I would, too. What do you say? It's not really a date, or anything. You'd save me from being the only one there under fifty, and it might give you a little distraction from a tough day."

It took Christy a full minute to digest his invitation. He smiled and added, "It's at the Relief Society president's home, for heaven's sake. How bad can it be?"

"It doesn't sound bad at all, actually," Christy admitted. "In truth, it sounds nice. I'd love to . . . if you're sure it's all right with your aunt and—"

"Oh, she's all for 'the more the merrier' when it comes to holidays. I'll pick you up about twelve-thirty, if that's all right?"

"That would be fine," she said. "Should I dress up or—"

"Oh, no. It's casual. Bea will probably be in her pajamas most of the day, if I know her."

"Bea?"

"My aunt."

"Oh, Beatrice. Of course. Aunt Bea. That's funny. Just like in Mayberry."

"Yeah," he said with a little laugh, "it is, actually."

Christy felt tempted to thank him for being an answer to her prayers, but before she could gather her words the doorbell rang.

"That's probably my ride," he said, coming to his feet. Christy hurried to the door and opened it to see an older gentleman wearing a ski parka with the hood pulled over his head. Not the typical chauffeur, she thought. *Assistant,* she corrected silently.

"You must be looking for Cameron," she said.

"That's right," he said with a nice smile, pushing the hood back to reveal a head of silver hair, topping a face that looked wise and distinguished.

Cameron appeared and the older man chuckled. "Hello there, boy. Looks like you found yourself a real winner here." He winked toward Christy.

She smiled and turned to Cameron, who looked downright sheepish, perhaps even embarrassed. While she was pondering the reason, he said to the chauffeur, "I'll be right out, William. Keep the car warm."

"Very good, Mr. Chandler," he said and left, closing the door behind him.

Christy put the pieces together and gasped audibly the same moment he turned to look at her, that sheepish embarrassment still hovering in his eyes. "Good heavens," she muttered and turned away. Hoping she was mistaken, she forced herself to say, "I assume you are some relation to Bruce Chandler, the subject of our conversation earlier."

"The very same," he said. She turned with questioning eyes. He took a deep breath, put his hands behind his back and stated, "I am

Bruce Chandler." She gasped again and he added, "Bruce *Cameron* Chandler."

"Good heavens," she said again. "I don't know whether to be angry or embarrassed."

"Neither, I would hope. If anyone should be embarrassed, it's me. I really didn't intend to deceive you, but—"

"But you did."

"No," he insisted gently. "You asked me if I worked for Bruce Chandler."

"But the statistics. You said—"

"I told you there was an article in the paper. I didn't say that's where I learned the information. Listen, Christina, I was really trying to get around to telling you, but . . . we've only known each other forty-five minutes, if that. Please don't let this come between us, because . . . I really think we could be good friends, and . . . maybe we should just start over . . . tomorrow." She felt briefly disoriented until he added, "You will still come to Christmas dinner with me, won't you? You can't possibly sit here alone when you have an option. Please, say you'll come."

Christy nodded firmly, but couldn't seem to find her voice. He chuckled with relief and moved toward the door. "Thank you again," he said, taking hold of the door knob. "You were an answer to my prayers . . . on more than one count." Seeing something almost chilling in his eyes, Christy wanted to ask what he meant, but he smiled and said, "I'll see you tomorrow." And then he was gone.

Christy stared at the closed door until she heard the car pull away, then she hit her head on the door and groaned. The less-than-forty-five minutes she had spent with Bruce Cameron Chandler replayed in her mind, forcing her to accept that she'd practically given her life story to a multimillionaire divorcé whom she had been blatantly criticizing over the last several days. If the guys at work got wind of this, she would never live it down. And he just had to be near her age and attractive. If he'd been an old man with a wife and grandchildren it would have been a lot easier to avoid the embarrassment of the entire situation.

Christy became gratefully distracted by the children and their excitement. She got the ham and scalloped potatoes out of the fridge that she'd prepared earlier, and put them in the oven. They worked together to tidy things up while the house filled with the fragrance of Christmas dinner. She was surprised at how well the children did with carrying out their usual traditions, and not drawing attention to the absence of their father. After the stockings had been hung and prayers were said, she tucked them all into bed, where they each admitted quietly that they missed their father. Christy agreed, then went to her own room and resisted the urge to curse Keith Hardy aloud. She prayed until her anger dissipated, then she wandered the house searching for something to kill time until she knew the children were sleeping soundly.

Plopping onto the family-room sofa, her eye was drawn to the stack of unread newspapers. She'd not opened one in weeks beyond searching for the coupons, but Charlotte often needed the paper for class projects, so she'd kept up the subscription. Besides, she never knew when she'd want to look up a movie listing. And they needed something to line the litter box.

Recalling what Cameron had said about an article in the *Deseret News*, she hurried to the stack and started perusing the last few days, wondering if she could actually find it. Less then five minutes into her search, she turned a page to see a photograph of Bruce Cameron Chandler staring back at her.

"Oh, help," she murmured and proceeded to read the article. She was probably the only person in the Salt Lake valley who wouldn't have recognized him. His charity *game* as she had so unkindly called it, had been something his father had often talked about doing, but he'd passed away recently, following a brief but traumatic bout of cancer. Bruce Chandler the third, upon inheriting his father's fortune, had quickly put together the project for the holidays in honor of his father. He was described as a humble, reticent man, reluctant to take credit for the vast amounts of charity and philanthropy he had quietly engineered for many years while working at his father's side.

Christy read the article twice before she tossed the paper back into the pile that would eventually be recycled if it didn't get in the litter box first. Peering into the children's rooms, she found them all asleep—or at least pretending to be. She quietly put out the minimal Christmas offerings, trying not to think of the vast differences in contrast to last Christmas. But she was unable to keep from feeling bitter over the reality of doing this ritual alone, when she had done it with Keith since that first Christmas when Charlotte was far too young to notice what Santa had brought her.

With the chore completed, Christy got ready for bed and curled up with the cat to read from the Book of Mormon. But before she drifted off to sleep, she returned to the family room and dug that paper out again. She cut out the article, read it once more, then tucked it carefully into her journal. After saying her prayer, she lay looking into the darkness, recalling how Cameron had said she was the answer to his prayers—on more than one count. She couldn't imagine what he might mean beyond the fact that he hadn't had to walk to his aunt's house in a blizzard. But she had to admit that he could very well be the answer to *her* prayers. If she never saw him again after tomorrow, he was offering some compassion to her situation, and a distraction to get her through this first Christmas of having to share her children. And at that moment, and for that reason alone, his appearance in her life made her grateful.

Chapter Three

Cameron lay in the darkness, staring toward the ceiling above him. "Unbelievable," he murmured aloud for the fifth time in the half hour since he'd gone to bed. The evening had been filled with the usual celebrations, made unusual by his father's absence. But the scrap of time he'd spent with Christina lingered with him, somehow buffering the emptiness he'd expected to endure. It was as if her very gesture of helping him, their commonalities, her apparent personal struggles, her very *presence,* all seemed to speak of divine intervention. He could never put what he felt into words, but their encounter had blatantly assured him that God was in His heaven, and He was mindful of the incidental personal struggles of Cameron Chandler. The grief he'd felt over losing his father had gradually merged into a hopeless despair that had enveloped his life with darkness. He wondered what had happened to the man he'd once been—a man with a wife, a son, a place to call home. And with his father's death, he'd begun to wonder what purpose he had for even making the effort to go on another day. The dwindling threads of purpose in his life had already been threatening to snap when his car had quit in that storm. And walking blindly through the snow had left him wondering if life could ever have any meaning whatsoever for him again. And then Christina had rescued him. Any offer for a ride would have given him some measure of belief that he was being looked out for, but the circumstances of her life, the comfortable nature of their conversation, and just the way she made him feel, all pointed to a meeting too incredible to ever be considered coincidental. His earlier despair now seemed difficult to comprehend. And he was grateful. Did this Christina have any idea of the impact she'd had on his life, already? And he didn't even know her last name.

Cameron finally slept and woke late. Since they had exchanged gifts the previous evening, there was nothing pressing him to get out of bed. He helped Bea prepare the usual Christmas breakfast, which they shared with the usual small talk until she said, "You're distracted. What's wrong?"

"I can't help thinking of Father," he admitted.

"Yes, I miss him, too. But it's more than that. What is it?"

Cameron smiled at his aunt across the table. His mother's sister had never married, but she had taken on much of his mother's role following her death in his twelfth year. Approaching sixty, Bea's age showed only in the lines of living in her face. She was active and healthy, with a cute little figure that could rival most of the girls that worked in his office. Her hair rarely showed any hint of the gray that she hid very carefully with a color that resembled burgundy more than any natural color that God would have assigned to hair. And that's the way she liked it. "When I create worlds," she'd often say, "there will be burgundy hair, and it will be greatly coveted by all women."

"Cameron?" she pressed, startling him from his thoughts. "What's on your mind?"

"I must confess," he said with some hesitance, "I've been rather preoccupied with . . . my encounter yesterday."

Cameron watched one of her penciled eyebrows raise into a distinct arch. "Your encounter? Are you talking about the very fact that you were stranded and rescued, or that your rescuer was Christina Hardy?"

Hardy, he echoed silently, feeling his heart quicken at the very mention of her name. "Both," he said and took a long sip of orange juice.

Bea smiled and did the same. "That's not a bad thing," she said, setting her glass down.

"You know her, then," he said, wishing it hadn't sounded so eager.

"Quite well, actually. Being Relief Society president brings you relatively close to a woman in crisis."

"Is she in crisis?"

"That's a very nosy question."

"Perhaps; I'd say it was more . . . curious. Actually, she told me she was recently divorced, and this was her first Christmas without her husband. I know how hard that can be. I guess I'm just wondering: is she *still* in crisis?"

"She's doing much better. It's been terribly difficult for her. Beyond that, my knowledge falls under the confidentiality of my calling."

"You know," he said, leaning his elbows on the table, "I had no idea you were Relief Society president until she told me. You should be ashamed of yourself for keeping such secrets."

Bea shrugged her shoulders. "You're a busy man."

"And apparently you're a very busy woman," he said.

"I enjoy my calling, for the most part. I was put in just before Keith left Christy."

Cameron raised a brow, much as she had done a moment ago. She seemed to grasp that she had let information slip when he smiled at her. "Finish your breakfast, Cameron. If you get the dishes washed, you can go and get her instead of sitting here trying to pry information out of me. And if you hurry, I can drive you down to see if your car will need to be towed."

"Oh yeah," Cameron scowled, "I forgot about *the car*. But you know what? It's Christmas day, and I'm not going very far from here until some time tomorrow. So why don't we just worry about it then?"

Bea smiled. "Excellent idea."

* * * * *

Following a good, long prayer, Christy found that she was able to enjoy Christmas morning with her children far more than she'd expected to. The dread of having the children leave was lessened by the prospect of having somewhere to go and someone to be with. She thought of the time she had spent in Sister Hammond's home following Keith's departure. As the Relief Society president, she had quickly taken Christy's wounded spirit under her wing. Along with her daily visits and seeing that her needs were met, she had guided

Christy to the right attorney, accompanied her to court hearings, and offered her home as a refuge when Christy had needed to vent anger that she hadn't wanted the children exposed to. The past few months had gone better, and she hadn't seen Sister Hammond beyond passing at Church meetings. She called occasionally to see how Christy was doing, but she'd never mentioned being related to the esteemed Bruce Cameron Chandler. Not that Christy would have cared if she *had* mentioned it. But now the coincidence seemed incredible. Christy had suspected that Sister Hammond was more than well off, and she'd known that she hired someone to see to the upkeep of the house and grounds. Now she knew that was the William who had picked Cameron up the previous day.

Preoccupied with her curiosity and attempting to put the pieces together, she managed to get through seeing the children off with their father and not fall apart the minute they left as she had done in the past. Once they were gone she had less than twenty minutes to get ready. She ignored the disastrous state of the house following the Christmas morning frenzy, and took a shower in record time before she dressed in a nice pair of jeans, with a white blouse and Christmas vest that she'd not worn yet this season. She brushed through her wet hair and pulled it into a ponytail, dabbed on the usual minute's worth of makeup, and checked the contents of her purse. Grateful that he hadn't arrived right on the dot, she programmed the phone to forward her calls to Sister Hammond's home. She turned down the furnace and unplugged the Christmas lights; then she realized she was ready and he hadn't come.

At twelve-forty she dug in and started stuffing all the discarded giftwrap and packages into a garbage bag. At two minutes after one she realized she'd actually conquered the mess rather well. She glanced at the clock, wondering if she'd misunderstood what he'd said, or perhaps he'd had second thoughts about his offer for some reason. She was wondering whether to feel angry or depressed just as the doorbell rang. She opened the door to see a huge basket wrapped in cellophane and tied with a big, red bow. It was filled with an assortment of meats, cheeses, crackers, and treats from Hickory Farms. She gasped just before Cameron Chandler peered out from behind the basket with a delighted grin.

"Merry Christmas," he said with no explanation for his tardiness. "My aunt sent this in gratitude for saving my life."

"Saving your life? I doubt it was *that* serious."

"Well, it could have been if I had honestly had to walk to the closest home in that weather."

"Well if you put it that way . . ." Christy laughed, feeling her bad mood dissipate as he pushed the basket into her hands. "Where did she come up with this at the last minute?"

"Oh, she keeps stuff on hand. That's the way she is."

"The children will love it. Thank you."

"Well, it will keep. So save it to open when they come back."

"Good idea," she said, setting the basket on the coffee table.

"Shall we go?" he asked and she picked up her coat.

"I'm ready," she said and he took the coat to help her into it. "Thank you," she said, unable to recall the last time a man had helped her with a coat. Keith had stopped doing such things a decade ago.

Christy picked up her purse and they stepped outside to bright, blue skies. She locked the door behind her and he opened the passenger door of a sedan she recognized as the car Sister Hammond regularly drove.

"You really don't have to open the door for me, you know," she said before she got in.

"Why not?"

"You said this wasn't a date."

"It's not. But I was taught to open doors for ladies. You won't get away with feminism around me."

Christy wasn't sure how to take that last comment, so she got into the car while she let it digest. After he'd gotten in and started up the road, she just came out and said, "Perhaps you should clarify that point on feminism, so I can decide whether or not I should be offended."

He smiled as if he appreciated the opportunity. "I'd be glad to. If you add up the issues that were behind the bulk of what we might call the feminist movement, I'm all for equal pay for equal work, and I don't know how any organization can function in this world without the input of women. Personally, as a whole, I think women are more intuitive and perceptive than men could ever dream of being. I think the feminist movement did a disservice, however, in trying to put equality between men and women, thereby weakening the concept that women should be treated with more reverence and respect *by* the men of this world."

Christy was stunned. She had never in her life heard her own feelings echoed so perfectly. Funny that she recalled having a strong *discussion* with Keith on the topic, where he had declared that either she was *for* equal rights for women, or *against* them. She had to ask, "Where did you come up with such beliefs?"

"Those were my father's beliefs. He spent his life serving in priesthood positions in the Church, and dealing with high-level business. But I never saw him in the presence of a lady when he didn't open the door, pull out the chair, or help with the coat. My mother died when I was twelve, but my memories are very clear. He treated her like a queen, and she treated him like a king in return. It always seemed like a simple enough equation for me, but . . ."

Christy heard a hint of sadness creep into his voice as he hesitated. "But?" she pressed.

"It didn't end up working for me. The more I tried to treat her like a queen, the more distant she became. Maybe I was trying too hard." He shrugged. "I don't know. I just know that my thoughts on feminism never impressed my wife."

"Well, they impress me, if it's any consolation."

He turned briefly and smiled. "Yes, it is, actually."

"I have to ask . . . do you really go by Cameron, or were you just trying to throw me off after that speech I made about . . . your little . . . game?"

He looked so surprised that she wondered if she'd offended him. Then he smiled. "Yes, I go by Cameron—with friends and family that is. My close associates at work have always called me Cameron. My father was always known as Bruce. At the high levels of the business, however, or relating to public issues, I go by Bruce Chandler, *the third,*" he added in a tone that seemed to mock the formal sound of it.

"I see," she said.

"Did you have anything else you wanted to clear up?" he asked.

"Not at the moment, but . . . what kind of business are you in . . . exactly?"

"Well, there's not really an *exactly*. My father made his own fortune; he did not inherit anything except a good work ethic and a strong value system. But he actually owns and oversees a number of different corporations." He sighed and shook his head. "Sorry, I mean, he *owned*. Sometimes I actually forget that he's gone."

"And now it's all yours: the companies, the money . . . everything."

"Yes," he said with a skeptical glance.

"I'm sorry. Did I say something wrong?"

"No. I'm just . . ."

"Yes?" she pressed when he hesitated.

"Well . . . to be quite honest, I've spent most of my adult life trying to discern if people want to be around me because I have money, or they *don't* want to be around me because I have money."

"That's terrible," she said emphatically.

"Yes, well . . . it's quite true. Many people have very strong opinions on money. Some people are firm on the adage that a camel could go through the eye of a needle easier than a rich man could go to heaven. They don't bother to look at the counterpoint that the *love* of money is the root of all evil. And I hope you'll believe me when I tell you that I don't *love* money. My place in my father's businesses is no different than a man who inherited a flower shop or a piece of farmland. And the truth is, technically I may be worth a great deal, but I don't have a huge cash flow. And I do have to work very hard to see that it all stays together." He glanced quickly toward her, seeming alarmed again. "I'm sorry. I guess I didn't need to tell you all that. I suppose I just needed to clear the air on that count. But I do get rather . . . vehement."

"Which is understandable. And as long as we're clearing the air. I don't love money either, which is easy because I don't have any. My money provides for my children and that keeps me going from day to day. It's been rough at times, but I find a great deal of fulfillment in working to provide for our needs."

He smiled as if he appreciated her attitude, then he pulled into Sister Hammond's driveway, which actually startled her. She had trouble connecting something so familiar with this man who was unlike anyone she had ever known. Christy opened her door to get out, then looked up to see Cameron scowling at her. She quickly closed it again and shrugged her shoulders. He chuckled as he opened the door, saying, "That's better."

"Sorry. Old habits die hard."

"You haven't been divorced *that* long."

"No, but . . . door opening was not one of his finer qualities."

"Is that why you divorced him?" he asked on their way to the front door.

Christy stopped. He took two steps then turned to face her.

"I'm sorry," he said. "That was probably way too personal. I seem to be having trouble remembering that we only met yesterday."

Christy took a long moment to consider him where he stood affably a few steps away. She wanted to admit that she was having the same problem. He was so easy to talk to that she could hardly believe they were practically strangers. She wanted to tell him that getting personal enough to pour her heart and soul out to him was exactly what she felt compelled to do in his presence. She simply cleared her throat and said, "I didn't divorce him. He left *me.*" She quickly moved past him up the walk to avoid having the conversation go any further. Already she'd had more stimulating exchanges with him in the total hour they'd been together than she'd had with Keith in the final year of their marriage. She needed time to digest all they'd discussed before she could absorb any more.

While Cameron was taking her coat just inside the front door, Beatrice Hammond appeared, wearing silly flannel pajamas just as Cameron had predicted, although her hair was dressed to perfection as usual, and her makeup was perfectly in place.

"Hello there, my dear," she said, taking both Christy's hands. "Forgive my attire. I've spent the whole of Christmas day in my pajamas my entire life, and I'm not going to start getting dressed now."

"I think they're ravishing," Christy said. "Very good taste."

Bea let out a delighted little laugh. "And how can I thank you for saving this poor vagabond from hypothermia?" She nudged Cameron who smirked sheepishly.

"It was not a problem, really. And you already thanked me. The basket of goodies was very sweet, thank you. I'm certain the kids will love it. And there's enough there to make a couple of meals."

"Well then, there's a couple of times you don't have to cook."

"I don't much anyway."

"Neither do I," Bea chuckled.

"Oh," Christy said, "I hope it's all right that I had my phone forwarded here, so the kids can call if they need me."

"Not a problem," Bea said. "Now, come in. Come in. Meet the gang."

Christy was officially introduced to William, then she met Mildred and Fred, lifelong friends of Beatrice's. Bea's brother Charles and his wife Linda were there, along with a few other people that Christy recognized as widowed members of the ward. They visited for a few minutes before a buffet was set out, and they loaded their plates with an amazing variety of salads, meats, cheeses, fruits, vegetables, and breads. Cameron helped Christy with her chair then he poured her a glass of sparkling apple juice before he sat beside her.

"Thank you," she said. "It looks wonderful."

"Bea knows how to throw a party."

"I can see that," she said and proceeded to eat.

Christy mostly listened to the conversation while she grasped some idea of why Cameron didn't want to be the only one younger than fifty. She guessed that Bea was likely the youngest of the others, and she was pushing sixty. Occasionally Christy exchanged a humorous glance with Cameron, as if they both perfectly understood the blatant evidence of the generation gap.

Following the meal, everyone worked together to do a quick cleanup, then they embarked on an animated game of charades. Christy couldn't remember the last time she'd laughed with such abandon. And when it was her turn, she felt rather proud of herself for putting the crowd into fresh peels of laughter. When the game ended, Christy took the opportunity to visit the restroom, and returned to find only Cameron sitting on the sofa.

"Party over?" she asked.

"Nah," he said, "this is siesta time. It's a great tradition of the more mature generation. I suppose when we pass sixty, we'll need siestas too. This is the time when my father and I would usually play Monopoly."

"I'm game," she said eagerly.

"You don't have to do—"

"No, I'd like to. I love board games, actually. But it would be nice to play it with an adult for a change. I bet I could monopolize you with little trouble."

"You're on," he said and left for only a minute before he returned to set the game up on the dining-room table.

"So, you and your father must have been very close," she said while he was passing out the rations of play money.

"Yes, very," he said. "After my mother died, he became very actively involved in my life. I mean . . . he was always involved to some degree, but I think the time that he would have shared with my mother became transferred to me and my sister."

"You have a sister, then."

"I do."

"And where is she?"

"She's living in New York City, actually. She works for a fashion design company, and absolutely loves it. She hasn't been active in the Church since her youth. But she's doing well. She went through extensive drug and alcohol rehab. Since then, she's kept her life straight and she's happy. It could be a lot worse."

"She's not married?"

"No, but she's got a live-in boyfriend. They've been together a few years, and he seems like a decent guy, but I guess it's just not vogue in her social circle to exchange vows."

"And is there anyone else in your family?"

"No one significant. My father was an only child. You've met my mother's siblings that are still living."

"That would be Charles and Bea."

"Precisely. I have some cousins scattered around, but we were never close."

"So losing your father was . . ."

"Devastating, to be truthful. I've worked by his side since I returned from my mission. We went to games together, played racquetball and tennis, traveled together. Especially since my divorce,

we were just like . . . two peas in a pod, if you'll pardon the cliché."
While he sorted the property deeds, he asked, "What about your family?
You have no one to spend Christmas with beyond your children?"

"I have two brothers and one sister. My parents are both living.
They are all in California, within a two-hour radius. The rest of them
do a lot together. I go out there once a year, usually, but I've not been
with them for Christmas for years, and . . ."

"And?" he pressed. "This is your first year alone with the kids.
You could have gone to be with your family. I mean . . . don't get me
wrong. I, personally, am grateful that you didn't. I'm just curious."

"Well . . . the thing is . . . Keith—that's my ex-husband—is
someone I grew up with. My family and his family are extremely close."

"Oh, I see," he said, as if she'd just announced they were cannibals.

"So . . . the few times I have talked to my family about the
divorce, I've heard things like . . ." Christy suddenly found it impossible to go on. "I'm sorry," she said. "I think I'd rather play Monopoly
than talk about that. It's still . . ."

"Too close for comfort?"

"Yes."

"Fine," he said with a dramatic positive lilt to his voice that made
her laugh, "you go first, and we're not doing the booty on free
parking thing. I like free parking to just be free parking."

"Okay, you can have your way this time, but next time, we do the
booty on free parking."

Cameron chuckled and handed her the dice. An hour later,
Christy owned the entire Boardwalk side of the board and Cameron
was running low on cash. When he yawned for the third time she
said, "Now, stop that. You're making me yawn."

"Maybe we should join the siesta after all," he said. "I confess, I
didn't sleep real well last night."

"Me neither, actually," she said. Their eyes met for a long
moment while she wondered if there was supposed to be some deep
meaning to such a silly coincidence. She turned away and tossed the
dice. "But you can't take a nap until I make you go bankrupt, once
and for all. You're not going to get out of losing properly just because
you're suddenly tired."

"Yes, ma'am," he said with that Texas accent, making her laugh.

"So, tell me," she said while rolling the dice, "do you use your middle name because it distinguishes you from your father, or was it a personal preference?"

"I grew up being Cameron," he said. "And Bruce was always my father."

"Well, I must admit that Cameron suits you better. Bruce is a nice name, but . . . you just look like a Cameron. I knew a guy named Bruce once."

"Was he charming?"

"Most of the time, I believe," she said. "He had this car that he hid in a cave, and he put this silly mask on occasionally to go out in his car and fight crime and—"

"Okay," he laughed, "I get the idea. You're not the first to bring up the *Bruce Wayne, hero and defender of right.*"

"Well, you don't look anything like Batman, in case you were wondering."

"That's a relief," he said and took his turn, groaning when he landed on one of her properties that sported a hotel. After he paid his rent and counted his little remaining cash, he asked, "So, might I ask what your middle name is? Something really good I can tease you about, I hope."

Christy chuckled. "If you only knew."

"I would know if you'd tell me."

"Actually, Christina is my middle name, and I didn't start using it until I got engaged to Keith."

Cameron raised his brows. "What? He had a problem with your name?"

"We both did, actually. I should have known then that it could never work." She chuckled again, realizing she'd just managed a light comment about her divorce. She hoped that was progress.

"And why is that?" he asked.

"My name is Laurel," she said.

"And?" he asked, obviously baffled.

"When I married Keith, I became Laurel Hardy."

Cameron laughed until she couldn't help but join him. He finally said, "Laurel is a beautiful name, but I see your point. If you must know, I think Christina suits you better."

"Well, I'm glad that's settled . . . Bruce."

"Now we can move on to more important things—Laurel—like how ruthless you are at this game. I should hire you. I could send you to New York to handle my business, and you'd leave them all flat on their backs."

She chuckled. "I'm flattered, but I wouldn't have the slightest idea how to even find my way around New York."

"One day, perhaps," he said.

"Perhaps," she replied, trying to ignore the subtle implication in his eyes that seemed to say he would love to be the one to share New York with her . . . one day.

Half an hour later, Cameron had gone fully bankrupt and together they cleaned up the game while he teased her about being such a cutthroat.

"So, how about that siesta?" he asked, looking around. "I don't think we'd miss anything. I'm sure we can find an empty room somewhere for you to rest."

Christy yawned. "That sounds nice, actually. It's been a long week."

Cameron showed her to a small bedroom that was decorated for a young child. But the twin bed was sufficient, and Christy quickly fell asleep, feeling somehow more secure than she had in nearly a year.

Chapter Four

Christy woke to find the room dark. A quick glance at the clock told her it was nearly six. "Oh, garbage," she muttered, wondering what her hosts might be thinking of her absence. She flipped on a lamp and stumbled into the attached bathroom to freshen up, grateful to have some blush in her purse. Without it, she looked ghostly.

Christy smoothed the bed and turned off the lamp before she went downstairs to find the group sitting around chatting casually. Cameron glanced toward her, as if he'd sensed her presence in the room when no one else had. She returned his smile as he stood and walked toward her.

"Oh, hello," Bea said, noticing Cameron's reason for getting up, then she returned to her conversation with her brother.

"Did you get some rest?" Cameron asked.

"I did, actually. Thank you. Did I miss anything?"

"Not a thing," he said. "In fact, if you hadn't shown up soon, I was about to go wake you, just to spare me from any more conversation on the physical ailments of every person in the room."

Christy chuckled. "Glad I could help."

"Would you like to—"

"Oh, look," Mildred said, pointing toward them, "you're both right beneath the mistletoe."

They both glanced up at the same time, then Cameron grinned at her as if he found the situation terribly amusing. Christy glanced away and said quietly, "I don't kiss on the first date."

"But this isn't a date," he said with mischief in his voice.

"All the more reason not to be kissing. The very idea is . . . ludicrous and unfathomable." She glanced around, grateful that no one seemed to be paying attention. Even Mildred was obviously gracious enough to not embarrass them further by pushing the issue.

"Ludicrous because you can't fathom kissing *me,* or ludicrous because you can't fathom kissing *any* man you've known about twenty-seven hours."

"What difference does it make?"

"It makes a great deal of difference to me," he said with such sincerity that Christy had to look into his eyes. The intensity of his gaze tempted her to turn away, but she returned it firmly.

"What are you implying, Mr. Chandler?"

"I'm implying that I would very much like to kiss you, Christina, but not at the expense of your respect, and not if the experience would be the least bit distasteful to you."

Christy shook her head in amazement. "Were you born this arrogant, or is it something you learned in order to cope with being a multimillionaire?"

His eyes widened and she wondered if he was intrigued or disgusted. She almost hoped the latter, which would more quickly put his apparent interest in her to a halt. His voice was toneless as he retorted, "Were you born this belligerent, or is it something you learned in order to cope with being divorced?"

Christy felt angry with the question, but it only took a moment to realize that she deserved it. And there was something so genuine—even compassionate—in the way he'd asked it, that she could hardly give in to such anger. She swallowed carefully and said, "There is only one man that I've kissed in the past seventeen years, and I didn't kiss *him* on the first date. If I ever stop wishing that he would come back to kiss and make up, I might consider a kiss with the right guy under the right circumstances, but not on the first date. And since this isn't a date, you're out of luck. Because you can't get to step two until you've completed step one. And since I'm not ready to date, and may never be at this rate, you're *really* out of luck. However, if this *were* a date; say our seventh or eighth date, I think it would be fair to say that the idea would be anything but distasteful."

Christy watched a smile creep slowly into his countenance, then he bent forward and pressed a lingering kiss to her forehead. She didn't know whether to feel delighted or defeated. He drew back and looked at her with eyes that seemed to echo the affection he'd just expressed so openly, without showing any disrespect for the boundary she had just clearly stated.

"And just so it's perfectly clear, that was a *friend* kiss. And friends don't date. They just . . . do stuff together, and they understand that healing and sorrow and joy are all very individual. And friends respect and accept each other unconditionally. And you asked me a while ago how you had been the answer to my prayers beyond your saving me from a blizzard and a boring party. Well, there's your answer—part of it at least. I'd been praying for a friend; someone who needed me, and someone that I could need; someone who could teach me to believe in the basic goodness of the human heart again; someone who could understand what it's like to be abandoned in a marriage that you thought was forever."

Christy was too stunned to speak while he gazed into her eyes, as if to gauge her reaction, then he took her hand and she said, "What are you doing?"

"Friends hold hands. It has a way of making you feel like you're not alone. Now, come along, Laurel Christina Hardy; they're about to start Santa Claus Bingo. And you don't want to miss that."

"No," she said, subtly squeezing his hand, hoping he would perceive the respect and appreciation she felt, "we certainly don't want to miss that. But what's the other part?"

"What other part?" he asked.

"You said that was part of why I was the answer to your prayers; what's the other part?"

He smiled and said, "I might just tell you the rest . . . maybe on our seventh or eighth date. But we can't get to step two when we haven't even had step one."

Christy smiled and followed him to the dining room table. She thoroughly enjoyed the Bingo game. She won a candy necklace, sidewalk chalk, and a beach ball. After Cameron won a plastic harmonica, he said, "Where do you guys get this stuff? Do you steal it from your grandkids, or what?"

"No," Mildred laughed, "but we usually pass it along to them eventually."

"Well, a lot of good that will do me," Cameron said.

"Oh, I've got kids you can pawn it off on," Christy said. He blew a horrible noise into the harmonica. She laughed and said, "Never mind. You can keep it. The last thing I want is one of my kids making *that* noise on a Sunday morning."

When the Bingo game finally drew to a close, Bea set out leftovers and everyone took their filled plates to the sofas where they watched *It's a Wonderful Life*. After they'd finished eating and had paused the movie to put the food away, Cameron sat beside Christy and took her hand as naturally as if they'd been friends for years.

When Christy began to feel sleepy, she realized she was more completely relaxed than she'd felt in months. Sister Hammond's home had been a source of security for her through some of the worst moments of her divorce. Being there amidst the serenity of Christmas only added to her contentment. She sighed and closed her eyes, attempting to absorb the tranquility of the moment to carry her through whatever might lie ahead.

Christy's next awareness was jolting her head upward in response to unfamiliar noises. She was embarrassed to realize she'd drifted to sleep before the movie had ended, and even more embarrassed when she turned to see that her head had been against Cameron Chandler's shoulder.

"Oh, I'm sorry," she said, sitting up straight and smoothing her hair.

"Nothing to apologize for," he said gently. "It's getting pretty late."

"Good heavens," she said, glancing at the clock. "I think you'd better take me home. I—"

"And who is going to miss you?" Bea interrupted and Christy looked up to see her standing in front of them. "Why don't you just stay the night? You told me your phone was forwarded, and the kids won't be back for a couple of days."

Christy chuckled. "Okay, you talked me into it. Can I use your phone?"

"Of course. Who are you going to call this late?"

"The kids," she said as Bea handed her the phone. "They won't be in bed for a while yet—not while they're on vacation with their father."

She was left alone while she talked for a few minutes with each of the kids, feeling a little down to hear their reports of an exciting day with many more gifts. She did her best to sound thrilled for them before she said good-night, then she returned the phone to Bea, who said, "If you look in the dresser drawers of the room you stayed in, there are some toothbrushes and a few odds and ends that I keep on hand for spontaneous visitors. If you need anything else, don't be afraid to tell me. You know where my room is."

"Yes, thank you." They embraced and Christy added, "It's been a wonderful day . . . all things considered."

"It's been a pleasure," Bea said. "But don't thank me." She motioned toward Cameron who was leaning back on the sofa with his eyes closed. "I think the two of you helped each other through a tough day."

Christy tried to come up with a comment, but Bea added, "Good night, dear. Sleep as late as you like. You're on vacation."

She left the room and Christy nudged Cameron, "You sleeping there?"

"Nah," he said with a chuckle, "just a little siesta."

"Well, I'm going to bed. I guess I'll see you in the morning."

"I'll look forward to it," he said.

"Thank you for everything, Cameron."

"I didn't do anything," he said.

"Thanks anyway," she said and went back to her room. She found everything she needed, just as Bea had promised, and was quickly between the covers, marveling at the contentment she felt, such a stark contrast to her nights without the children in the past. She slept before she had a chance to analyze her feelings too deeply; she only knew she was glad to not be at home alone on Christmas night.

Christy slept soundly and woke up mid-morning, feeling deeply rested. She was embarrassed to see how late she had slept until she remembered Bea telling her that she was on vacation. She showered quickly, combed through her hair and straightened her room before she went downstairs to find Bea stretched out on the sofa, reading a book, and Cameron sitting across from her, reading the paper.

"Good morning," Bea said brightly. "Did you sleep well?"

"Oh, yes! And you?"

"Of course," Bea said.

Cameron smiled at her over his newspaper, and she smiled back; he was wearing wire-rimmed glasses that made him look even cuter than he had the day before. "Good morning," he said.

"*Wall Street Journal*, huh?" she said with a teasing lilt.

"Yeah," he almost moaned, "it's a tedious habit."

"It's awfully quiet," she commented.

"The others all left, either last night before the movie was over, or early this morning," Bea reported while Cameron went back to his paper. "Help yourself to some breakfast, my dear. There are bagels and cream cheese, a variety of fruit, and leftovers from yesterday. You'll just have to make yourself at home."

"I can do that," Christy said and went to the kitchen. She started with a glass of orange juice, then dug into the fridge, pulling out a little bit of everything. Spreading the fare out over the table, she thoroughly enjoyed herself.

Cameron appeared in the kitchen doorway and folded his arms, chuckling warmly. He still wore his glasses, and she decided she quite liked them. "I see you found something to eat," he said, moving closer. Christy chuckled to realize she was surrounded by food, with a bagel in one hand, and a cracker layered with beef stick and cheese slices in the other. "In fact," he said, sitting across from her, "you seem to be quite enjoying yourself."

"Oh, I am. Thank you. I mean . . . most of this is luxury food, and it's been so long since we've had any luxury food around the house."

"Luxury food?"

"Yeah, you know, stuff that's not practical when you're feeding a family on a tight budget. So, this is just . . . fun."

Cameron chuckled and began sampling bits and pieces of all that was laid out. He wasn't necessarily hungry, but he enjoyed the opportunity to watch Christina Hardy without seeming too obvious. He was amazed at how thoroughly fascinated he'd become with her—from the very first minute he'd climbed into her car. He had no trouble admitting that she was attractive, but what he felt for her was not necessarily romantic. Or was it? The very fact that he had trouble defining how she made him feel only enhanced his fascination. He'd never met anyone quite like her. He'd lost count of the women he'd dated since his divorce, most of them once each. It didn't take him long to see that most of the women who were drawn to him were actually drawn to the good looks he considered a curse, or the money that he wished he could pretend he didn't have. After a few years he'd given up for the most part. And through his father's illness and death, he hadn't had the time or inclination to date. And now, here sat Christina Hardy, adamantly declaring that she wasn't dating, and didn't know when—or if—she would be. But that was okay. While he'd had a great deal more time to heal from his divorce, he couldn't help wondering if what he felt now would mislead him, the way he'd been misled by his feelings for Jolene. Initially everything had seemed all right, but time had only proven that everything was all wrong. And he had to wonder if it always had been. Logically he'd sorted all of that out a long time ago. He'd analyzed, he'd grieved, and for the most part he'd healed. But what he felt now made him wonder just how deep that healing had gone. While a part of him wanted to get down on one knee and beg this woman to marry him, a much bigger part was grateful for her clearly defined declaration that had prompted him to make the boundaries of friendship very clear. He doubted she would accept spending time with him any other way, and he felt certain that being friends was by far the best way for him to come to terms with where he was in his life right now.

When he realized she was clearing the table, he stood to help her and said, "Hey, could I get you to do me a favor?"

"Sure," she said, pouring herself a little more orange juice before she put the pitcher into the fridge. "What do you need?"

"Could you ride down with me to see if the car will start? If it does, I won't be able to drive them both back." He really didn't expect it to start, but it was a good excuse to have Christy along while he made certain he needed to call a towing company.

"I'd be happy to," she said and he helped her put the kitchen in order.

"Thanks," she said.

"You're welcome."

"Hey, I think I really like having you as a friend."

"Why is that?" he asked, leaning against the counter and folding his arms. He almost expected her to say something about his family being wealthy, which gave her the opportunity to eat luxury food. He was glad to give her that opportunity, but the money issue was just too sore of a point for him.

"Well," she said, "being friends, as we are, I don't have to be embarrassed to start snoring during the movie, and I can eat as much as I want without wondering if I'm leaving a good impression." Cameron smiled and she added, "I don't have to impress you, do I? Because we're just friends."

"That's exactly right," he said and reached for her hand. "But you didn't snore during the movie."

He told Bea where they were going and they walked together to the garage. After he put some things in the trunk, he noticed Christy purposely waiting for him to open her door. He smiled and said, "You learn quickly."

"Yes, I do," she said as she slid into Bea's car.

The conversation that had flowed easily between them since they'd met less than two days ago, had now become stilted and minimal. While he felt preoccupied with thoughts of deeper implications in all of this, he couldn't help wondering if she felt the same. The darkness of his life that he'd almost become comfortable with had dissipated drastically, and he almost had difficulty accepting that the light he felt in her presence was real. The need he felt to be close to the light she offered was almost frightening.

"Oh, this ought to be fun," he said when they came upon his abandoned car. The snow plows had obviously passed by a few times, and it was buried in snow and ice.

"I hope you brought a scraper or something," Christy said.

"Oh, I did. But this could take a jackhammer."

Cameron got out of the car and opened the trunk to take out a shovel. "Ooh, you've come prepared," Christy said, appearing beside him.

"Yes, I predicted this," he said and headed toward the car. He was relieved to find the snow somewhat soft and easy to move. And he was surprised to look up and see Christy, wearing gloves, standing knee-deep in the snow on the other side of the car, attacking the ice and snow stuck to the windshield. "You really don't have to—"

"It's okay," she said. "I could use some exercise."

They worked mostly in silence for nearly twenty minutes, while Cameron couldn't keep from discreetly watching her. Not only was she beautiful, she was obviously not intimidated by hard work. He couldn't help thinking of Jolene, who would have sat impatiently waiting for him in the car, or more likely, she wouldn't have come at all. He cautioned himself against comparing the past to the present, but he could hardly help it when his greatest desire was to avoid the mistakes of the past.

When he was finally able to get into the car, the engine started immediately. They both laughed, then Christy said with sarcasm, "Oh, great. It's probably one of those things that only doesn't work when the mechanic's trying to find the problem."

"Maybe," Cameron said, realizing that in spite of his expectations, he wasn't completely surprised that it had started, "and maybe not."

Christy drove Bea's car back to her home, and Cameron pulled into the driveway right behind her. They entered the house to find Bea just putting lunch on the table. "I don't know what your plans are," she said to both of them, "but you must eat."

"I only ate an hour ago," Christy said, washing her hands at the kitchen sink.

"So, top it off," Bea insisted, "and then you can go do whatever it is you need to do."

"I don't need to do anything," Cameron said, washing up as well.

Cameron helped each of the ladies with their chairs, and Bea asked him to bless the food once they were all seated. While he was fixing himself a turkey sandwich, Bea asked, "So did the car start, or—"

"Yes, it started," Cameron said.

"Don't you just hate that?" Christy asked. "I just hate it when there's something wrong with the car, but when it comes to trying to fix it, they can't find anything wrong."

Bea smiled and perfectly expressed what Cameron was almost afraid to say, "Maybe there's nothing wrong with the car. Maybe the good Lord wanted Christy to spend Christmas with us."

Christy felt a little alarmed over the statement for reasons she couldn't quite pinpoint. Her mouth was too full to comment, but Cameron said, "Or maybe the good Lord knew I needed someone like Christy to rescue me."

Christy swallowed and asked, "Rescue you from what? I'm certain this situation has turned out far more to my benefit."

"That's a matter of opinion, I suppose," he said with a little wink.

Christy wanted to press him on that, but felt safer dropping the subject. She was glad when Bea asked, "So, are you kids in a hurry to be going, or—"

"What did you have in mind?" Cameron asked.

"Well, I've been wanting to see that movie I told you about. It's playing downtown, and I thought a late matinee might be a fun way to finish up the holiday."

"I'm in," Cameron said. "I told them I wouldn't be back into the office until Monday morning. What about you, Christina, my friend?"

"The same. I'm not going back to work until Monday; I've already put in far too many hours for this pay period. And the kids won't be back until after church tomorrow. I'd love to go to a movie. Quite frankly, I can't remember the last time I did."

"Well, lets get going then."

As soon as lunch was cleaned up, they drove down to the city in Bea's car. Cameron drove, but he insisted they both sit in the front seat with him, and Christy ended up in the middle.

"This is my treat," Bea said as they got into the ticket line.

"That's fine," Cameron said with mock belligerence, "but I get to buy the popcorn."

Christy groaned. "I couldn't eat popcorn right now if my life depended on it."

"Well, you'll just have to save it for later," Cameron said and took hold of her hand as they entered the theater.

Christy enjoyed the movie almost as much as she enjoyed having Cameron Chandler's hand in hers. It felt good to be out; and it felt good to have a friend without the pressure of romantic involvement that she had felt in her previous efforts at dating.

It was dark when they came out of the theater and Bea said, "Oh, let's go to the square. The lights are so beautiful, and it's such a pleasant evening."

"It's fine with me," Cameron said. "What about you, Christina?"

"I've got nothing to get home for," she said, not admitting to the way she'd avoided Temple Square since Keith had left. She often enjoyed the Main Street garden, and exploring the Joseph Smith Building and the Conference Center, but she'd avoided Temple Square in spite of her occasional temple attendance. Walking through the square had been a common pastime with Keith, and the memories were just too ironic to swallow. As they drove deeper into the heart of the city, she reminded herself that it had been nearly a year, and it was time she got past such silly sentiments.

Christy was lost in thought when Cameron stopped the car and she looked up to see him rolling down the window where a gentleman in uniform was standing. "Oh, Mr. Chandler. It's you."

"Hello, Ben," Cameron said. "Did you have a good Christmas?"

"Very good, thank you. And you?"

"It was much better than I'd expected," Cameron answered as he got out with the car running, and reached out a hand for Christy. She slid out as Ben opened the door for Bea and Cameron added to Ben, "We're just going to have a walk around the square; we won't be long."

"Very good, sir," Ben said and got into the car. Christy watched it become swallowed into the building they were parked in front of. She craned her neck and couldn't see the top from this point of view. As her gaze moved back down, she noticed the elegant sign that was lit up beside the huge glass doors. *Chandler Corporation.*

"Come along," Cameron said. "If we don't keep moving, we could freeze."

Christy quickly dug into her pockets for her gloves and put them on while they were walking. She then took Cameron's hand and he smiled. Getting her bearings, she realized they were less than two blocks from Temple Square, and only a block from where she worked.

"So," she said for the sake of conversation, "I take it that's where you work."

"That's where," he said.

"And is someone there all the time?"

"There are security people there all the time, yes. They do little odd jobs to stay busy."

"Like parking cars," she said.

"Yep," he answered, then Bea began telling them about an article she'd once read about the Christmas lights at Temple Square. She gave some statistics of the number of lights, and the hours it took to put them up and take them down.

"Well, it's worth it," Cameron said as they entered the square.

They slowed their pace as they moved through an atmosphere so warm and peaceful that Christy had to question her resolve in avoiding this place. They paused to gaze at a beautiful nativity scene, while the story was told over a loud speaker, with corresponding music. In the distance Christy could see the Christus statue in the north visitors center. And she hated the way something inside her felt unworthy of the Savior's love. At some level, she knew her thinking was illogical. She knew the Atonement had already paid for her sorrow and grief. But accepting the reality of that emotionally was something she continued to struggle with. In spite of her efforts at prayer and study, she felt as if her heart had become enveloped in something crusty and cynical, something that made it difficult for her to move beyond the pain of her loss.

Bea occasionally made a comment, but not much was said between Cameron and Christy as they wandered aimlessly, absorbing the Christmas spirit of their surroundings. Christy's thoughts regularly strayed to the reality of holding hands with this man who had so recently been a complete stranger in her life. She marveled at how thoroughly comfortable she felt with him, and the way his companionship made her feel more secure than she'd felt in nearly a year—perhaps much longer. While she couldn't bring herself to think beyond the moment, she couldn't help hoping that his friendship was not something short lived. The very idea of losing this security she had suddenly found made her fear that she'd already allowed herself to become too emotionally involved; not romantically, she reminded herself—but emotionally.

They went into the mall to get warm and eat a light supper, then they walked back to the Chandler building, where a different security guard drove the car out to the street from the underground garage. Cameron spoke amiably with him as well, and she couldn't help but admire his genuine diplomacy. And this from a man she had once ignorantly called a vain and lofty snob.

The drive home made it evident they were all tired. While the radio quietly played Christmas music, Cameron held Christy's hand, and Bea dozed in her seat. Christy almost felt afraid when he pulled the car into her driveway, and it became apparent she would be alone with her empty house and hollow heart. She steeled herself to face both as she slid out of the driver's door in order to not make Bea relinquish her comfortable seat.

"Thank you for everything," Christy said, bending over to squeeze Bea's outstretched hand.

"It's my pleasure, dear. You call me anytime . . . if you need anything at all, or if you just need to talk."

"I will, thank you," Christy said and Cameron walked her to the front door while she dug in her purse for the keys.

Once she had the door open, she turned to Cameron and he said, "Hey, I had a great time. You helped me get through . . . more than you know." Again, Christy wanted to ask what he meant, but she didn't know how.

"Same for me," Christy said. He nodded and moved down the walk. "Hey," she called and he stopped and turned, "thank you . . . for everything."

"It's my pleasure . . . truly."

He took a step backward and she took a step forward. "Listen," she said and he stopped, "I . . . need to say that . . . I really appreciate this . . . friend thing, because . . ."

She faltered and he stepped closer. "Because?" he pressed.

Christy looked up at his face, illuminated by the porch light. "Because I can't even consider dating somebody—*anybody*—when I'm still wishing that he would come back and make it right. But I really do need a friend, even more than I thought I did. So . . . at the risk of gushing: thank you, Cameron."

"You're welcome, Christy, but don't go thinking I'm all noble in this. I needed a friend, too—more than you could possibly know." The severe expression in his eyes was so compelling that she had to force herself to look away.

"Well, then," she smiled, "we seem to be in a position to do each other a big favor."

"We seem to be." He smiled in return. "I'll be in touch."

"I'll be counting on it."

He smiled once more and hurried away.

Chapter Five

Christy called her children to hear their report of another fun-filled day, and no apparent homesickness. She cried a little, then reminded herself that they would be home tomorrow. She crawled into bed and slept well. After coming awake slowly, she luxuriated in the comfort of her bed and the quiet of the house. She had to admit that in spite of missing her children, it was nice to have some quiet time to rejuvenate. Absorbing that thought, she concluded that it would be far better to appreciate the advantages of this situation, rather than focusing on the negative.

Christy lay in bed and read some articles from the current *Ensign*, glad that Church meetings didn't start until one. Following a long bath and some Christmas dinner leftovers for lunch, she arrived at sacrament meeting ten minutes early. She took a seat about halfway up in the chapel and opened her scriptures. A few minutes later, Bea tapped her on the shoulder and said with a warm smile, "May I sit with you, my dear?"

"Of course," she said eagerly. It wasn't the first time Bea had sat with her; in fact it was fairly common. But Christy's heart skipped a beat when Cameron sat on the other side of Bea. Putting her mind in the proper frame, Christy leaned over and whispered, "What are you doing here?"

Cameron looked comically over his shoulder and said, "The sign outside did say visitors were welcome." Christy laughed softly. "I decided to come to church with my sweet little old aunt."

"Be careful who you're calling old," Bea said with mock offense.

"Do you come to church with your aunt often?" Christy asked.

"On occasion," he said.

"Then why have I never seen you here before?"

"The last time he came with me was more than two years ago," Bea said.

"So, why today?" Christy asked with exaggerated suspicion.

"I was hoping to see an old friend of mine." He winked.

"Be careful who you're calling old," Christy said, imitating Bea's tone.

Through sacrament meeting, Christy's mind wandered to the wonderful holiday she'd spent with Beatrice and Cameron. Then she thought of the contrasting empty hours left until the children returned late this evening. While she contemplated fixing the meal she'd planned for herself during the children's absence, she impulsively decided to invite Bea and Cameron over for dinner. Feeling both excited and a little nervous with the prospect, she reminded herself that her invitation had no romantic implication whatsoever, and he certainly wouldn't expect it to—especially with his aunt around. It was merely a way of reciprocating their hospitality. As soon as the closing prayer ended, she quickly turned to them and said, "Hey, do you have plans for dinner? I'd like to have the both of you over . . . if you're not busy or—"

"Oh, I'd love to, dear," Bea said, "but I've got some meetings and Relief Society visits that need to be seen to. I'm sure Cameron would love to, however. Wouldn't you, Cameron?"

Christy was wondering what she might have gotten herself into when he grinned and said, "Yes, I would, actually . . . if that's all right . . . my coming without supervision, or anything."

"That would be fine," she said, feeling her nerves heighten. "How about six? The kids shouldn't be home until nine or ten."

"Six is perfect. Can I bring anything?"

"Just you," she said, then she added to Bea, "And if you get finished, stop by and I'll feed you."

"Thank you, dear," she said and Christy hurried off to teach her Primary class.

Christy didn't see Cameron or Bea before she left the church following Primary and hurried home to put the meal together. Cameron arrived right on time, and she was relieved to feel her nerves lessen with his presence. He had a way of making her feel completely comfortable, with no hidden pressure or romantic implications.

"Well, it's ready," she said, motioning him toward the table, which she had set for three—just in case.

Following a blessing on the food, Cameron took a savory bite and made a pleasurable noise. "Oh," he said, "this is luxury food."

"This is lasagne," she said, as if he hadn't figured it out.

"It's homemade lasagne, and it takes me back to my childhood. My mother loved to cook, and Italian was her specialty. My home-cooked meals since her death have been relatively minimal."

"I guess luxuries are relative."

"They certainly are."

"Well, I love lasagne, personally. But my children aren't real fond of it, so I plan to cook it occasionally when they're with their father."

"Well, thank you for sharing it with me."

Christy just smiled. He closed his eyes as he bit into the cheesy garlic bread, as if it were a rare delicacy. Following a few minutes of silence, she said, "Well, since I feel like I've known you for about a hundred years, I was thinking it might be a good idea to get to know you."

"Sounds reasonable," he said with a little laugh.

"So, forgive me if I'm starting out on a sensitive note, but . . . may I ask how long you've been divorced?"

"Nearly five years," he said with no hesitation or apparent concern.

Christy leaned forward and set her fork down. "Does it get any easier?"

"I don't know if I have an intelligent answer to that question. I've been wondering the exact same thing in regard to my father's death. Bea told me just the other day that since she'd lost her mother eight years ago, she's never stopped missing her, and sometimes the ache comes back all over again. But she says that she's gotten used to it. She also said that the peace she feels in knowing it was her time to go has made the loss bearable. I think I can agree with all of that in the respect that . . ." He glanced down and she sensed some added sadness when he said, "That's basically how it's been with losing my son."

Christy gasped softly, grateful that he didn't seem to notice. She'd honestly forgotten that he'd told her he'd lost a son. Before she could comment, he went on, "But . . . when it comes to divorce, it's difficult to find peace when you can't even understand what went wrong. I mean . . . my father died of cancer. It happens. It's nobody's fault. My son died in an accident, but when you get past trying to place blame somewhere, it comes down to the same thing. It was his time to go, and I know it beyond any doubt. But I've had to ask myself, does the same apply to divorce? Was this just the way it had to be? Or did I do something wrong somewhere?"

Christy forced back an unexpected rise of emotion and managed to say in a steady voice, "After all these years, have you come to any conclusions? If you have, I'd sure like to know, because I'm tired of losing sleep while I wonder what I might have done differently to keep him here—or what I might do differently to bring him back."

Cameron took a good, long look at Christina while she was concentrating on keeping her emotions in check. He was so keenly aware of how she felt, that the empathy threatened to choke him. He wondered if she had ever opened up—*really* opened up—to anyone who had been through it. He wanted to beg her to tell him everything that had happened, if only so he could know more how to help her, to console her, to give her hope. He broke the silence by saying, "You know, at one point when I was still wishing for Jolene—my ex-wife—to come back, I was sitting in a business meeting while some guy was analyzing the pros and cons of going into a certain situation, as opposed to staying in a certain situation. And all I could think about was her. She'd been gone more than a year. The divorce had been final for months. And I just couldn't let go. I just kept hoping and praying for some miracle that would change her heart and bring her back. While I was sitting in that meeting, it occurred to me out of nowhere that maybe I had been praying for the wrong thing. While they were writing this huge list of pros and cons on these whiteboards in the room, I starting making a list in my planner of the pros and cons of being divorced. I was actually shocked to see on paper that my life was far better off without her. I went home and cried for an hour. I think that's when I truly let go, and I had to mourn a part of the loss I'd never accepted before. But it got better for me after that. I don't know if that would work for you, but it might give you something to think about."

Christy sighed and took a bite of lasagna. "I certainly wouldn't want *him* to make a pro and con list, or should I say a *her-or-me* list. She's got everything I haven't got. A cute little figure. A high-paying career. A home that's paid for."

"So, is that what he bases a woman's value on? Is she a financial investment? An ornament? The *her-or-you* list could be much different, depending on who wrote it."

Christy only sighed again, and Cameron felt certain she had a long way to go before she could let go of this man who had left her. Hoping to push her just a little further, he said, "Okay, well, you don't have to make a whole list right now, but just name one thing that's better with him gone. I'm not suggesting you be flippant about a failed marriage, because it's a horrible thing. I just think it helps to get a little perspective."

"Okay," she said, but she said nothing more.

"So name just one thing that's better with him gone."

"Well, I really like being able to eat whatever I want and not feel guilty." Cameron raised his brows but bit his tongue to keep from saying what he was thinking. "When I got married I was a size eight. After three kids and pushing middle age, I am now a size twelve. I don't mind being a size twelve. When I look at myself in the mirror, I like what I see. But he never did. It seems he was disillusioned to some degree once I'd had a baby and didn't bounce right back into skinny jeans."

While Cameron was fighting a vehement anger on her behalf, he was surprised to hear her giggle. "You know, it felt good to say that. I've never told anyone that. And it's a good thing we're friends, because I sure as heck wouldn't have said something like that on a date."

Cameron chuckled. "Yes," he agreed, "I think it's a good thing we're friends." They ate for a few more minutes in silence, until he felt compelled to say, "If you don't want to talk about it, that's fine, but I can't help wondering what the divorce was about. If this was a date, it would be far too nosy a question, but since we're just friends . . ."

He was relieved when she smirked. "I'll tell you about mine, if you'll tell me about yours."

"Deal."

"Well," she said, putting one arm up on the back of the chair behind her, "early last January, he walked in the door and told me he'd been leading a double life and it was time to come clean. He was leaving me for another woman. He left it up to me to tell the kids. He told me he'd send some money. What he sent didn't even pay the mortgage. That's when your sweet aunt scraped me up off the floor, almost literally, and got me on my feet. She got me a great attorney, went to all the hearings with me. She got me out of my depression so I could take the job I've got now—which was actually offered to me the day he left. A miracle, of sorts, I believe."

"And what do you do?"

"I manage a mall gift shop downtown."

He made an expression to indicate he was impressed, then he motioned for her to go on.

"So, I managed to get a fair settlement of child support, but it doesn't begin to cover what he contributed before he left. Three days after the divorce was final, he married *Patricia;* a woman he calls his 'eternal soul mate.'"

"Ouch," Cameron said with disgust.

"And yes, she is a size eight. I look back and I can see all kinds of signs that our marriage wasn't good, but at the time, I really believed we were doing okay. Not perfect, by any means, but okay. So, I wonder what I might have done differently. Was I in denial? Or just a fool?"

"You're overlooking something important, I think."

"And what is that?"

"He deceived you, Christina. You were not committing a sin to be assuming that he loved you and was committed to you, the way you were to him. But he was cheating on you."

With a cracked voice, she said, "Thank you. I've tried to tell myself that. But it's nice to hear someone else say it. I think the worst of it all for me is just . . . wondering how long it had been going on. How long was I sleeping with a man who was sleeping with someone else? When I fully realized that was the case, I threw up for an hour.

The thought still makes me nauseous. He assured me that he'd taken precautions and I was not going to get some horrible disease, but if he cheated on me, how can I believe he's telling the truth about that?"

"You just have to move forward and put it behind you."

"Yes . . . that's easy to say, but . . . would *you* want to marry a woman who might have been exposed to . . . Oh good heavens!" Christy felt herself blush and put both hands over her face. "I can't believe we're having this conversation."

"We live in a tough world, Christina. Better that we talk about such things and come to terms with them, than to bury our heads in the sand and hope they'll go away. And the answer is *yes*. If I knew in my heart she was the woman for me, I would take her on with whatever her past might have been."

Christy closed her eyes and inhaled one more layer of validation. "How do you do that?" she asked, still keeping her eyes closed.

"Do what?"

"You just . . . have this way of making me feel good and right about things that have felt all wrong since the day he left."

"I suppose I just . . . know how you feel."

Christy opened her eyes. "Did Jolene cheat on you?"

"Yes," he said with hard eyes. "But the marriage had pretty much fallen apart before it happened. I strongly suspected, and . . . well we hadn't been intimate for a long time. So I made sure it didn't happen again."

"How *did* it fall apart, Cameron?"

Cameron sighed deeply and pushed his chair back, setting a hand firmly on the table, as if he needed its support. "I met Jolene about a year after my mission. We dated for several months, but after we married I quickly realized that we hadn't talked about any of the important things before we got married. I disagreed with her attitude on many things, but I took my marriage covenants very seriously. I worked to improve myself. I tried to be tolerant and love her unconditionally without spoiling her. I suggested some counseling. She refused. I went anyway, if only to know how to handle the struggles appropriately. I learned a lot about myself that helped, and I learned a lot about communicating and commitment that really helped. She seemed convinced that having a child would make everything right, and for a while I believed her. Through the pregnancy and those first few years of Daniel's life, I believe we truly were happy."

Christy noticed his grip tightening on the table, and she felt it coming even before he said, "Daniel had just turned three when the accident happened. Jolene was driving. He was in his car seat in the back. She was rear-ended. It wasn't her fault, by any means. But Daniel died a few hours after the accident, and she walked away with some cuts and bruises. She just couldn't come to terms with it. Losing him was the hardest thing that had ever happened to me, but before he was buried I knew beyond any doubt that it had been his time to go. I felt an undeniable peace that got me through. But no matter how much I shared my feelings with her, and challenged her to find her own peace, she just couldn't deal with his death. It reached a point where she began to resent the fact that I had found peace, as if that in itself was somehow an affront to her grief. She did agree to some counseling, but she didn't go more than a few times. And that's when she started staying out all night with no explanation. One day I came home and she'd completely moved out. The divorce papers were on the kitchen table. It certainly wasn't a complete shock, but the reality of seeing those papers still sent me over the edge. I didn't leave the house for days. My dad left me alone for a while, then he forced me to sit down and face the facts. He talked about losing my mother, and even though it was a different kind of loss, the grief was still the same. I knew that if he had survived, I could too. My father gave me hope that day. And from then on, we were best friends."

He looked down and Christy could almost literally feel his pain. "And now you've lost him."

"Yes, now I've lost him. However," his voice brightened, "the loss of my son and my parents are only temporary. Losing Jolene was permanent. It's a different kind of grief from death, but as I said, it's still grief."

"Yes, it certainly is," she said distantly. They both fell into silence until Christy forced a chuckle. "I think we need to lighten the mood a little, and it wouldn't hurt to warm our dinner up, as well."

She quickly picked up both their plates and heated them in the microwave. "Thank you," he said when she set it back in front of him. "So, tell me more about your job," he added in a lighter tone.

Christy told him about the people she worked with, her frustrations and fulfillment.

"And what exactly do you sell?" he asked.

"Oh, all kinds of mostly useless gift items. Much of our inventory borders on the unusual, but it boils down to figurines, wind chimes, candles, and a number of strange objects that you just have to see to believe."

"So tell me, what's the most beautiful thing you have for sale?"

"Oh, that's easy," she said. "It's the porcelain seagulls. They're exquisite, really. And they remind me of the pioneer cricket story. When I look at a seagull, I think of the miracle of God rescuing his people from evil and destruction. In my opinion, that makes the seagull a wonderful symbol of hope."

"Well said." He took a bite and swallowed before he asked, "So, do you own one of these seagulls?"

Christy gave him a sad smile and simply said, "Someday."

When the meal was finished, Cameron complimented her once more then offered to help with the dishes. She protested only a moment before he started clearing the table and making himself completely at home in the kitchen. "So, are we loading the dishwasher here, or—"

"Yes, but it's not a real great dishwasher. They have to be rinsed with that brush there, and—"

"I can do that," he said and quickly set to work. By the time Christy had the food put away and the kitchen cleaned up, Cameron had the dishwasher neatly loaded and ready to run, but with room for more items.

"Thank you," she said.

"Not a problem. Dinner was wonderful."

"I'm glad you liked it," she said. "I was going to make some dessert, but I just didn't have time. If you want to stick around a while, I could whip up a brownie mix. Or if you need to go, then—"

"Brownies sound great," he said. "Unless you have other things you need to do. You certainly don't need to feed me dessert. I just . . ."

Christy saw his eyes say what his words didn't. He didn't want to leave, and that suited her just fine. She pulled the brownie mix out of the cupboard and they worked together to get them into the oven.

Again, they cleaned up the kitchen, and Cameron declared that the dishwasher was now officially full. Christy put some soap in and started it before they went to the front room to sit and visit while the brownies baked. They talked and laughed while sharing stories of their childhoods, which were not far removed from each other. In spite of growing up in different states, they had both been raised in the Church, with strong values. And they had both gone through a fairly normal education experience, being just average students with no great difficulties or amazing accomplishments.

They ate the brownies warm with vanilla ice cream and chocolate syrup. "If I keep this up, I'll be a size fourteen," Christy said lightly.

"And still beautiful," Cameron said so sincerely that she stopped to gaze at him, wondering how to respond. The moment became almost unbearably tense until he stuck his finger in his chocolate syrup, then touched her nose. "You look great in chocolate," he said and they both laughed while she wiped it away and licked her finger.

"So," he said, "the children are expected home this evening?"

"That's right. But I doubt they'll get here before nine-thirty or ten." She glanced at the clock to see that it was just past eight.

"I assume you have to do this alternating holidays thing that I've heard about," he said.

"Yes," her voice expressed her dismay. "Next year he gets them for Christmas Eve, until one o'clock Christmas day. He's actually supposed to have them through New Year's, but he's got plans with his *wife*. He's actually been pretty good about the visitation thing, mostly because he really doesn't want the kids as much as the guidelines state. I mean . . . he seems to like having them, but he also doesn't seem to want them to intrude on his life too much. A fact that I'm grateful for, really."

"Still, sharing them at all must be difficult," he said.

"It is," she admitted. "But I think I'm adjusting. I had a nice peaceful morning today, and . . ." she reached for his hand, "it's nice to have a friend to fill in the hours." He smiled and she added, "I mean . . . I'm sure I could find something to do, like cleaning the basement, or something. But there's only so much work a person can do in a day."

"That's true," he said. "You can't be too hard on yourself for what you *don't* get done. You just have to focus on what you *do*. It's evident you're raising great kids."

She chuckled. "You've barely met them."

"Yeah, and they're great kids."

"How do you know?"

"They have a great mother."

For the second time in ten minutes, he was complimenting her in a way that she didn't know how to respond to. Rather than ignoring it, she simply glanced away and said, "You're being far too kind for a friend, Cameron. If you're not careful, I might think you have ulterior motives."

"Maybe I do," he said so seriously that she had to look at him to gauge his intent. Their eyes met in a way that was becoming almost comfortable, as if they could openly search each other's souls with no embarrassment.

"And what might that be?" she asked.

"I just . . . hope that we can be friends forever."

"And that's why you're flattering me?"

"It's not flattery, Christina, if I'm being honest. I think you're a beautiful, amazing person, so why shouldn't I let you know?"

Once again, Christy inhaled his sincerity, amazed at how good she could feel about herself in his presence. "You're very kind," she said. "And if you must know, the feeling is mutual. I think you're a beautiful, amazing person, too. In fact, you're so cute that I wonder if I should be hanging around with a man who is better looking than me."

"Hardly," he said with an edge, then he glanced down, apparently uncomfortable.

"Did I say something wrong?" she asked.

"No, of course not. I just . . ."

"What?" she pressed. When he hesitated, she said, "Friends are supposed to be honest with each other."

"Okay, but . . . that doesn't mean I have to spill my every secret."

"A secret, huh?" She lifted her brows several times and he chuckled.

"Not really. It's just . . . something I have a hard time with."

"What? Tell me," she gently persisted. "Unless you really don't want to, of course."

"I don't mind telling you," he said. "I just wonder how it will sound."

"I'm not passing any judgment here, Cameron. Just tell me."

"Well, I guess this is one of those sore points I have that kind of goes along with the money issue."

"You mean the way people behave toward you because they know you're wealthy."

"Precisely. Well, the thing is . . . I actually did some modeling in college. I didn't spend my youth looking in the mirror and being impressed with what I saw. It was just me, and I struggled with acne and finding the right hair cut in my youth just like everybody else. But after hearing about a hundred times that I had the right looks to be a model, I finally decided to try it out. I made good money and it put me through college."

"Your dad didn't pay your way through college?"

"Not at all," he said. "My father made it clear that he had made his own fortune, from the ground up. He'd seen how first-generation millionaires were usually decent people, but the ones who inherited their fortunes often had problems. He expected me and Sherry to work for what we got."

"Sherry must be your sister."

"That's right.

"So, I have to admit, I tried a number of temporary professions to get myself through school, and I wasn't very good at any of them. But the modeling worked for me, and I felt blessed to have the means it gave me to make money when I needed it. On the downside, I think the experience made me almost resent the way I look."

"For the same reason that you have to wonder if people are drawn to you because of the money."

"That's right," he said. "I've found that I tend to attract people who are very superficial. I've always tried to dress conservatively and not draw attention to myself. You know the car I own is pretty average. But I often find people just . . . looking at me, and it's uncomfortable. It's funny how people can see me from the outside and think, 'He's handsome and rich. What else could he possibly need?' And they have no idea that while I'm grateful for what I've been blessed with, it can be a curse sometimes. They also have no idea that my life has not necessarily been easy. Money doesn't keep people you love from dying . . . or leaving you."

"Well," Christy said, hoping to brighten the mood, "I promise to always be your friend, even though you're handsome and rich."

"And if I were ugly and poor?"

She smiled and took his hand. "Do you really think I invited you over tonight because you're handsome and rich?"

"No," he said firmly. "That's why I'm here."

"But I can still enjoy looking at you, right?" she said with mischief in her voice.

"Only if I can enjoy looking at you," he said with such a blatant sparkle in his eyes that she almost blushed. She hadn't felt attractive since she'd blossomed with her first pregnancy. But when Cameron Chandler looked at her, she felt beautiful and valuable without even trying.

"As long as we're on the subject," she asked, glancing away, "may I make a confession?"

"Of course. It seems to be fashionable at the moment."

She chuckled and said, "I must admit that when I first saw you, your appearance made me leery." His eyes widened and she went on. "You see . . . Keith is actually very good looking, and he just seems to get more so with age. I think I always felt somehow inferior because I'm just so . . . average looking, I suppose."

"No, Christina," he said, actually touching her face, "you're a very beautiful woman."

"Funny," she said, unable to camouflage the emotion in her voice, "I haven't felt beautiful for such a long time."

"Have you ever considered that such a feeling had nothing to do with you? It's evident you take good care of yourself. I think it's more likely a result of the way you were treated."

Christy felt a sensitive point validated and quickly wiped her eyes before the tears had a chance to brim over. "As I said, you're very sweet. And it's really nice to hear you say that. I think you're right . . . at least to some degree. The fact is . . . my husband was very vain, and his good looks obviously attracted another woman; at least one that I know of."

"You know, Christina, it wasn't your husband's appearance that made him the way he was; it was the way he used his appearance."

Christy smiled and said, "Just like it's not money that's the root of all evil, but the *love* of money."

"Precisely," he said and together they laughed.

Chapter Six

"So, where do you live exactly," Christy asked, "when you're not staying with your aunt?"

"I'm homeless," he said soberly, then he chuckled. "Actually, I had a home once, about the size of this one, I believe." He glanced around. "After the divorce, Jolene moved to Florida to make a fresh start. I sold the house and just started staying in the apartment at the top of my office building."

"Ooh," she teased, "a penthouse."

"Sort of, I suppose. It's just a little studio apartment. Nothing spectacular. But it is convenient. Occasionally I—or my father—would stay there when work demanded long hours. But after the divorce I became somewhat of a workaholic, and it just seemed that the house was an unnecessary expense. I think there were times when I hardly left the building except for church and business trips. I had one of the assistants bring in food here and there. My life was pretty pathetic.

"When my dad got cancer, my priorities took a drastic shift. We basically put the company into maintenance mode, and let the vice presidents and officers do what they were paid to do. I spent every possible minute with my father, and hardly gave the business a second thought. They seemed to manage well enough, but there were some problems that resulted. Since my father's death, I've been able to achieve a little better balance. I now know how to put in a good work week and still have somewhat of a life. I buy my own groceries now."

"I'm impressed," she said lightly. "So, have you been dating, then?"

He chuckled. "Not for a long time."

"So, what exactly does having somewhat of a life outside the office entail?"

"Oh, I have some friends I spend time with, although most of them are married. I do a lot of wandering around—window-shopping, I guess. Museums and stuff like that. And there's a certain amount of travel required in my work. I'm back and forth between New York and LA quite regularly. Oh, and I work one night a week at the temple."

"Really?" She couldn't help being surprised, because most of the temple workers were elderly people. "That's great."

"Yeah, it is. I really enjoy it. I think it helps me keep perspective."

"I'm ashamed to say I haven't gone much since . . . Keith left."

"Well, you're very busy. There's a big difference in having extra time that gets wasted, and spending your whole life taking care of a family. It's a matter of seasons in our life, I believe."

"That's true," she said, appreciating his perspective.

Christy was startled to hear the door open in the other room, then Lucy and Tim appeared, assaulting her with hugs and laughter. "You're home early," she said after a quick glance at the clock.

"Dad's got to go somewhere early in the morning," Lucy said.

Charlotte appeared in the doorway the same moment the other children took notice that their mother had company. "Hello," Christy said to her daughter, then she motioned toward Cameron. "You remember Mr. Chandler."

"Hi," she said, just as she had the last time he'd been here. Christy sensed some tension from Charlotte and wished she knew what the child was thinking. Lucy and Tim seemed to take Cameron's presence in stride. Perhaps they sensed the friendship that had been established between them, while Charlotte could perhaps be reading something deeper into the fact that her mother had a male friend.

"Hello," Cameron said and came to his feet. "Well, obviously I should go and let you visit with your children. I'll just—"

"This is quaint," Keith's voice said and Christy looked up to see him standing in the doorway behind Charlotte. His eyes were focused on the man standing in front of him, and she sensed his anger. Noting the way Cameron returned his gaze almost defiantly, she willed her heart to slow down and said in an even voice, "Keith, this is my friend, Cameron. Cameron, my ex-husband."

"Hello," Cameron said, but Keith didn't say anything.

"Cameron is Sister Hammond's nephew," she said, hoping to ease the obvious tension.

"How nice," Keith said. Christy almost expected Cameron to hurry away as quickly as possible, now that the situation had become uncomfortable. But she couldn't help hoping he would stay—at least until Keith left. She could never explain how safe Cameron made her feel. She knew Keith would never physically hurt her, but they never shared an encounter where his words were not wounding.

"Did you need something?" Christy asked, attempting to focus on the moment at hand. Keith finally turned to look at her.

"Tim ran into the door this morning and cut his forehead. He's got a few stitches. Doctor said to keep it clean, put ointment on it, and to get them removed in ten days."

Christy lifted Tim's hair to examine the wound while Keith spoke. "Did it hurt, buddy?" she asked.

"Yeah. Mostly when I got the shot to numb it."

"Well, I'm glad it wasn't any worse," Christy said, then she became acutely aware of the silence in the room. She glanced at Cameron and saw him watching her, apparently waiting for some cue as to what she wanted him to do. She could only briefly return his gaze, praying that he would read her need for him to stay. He turned to look at Keith again and put his hands in his pockets, as if to make himself comfortable.

Christy was ready to politely dismiss Keith, now that he'd reported the news, when he said snidely, "Do I need to take the kids back home with me?"

"What are you implying?" she retorted, fighting to keep her voice steady. Her gratitude for having Cameron here to buffer the situation far outweighed her embarrassment.

"I'm not implying anything. I'm not leaving my kids here to be exposed to whatever you might be doing with a strange man in the house."

Christy swallowed hard and counted to ten, while she glanced at Cameron, praying he would see this for what it was. His expression—if not his presence—boosted her confidence. She calmly said, "You children go to your rooms and start unpacking. I'll be there in a few minutes."

As soon as they had all left the room, and Christy took a quick peek in the hall to make certain they weren't eavesdropping, she turned to Keith and said firmly, "You have a lot of nerve to come in here and make such accusations after what you did to this family. Don't you ever come here again and make threats and assumptions when you have no idea what you're talking about. Cameron and I are *friends,* but even if it were more than that, it would be no business of yours."

"It's my business when you're exposing my children to—"

"Get out of here," she insisted, clearly recognizing the symptoms of a growing argument that would never come to anything positive. "If you have something to say, you can call my attorney."

Keith glared at Cameron, who drew back his shoulders and put his hands on his hips—a gesture that clearly challenged Keith. He tossed one more glare at Christy and snapped, "You keep this up and you will be hearing from *my* attorney." He left the house and slammed the door.

Christy blew out a long breath and pressed her hands over her queasy stomach. "Did that make any sense to you, whatsoever?"

"Yes, actually," Cameron said. "He's guilty, he's delusional, and he's judging you by his standards." He chuckled sardonically. "You would be amazed at how close that came to conversations I had with Jolene after the divorce, except that there were no children involved, of course."

"Really?" Christy asked, amazed to feel so thoroughly understood.

"Really," he said earnestly, and she took a deep breath to absorb a new layer of validation. "Well," he added, "I should go and let you catch up with the kids. Thank you for a wonderful evening."

"I enjoyed it," she admitted.

"I'll be in touch," he said, and Christy locked the door behind him.

She spent a short while each with Tim and Lucy in their rooms, seeing the gifts they'd received, and hearing of the activities they'd done with their father and Patricia. She had to fight feelings of resentment to hear them talk about how they liked Patricia and how much fun she was. She reminded herself that she wouldn't want them to have a difficult and ornery stepmother. It was simply their having a stepmother that disturbed her. She left them to get ready for bed and went to Charlotte's room to find her unpacking. Charlotte too showed Christy the gifts she'd received, but she didn't say much about what she'd done since Christmas day.

"So, how did it go?" Christy asked.

"Fine, I guess."

"Didn't you have fun?"

"Well . . . yeah, most of the time. I just . . . wish it didn't have to be this way."

Christy was grateful to hear Charlotte talking so openly, but there was a contrasting heartache on her daughter's behalf. Still, she felt a deepening of their bond when she was able to take Charlotte's hand and say, "I know exactly how you feel, honey. I wish every hour of every day that it didn't have to be this way. And I wish there was something I could do to change it."

Charlotte smiled sadly and wiped at a sudden rush of tears. They talked for a few minutes about the emotions she had gone through concerning the divorce, in a way they had never been able to do before. When it became evident she'd said all she was going to, Christy hugged her and murmured, "I love you, Charlotte, and I don't ever want to see you hurting. I hope you'll always come and talk to me so that we can get through this together."

Christy was moved to tears herself when Charlotte tightly returned the embrace and said, "I love you too, Mom."

Charlotte pulled back and grabbed a tissue to blow her nose before she asked, "Is this Cameron guy your boyfriend?"

Christy was taken aback by the abrupt change in the conversation. She figured it was a good sign that her teenage daughter didn't seem displeased with the idea of her mother dating, as she had previously, but she insisted, "No, honey, we're just friends. We've made that very clear. I'm not ready for anything romantic yet."

"But if you were, Mom, wouldn't he be the kind of guy you'd want to date?"

Christy smiled and had to admit, "Yes, actually, he would be."

"He's rich, isn't he?" Charlotte said with a little smirk.

"How did you know that?" Christy retorted, wondering what she might have absently said in front of her daughter.

"I'm not deaf, Mom," she said, but gave no further explanation.

"Yes, he's rich," Christy said. "But—"

"And he's really cute," Charlotte added.

"Yes," Christy chuckled, "he's that, too. But that has nothing to do with my reasons for spending time with him. Good looks and money don't make a person worthy of our admiration. In fact, I tend to generally be put off by such things. However, Cameron is not vain or arrogant in the slightest. He's a good man with a good heart, and I think Heavenly Father knew I needed a friend."

"That's good, Mom, but . . . you have to admit that having a friend who is rich and handsome certainly has its appeal." They laughed together, while Christy reminded herself that it was typical for teenagers to be more concerned with superficial qualities.

"I suppose it does," Christy said. "But seriously, he's extremely kind and gracious. And he's divorced, too. He's been through a lot, and he understands how I feel. It's nice to talk to someone who does."

Charlotte smiled. "That's neat, Mom. I'm happy for you."

Christy squeezed her daughter's hand, silently thanking her Father in Heaven for giving her one more glimpse of light. Charlotte's distance and belligerence had been just one more difficulty to deal with the past year. She couldn't help wondering if something had happened during her stay with her father to give her some perspective and appreciate the relationship they shared as mother and daughter.

That, combined with her growing friendship with Cameron, made her feel more tangible hope than she'd felt in a long time. She found it easier to go to sleep, and easier to get up in the morning and go to work, knowing in her heart that God was truly mindful of her. What else did she need to know?

* * * * *

After hours of finding it difficult to focus on his work, Cameron took an early lunch and wandered both of the downtown malls, searching for an elite gift shop that sold the type of items Christy had described. He finally wandered into a spacious shop, tastefully arranged, and invitingly warm. He felt relatively certain he'd found the right place, simply by the way he felt as he stood there. It had a certain refined quality that reminded him of Christina Hardy herself.

Rodney was concentrating on the book on the counter in front of him when he heard Mazie say in a hushed voice, "Oh, my gosh. Is that . . . Holy Toledo, it is!"

"Is what?" he asked in the same hushed tone.

"That man who just came in . . . that's Cameron Chandler."

"Yippee Skippy," Rodney said tonelessly. "Is this supposed to mean something to me?"

"Yes, you idiot. Cameron Chandler, also known as Bruce Chandler the third."

"The charity game guy?" he whispered, aghast, trying to discreetly get a good look at him through the wind chime display.

"The very same."

"How do you know?"

"Remember, I told you I knew him as a kid," she said. "But his picture has been all over the news lately. Where have you been?"

"Reading, if you must know." Rodney chuckled. "Oh, man; too bad Christy's gone to lunch. She would freak out. I bet she'd like to give him a piece of her mind."

"No doubt," Mazie said. "That's because she's not clever enough to know how to treat a rich man. Keep your distance, Rod. If I can't get him to buy something expensive, I'll buy you a pretzel."

"Go for it," Rodney chuckled and watched her walk away, smoothing her hair and skirt.

Cameron was startled by a high feminine voice asking, "May I help you?" He turned to see a skinny blonde girl with too much makeup, and clothes that were too tight. Her name tag read *Mazie*.

"Yes, actually," he said. "Do you have porcelain seagulls?"

"We do," she said eagerly and he followed her around a display of wind chimes to a glass case where a number of porcelain items were displayed. He chuckled delightedly to see exactly what he'd been searching for. While he was pondering which one he liked best, Mazie interrupted his thoughts with her high-pitched voice, "Forgive me for being presumptuous, but aren't you Cameron Chandler?"

He turned in surprise, searching for some kind of familiarity. Few people knew him as Cameron, but for the life of him, he couldn't place her face in his memory. "Yes," he said, wishing it had sounded more polite. He didn't necessarily like the crustiness he'd developed toward people. "Do I know you?"

"Well," she snorted a laugh, "you probably don't remember me, but we grew up in the same ward."

"Oh," Cameron said, feeling somewhat relieved.

"I was just a kid when you got married, but I know my dad worked with your dad in the bishopric."

"Oh," he said again, feeling more pleasant. "And his name would be . . ."

"Eldon Johnstone," she said and Cameron smiled.

"Of course," he said, "I remember your father well. And how is he?"

"Doing well, actually. And yours?"

Cameron felt his expression darken. He looked away and forced back the bite of envy; this woman's father was still living. "He, uh . . . passed away a few months ago—cancer."

"Oh, I'm so sorry," she said, but a quick glimpse at her eyes told him she was being more patronizing than empathetic.

Cameron cleared his throat and pointed to the seagulls. "They're very beautiful," he said, wanting only to change the subject.

"Yes, they are," she said and embarked on a well-memorized oration of the sculptor who had created them, and the process of their fine creation. "Are you looking for a gift?" she asked. "Or something for yourself?"

"Oh, it's a gift," he said decisively.

She turned a key in the glass door and swung it carefully open. "A special occasion, or—"

"It's for a friend," he said firmly. "Kind of a thank-you gift."

"This friend must have done something pretty wonderful," she said, absently fingering one of the price tags.

"Yes, actually," he said, "it was."

While Cameron carefully picked up each of six different varieties, pondering which he liked best, Mazie rambled on about how she'd heard about the death of his son and his divorce, and how terrible it must have been for him. Something in her voice seemed to say she'd be more than eager to help console him—given that he was rich. How could he not recognize the symptoms, when he'd been exposed to the disease so many times before? He grunted to indicate he'd heard, while he did his best to shut her out and focus on his intended purchase. She droned on about how marvelous she thought his charity project had been, and he wished once again that he had declined the media interviews that had attached him so blatantly to a project he had such mixed feelings about.

Cameron finally narrowed his choice down to two, and he set them forward on the shelf while he contemplated their differences. "I really like this one," Mazie said, pointing to the one on the left.

"I'll take this one," he said, picking up the one on the right.

She tossed him a subtle scowl and he couldn't help but smile. He'd come to easily recognize the people who were attracted to all the superficial qualities of his life—most specifically, his money. And this was one of them. If he were old, ugly, and poor, she wouldn't be giving him the time of day. And he resented it. But his thoughts lightened as he more closely observed the work of art in his hands. It so much reminded him of Christina Hardy. And she was different than any woman he'd ever known.

"Would you like it wrapped?" she asked, taking it from him.

"Yes, please," he said, "and do you have any cards?"

"Right over there." She pointed to a circular rack near the counter.

Cameron perused the artistic selection of cards for only a couple of minutes before he found the perfect one. On the cover was a photograph of a dark sky, with a sliver of a yellow moon, and one bright star. Inside it read: *Thanks for bringing some light into my life.*

Mazie rang up the card and the seagull. He handed her a credit card which she handed to a young man behind the counter. "You finish this while I wrap it," she told him and disappeared into a back room.

Cameron pulled a pen out of his inside jacket pocket and wrote: *And thanks for being the kind of person who is receptive enough to answer prayers for Him who counts on human hands to do His work. You've helped me through a dark time more than I could tell you. I hope to see you soon. Lunch tomorrow, perhaps? Your friend, always, Cameron.*

He sealed up the card, signed the receipt and put it into his wallet along with the credit card. Mazie appeared with a beautifully wrapped package and set it on the counter. Cameron wrote *Christina* on the envelope and tucked the card beneath the ribbon on the package.

"Now," he said, "I assume your manager is not in at the moment."

"That's right," Mazie said, screwing up her forehead in obvious bewilderment. The other clerk, whose name tag read *Rodney*, stood looking on.

"And I assume your manager would be Christina Hardy."

"That's right," Mazie said again, her brow furrowing more deeply.

"Well, when she comes back, give her this." He pushed the package into Mazie's hands, took a long look at her shocked countenance, and left the shop.

* * * * *

"Unbelievable!" Mazie gasped, startling Rodney out of a daze.

"You can say that again."

"Unbelievable!"

Rodney chuckled and she demanded, "What's so funny?"

"The whole thing is funny. I can't wait to hear how Christy managed to get an expensive *thank-you* gift from the very man she was badmouthing last week. This has got to be good."

Mazie grunted and got busy dusting the array of tiny statuettes along the north wall of the store. A few minutes later Christy walked in and headed straight for the back room. Rodney fell into step behind her and Mazie met her at the door with a gift in her hands.

"What is this?" Christy demanded, questioning their behavior as much as the package.

"A gentleman came in a while ago," Rodney said with a smirk. "He bought this and asked us to give it to you."

Christy's heart quickened but she forced a subdued voice as she said, "Really?"

She took the package and attempted to move past them to the back room, but together they blocked her path. "What?" she demanded.

"Fess up, Christy," Mazie said. "We want to know how you managed to earn an expensive gift from the same Mr. Chandler you were badmouthing last week."

Christy knew her shock was evident by their pleased expressions. She felt like a very small mouse looking into the faces of two very large cats. She wasn't going to lie, but she had no desire to tell these people every detail of her holiday encounter. While she was attempting to gather the right words, three people walked into the store. Christy nodded in their direction and said, "See to the customers. I'm still on my lunch break."

Mazie scowled. Rodney pointed a finger and said, "You're not going to get out of this. You've got egg on your face, and I want to hear about it."

"I'll tell you, okay? Just give me a few minutes."

Christy escaped to her office and closed the door. She couldn't help laughing at the very idea of Cameron Chandler giving her a gift. Wanting to savor the experience, she slowly opened the envelope and drew out the card. She recognized it as one he'd purchased here, but his hand-written words tempted tears into her eyes. She quickly blinked them back and opened the gift, slowly enough to enjoy the moment, but not so slowly as to be interrupted by her coworkers. Christy didn't know what she'd expected, but when she pulled back the tissue to reveal the familiar porcelain seagull that she had longed to own for many months, the tears she'd been fighting misted her vision. Her conversation with Cameron regarding seagulls and miracles washed over her with a warm tingle. *Hope.* That was what he had brought into her life. She silently thanked God for sending her such a friend, then she cautioned herself to not become too dependent on such a friendship.

Hearing someone in the storage room next door, Christy quickly tucked the card into the box with the seagull and closed it. She blinked back the tears and stole a quick glance at herself in a mirror to make certain her eyes didn't show any hint of emotion. She quickly prepared an honest but cautious response to their questions, then she impulsively made a business call that would give her a few more minutes to get her composure. When the call was completed, she found Rodney and Mazie both behind the counter, and the store void of customers.

"Okay," she said in response to their expectancy, "I have egg on my face. I admit it. So, I'll tell you what happened, but it stays between the three of us."

"Of course," Rodney said.

"Absolutely," Mazie added, quickly crossing her heart with her hand.

"Well," Christy drawled sheepishly, "I was on my way home on Christmas Eve, when I passed a stalled car, and this guy walking. The storm was horrible, and the road was basically deserted. So I picked him up."

"You found Bruce Chandler in need of charity?" Rodney chortled. "Oh, that's just too precious!"

"It was a setup," Mazie said. "It had to be."

"It wasn't a setup," Christy insisted. "It had nothing to do with that other thing, whatsoever. Turns out his aunt lives in my ward, and I know her quite well. I had Christmas dinner with them while my kids were gone. There. That's it."

"So," Mazie said with that cat-chasing-the-mouse expression, "is this some . . . romantic thing or what? Is he—"

"Of course not!" Christy insisted. "We're friends. We had a lot to talk about, but I made it very clear that I'm not dating. End of story."

That evening after she'd played a game with the kids, supervised getting the dishes washed and the house picked up, and tucked the children in bed, Christy mustered the courage to call Cameron's home number. She was almost relieved to get his machine, and she chuckled at his recorded voice saying: *If you know who you're talking to, leave a message. If not, call somebody else. Either way, have a nice day.* The beep startled her into speaking. "Hi, it's me, Christy. Thank you for the beautiful gift. You made my day, really. Maybe I'll see you tomorrow. Good night."

Reminded of the gift, Christy took it out of the box and set it reverently in the center of her dresser, where it was reflected in the mirror. A symbol of hope. She read the card once more, then tucked it into the side of the mirror before she got into her nightgown and brushed her teeth. She'd just finished checking the doors and lights when the phone rang. The caller ID said *private* and she felt relatively certain that it was him. "Hello," she said.

"You're welcome," she heard him say. "I'm glad you like it."

They ended up talking over an hour, until Christy was just too tired to stay awake any longer. But long after she hung up the phone, she stared at the ceiling, wondering why she felt more alive inside than she had in years.

Chapter Seven

The following morning was business as usual, while Christy enjoyed the extra little light she felt in her life from Cameron's presence. Late in the morning, while Rodney was straightening the candles on the far side of the store, Christy had her back to the counter, going over some invoices. She had no reason to believe there was anyone else in the store when she heard a loud, "Hello there."

She screamed and turned abruptly to see Cameron Chandler chuckling at his obvious intent to startle her. "That was rude!" she insisted.

"I know, but . . . I'm certain you'll get even eventually."

"I guess I'll have to," she said. "So, what are you doing here?"

"I was hoping you didn't have plans for lunch, because I'm starved . . . for your company as well as a good bowl of soup. What do you say? My treat."

Christy was almost afraid to admit—even to herself—how absolutely delightful his invitation sounded. She couldn't come up with a single reason to say no, so she glanced at the clock and said, "I can leave in ten or fifteen minutes."

"Great," he said. "I'll be back to get you."

"I'll be ready," she said and watched him walk away.

She found herself staring after him when Rodney said beside her, "Just friends, eh?"

"Yes, just friends," she insisted.

"Maybe so," he said. "But most friends don't look at each other the way you do."

Christy willed herself not to turn warm over the implication. She couldn't possibly have romantic feelings for *any* man when everything inside of her wanted nothing more than to have Keith come back and make everything right. Unable to respond, she hurried to the restroom to freshen up before Cameron came back. She stepped out of the back room with her purse to see a young woman with a camera talking to Rodney. They both turned toward her as Rodney explained, "She's doing some promotional stuff for the mall and wants to take a few pictures."

"Okay, fine," Christy said to her. "I'm on my way out, but Rodney can help you with whatever you need."

"Oh, I've got what I need," she said, indicating her camera. "Just do your thing. You won't even know I'm here."

Christy smiled and hurried to straighten a few items, then she glanced over some papers behind the counter while she was aware of a flash going off occasionally. She felt mildly annoyed to realize that Cameron been gone nearly twenty-five minutes, but she forgot all about it when she looked up to see him walking into the store, carrying a small sack from a nearby music store.

"Hi," they both said at the same time, then laughed.

To ease a sudden tension, Christy said, "By the way, this is Rodney, my assistant manager and a dear friend. Rodney, Cameron Chandler." She ignored the photographer who was on the other side of the store.

"It's a pleasure, Rodney," Cameron said with genuine sincerity and a hearty handshake.

"The pleasure is mine," Rodney said in return.

"Shall we go?" Cameron asked Christy and held out a hand.

Christy loved the feel of walking with Cameron's hand in hers. She felt a sense of belonging that she'd not felt since Keith's departure from her life—perhaps longer. As he guided her through the busy mall corridors, she pondered the innate desire of human beings to be connected to other human beings. God had created men and women to be together, and being alone just felt all wrong. She cautioned her thoughts to stay in a hypothetical mode, and not to apply the concept literally to the present circumstances. She was grateful for his companionship; simple as that. She didn't expect—or even want—

anything more to come of it. And she refused to even ask herself why the idea of never seeing him again caused her grief. She pushed such thoughts away and determined to make the most of the moment. He was a pleasant distraction, and she could bank on nothing more. If Keith came back, Cameron would have no comfortable place in her life, and she couldn't lead him—or herself—on with ideas that were preposterous under the circumstances.

At the entrance to the food court, he stopped and asked, "So, what would you like to eat?"

"You said something about soup; sounds good to me."

"You sure?" he asked. "You don't have to have soup just because I'm having soup."

"I said it sounds good to me."

He smiled and led the way to the right counter, where they waited in line only a few minutes before they both ordered potato cheese soup in bread bowls. It was dished up quickly and he carried their tray to a table right next to the huge window facing north toward the gardens between the Joseph Smith Memorial Building, and the Church office high-rise. "My favorite spot," she said and he smiled.

A few minutes into the meal, he passed the little sack he'd been carrying across the table and said, "This is for you."

"A gift a day," she chuckled. "I don't think you can keep this up."

"I really didn't intend to," he said. "It just . . . occurred to me this morning that you needed one of these."

Christy reached into the sack and pulled out the CD, wondering what it would be. She gasped when she realized she was looking at the soundtrack to *Jonathan Livingston Seagull*. "How did you know?" she asked and impulsively reached over the table to kiss his cheek.

Cameron laughed. "I didn't *know* anything. I just . . . sort of grew up listening to that. I came across the CD a while back and bought myself one, and I've enjoyed it. With the whole seagull thing, I thought you might like it. So, what is it that you think I know?"

"Well," she said, touching the cover almost reverently, "I had this on one of those antique record things when I was a kid. Even *if* I still owned a record player, the thing is so scratched and worn out. But I *love* this music, and I haven't heard it for years. Thank you."

He smiled. "You're welcome."

"You know I can't afford to buy *you* nice gifts."

"And I wouldn't expect you to," he said with a subtle scowl. "We're not keeping score here. We're just friends, and if all I could afford as a thank-you gift was a candy bar, then that's what you would get, but the sincerity would still be the same."

"Provided it was chocolate, of course."

"Of course," he chuckled and squeezed her hand across the table.

A few minutes later she said, "There's something I need to clear up."

"Okay," he said eagerly.

"Well . . . on Christmas Eve, after I'd picked you up, I think I said some things about you that weren't very favorable." He smirked and she went on. "Of course, I didn't know it was you, but still . . . you've taught me something about judging people and situations I know nothing about. Before I met you, when I was grumbling to Rodney about this very thing, he accused me of getting angry over silly things that had nothing to do with me, because I couldn't let myself get angry with Keith. Maybe he's right; I don't know. The thing is . . . I want to formally apologize for anything I might have said to you, or about you, that simply had no warrant."

"Apology accepted," he said with a warm smile. "But you must know that in a way you were absolutely right, and I agree with you."

"You're kidding," she said dubiously.

"No," he said, "I confess that I have very mixed emotions about the whole thing. This charity game was an idea my father had toyed with off and on for years, but he could never quite work out what he thought were potential flaws. When he died, there was a fund set aside for this very thing, and I just felt like I needed to do it. I'm afraid I did it impulsively, and a bit overzealously." He sighed with a deep sadness in his eyes, and Christy put her hand over his. "So there you have it," he finished.

"I'm sorry," she said.

"For what?"

"Well . . . just that things have been so obviously difficult for you lately."

He smiled, although the sadness still hovered in his eyes. "As they have been for you."

When they had finished eating, Cameron asked, "Have you got time for a walk in the gardens?" He motioned across the street.

"It's freezing out there," she said, not wanting to admit that she'd spent countless hours in the gardens, in any kind of weather.

"That's why we'll make it a quick, brisk walk, and it will make us appreciate the warmth of the mall all the more when we come back."

"I'd love to," she said and took his hand. She loved holding his hand, but the tiny inkling that she might actually be attracted to him was quickly squelched. How could she even entertain thoughts of another man, when her heart was still with Keith? Cameron was her friend, and that was just the way she liked it.

They both pulled gloves on as they stepped out of the building onto the wide sidewalk. Cameron took her hand as they started across the street, walking in time with the mechanical bird that signaled their right-of-way. They chatted comfortably as they turned and ambled into the Main Street garden. Standing for a minute next to the glass pond, Christy looked up at the temple spires and sighed. She wondered if she'd ever come to accept that the vows she had exchanged there had been shattered. She pushed the thought away and was glad to hear Cameron speak.

"I'm leaving town tomorrow," he said and she hated the intense disappointment she felt, almost as much as she hated the fact that she'd allowed that disappointment to blatantly show.

"Where you going?" she asked, forcing a light voice with the hope of counteracting her initial reaction.

"New York," he said and looked up toward the spires. "Remember, I told you Sherry, my sister, lives there. I worked out some business I need to do there, so that I could spend New Year's with her. The trip's been planned for weeks."

"Well, that will be nice for you . . . to be with your sister and—"

"I'd rather stay here with you, if you want to know the truth."

Christy looked away, wanting to tell him that she didn't want him to say such things, especially since she agreed. But she couldn't bring herself to admit or deny it, so she simply smiled and said, "When you get back, maybe we could . . ."

"What?" he asked when she hesitated.

She chuckled tensely. "Well, I was thinking maybe you could join us for family night, or something, but maybe you'd rather not or—"

"I'd love to join you for family night. I'll call you when I get back."

"I'll be counting on it."

He smiled and they began to walk back toward the mall. "Hey, do you have the kids for New Year's?"

"Keith was supposed to have them, but he's taking a ski trip with . . . his wife. Why?"

"I was just thinking that . . . I didn't want you to be alone, and if you didn't have them, well . . . you could come with me."

Christy laughed. "Me? Go to New York with you? That would be . . ."

"What?" he asked, but she couldn't put any words together to answer. "It would be totally appropriate, I promise. No hidden agendas; just a chance for you to get out of your rut."

Christy had to admit. "It sounds nice, actually. But . . . I have the kids, and well . . . maybe we should get to be a little better friends before we go exploring the world."

"Have you ever been to New York?"

"No," she laughed. "I've never been *anywhere.*"

"Well, we'll have to work on that," he said. "It's an incredible place to see. I wouldn't want to live there, but I truly enjoy being able to visit regularly."

"When are you leaving?" she asked as they neared the store.

"Tomorrow, early," he said. "But like I said, I'll call."

"Be careful," she said and they stopped just outside the store. "And . . . thanks for lunch."

"My pleasure."

"And for the CD."

"My pleasure," he repeated. He walked away and waved. Christy tore herself away from watching him and hurried into the store.

The remainder of Christmas vacation dragged for Christy. She kept busy with the kids through the hours she wasn't working, but her work hours droned on slowly. She found her mind absorbed far too much with Cameron Chandler, and she wondered how she could feel as if she'd known him forever, and at the same time feel as if he was a stranger. But then, the man she'd been married to for fifteen years felt like more of a stranger to her than any man she might pass on the street. She didn't know Keith at all—not any more. While she contemplated the comparisons, it occurred to her that with Cameron on her mind, she had hardly thought about Keith at all for several days. The idea was disturbing in the respect that she'd been practically obsessed with Keith since he'd left. She'd spent endless hours trying to analyze his motives and cope with his attitude, all the while praying that he would come back to her and make everything right. But now, those longings had been superceded in her mind by this new *friend* who had appeared in her life. She credited her thoughts about Cameron to the fact that he was new and intriguing, but instinctively she felt there was more to it than that. And the more she tried to come to terms with what she was feeling, the more weighed down she became.

The day before New Year's Eve, the phone rang while she was cleaning up after supper. She picked it up absently and heard Cameron say, "Hello, my friend."

"Hello," Christy said and exhaled with deep relief to hear his voice through the phone, sounding as close as if he were just up the street.

"How are you doing?" he asked.

"Do I have to be honest?"

"Of course. I wouldn't have asked, if I didn't want to know." She hesitated and he demanded, "What's wrong?"

"I've just . . . been thinking—a lot. Maybe too much. I mean . . . not really, because . . . well, I think the problem is that I haven't been thinking at all for so long, and now I'm thinking and I'm not sure I can handle it."

"Thinking about Keith, you mean."

She sighed. "Yeah."

"So, tell me."

"I'm not sure this is a good time to get into it."

"Do you need to be with the kids?"

"No, they're watching a movie that just started, but—"

"You've got an appointment or something?" he asked.

"No, but . . . it's long distance and—"

"I can afford it. And even if I couldn't, I'd pawn my watch or something to pay the phone bill." Christy laughed and he added, "I think you need to talk. So talk."

"Okay . . . well, I'm not sure where to begin, but . . ."

"You've been thinking. What have you been thinking about?"

"Well, this sounds really kind of stupid, but . . . I feel as if . . . it's just occurred to me that the man I thought I knew so well is actually a complete stranger to me. And maybe he always was. I think I've spent all these months trying to make myself believe that I know him better than anyone, and that I knew there was something inside of him that would realize he'd made a mistake, and he'd come back to me."

Christy heard a deep sigh before he asked, "Is that what you want? For him to come back?" She hesitated and he added, "Do you really think you could take the full enormity of everything that's happened, and put it behind you? You're talking about a great deal of betrayal, broken trust, and some very deep hurt. Do you really think that's possible?"

Christy quickly said, "If he wanted it, too. If he had the right attitude, and was truly sorry."

"And that's the clincher, isn't it, Christy? There's a great big fat *if* attached to *his* attitude. Has he said or done anything since he left you to indicate that he could ever come up with that much penitence?"

It took several seconds of silence before Christy could choke out the word, "No."

"So, are you . . . what? Waiting for a miracle? What?" His words were firm, but spoken with compassion.

"I don't know," she said, unable to hide the fact that she was crying. "I guess I just . . . keep hoping that he'll come back and . . . give me another chance to make things right, and . . ."

"Wait a minute. Did you say: give *you* another chance? Are you saying you have accountability in what he did?"

"Well . . . yes . . . I . . ."

"What, Christy? Is there something you haven't told me? Were you cheating on him? Secretly abusing the children? Were you lazy? Rude? Selfish?"

"No!" she insisted and took the phone into the bedroom and closed the door, where the children wouldn't overhear.

"Then what exactly did you do that brought this on?"

"Well . . . I guess I just stopped being . . . fun and intriguing. Everything became so caught up in raising the kids and paying the bills and . . ."

"You and millions of other middle-America families. Is there something wrong with that?"

"Only that the marriage obviously took a back burner. I should have been . . . trying harder to keep him . . . interested and . . ."

"And what should he have been trying harder to do, Christy?" She didn't answer and he went on. "Now, let me give you some perspective that took me a long time to get myself. First of all, even *if* you had been a very poor wife, even *if* you'd had some serious struggles that affected your relationship, he could have come to you at any time and said, 'We've got some problems and we need to work on them.' If he was feeling unfulfilled and bored with your relationship, he could have let you know. He could have done something about it."

Christy pressed a hand over her mouth to keep from whimpering into the phone as his words began to penetrate the very heart of her pain. "I'd bet a great deal," he went on, "if he'd put half the effort into making you happy that he put into impressing this *eternal soul mate* of his, you'd be living in marital bliss. I realize we haven't known each other long, Christy, but I know you well enough to know that you're the kind of woman who genuinely wants to do the right thing. I also know you're human. But listen carefully when I tell you that you don't have to be perfect to expect a husband to stay loyal and committed."

Christy melted from the inside out as that last statement broke open the festering wounds that had plagued her since Keith's departure. The pain oozed from her heart into every nerve of her body and she curled up on the bed, barely managing to hold the phone against her ear. The blackness that she had felt surrounding her for nearly a year suddenly became so thick that she feared it would swallow her. While she was praying inwardly that she would be spared any more pain, she was startled to hear Cameron say through the phone, "You okay?"

Christy could only whimper a noise to indicate that she was still there. She knew she could never form words without setting free the torrents of emotion stuck in her throat.

"Talk to me, Christy," he insisted gently.

She moved a trembling hand from over her mouth to press it against the throbbing between her eyes. Gathering every grain of self control, she forced herself to say, "Maybe I should go." A heaving sob came in the wake of her words and she clamped a hand over her mouth again.

"And maybe you shouldn't," he said. "If I could hold your hand, I would, but I can't right now. So you're just going to have to hold onto the phone until you get it out of your system. I've got all night. So, just cry all you want; scream if you have to. You've lost something, Christy, and it hurts. You have a right to mourn and to grieve, and I'm here for you. Because I know *exactly* how you feel. As long as I live I will never forget the night I finally came to accept that Jolene had hurt me, and abandoned me, in spite of anything I could have done. And she wasn't going to come back."

A sob pressed through Christy's hand as she heard him perfectly validate, once again, the full perspective of what she felt—and what she had to accept. She finally succumbed to the force of her emotion, and accepted Cameron's permission to mourn. She lost track of the time she spent crying into her pillow, with the phone turned away from her mouth, but pressed tightly to her ear. When she finally calmed down, she heard him say gently, "Are you still with me?"

"Yes," she said, her voice cracked and hoarse.

"Feel any better?"

"It's hard to say. I just . . ." The tears rushed forward again, but at least she was able to speak through them. "Now I know why I've hidden from my feelings all this time."

"But you can't hide from feelings; they always catch up with you eventually, and the longer they've been hidden, the harder they are to face."

"Yes, I can testify that's true." She forced a chuckled that turned into a sob. "But . . . how can I go on with this kind of pain? How can I ever . . ." She became too emotional to speak.

"You don't have to, Christy." She didn't respond and he asked, "Are you with me?"

"Yes."

"There's something you need to hear that is by far the most important thing that I, or anyone else, could ever tell you to get you through this, or anything else you might come up against in your life. I know you already know it, but sometimes I think that we as humans don't fully comprehend, or know how to accept it. Are you listening?"

"Yes."

"Christy, you don't have to go on with the pain, because the price for that pain has already been paid. The Atonement covers it all. He already suffered this for you, Christy. You don't have to suffer any more when it's already been taken care of. He paid the price, not only for our sins and mistakes, but for our sorrow, our grief, our pain. Just ask Him to take the burden, Christina, and He will." She heard his voice break with emotion. "I testify to you that He will. And that doesn't mean life suddenly becomes easy. It doesn't mean you don't have to live with the ramifications of this situation. But it does mean you can find peace, and you can move forward, and you can find a way to be truly happy, perhaps happier than you've ever been."

He allowed her a few minutes of silence to absorb what he'd said. As the words rolled through her mind again and again, she felt them very naturally turn to prayer. With all the energy of her heart and soul, she prayed inwardly for the pain to be taken away. As she contemplated the Atonement in a way she'd never fully considered before, the idea began to penetrate her soul with the tiniest spark of hope against a black horizon. She squeezed her eyes shut and attempted to take hold of that spark and absorb its warmth. While Cameron's silent support continued, she felt the light begin to soften her heart, until it infused slowly, but wholly, her entire being, driving away the darkness and despair that had bound her.

Following another long silence, Cameron said, "Christina? Are you okay?"

"Yes, actually," she said and sniffled, "I think I am. Thank you. I think I need some time to just . . . digest everything. But you've said a lot that's helped me. I hear the kids; the movie must be over, but . . . thank you, Cameron."

"Hey, what are friends for?"

"Well, you're the best friend a girl could ever ask for."

"I'll call tomorrow and see how you're doing," he said and Christy hurried to say good-bye and wash her face before the kids searched her out.

Chapter Eight

Through that night and the following day, Christy marveled over and over at the miracle. She'd always believed in the Atonement, and had felt she'd understood it. But she had struggled with subtle nagging doubts that had tempted her to believe she wasn't worthy of such blessings. Never had she imagined that her pain could be so quickly—and so tangibly—eased through its healing power. It truly was a miracle. And as Christy pondered the changes taking place in her thought processes, the miracle deepened. The validation of the Spirit had soothed her aching soul and calmed her battered heart. She felt the truth of what Cameron had told her settle firmly into her mind: *You don't have to be perfect to expect a husband to stay loyal and committed.* She knew in her heart that in spite of her imperfections and challenges, she had been blatantly wronged by her husband. In fully acknowledging his crimes against her, she became consumed with anger. She prayed to come to terms with her feelings toward Keith and find peace, but the anger didn't subside as quickly as the pain had.

She was still absorbed with her thoughts when Cameron called early that evening, as he'd promised. "You sound upset," he said right off. "What's wrong? You're not digressing here, are you?"

"No . . . I don't think so. I mean . . . don't they say it gets worse before it gets better?"

"Yes, I believe that's how it works. So, what's worse?"

"Well, I think it's been really good for me to acknowledge how much he hurt me, and that he wronged me, but now I just feel so . . . *angry!*" She ground out the last word through clenched teeth. "I want to just . . . call him up and scream at him and tell him exactly what I think of him, but . . . I know that wouldn't help anything. Did you ever feel this angry?"

"Did I?" he chuckled. "Boy, did I! And you're right, screaming at him won't accomplish anything good. On the other hand, if the opportunity ever presents itself for you to express your feelings *appropriately* . . . then that might be a good thing. If you must know, I actually had a really hard time with this anger thing."

"So, how did you come to terms with it?"

"Well, I spent a lot of time talking to my bishop, and he actually referred me to a few sessions with a counselor, which helped immensely. She helped me understand that anger is a secondary emotion, which means it's generally a mask for hurt, or fear, or frustration. When you learn to recognize *why* you're angry, then you can deal with those feelings appropriately. In this case, you're angry because you're really hurt and betrayed."

Christy thought about it. "Yeah, I can see that."

"So, if you can find peace with the hurt and betrayal, then you can be free of the anger. And then you can forgive him, and let what he's done stop affecting your life."

"But right now I can't even comprehend forgiving him. And that makes me feel like a bad person."

"Do you want to know what that counselor told me about forgiveness?"

"Yes, I do," she said eagerly.

"She told me that forgiveness comes in layers, along with healing from the hurt. You can't just snap your fingers and say you've forgiven someone if you don't truly feel it. When justice is met, it can help forgiveness along. But often justice isn't met in this world, and that's where trusting in the Lord, and knowing that He will take care of it, helps shift the burden to Him. Another thing that really helped me was understanding that forgiveness and trust are not the same thing. Forgiveness should be given unconditionally, because that's what the Lord told us to do. But trust has to be earned. I learned that when I was saying, 'I can never forgive her,' what I really meant was, 'I can never trust her.' Big, *big* difference."

"Yeah, it sure is," Christy said thoughtfully, then said nothing more.

"You okay?"

"Yeah . . . I think so. You've just given me a lot to think about . . . again."

"Well, I can give you plenty of time to do that," he said soberly.

"What do you mean?"

"I'm going to have to stay a few more days than I'd anticipated."

Christy didn't know what to say. She didn't want to admit how very much she missed him, and perhaps even more difficult, was the evidence in his voice that he was missing her, too. His firm declaration that they were *just friends* was the only thing that kept her from wanting to run from these feelings fast and far. She couldn't even consider any other possibility; she just *couldn't!*

She finally broke the silence by admitting, "Let me know when you'll be back, and it will give me something to look forward to."

"Does that mean you'd go out to dinner with me when I get back?"

Christy had no trouble addressing *that* head on. "You're not asking me on a date, are you?"

"Heavens no," he insisted with no trace of humor. "You're in no condition to be dating. In my opinion, it's impossible to come to terms with a broken relationship when you're caught up with a new one. Everything has its proper order, don't you think?"

"Yes, I do. And that's one of many reasons why I appreciate having you for a friend."

"The feeling is mutual, Christina."

"And why is that?"

"I've told you before, you've been the answer to my prayers on many counts."

"Yes, you've told me that before," she said, "but you've never told me why, exactly."

"And one day I will."

"That gives me two things to look forward to."

Cameron chuckled. "So it does."

"Thank you, Cameron, for everything. You've helped me more in the last couple of days than you could possibly know."

"You're welcome. I wish I could be there . . . to give you a shoulder to cry on, or to hold your hand, if nothing else."

"Yeah, me too."

"But when I get back, I've got a really great hug all stored up for my best friend."

"Your *best* friend?" she said. "So now I'm your *best* friend? What were you doing before last week?"

"Grieving . . . for the loss of my best friend."

"Your father?"

"That's right. And what about you?"

"I always thought Keith was my best friend. I realize now that I haven't had a really good friend in a long time. I talk to Rodney quite a bit when we're working. He' a good guy, but he's got a wife, who is his best friend. So, as I said, I truly appreciate your friendship."

"It works two ways, you know. I'll call and check on you. And you have the number here if you need me."

"Yes, thank you."

"Oh," he said, "read second Nephi, chapter five, and we'll talk about it."

"Okay."

"Oh, and Happy New Year."

"It just might be," Christy said. "You know, last year at this time . . . I felt so good about my life. It's been a rough year, but I really think I can head into *this* new year, much better prepared to face life realistically."

"That's great," he said, and they said their good-byes.

Christy did her best to table her emotions and enjoy New Year's Eve with the children. They played Monopoly and Uno, intermittently eating junk food and checking the countdown from New York City. She couldn't help thinking of Cameron being there, and realized that with the time zone difference, it was already the New Year there, and she had to explain to the children why the broadcast from New York wasn't live for that reason.

After going to bed late and sleeping in, Christy finally got around to reading the chapter in the Book of Mormon that Cameron had suggested. She gasped just reading the first line of the chapter heading: *The Nephites separate themselves from the Lamanites.* As she studied the chapter through a new perspective, Christy tried to apply the separation of these two brothers and their people, to the concept of divorce. She had trouble pinpointing exactly how they related, but she did feel an intangible comfort to realize that even divorce was metaphorically handled in the Book of Mormon. And she couldn't wait to hear what Cameron had to say about it. He called the afternoon of New Year's Day and they talked for nearly an hour about the concepts he'd learned from the Nephites that had helped him make sense of how to handle his divorce righteously. Christy felt her testimony of the Book of Mormon deepening as she felt this new level of understanding settle into her.

The kids weren't excited about returning to school, but Christy felt better knowing they weren't home on their own for hours every day. She felt a little down as she settled back into a routine through the days while Cameron remained out of state. The thoughts and emotions she'd been dealing with continued to hover around her. She knew that she'd taken some marvelous steps forward, but there was still a great deal that she had to come to terms with. She continued to study the Book of Mormon and prayed fervently to be guided to the answers she needed.

She often thought of Cameron and how much he had helped her. With the shift in her attitude toward Keith, she couldn't help wondering if something might evolve between them eventually. But in her heart she knew she wasn't ready to even consider such a thing, even though she was making progress. She recalled her bishop once telling her that the healing from a divorce had to be independent of any other relationship in her life, and she soundly agreed with that advice. But she'd never really worked very hard at healing, because she'd been too focused on hoping Keith would come back. She could only hope that she would be able to keep moving forward and come to terms with all that had happened in the past year.

Later that afternoon Rodney answered the phone at the store, then handed it to Christy. "It's a *man*," he said somewhere between humor and disdain.

"Hello," Christy said, hoping it was Cameron.

"Hello, my friend," she heard him say. "How are you?"

"I'm okay. How are you?"

"I'm great, now that I'm back in the glorious state of Utah. My plane just landed. Can you meet me for an early dinner before you head home?"

"I can do that," she said, trying to conceal the full depth of her excitement. Not only had she missed his company, but there was still so much on her mind that she wanted to discuss with him.

"Good," he said, "because we have a lot of catching up to do."

"Yes, I believe we do," she said. "Where do you want me to meet you?"

"I'll pick you up outside the door where we ate soup. Is five okay?"

"I'll be there," she said.

After making certain that everything was under control at the store, Christy called the kids and talked with each of them for a few minutes to make certain all was well. Then she hurried to the spot where Cameron said he would pick her up. For nearly half an hour she waited, glancing at her watch and wondering if something had gone wrong. Car trouble? An accident? Or had she misunderstood what he'd said? She tried his cell phone a couple of times but only got a recording. She was nearly ready to just go get her car and leave when he pulled up in the No Parking zone and she slipped into his car. He laughed and she asked, "Is something funny?"

"Not funny," he said, taking her hand. "It's just so good to see you."

"The feeling is mutual," she had to admit in spite of her frustration.

"So," she asked, trying not to sound irritated, "did you run into traffic or something?"

"No," he said nonchalantly, "just had a couple of calls to make."

"I was worried," she said and he looked surprised.

"Sorry," he said and seemed to mean it.

Christy forced the incident out of her mind and focused instead on just being with him. While he drove, she asked, "So, how's your sister? All that time we talked on the phone, and I didn't once ask about your sister."

He smiled. "You had other things on your mind."

"True, but . . . I'm asking now."

"She's fine . . . relatively speaking."

"Is there a problem?"

"That all depends on how you look at it. She's basically a responsible adult, holding down a good job, and she's been with the same guy for more than three years. That's definite progress from years past, and I'm grateful. Jeff is really a great guy. It was good to see her, and I love her dearly. But we just have so little in common, when her life is so thoroughly different from mine. How much can we possibly talk about, when she simply has no interest in religion, or any comprehension of spirituality? We have fun together, but having any kind of deep conversation is impossible. And I worry about her because I can see the bigger perspective of what she's doing with her life. I mean . . . I can't imagine living without the guidance and protection of the Spirit. But . . . she's simply not living in a way that could warrant that being a part of her life, and . . . well, I worry. I already said that."

"Well, it's understandable. Did you have a good visit, anyway?"

"Yes, we did. At least we keep up on each other's lives, and I know she respects me, even if she doesn't agree with me. I guess that works both ways." He smiled and added, "I'd like you to meet her one day."

"Well, you did say you wanted to take me to New York. Perhaps I will get to meet her eventually."

"I hope so," he said.

"And your business went well?"

"It did, actually."

"Tell me about it."

"It's really just a bunch of tedious meetings, but I enjoy being in the heart of Manhattan. It's an amazing place, really. As I said, I wouldn't want to live there, but—"

"But it's a nice place to visit."

"Exactly." He glanced toward her and asked, "So, how are you doing, Christina, my friend?"

"I'm okay," she said.

"That doesn't sound very positive. Talk to me."

"Well . . . I've been thinking, and studying, and praying. I feel like I'm moving forward, but there are still some things I'm having trouble with."

"Like what?" he asked and put the car into park. She looked up to see that they were in the parking lot of a restaurant.

"Let's go in and I'll tell you . . . if I can manage to put it into words."

Cameron smiled and got out, coming around the car to open her door. After she got out and he closed the door, she was surprised to hear him say, "I owe you a hug, you know."

Recalling what he'd said the night she'd fallen apart on the phone, she said, "So you do."

He took her in his arms and hugged her tightly, adding a new dimension to the security she had always felt in his presence. She returned his embrace with fervor, then found him looking into her eyes. "It's good to be back," he said. "I missed you."

"I missed you, too," she said and took his hand to go inside.

After they were seated and had ordered their meal, Cameron said, "So, tell me."

"Well," she said, trying to gather her thoughts, "I guess I've just been thinking about the whole breakdown of the marriage from a different perspective. Keith's announcement that he was leaving me came as a complete shock. I've probably said this before, but I've had to ask myself if I was that deep in denial, or just a fool. I honestly had no idea that anything was wrong. I knew we didn't have a fantastic marriage, but I'd always figured we were both tolerably happy, and we had a lot to be grateful for. Obviously my expectations were not nearly as high as his. Still, I certainly wasn't oblivious to the marriage. I'd always made a conscious effort to be a good wife and make him happy, without going overboard and spoiling him. But then he'd never given me the message that he wanted to be spoiled or that he wasn't content. I know that all probably sounds pretty obvious, but I've spent so much time trying to be responsible for the breakup, that it's taking some adjustment to see the truth." She shook her head and sighed. "Why would I do that? Why would I want to take responsibility for him doing something so heinous?"

"You know what? I can answer that, because I once asked that counselor the same thing. Although, I must say it took me a little more work to get where you've gotten. But she told me that I wanted to find a way that showed I was responsible for the breakdown of my marriage, that way, I could find a way to fix it, and I wanted to be able to do that. In accepting Jolene's accountability, I was able to accept that there was simply nothing I could do to fix it. Jolene was a free agent and she had made her choices—choices that I had no control over."

Christy absorbed that for a minute, then sighed deeply. "Wow. That makes sense, so much sense that it's almost eerie." She shook her head again and chuckled somewhat bitterly. "Looking back now, I can see a lot of warning signs that things weren't good between Keith and me, and little hints that he wasn't being loyal. But I think I just took for granted that he was trustworthy, and was as committed to the marriage as I was."

"There's no crime in that," Cameron said.

"I suppose not," Christy sighed. "But it sure feels wrong to have believed all along that he . . . loved me the way I loved him." Her voice broke with emotion and Cameron reached across the table for her hand.

After a minute he asked, "You okay?"

"Yes, actually," she said, dabbing her eyes with her napkin. "I think I'm doing a little better every day . . . or should I say, a little better every time I talk to you?"

"Glad I can help," he said.

They chatted comfortably—mostly small talk—during the meal. Christy's cell phone rang twice, with the kids asking questions, but she admitted to Cameron, "I consider the cell phone a huge blessing. Except for when I'm in the Bermuda Triangle, I can keep in contact with my kids almost all of the time."

"It's the next best thing to being there," he said with a smile.

"Hey, I've been meaning to ask you," he said after their plates had been taken away, "did you ever write that pro and con list I suggested?"

"Actually no," she said. "I'd forgotten about it."

"Maybe you weren't ready."

"Maybe I am now," she said. "I'll give it some thought."

*****

After spending some time with each of the children, doing a load of laundry, and putting the kitchen in order, Christy went to bed early. But she found it difficult to sleep as her recent discoveries concerning her marriage and the present state of her life roiled around in her mind. When just lying there began to make her crazy, she got up and found a notebook. Now seemed as good a time as any to make that pro and con list Cameron had suggested. At first it was difficult to actually put in writing all of the negative aspects of her marriage. She felt as if she were being somehow selfish or disloyal, but as she reminded herself of all that Keith had done to hurt her, she was able to approach the project more objectively; she was simply making a list of facts. Trying not to taint those facts with her emotions, she was amazed at the lengthy list of difficulties she had endured in her marriage, as well as the possible repercussions that would have to be faced if they were to get back together. On the pro side of the list, Christy tried to write down everything good that would make her want to patch up her relationship with Keith and put their family back together. She wrote down that they shared three children, and their parents were friends. It took her several minutes to come up with the fact that they had many years of history together. And after another twenty minutes, she realized that she couldn't honestly come up with any other positive reason for getting back together. Of course, if he humbled himself enough to ask her forgiveness, make retribution, and once again become active in the Church, the list might be different. But she had to gauge the reality of the present, not an obscure image of the past or her hopes for the future that had no sound basis in reality. To say nothing of the fact that Keith was now married to someone else.

Looking at the list long and hard, Christy began to cry. She was finally realizing that it was over between her and Keith, and it would simply never be the same again. Her tears continued while she felt herself grieving deeply for her loss. She grieved over the years they would never share, the lost hopes and dreams, and the long months of heartache. But once she had spent the better part of the night working through that grief, she had to admit that she felt better. Now that she had become realistic enough to remove Keith from the picture, the prospect of a bright future became more defined. As she prayed to be able to deepen her understanding and press forward, she felt the validating warmth of the Spirit. She knew she had finally found the right path for her life—and that path led away from Keith Hardy.

Christy finally slept around four, and when the alarm woke her, she knew it wasn't going to be a good day if she didn't get some more rest. She called Rodney at home and asked if he'd open the store and cover for her until this afternoon. He gladly agreed, and once the children were off to school, Christy went back to bed for a few hours. She arrived in the city a little after eleven and drove directly to the Chandler building. She was guided into the parking garage, then walked into the building and was met by a security guard who asked her destination.

"I need to see Mr. Chandler," she said. "I can wait if he's busy."

He looked dubious, but he motioned her toward an elevator and told her to go to the twelfth floor. She stepped off of the elevator into a completely different atmosphere from the basement where she'd come in. The lobby in which she stood was elegant and fine, without being extravagant. She approached a young man seated at a low counter.

"May I help you?" he asked.

"I'm here to see Cameron Chandler. If he's busy I can wait."

Again she was given a dubious glance. "Apparently you don't have an appointment."

"No, but—"

"Is there a problem?" a woman in her fifties asked as she emerged through a tall, polished wood door.

"This woman would like to see Mr. Chandler, but she doesn't have an appointment, and—"

"What would this be regarding?" the woman asked. She wasn't the least bit condescending or rude, but Christy still felt uncomfortable. She had certainly known that the Cameron she had come to know so well was an incredibly important man, but seeing the evidence left her feeling a little unsteady. She reminded herself that they were just friends, and his way of life would in no way ever affect hers.

In response to this woman's expectant gaze, Christy answered, "I just need to talk to him."

The woman raised a brow. "And your name?"

"Christina Hardy," she said.

The woman went back through the same door, then returned only a minute later to say, "You can go in. He's between meetings."

"Thank you," Christy said, catching the speculative glance that passed between the woman and the young man at the counter.

She walked through the door to find herself in what appeared to be a secretary's office. The woman who had shown her in said, "He's in there." She motioned toward a set of double doors before she sat down at the desk close by.

Christy had almost reached the door when Cameron opened it. "What a pleasant surprise," he said and laughed. "Hey, Bertie," he said to the woman at the desk, "this is Christina. The woman who saved me from freezing to death."

"Oh *that* woman," Bertie said. "It's a pleasure to meet you."

"And you," Christy said.

"Come on in," Cameron motioned her through the door ahead of him. Over his shoulder he said, "If somebody calls, take a message. I'm busy."

"Whatever you say," Bertie said just before Cameron closed the door.

"Wow," Christy said, pausing to take in her surroundings. "This is pretty impressive."

Cameron gave a disinterested grunt and sat on a leather sofa. "Have a seat," he said. "To what do I owe this pleasure?"

"Well, I know you're busy, and I didn't know if I could even see you . . . dropping in like this. But I thought it was worth a try."

"I'm glad you did. And your timing's good. So, what's up?"

"Well, I actually spent half the night making that pro and con list you suggested, and the other half thinking about what I learned from it. I got out of going to work this morning so I could get a little more sleep, and then I just . . . wanted to tell you, once again, how much I appreciate your perspective . . . and your suggestions. You're beginning to make me wonder how I ever got along without you."

He smiled and said, "I've been wondering that myself." Then, somewhat nonplused, he clarified, "I mean . . . how *I* ever got along without *you.*"

"I find that difficult to believe," she admitted. "I feel so horribly . . . *needy* all the time, while you seem so . . . Oh, I don't know."

"Listen to me, Christina," he said with an intensity in his eyes that quickened her heart. "My needs may not be as visible, but that doesn't mean I need you any less." He faintly touched the back of his fingers to her face and she became briefly lost in his eyes. "You have given me purpose and meaning, my friend, and I would be utterly lost without you."

Christy didn't know whether to feel thrilled or alarmed. She simply gave a soft laugh and glanced down, relieved when he asked, "So, what did you learn? Or is it too personal?"

"No, actually. It's difficult to put into words, but . . . Well, I think it boils down to one thing: I've spent so many months praying that Keith's heart would be softened; that he would realize he'd made a mistake and come back to me. I knew it would take time for the wounds to heal, but I spent countless hours imagining us being together again as a family, as if my positive thinking alone could make it happen. I began to wonder if my prayers weren't being heard, or if I was somehow unworthy of being blessed with what I'd asked for." She turned to look into his eyes. "Now I realize that I've been praying for the wrong thing. I know now that He *has* heard my prayers. I just didn't hear the answer because I was looking for the wrong solution. Now I have my answer."

"And what is that?" he asked when she didn't go on.

"The answer is that . . ." Her voice broke with emotion as the Spirit verified once again the truth in what she'd felt. "Even if Keith were to come back, it would be all wrong. The answer is that I don't need him to come back, because he would never change enough to be the kind of husband I deserve." She laughed softly and wiped at a sudden surge of tears. "Do you have any idea how liberating that feels?"

Cameron glanced away and clasped his hands together. "Yes, actually, I do." He turned to look at her again. "I know exactly how it feels." He smiled. "And I've been praying that you would be able to realize that very thing."

"Really?"

"Really. Because you *do* deserve better than that, Christy. You're a daughter of God. You're not perfect; nobody is. But I believe you were a good wife, and you gave him no just cause to do what he did. I'm not saying you shouldn't forgive him. But forgiving does not mean opening your heart to allow him to hurt you again. He doesn't have to make restitution in order for you to forgive him. Forgiving him allows *you* to progress and get on with your life. You deserve to be happy, Christy."

"Yes, I do," she said, then she laughed, relishing the liberation she had just endorsed for herself. "And you know what? I feel better about myself as a person than I've felt since . . . oh, long before Keith left."

Cameron sighed and smiled. "That's maybe the best news I've heard this year."

"This year is very new," she said.

"Which gives us a lot to look forward to."

"Yes, I suppose it does." She glanced at the clock and cleared her throat. "Well, that's all really. I'm sure you have work to do, and—"

"Actually," he said, "I could do an early lunch, if you're game."

"That would be great," she said readily. He stood and took her hand.

Walking past Bertie's desk, he said, "I'm going to lunch. I'll be back for that meeting."

"Do you want your car brought around?" she asked.

"Yes, please," he said. "You're a gem, as always."

"I know," she said with a little smirk as he pushed his back against the door to open it.

Walking past the counter in the lobby, he said, "Have you taken a break, Matt?"

"Yes, sir," he said stiffly.

"You'd better," Cameron said to him. Then, while they waited for the elevator, he said to Christy, "Poor kid's a workaholic. I have to threaten him to take his breaks."

They got into the elevator and as it started down, Cameron laughed for no apparent reason. "Is something funny?"

"Not funny," he said, much as he had the previous day. "It's just good to see you."

Christy smiled and watched the red digital numbers count the floors they were descending, while she contemplated just how good it felt to be holding Cameron Chandler's hand.

Chapter Nine

While they shared a leisurely lunch, Christy couldn't help contemplating how good she felt. She'd become accustomed to being weighted down with grief that she had been afraid to look at, and an acute hopelessness in wanting Keith to come back, but logically unable to believe he ever would. The contrasting joy of her new perspective gave her an almost tangible hope. Pondering her feelings while Cameron entertained her with comical stories of business meetings gone amiss, she couldn't help but see him at the center of her hope. The thought caught her off guard and she glanced down while he continued to talk, not wanting him to notice how distracted she was. She told herself that the help and support he'd given her had no relation to the path of hope that had opened up before her. Her healing had to be completely separate from any relationship she might get into. The fact that Cameron had helped her through the healing process did not necessarily mean he would ever be anything more to her than the friend he had come to be. She had to keep that objective very clear. But something in her heart made her almost afraid to look at the reality of how close she and Cameron had become through conversations more emotional and stirring than she'd shared with Keith in a decade. And she only had to look at him to be reminded that she was attracted to him, and if she were truly honest with herself, she had to admit that she always had been. He was handsome, yes. But her attraction went far deeper than that. She would have been turned off by his good looks at the first hint of arrogance or insensitivity. But the more she got to know him, the more attractive he became—as a whole person, not just a man who had once made a living modeling, and certainly not as a man who was now king of a corporate empire. It was the heart and soul of Cameron Chandler that she had grown to care for so deeply. And the very idea that perhaps somewhere deep inside she actually *wanted* this relationship to blossom into something romantic frightened her.

"Hey," he said and startled her, "are you with me at all?"

"Sorry," she laughed softly, "I'm afraid my mind was wandering a little."

"That's okay. It was a silly story, anyway."

"But I love your silly stories," she insisted.

"What's on your mind?" he asked.

She shrugged her shoulders. "Nothing important, really. Maybe I'm just tired."

"Understandable." He glanced at his watch. "And I hate to go, but I've got a meeting to get to."

"Yes, and I need to relieve Rodney at the store. But it's been wonderful, as always."

"You got plans this evening?" he asked.

"Nothing particular," she said, "other than needing to be with the kids, since I was gone part of the evening yesterday."

"Well, what I had in mind was . . . . when I was in New York, you mentioned something about family night, and I know it's not Monday, but . . . Would it be a problem if I brought pizza over, and . . . we could play a game or something? If it's not cool, I understand. I must confess that the family thing sounds really nice, so this is a totally selfish request, but—"

"I think it sounds wonderful," she said. "I wouldn't have brought it up last week if I hadn't wanted you to come. But I do have one condition."

"Anything," he said eagerly.

"Well," she sighed, "this may not come out sounding right . . . so be patient."

"I'm listening."

"The thing is . . . the divorce has been tough on the kids, as it would be for any kids. They're doing much better the last few weeks, and I think you could bring some light into their lives, just as you have mine. But I don't want them getting attached to you and then have you disappear from our lives. This friendship we've established means a great deal to me, Cameron, and I would hope that wherever the future takes us, we can always maintain what we've come to share. But the same has to apply to my kids. If you're going to befriend them too, then it can't be temporary. I'm not saying you have to become a prominent figure in their lives, or that an occasional evening of pizza and games is going to make them dependent on you. I just don't want you giving them expectations that aren't realistic. I suspect they're starved for positive male attention—especially Tim. And it could be good for them. But you've got to promise that whatever might happen in the future between you and me will be independent of whatever relationships you might develop as *their* friend. Is that making any sense?"

"Absolutely," he said. "And I appreciate your bringing it up. It's a valid concern. And I promise that I will be careful and honest. And I'll expect you to let me know if I'm doing all right."

"It's a deal," she said. "We like pepperoni, mushrooms, and olives. And Tim can eat half a pizza all by himself."

Cameron chuckled. "I've got it covered."

Christy arrived at the store to find everything in order. There were no customers, and Rodney was reading behind the counter. But the numbers on the register showed that they'd had a good morning's sales.

"How are you?" she asked once he'd updated her on all that had happened in her absence.

"I'm fine," he said. "How are you?"

"I'm great, actually," she said and couldn't hold back a little laugh.

When Cameron showed up that evening with pizzas and his deluxe Monopoly game, she was so thoroughly glad to see him that it almost scared her—in spite of his being twenty minutes late. She forced any criticism of this annoying habit of his out of her mind in order to enjoy the moment. The kids warmed up quickly and obviously liked Cameron a great deal—which was understandable. And it was also evident that Cameron genuinely liked the kids as well. At one point, while she was observing his interaction with Tim and Lucy, she thought of the little boy he'd lost years ago, and wondered if Cameron looked at Tim and contemplated how old his little Daniel might be now. Christy actually had to choke back tears as she thought of how lonely Cameron must have been all these years, after once being a father.

She forced her focus back to the game, but more than once she found Cameron looking at her in a way that made her wonder if what he felt for her went beyond the friendship he declared. Was this well-established boundary something he upheld out of respect for the healing she was going through? Or did he simply see nothing in her beyond a friend? Was she somehow reading her own desires into the situation? And for that matter, did she even really know what her desires were? The answer to every question was simply time. She knew it would take time for her healing to be complete, and time to get to know Cameron better before she could even consider such feelings.

Again, she had to force her thoughts to the moment and enjoy the rousing game of Monopoly, the highlight being when Charlotte forced Cameron into bankruptcy and he fell off his chair with an elaborate death scene that had the children rolling with laughter. But that night in bed, Christy's mind posed the questions to her all over again. Whether or not her feelings for Cameron were creeping into something romantic, there was no denying that she had become extremely emotionally attached. And it scared her. Was she setting herself up for another fall? Could they really be friends in spite of anything else that might happen? She imagined him coming to her and telling her that he'd fallen in love with an incredible woman and he would be getting married. How could they possibly remain as close as they were under such circumstances? Could she ever stand back and feel emotionally detached from such an occurrence? In spite of her recent progress, Christy found it difficult to believe that a man like Cameron Chandler could ever see anything more in her than a friend. Not only was he good-looking and rich, he was emotionally healthy, spiritual, and sensitive. She felt certain he had his faults and weaknesses, as anyone would—being habitually tardy could be at the top of the list. But instinctively she knew that he was what he seemed to be. And she was falling for him.

Knowing she needed to get some sleep, she resigned herself—once again—to just giving the situation some time. Their friendship had grown quickly and deeply, as had the progress in her healing. But she needed time to let both settle. She knew better than to jump into anything on a rebound, which was the reason her attempts at dating last summer had been so ridiculous.

With the goal of giving everything some time set firmly in her mind, she finally slept soundly and woke up with the realization that she was feeling a little better about her life every day.

Christy arrived at the store feeling bright and motivated. She walked in to see Rodney and Mazie both loitering at the front counter. She glanced at the clock. Mazie was actually early. It had to be a first. Walking toward the back room, she noticed them both watching her skeptically.

"What?" she demanded.

"What do you mean, what?" Rodney asked with a poor effort to sound innocent.

"What's up?" Christy asked. "The two of you look awfully glum."

"Obviously you haven't seen this," Mazie said, turning a magazine around on the counter.

Christy chuckled. "I haven't opened a tabloid in more than a decade."

"Well, maybe you should open this one," Rodney said.

Christy felt a prickle at the back of her neck. "Why?" she demanded.

Mazie picked it up to find a particular page, then she set it back down on the counter for Christy to see. She gasped and grabbed the edge of the counter, but it took her a full minute to realize what she was looking at and digest what it meant. In front of her was a two-page spread, with color photos of herself working in this store, and her and Cameron walking in the mall, and sitting at a table in the food court—holding hands. The huge headline across the top read: *Winner in millionaire's charity game goes home with a lot more than a hundred grand.*

"This is unbelievable!" she snarled and grabbed the magazine before she stormed into her office and slammed the door. She threw down her purse and slumped into the chair, staring at the pictures and headlines, not believing her eyes. Forcing herself to focus, she read through the brief article that gave an exaggerated version of what had happened on Christmas Eve, claiming that she had unwittingly received the grand prize of his game. A romance between them was strongly implied, referring to the photographs as evidence. Christy felt her blood turn hot with embarrassment and anger. She felt so furious and appalled that she couldn't even think straight. And there was only one conceivable target for her anger. Grabbing the magazine and her coat, she rushed out of the store, barely saying to Rodney and Mazie, "I don't know when I'll be back."

Christy all but ran to the building where Cameron worked. She scowled at the *Chandler Corporation* sign beside the huge glass doors, and went directly to the twelfth floor. She walked past Matt at the counter, who shot out of his seat and followed her, insisting that she couldn't go in there unannounced. Bertie rose to her feet as Christy stormed past her desk, ignoring anything but her purpose. She pushed open the door to his office and saw him sitting at his desk, with another man seated at his side.

"Christy," he said, coming to his feet. "Is something wrong? You—"

"You'd better believe something is wrong. Maybe you could explain *this!*" She snapped the open magazine down on his desk in front of him and watched him for a reaction. She felt some degree of relief to see the obvious shock in his expression, but it was quickly squelched by her anger.

"This is unbelievable," he muttered. He shook his head and gave a humorless chuckle before he said, "Dean, would you excuse us please. We can talk later."

"Sure, no problem," the other man said and hurried from the room.

"Unbelievable doesn't begin to explain," Christy barked. "This is the most ludicrous thing I have ever seen in my life."

"Where did you get this?" he asked, slumping into his chair, his eyes glued to the pages in front of him.

"My employees showed it to me, which goes over really well for maintaining my dignity with the people I have to work with every day." He squeezed his eyes shut and groaned.

Christy became impatient while he was obviously reading the article, then he leaned back and sighed. "So," she said, "you'd better come clean here, Chandler."

"What?" he retorted. "Are you implying I had something to do with this?"

"It's right there in front of your eyes, in a slimy tabloid, of all things. It says that a Chandler Corporation employee verified that I had won a hundred grand for picking you up by the side of the road on Christmas Eve. Where could such information come from if—"

"Forgive me," Bertie's voice interrupted and Christy turned to see her standing just on the other side of the door—that had been left open. "I couldn't help overhearing, and . . . I think I might offer some enlightenment, here."

"We're all ears," Cameron growled.

Christy folded her arms and leaned against the huge desk. Bertie glanced briefly toward Christy, but focused her attention on Cameron, who was still sitting behind the desk. "I got a phone call while you were in New York; someone saying they were from a local newspaper. They said they wanted a comment from Mr. Chandler on the grand prize that had been awarded over the Christmas holiday. You know I'd been out of the office for a week, and I just assumed that it had happened. I told them you were out of state, and I couldn't tell them anything. But they asked a few questions about the contest, and I answered them. When I got off the phone, I felt uneasy. It only occurred to me afterward that the local papers had never fished for information that way. If I'm to blame for this, I am so sorry." Her voice actually cracked and Christy sighed. How could she be angry with this sweet woman who had done nothing wrong?

"It's all right, Bertie," Cameron said. "It's not your fault. Thank you."

She nodded and left, closing the door behind her.

Following a miserable silence, Cameron said, "I'm so sorry, Christina. I never dreamed that something so . . . ridiculous could have happened."

"Well, what are you going to do about it?"

"What do you want me to do about it?" he retorted. "It's a cheesy tabloid, for crying out loud. Most decent people don't even read those things. I could sue them, but for what? The legal fees would be ridiculous, and where would it get either of us? I understand your being upset. I'm upset, too. But it's gossip. It will die down. There's nothing here that defames your character, or mine. These people are skilled at twisting and manipulating the truth. They sensationalize for the sake of a story. You and I and the people who really matter in our lives will know it's not true. I don't see any possible way that there could be repercussions from this. It's just a stupid tabloid!"

"But where did they get this?" she asked, slapping the magazine where it lay. "This thing is published back east. Someone had to give them the story, the photographs."

"I can have my employees questioned, but if one of them leaked something like this for a few extra bucks, do you really think they're going to admit it and jeopardize their job? And all it would really accomplish is bringing the story to the attention of people who would have been oblivious to it, otherwise."

Christy sighed with frustration. Everything he said made sense, but it left her with nowhere for these feelings to go. "But who would have known?" she demanded. "I told practically no one. And you?"

"I told less than a handful of people; people I trust; people who are *not* gossip mongers. I don't know where the story came from. But I do know that for either of us to waste our energy and emotion over this is as ludicrous as the story itself."

"And what about the money?"

"What about it?"

"If you hadn't been offering this great big carrot to draw people into this game, none of this would have happened."

"That's probably true. You've got me there, Christy. But you know what? There was no hundred-thousand-dollar grand prize. I gave it to the American Red Cross. The official announcement ran in the *Deseret News* and the *Tribune* last week."

She sighed and looked away before he added, "So why don't you calm down, and we can talk about this."

"I don't want to calm down," she snapped. "I just . . ."

"What?" he pressed when she hesitated.

"I just need to get out of here," she said and left the magazine on his desk.

"Hey," he said as she reached for the door knob, "can I see you later?"

"I don't know if that's a good idea," she said with all the coldness she felt.

Christy left the building as quickly as she had stormed in. Once outside, she slowed her pace and returned to the mall as slowly as she could possibly manage. She just couldn't believe it. She knew it was a stupid thing to be so upset over. But she *was* upset. And she could never explain how the hurt and betrayal that was still so close to the surface had suddenly erupted with fresh torment. She found herself sitting on a bench at the back of the chapel in the Joseph Smith Memorial Building, listening to quiet organ music being played. She was alone beyond the organist, while her mind played through all that had happened in her life since she'd picked Cameron Chandler up by the side of the road. While she couldn't deny that he'd done a great deal to help her, at the moment she could only feel that trusting *any* man would leave her suffering in the end. She wondered for just a minute if the anger she felt was masking something deeper, but the minute passed quickly with the determination that she was just plain angry, and she had a right to be.

Christy finally went back to work. Mazie's shift had been taken over by a relatively new employee named Ruth. Rodney met her near the office door. "You okay?"

"Not really," she said.

"What are you going to do?"

"I'm not sure there's anything I can do, but if I ever find out who's responsible, I'll . . . I'll . . . I don't know what I'll do. I don't know that it makes any difference." She sighed. "I need to get some paperwork done here. I've already lost half a day. Will you—"

"Of course. Everything's covered out here."

"Thank you."

He popped his head back in a minute later and said, "Oh, your ex-husband called."

"Great," she said with sarcasm. "Did he say what he wanted?"

"I'm not your mediator, Chris. I just told him I'd tell you he called."

"Great," Christy said again, and attempted to concentrate on the work in front of her. Half an hour later, she still hadn't accomplished much. She felt distracted and confused, and when her stomach rumbled, she realized she hadn't eaten.

When the phone rang she let them answer it up front, but then Rodney came to tell her it was for her. She knew it was Keith before she picked it up.

"Yes," she said in a tone that fully represented her mood.

"It's amazing," Keith said, "the things you can learn about the mother of your children in a tabloid."

"Oh help," she muttered under her breath and pressed her face into her hand. Of course, Patricia Hardy just had to be the kind of woman to read tabloids.

"A hundred thousand dollars, eh?" he said. "That puts a new twist on the child support issue, now doesn't it."

Christy's heart sank to the pit of her stomach. "The story was completely false, Keith. I don't have any more money now than I did when this divorce was settled."

"They have ways of proving how much money you have, you know. It can be tracked."

"Well, you just go ahead and do that, because you won't find anything," Christy insisted.

"I think our lawyers are going to be getting together."

"You go for it," Christy said and hung up the phone, tallying up a potentially new set of legal fees, when the last ones hadn't even been paid off yet.

Staring at the wall for twenty minutes, she felt her anger melt into depression. She wanted to just go home and curl up in her bed and never get out. She was contemplating telling Rodney that she was useless and needed to go home, when the phone rang again. And again Rodney came to say that it was for her.

"Hello," she said, hoping this was business. Maybe it would get her back into a working mode.

"Hello," she heard Cameron say. "We need to talk . . . if you've calmed down."

"I'm calm," she said, "but I don't think you want to hear what I have to say."

"I'll listen to anything you have to say," he said.

"Okay, well . . . Keith just called. He's seen the article. He thinks I'm lying when I tell him that I don't have a hundred-thousand dollars, and he intends to prove it, so that he can renegotiate child support."

She heard him sigh loudly. "I'm so sorry, Christy."

"Well, as you pointed out, it's obviously not your fault. I don't know whose fault it is, but I don't have the fortitude to deal with this right now."

"I want to help you deal with it, Christy. Surely we can sit down together and figure out a way to weather this storm. You should know I would never let you or your children go without, or—"

"I don't *know* anything, Cameron. But maybe I don't know you as well as I thought I did. You've been very kind to me, and you've helped me through some tough things, but I just . . . think it's better that we don't see each other any more."

Following a long moment of stunned silence, she heard him say, "You've got to be kidding. You're going to just toss what we have out the window over *this?*"

She hesitated. "Yes, I suppose I am."

"Well then," he sounded angry, "apparently I don't know *you* as well as I thought I did."

"Maybe you don't," she said, unable to help the cynical tone.

"You know what I think your problem is?" he said, sounding even more angry.

"I'm sure you're going to tell me."

"Yes, I am. Because that's what friends do. Your problem, Christina Hardy, is that you're scared. Whatever our relationship may be or become, I'm a man and you're just plain scared to get too close, because in spite of everything you might feel, you can't help wondering if I'm just another selfish jerk that will leave you high and dry. So you're jumping all over this as an excuse to stop something that you don't know how to deal with. That's the bottom line. You're just plain scared."

"What have I got to be scared of?" Christy retorted, hating the uneasiness his words stirred inside her. "You and I were friends and nothing more."

"Apparently friendship is relative," he said. "But I have done *nothing* to warrant your lack of trust, Christina, *or* your belligerence. If you're scared, so be it. But have the maturity to come out and admit it, instead of masking it behind these ridiculous accusations. If we're friends you can sit down and listen to what I have to say before you start assuming that you've got it all figured out. I'm as much a victim here as you are. And I am as much in the dark. Not only that,

I'm scared too, because I have no idea how I can even get through another day without . . ." She heard a subtle crack in his voice and wondered if he could actually be near tears over her rejection. But when he spoke again, his voice was steady and cool. "Now, do you want to work this out and get through it together? Or do you want to yell at me a little more and go crawl back into the hole I found you in?"

Christy felt her defenses rising and knew she had to get off the phone before she exploded. "I have nothing more to say to you," she said.

"Fine," he retorted. "At least I know where I stand."

Christy hung up without a good-bye, then she locked the door to her office and cried.

Chapter Ten

Christy managed to stumble through life the next couple of days, reliving again the memories of Keith leaving her. She felt confused and afraid, and refused to answer Cameron's calls or return his messages. Bea stopped her at church on Sunday to ask if she was all right; Christy insisted that she was and hurried away.

On Monday Christy went to work with the resolve to put this behind her and move forward. But she wasn't sure how she would do that, when she felt as if her feet were stuck in quicksand, which threatened to suck the rest of her down. She got to the store nearly an hour before it opened to catch up on some paperwork. Rodney came in half an hour later and stood over her desk.

"Hello," she said, trying to sound cheerful.

"Hey, there's something you need to know."

"What?" she asked, wondering what other grim news she could be faced with.

"Saturday I came in to check those things, like you asked me to, and . . . I overheard Mazie on the phone."

"Yes?" she said when he hesitated.

"I may be jumping to conclusions, but it sounded pretty clear to me that she was responsible for feeding that story to the tabloid."

Christy gasped. "Are you serious?"

"I can only tell you what I heard."

"Which was?"

"She said something like, 'I sure owe you for taking those great pictures.' And something about with the money she'd gotten for the story, they'd be going out to lunch."

"I can't believe it," Christy said.

"So, what are you going to do?"

"I don't know," she said. "What do you think I should do?"

"I think you should confront her, personally."

"And if she lies?"

"Well, you just have to try. But her employment here has been in jeopardy for weeks anyway. I'm amazed that you've kept her on this long."

Christy sighed. "Yes, that is amazing, isn't it. Maybe this would be good practice in assertive management."

"Well, you'd better start practicing. She's supposed to be here in twenty minutes."

Rodney left the office and Christy closed the door. She sat back down and pressed her face into her hands. The harsh judgment she had thrown at Cameron came back to her and she groaned. Attempting to focus on one thing at a time, she contemplated how to address this new turn of events with Mazie. She prayed for guidance—and forgiveness, for her anger, her judgment, and for indulging her fear. It was that last one she had the biggest trouble with. When her prayer was finished, she quickly wrote a list of the reasons why Mazie had put her job in jeopardy, aside from telling lies to tabloids. Then she attempted to write a list of the reasons she should let Mazie keep her job. She couldn't think of anything.

She had barely completed the list when a knock sounded at the door. "Yes?" she called, and Mazie entered the room.

"Rod said you wanted to see me."

"That's right." She stood to face her. "I understand you were responsible for that story in the tabloid," she said, thinking it would be better to get her to defend her innocence—if she had any—than to give her a subtle implication that would be easy to evade.

"Where did you hear that?" she countered hotly, but Christy recognized something in her eyes that reminded her of Keith when he belittled and demeaned her.

"It doesn't matter where I heard it. If you're responsible for that kind of underhanded betrayal, you will not be working for me another hour. That, on top of your long-time record of irresponsible behavior, makes my decision very clear."

"What?" Mazie croaked. "You're firing me?"

"That's right. If you have something you'd like to say in your defense, now would be the time."

"You've already passed your judgment, that's obvious," Mazie snarled. "What good would it do me to say *anything?*"

"I think I'm intelligent enough to know the truth when I hear it. If you—"

"I don't have to stand here and listen to this," she interrupted and stormed through the open door.

Rodney appeared a moment later, just as Christy slumped into her chair. "Very good," he said.

"Did you hear any of that?"

"I did; eavesdropping is one of my vices. You want my opinion?"

"Yes, I do."

"She's guilty. If she had been falsely accused, she would have done her best to convince you of that, but she didn't even try."

"Well," Christy sighed, "this means we'll be working extra hours to cover her shifts."

"I can work the extra hours. I can use the money, and I get paid by the hour. You already put in too many hours for the salary you get. We have a few new applications. If you want, I'll look them over and arrange some interviews. In the meantime, I'll see who else might be able to cover some shifts."

"Thank you, Rodney. You're a darling. I admit . . . I'm not real clearheaded lately."

"This whole tabloid thing really upset you, didn't it?"

"Yes, it did."

"Why? It's just a silly magazine, with no reputation beyond stretching the truth."

"I don't know, Rodney. I guess I just need some time to sort it all out. I'm sure I'll be fine."

Christy tried to convince herself of that through the remainder of the day. The kids each called her when they got in from school, as they always did, to let her know all was well. She gave them assignments for their chores and homework and asked how their day had gone, then she tried once again to settle into her work without the distraction of tabloids, difficult ex-husbands, deceitful employees, and at the center of it all: Cameron Chandler.

Little more than an hour later, Christy answered the phone to hear Keith say in an unusually humble voice, "I need to talk to you. Could you meet me in the lobby of the Joseph Smith building?"

"What for?" she demanded.

"Hey, I don't blame you for being skeptical, but . . . I promise I'll be nice and . . . I just need to talk to you. Give me ten minutes."

Christy quickly searched her feelings. It was a public place, and easy to walk out of if he became difficult. "Okay, ten minutes."

On her way out the door, she said to Rodney, "I'm meeting my ex-husband in the lobby of the Joseph Smith building. If I don't call you on my cell phone in twenty minutes, you call me. If I don't answer, call the police."

Rodney looked shocked. "You really think that's a necessary precaution?"

"No, but if he gets obnoxious, I can tell him I told you that." She smiled and he seemed relieved.

Christy hurried across the street and sat in the lobby for only a few minutes before she saw Keith enter through the revolving door. An older woman accidentally bumped into him and his response to her was blatantly rude. Christy wondered if he'd always been that rude with people and she simply hadn't noticed. Perhaps not *quite* that rude, she concluded, but she could see now that he'd always had a certain abrasiveness about him. She knew now that she had been more in love with his potential than the reality of the man he was—or ever had been.

He looked around and caught sight of her, then he showed a warm smile that seemed completely out of place, considering the state of their relationship.

"Thanks for coming," he said, sitting beside her.

"I don't have much time," she countered.

"Well," he said, "there's something I need to say to you. It's not . . . easy, so bear with me. The thing is . . ." He glanced down and rubbed his hands together, as if he were terribly nervous, but she sensed that it wasn't completely genuine. Or had she just become cynical? "The thing is . . ." he started again, "I've been thinking a lot lately and I've been wondering if maybe I made a mistake."

Christy sucked in her breath and turned fully toward him, shocked beyond words. She thought of the endless weeks and months she had longed to hear him say those very words, and now that she was hearing them they sounded hollow and meaningless. Had she become so callous? Yes, she likely had. But for good reason. Funny that she would recall Cameron telling her, *Forgiveness and trust are not the same thing.*

"Well, say *something*," Keith finally said.

"What can I possibly say?" she asked. *"Maybe* you made a mistake? Sweetie, you made the biggest mistake of your life. But exactly *why* are you bringing this up now? Has it taken you this long to figure it out?"

"Listen, I don't blame you for being angry, Chris. I know I was unfair, but—"

"Angry? Oh, Keith," she said in a voice that expressed her pity for him, "I've gotten over being angry. Quite frankly, you're not worth my anger any more. And as far as your being unfair, I think you need to come up with some stronger adjectives if you're going to try and convince me that you're truly sorry."

He sighed and she sensed his rising frustration. "We have three kids, Chris, surely you could at least consider trying again to—"

"Listen, Keith," she said, "and listen very carefully. I recall saying those very words to you, a number of times, in fact. And you told me to get a grip and get on with my life. You know, I never did anything to warrant having my husband *cheat* on me, and *walk* out on me. But you did that anyway. Well, I've gotten a grip and I'm getting on with my life. So, what makes you suddenly come to this grand change of course, Keith? Is Patricia starting to get on your nerves? Is the grass not greener with your *eternal soul mate?* Or is it because, in spite of your knowing that I'm pathetically honest, you're secretly hoping that I really did win a hundred thousand dollars?"

Keith sighed again. "I know I deserve your belligerence, Chris. But I would hope you could at least consider what I'm saying."

"What exactly *are* you saying, Keith?"

"Well . . . I guess I want to know if you would . . . consider having a go at it again?"

"A go at it? What exactly is a go at it? Would that be turning my life upside down all over again so that you could test the waters and see if they're any warmer?"

"So, what?" he asked in a voice that sounded awfully belligerent for a man who was trying to win her back. "Are you saying you'd never even consider it? If so, just say it. Cut through all the garbage and get to the point."

"Okay, fine. I understand that we share three children, and we once shared eternal covenants. I always placed a high priority on those things; I still do. But the bottom line is this: the hurt that you have inflicted in my life is deep, and I will not open myself up to be hurt all over again. It would take a huge amount of restitution and penitence to even begin to win my trust again, and love is variable beyond that. Words are not enough to make me believe you want to try again. It would take demonstration—and lots of it."

"Like what?" he asked, sounding more angry than humble.

"If you have to ask, then—"

"Just tell me what you think I should do, Chris!"

"Fine. I think you should make the most of your marriage with Patricia. She's your wife now. She deserves your commitment for that reason alone."

He sighed loudly. "So, you're saying there's no chance for us to get back together?"

"And what are you saying, Keith? Are you ready to start going to Church again? Go through a disciplinary action with the Church? Make restitution with me? The children? How much groveling would you be prepared to do?"

His disgust was evident as he said, "I can't believe you would expect me to actually . . . *grovel.*"

"I can't believe you would expect me to take you back for anything less. In my opinion, groveling would just be a good start."

"You're out of your mind."

"That makes two of us. You made it clear a long time ago that there was nothing left between us. It took me a long time to accept that. But I've accepted it now. So, why don't you go home and patch things up with Patricia? The two of you deserve each other."

Christy stood up and walked out of the building, feeling better about herself than she had in years. She was contemplating the reasons when she looked up to see Cameron coming directly toward her, his hands deep in the pockets of a long wool coat. She stopped abruptly and found herself facing him in the middle of the sidewalk, while people maneuvered around them, going both directions.

"What are you doing here?" she asked, sensing that this was not coincidence.

Cameron glanced at the crowds surrounding them and took her arm, manipulating her out of the flow of traffic. He leaned against the building and said, "I called the store and Rodney told me where you'd gone . . . and what you'd said. I had no reason to assume you needed any help, but I just . . . wanted to make sure you were all right."

"I'm fine," she said, unable to look into his eyes the way she had become accustomed. She almost hated the reality of how thoroughly good it felt to see him. "Thank you, anyway."

He glanced down and shuffled his toe over the ground, obviously as lost for words as she was. "Why did you call the store?" she asked and he looked up, apparently put on the spot.

"I, uh . . . was just hoping you'd talk to me, because . . ." When he hesitated, Christy could almost feel the words he hadn't finished. *Because this rift between them was all wrong.*

"So," he went on, "could we talk, because . . ." Again he didn't finish.

Christy briefly met his eyes and felt hard-pressed to keep from crying. There was so much that needed to be said between them, but now was not the time. "Sure," she said, looking down. "But not now. I need to get back and . . ." She began to move away, fearing she would burst into tears.

"Hey," he yelled as she moved up the sidewalk, "if I call will you answer the phone?"

Christy felt embarrassed by the implication, and guilty for the chasm she had put between them. But she needed time to sort her thoughts. "I'll call *you*," she hollered back and the signal sounded for her to cross the street. A quick glance at Cameron's expression made her wonder if her effort to say that she needed to take the next step had been interpreted as his calls being unwelcome. Of course, he had good reason to think such a thing. But she would make it up to him . . . tomorrow, after she'd had some time to think.

She was startled when a woman walking beside her said, "If you don't call him, you're crazy."

"Yeah," Christy muttered, "maybe I am."

Christy kept far too busy the remainder of the day to think about Cameron at all. But when she crawled into bed that night, she couldn't get him out of her mind. Playing through the events that had taken their friendship from practically perfect to horrible, Christy asked her Father in Heaven to guide her in patching up the problems she had created with this wonderful friend He had sent into her life. Resolving to call him first thing in the morning, she finally slept.

Christy tried to call Cameron at his apartment right after the kids left for school, but she only got the machine. She called the office as soon as she got to work, and was told that he wasn't available. Three more calls through the day gave her the same answer. She tried his cell phone, but got only his voice mail, and she couldn't bring herself to even leave a message beyond, "Hi, it's Christy. I tried to call." What she needed to say had to be said to his face, under the right circumstances.

Through the afternoon, Christy became completely preoccupied with the conversation she needed to have with Cameron, until she checked on the kids after school and Lucy reported that she didn't feel well. She called back half an hour later to say that she'd thrown up. Christy told her not to eat or drink anything except some apple juice, and she'd be home soon. She arrived to find Lucy free of any fever, but feeling a little achy. She said her stomach felt better now that it was empty, and Christy concluded that it was likely just a little flu bug. She'd learned years ago not to stress over every little illness.

Certain that Lucy would be fine, her thoughts returned to Cameron. When his office closed and the phones were no longer being answered, she tried his cell phone again and found that it was still turned off. Now that she'd made up her mind about what she needed to do, she felt as if she'd never be able to sleep until the issue was resolved. After trying his home and cell phone again, she finally broke down and called Bea. "I don't suppose you'd know where your nephew is."

"Actually, I think this is the night he works in the temple," she said.

"Does that mean he'll be late?" Christy asked.

"Well . . . if his schedule hasn't changed, he's usually there the entire evening. I know he eats supper in the cafeteria between sessions."

Christy's frustration turned to hope as an idea formed in her mind.

Bea startled her when she asked, "You sound stressed, dear. Is there anything I can do to help?"

"Uh . . . no, Lucy has a little flu bug, I think; nothing serious. And I'm fine, thank you."

"Well, fine is relative," Bea went on to say. "Cameron told me about the tabloid story; he was terribly upset. I'm sure you must have been, too."

"Yes, I was," she admitted. "But I'm doing better now. The problem is . . . well, I didn't handle the whole thing very well, and . . . I really need to talk to Cameron, but . . . Hey, can you hold on? I'm getting another call."

"Of course."

"If I'm more than thirty seconds, I'll call you back," she said and pushed the button to get the other line. Then she groaned inwardly to hear Keith say that Lucy had called and told him she was sick, and he wanted to drop by in about half an hour to see her for a few minutes and bring the kids a surprise. He promised to make his visit brief and be amiable, and Christy knew it would mean a lot to the kids, so she agreed. She said good-bye and connected back to Beatrice. "Well, that was Keith. He's coming over to see Lucy. I couldn't find a reason to tell him he couldn't come, after what happened. But I don't want to be here with him, and I don't trust him in my house without me here."

"Well, there," Bea said. "I'll come and sit with the children while you get out for a while. I knew there was something I could do to help."

"I wasn't fishing for help, Bea. I was just grumbling."

"I know that. I'll be there in ten minutes. And I can stay as long as you need me to."

When Bea arrived, Christy readily declared, "You must be inspired. I must admit I never would have thought of having someone else here, but it solves every problem, and if anyone can keep him on his best behavior, it's you."

Bea laughed softly. "Glad to help. Is there anything I can be doing while you're gone?"

"Just . . . remind Tim and Charlotte to do their chores and their homework. They know what that entails. I've got a casserole in the oven that should be ready in about ten minutes, but Lucy shouldn't eat. There's some Jell-O in the fridge for her. I think I'll go get something to eat at . . ." She head herself laugh and added, "The truth is . . . since you're going to be here, I think I'll try and catch a bite at the temple cafeteria."

Bea smiled so widely that Christy couldn't help wondering if she had been secretly hoping for that very thing. "That's an excellent idea, dear. You might as well dress for a session and get some respite while you're there. I can stay as late as you need; I can see that Lucy and the others are perfectly fine."

Christy took a deep breath, then embraced Bea. "Thank you," she murmured, her voice turning teary. "Cameron's very lucky to have an aunt like you. With all you've helped me through, I hope it's not presumptuous to say that you feel like my aunt, as well."

"The feeling is mutual," she said. "And Cameron is very lucky to have a friend like you."

"I don't know." Christy glanced down. "I think my friendship skills need a little honing."

Bea touched Christy's chin to lift her face. With severe eyes and a compassionate voice, she said, "He understands, Christina. Just talk to him, and all will be well."

Christy nodded and choked back a new batch of tears until she was in the car by herself. She cried all the way into the city, then she touched up her makeup in the rearview mirror and walked into the temple, praying that her attempts to cross paths with Cameron would not fail.

Chapter Eleven

Christy was barely inside the temple when she felt better. She only prayed that she hadn't missed Cameron coming to the cafeteria already. Or for that matter, she wasn't completely certain he was even here. Either way, just being within temple walls helped put her feelings into perspective.

She went to the dressing room and changed into her white clothes before she went to the cafeteria and loitered discreetly where she could see those who came to get in the food line. Rather than getting impatient when minutes passed and she didn't see him, she focused on sorting out all that had happened, by going deeper into her feelings and being completely honest with herself. More than forty minutes after she'd arrived at her vantage point, she was almost startled to see Cameron. Watching him while he wasn't aware, she was struck with his dignity and undeniable aura, which was enhanced by the white suit and tie that he wore. Praying that it was not too late to regain all that had been lost between them, she took a deep breath and moved discreetly behind him just as he reached for a tray.

"I hear the chicken stuff is pretty good," she said. He turned abruptly then seemed to freeze, obviously not knowing how to respond. Hoping to ease the tension, she added, "Are you buying? 'Cause I left my purse in my locker."

He sighed audibly and put one arm around her in some semblance of an embrace. His relief was so evident that she felt even more guilty for dragging this out so long. He looked into her eyes and she marveled at the obvious adoration she saw there. As much as she had desperately needed his friendship in her life, she had to wonder what his need for a friend might have meant to him. She suspected there was more hurt inside that he'd not yet admitted to. And that was fine. For now, she simply had to take the steps to put their friendship in order. She needed him, and it was readily evident that he needed her, too.

"What are you doing here?" he asked, much as she had when he'd shown up downtown the previous day.

"I need to talk to you, and what better place than here to be humble and get to the truth?"

He smiled and said, "Yes, I'm buying. But I'm having the pasta stuff. I had chicken stuff for lunch."

"I tried to call you today; I really did."

"Really?" He was genuinely surprised. "I was in one of those all-day meetings. They brought lunch in, and then I rushed here and was almost late. I haven't checked my messages."

They got their food and moved down the line where Cameron paid for it, then they moved to a vacant table in the corner where they could talk quietly. He said nothing and she knew that it was up to her to begin—if only she knew how. After a few minutes of eating in silence, she concluded that she just needed to get to the point.

"I owe you a very big apology," she began and he looked up from his meal. Now that she had his attention, she hurried to add, "What you said was absolutely right, and I was too proud and too angry to admit it. So, I'm sorry."

He smiled kindly and reached across the table for her hand. "Apology accepted," he said. "But you're going to have to remind me what I was absolutely right about. It's been a long week."

"You can say that again," she said with a humorless chuckle.

"So, what was I right about?" he asked.

"You said that I was scared, and I was just using the tabloid thing as an excuse to be angry with you. Well, you were right."

Cameron leaned closer and tightened his hand over hers. "What are you afraid of, Christina?"

She set down her fork and put her other hand in her lap. "I guess you were right about that, too. You said that whatever our relationship may or may not be, you're a man and I was afraid you would leave me high and dry. Maybe somewhere deep inside, I was thinking if I left you first, then . . ." Emotion prevented her from saying anything more.

"And now?" he asked.

"Now what?" she said with a broken voice.

"Are you still scared?"

"Yes, actually."

"But you're here."

"Yes, I'm here, because nothing has felt right without knowing that you were there to turn to if I needed you. It's probably selfish of me, Cameron, but I need your friendship. I believe our coming together was not a coincidence; and if God sent you into my life to help me, then I can't expect to have my prayers answered if I've pushed you out of my life because I was afraid to trust or open my heart. So, I'm here to say: thank you for being my friend, and please keep being my friend, even though I've been awful."

"That will not be a problem, Christina, I can assure you. Now, let me clarify something. I am *not* going to leave you high and dry—not ever. No matter where our lives take us, or what may change, we will always be friends."

Christy watched his face and resisted the urge to confess that what he'd just said was at the root of her deepest fear. Could she ever cope with having him forever be her friend? Could she stand by and see him marry another woman, all the while considering her *just a friend?* She swallowed carefully and reminded herself to keep perspective. She knew that the only way to learn to trust again, was simply to trust. She had to believe that whatever happened in the future, he would keep his word and always be there for her, as far as it would be possible. In that moment, she resigned herself to stop worrying about the future, and enjoy the present with Cameron Chandler wanting to be her best friend.

"Now, I have something else to say," he went on, bringing her out of her thoughts. "You had a right to be upset over that tabloid thing. It was pathetic, to say the least. But I want you to know that the hardest part for me was to see our relationship cheapened that way. I have a deep regard for the forces that brought us together, and what I saw in that magazine was just one more example of how Satan takes something good and wonderful, and turns it into something ugly.

"I also think it's important to clarify that I don't want you to make anything of the romantic implications there, and don't think that I'm going to, either. I know where you're at, and that's not what this relationship is about."

Christy nodded in agreement, at the same time trying to convince herself that what she felt for him was simply a rebound reaction from finally putting Keith behind her. Only time would prove if her feelings could ever be anything else, and she needed to be patient and allow time to take its course.

"I owe you an apology as well," he said and she looked up, surprised. "That story never would have run if I hadn't done that pathetic game to begin with. And I apologize for your getting caught up in it. I really think the story will die quickly; in fact, I believe it already has. People who know us—the few who were even aware of the story—know it's not true. If anyone who mattered to either of us had read it, we probably would have heard from them by now. Those magazines are old news almost before they come off the presses, especially for people like us who are so terribly low profile compared to real public figures they feed off of. My biggest concern is how this might affect the situation with Keith. I'm afraid that in spite of not being able to prove you have that money, that he will delay child support, or push you into more court costs."

Christy shrugged her shoulders but couldn't comment. She'd considered the possible court costs, but it hadn't occurred to her that he might delay child support as long as legally possible, just to be difficult. The idea made her more concerned than angry. Her finances were already stretched to their limits.

"So," he continued, "just know that I'm not trying to hone in where I'm not wanted, I'm not trying to wound your pride or be a hero. I just want to be there for you, and help where I feel like the Lord wants me to help." He squeezed her hand. "I'm here for you, no matter what. Do you hear me?"

Christy nodded again, trying to absorb everything he was saying. They forged on through their supper while he seemed to sense her need to allow her thoughts to catch up with everything that had been said. She finally broke the silence to say, "I'm relatively certain I know who tattled to the tabloid."

"Really?" he said, lifting his brows. "Don't leave me hanging."

"It's a girl who works for me. I have no idea why she would do something like that, unless she simply doesn't like me. But I don't like her, either."

"So, now what?"

"Well, I've already fired her."

"Really?" he said again with a pleasant smirk.

"Her credibility as an employee was already hanging by a thread. Rodney overheard her talking on the phone, saying some things that made her involvement obvious. When I confronted her she didn't deny it, so I let her go. I hope to never see her again."

"Well, at least the mystery is solved," he said evenly, but his irritation was evident. "But how did she know that—"

"Well, that's the embarrassing part. I told her. I wouldn't normally tell her *anything* about my personal life, but she was the one who helped you when you bought the seagull, and she insisted on knowing the reason for the gift."

"Oh, *her*," Cameron said with a scowl. "It all makes sense, I suppose."

"Yes, I suppose. Anyway, I want to apologize . . . for the way I behaved, and for any trouble I may have brought into *your* life."

"It's not a big deal, Christy. It's over and done. And in the whole big scheme of life's challenges, it's just . . . not a big deal."

"Yes, I can see that now; now that I've gotten to the truth about what was upsetting me."

Following a minute of silence, he asked, "You okay?"

"Yes, actually, I believe I am; better than I've been in days."

"That's great," he said. "But I have to ask . . . What was this meeting with Keith downtown yesterday?"

Christy sighed. "He called and asked me to meet him. He promised to be nice, so I went."

"Yes," Cameron drawled expectantly, finding delight in the subtle sparkle that had returned to Christy's eyes. The darkness he had felt in her absence was too frighteningly familiar. He was grateful to have his friend back, and he hoped that they could always be as close as he felt to her now—no matter what.

"Well, in essence, he told me he'd made a mistake, and he wanted to try again."

Cameron felt his heart drop like a rock. He forced his expression to remain steady, but he couldn't even fathom how he would feel to see her go back to the man who had treated her so badly. He'd hardly dared give a conscious thought to the hopes he had for himself and Christina, but looking at the possibility of those hopes being dashed, he knew he'd become far too emotionally involved. Knowing that whatever the future might hold had to be independent of their pasts, he forced logic to his mind and said evenly, "That must have come as a surprise."

"Yes," she chuckled tensely, "it certainly did."

When she didn't go on, he had to ask, "And . . . what did you tell him?"

"Well, I basically told him that the hurt he had inflicted in my life was deep, and I wouldn't open myself up to be hurt all over again. I told him it would take a huge amount of restitution and penitence to even begin to win my trust again, and love was variable beyond that. I told him words were not enough to make me believe he wanted to try again. It would take demonstration—and lots of it."

Cameron sighed, feeling a degree of relief. She'd given him the right answer, and he was proud of her. But if Keith had been willing to do all she'd asked, would she go back to him and put an abrupt halt to this friendship that could never practically continue with either one of them committed elsewhere?

"I also told him," she went on, "that he was married to Patricia now, and he should make the most of that marriage. I told him that Patricia was his wife now, and she deserved his commitment for that reason alone."

Cameron couldn't keep from smiling, although he managed to keep it subdued. "Is something funny?" she asked.

"Not funny, Christina. I'm just proud of you. You've come a long way these last couple of weeks. He did the very thing you'd been hoping he'd do for months, but you didn't melt and grovel and fall apart."

"Ironic, isn't it?" she said with distant eyes and a sad voice.

"Yes," he agreed, then forced himself to ask, "So, did Keith agree to your conditions, or take your suggestion to stick it out with his *eternal soul mate?*"

Christina chuckled at the nonchalant way he said something that had once caused her such grief, and to know that she could hear it and not feel pain. "He didn't seem at all impressed with my conditions," she said, "especially when I suggested groveling would be a good place to start."

Cameron couldn't hold back a little laugh of relief. Again he justified his response by saying, "I'm really proud of you."

"Yeah, I'm proud of me, too. I saw right through him. I know the Spirit was helping me. I'm just glad it's over—all of it. Tabloids, proposals from ex-husbands. And most of all, I'm glad that you're still my friend."

"Forever," he said, then he glanced at the clock. "Hey, I've got to get back to work. Are you going home now, or were you going to—"

"I thought I would go through a session while I'm here. Bea's with the kids, and she made it clear I could stay out as late as I needed to."

"Well, bless her heart," he said. "If it's all right with you, I'll meet you in the celestial room."

"I'll be there," she said and they rose at the same time to take away their trays.

Sitting through the endowment session, Christy felt peace envelop her. Knowing she had cleared the air with Cameron, by apologizing and setting the record straight, her conscience felt clear and she felt the Spirit close. Contemplating her encounter with Keith, and the way she'd handled it, she felt added peace in knowing she had done the right thing. She felt another layer of healing take place within as she expressed silent gratitude to her Father in Heaven for all she had been blessed with, most especially the Atonement of His Son that made peace possible.

At a certain point in the endowment presentation, Christy caught her breath to see Cameron enter the room as one of the officiators. Watching him discreetly, she couldn't help feeling her gratitude deepen over having him in her life as she tallied all he had done for her. Thoughts of Keith pressed a panic button that made her wonder if she might be blinding herself to the possibility that Cameron might have deep, underlying problems that could bring difficulties into her life. Turning her thoughts to prayer, she felt peace come again. She simply knew that in spite of any imperfections he might have, he was a man of integrity, and by staying close to the Spirit and giving her feelings some time, she would be able to know what was right for her.

When the session was over, Christy sat in the celestial room for only a few minutes before Cameron sat beside her and took her hand. She caught a definite sparkle in his eyes as he looked directly into her face. While she was pondering over the possible reasons, he said quietly, "Forgive me; it may not be appropriate, but I just have to say: I've never seen you look more beautiful than you do now. That ex-husband of yours was a fool to ever believe he could find something better than what he already had."

The sincerity behind his words was readily evident, and Christy felt the depth of his compliment penetrate her heart with one more layer of validation. They talked quietly for a long while in a way that Christy had never experienced with Keith. Being within temple walls, they discussed spiritual principles in a way that opened her understanding and deepened her gratitude. She came to more fully understand the Atonement, and she felt the warmth of the Spirit strengthening her hope for a bright future—whether it included Cameron or not. One of many lessons she had learned through the past year was to separate the temple and all it represented from the man she had married there, who had so sorely disappointed her. And she had to keep the same principle clear now. Sharing spiritual moments inside the temple did not necessarily have anything to do with Cameron, himself. But it did make her appreciate having a friend who could share her spiritual beliefs and ideals. Only now did she realize that, while she and Keith had shared a temple marriage, they had not shared a spiritual relationship. She couldn't recall having conversations of a spiritual nature, or working with him to make decisions in their lives by spiritual means. It seemed the more time that passed, the more she realized how many difficulties there had been in the relationship. Of course, if he had remained committed to her, she would have done everything in her power to work those problems out. But as it was, such realizations helped her perspective.

Christy and Cameron finally separated to change into their street clothes, then they walked out of the temple together and sat in the Main Street park, gazing up at the temple spires, saying very little, as if they were each silently replaying the blessings of the temple that were too sacred to discuss outside its walls. When they started to feel cold, Cameron walked Christy to her car, then she gave him a ride to his. Before he got out, he squeezed her hand and said, "Thank you. This day didn't start out real great, but it sure ended that way."

"Thank *you*," she said. "For everything."

"I'll call you," he said. "Or you call me."

"I promise," she said and he got out and closed the door. He waved as she drove away, and Christy was filled with peace and gratitude that simply had no choice but to overflow in tears that ran quietly down her face throughout the rest of the drive home.

The following morning, Christy had only been at work an hour when Rodney told her she was wanted on the phone. "It's a man," he whispered, "but it doesn't sound like Keith *or* the Chandler guy."

Christy felt a little nervous as she put the phone to her ear. "Hello?" she said.

"Ms. Hardy?"

"Yes."

"My name is Stanley Kent; I'm an attorney representing Chandler Corporation. I wonder if I could meet with you for just a few minutes this morning."

Christy's mind momentarily swirled with what this might mean, but she couldn't come up with a single possibility. "Uh . . . that would be fine."

"Would you be able to come to my office, or would you prefer that I meet you somewhere else?"

"Uh . . ." she said again, "where is your office, exactly?"

He told her an address that was little more than a block away, and she said, "I'll come there. What time?"

They agreed on eleven o'clock, which gave Christy very little time to stew over what in the world he might want to discuss with her. Arriving at the legal office, she waited in a lobby for only a few minutes before the middle-aged, balding Mr. Kent appeared and led the way to his office. She had barely taken a seat when he said, "I have a matter of business that was assigned to me the end of last week, but I ended up needing to be in court, and this has been my first possible opportunity to meet with you. I appreciate your being willing to come on such short notice."

"No problem," she said warily.

"I'm sure you're wondering what this is all about, so I'll get straight to the point."

"That would be good," she said, "because I can't even guess what that point might be."

He erupted with a good-natured chuckle and leaned back in his chair. "Apparently there was some incident of a recent tabloid story regarding you and Mr. Chandler."

"That's right," she said, wondering what kind of horrible legal ramifications might have resulted that would involve her. Or had Cameron made the decision to sue the tabloid? Or Mazie? She couldn't imagine him doing such a thing, but what else could this possibly mean?

"Mr. Chandler explained the possible difficulties the situation might bring in regard to your ex-husband getting wind of the story, and he asked me to see that you were given some meager compensation that might help you ride out the storm."

Christy furrowed her brow and attempted to put the pieces together. "I don't understand. Is this some kind of settlement? Is he afraid that I might sue or—"

"No, of course not," he chuckled again. "He simply asked that I present you with this check to help compensate for any trouble the situation might cause. You don't have to sign anything." He leaned forward and his gentle tone became gentler. "May I be frank, Ms. Hardy?"

"Of course."

"This is far from the first time that Mr. Chandler, or his father, have asked me to do this very kind of thing, for a number of reasons. You certainly have the option to not accept the money, but I can assure you that it is given with only the purest intent, with concern for your well-being, and it will be kept completely confidential. No one beyond you, me, and Mr. Chandler will have any knowledge of the transaction."

In spite of this attorney's perfectly logical explanation, Christy still felt tempted to be angry. She quickly reminded herself that anger was a secondary emotion, and it wasn't difficult to figure what was beneath it: *pride*. The very idea of taking money from Cameron Chandler bristled her every nerve. While she was trying to come up with the words to politely refuse the offer, Mr. Kent slid the check across the desk. It took her a moment to digest an amount typed there that would free her of her financial burdens, and then her vision misted over. She quickly grabbed a tissue from her purse when the tears spilled before she could force them back. How could she not recall the fast offering check she'd written out with the hope that giving something extra to the Lord would be the best investment she could make toward helping her become free of her debts? Her pride melted into perfect humility as she realized that Cameron Chandler had unwittingly been the means to provide an answer to her prayers.

Christy quickly wiped her tears and managed to get her emotions under control before she made a fool of herself. She pressed her hand over the check and muttered quickly, "Thank you, Mr. Kent. And pass my gratitude along to Mr. Chandler. The money will be very much appreciated."

The attorney smiled and nodded his head before he stood to walk her back to the waiting area. He shook her hand and thanked her again for coming. Christy looked at the check once more before she tucked it into her purse, then she walked directly to the bank and put it safely into her account where she could pay those overdue legal bills. *It was a miracle.*

Noticing what time it was, she called the store on her cell phone to make sure everything was covered so she could go ahead and take her lunch hour. Rodney assured her that he would keep everything under control. Christy then called Cameron's office and was pleased when Bertie put her straight through.

"Hi," he said eagerly, obviously having been told who it was.

"You got plans for lunch?" she asked. "It's my treat."

"Ooh," he said dramatically. "It must be a special occasion."

"It is actually."

"Sure, where do you want to meet?"

"I was thinking about soup . . . our usual table."

"Sounds great," he said. "I'll be there in ten minutes."

At the risk of putting tension between them, she asked, "Will that be ten or thirty?" When he said nothing she added, "Are you there?"

"I'm here," he said, sounding subtly irritated. "I'll be there in ten minutes," he repeated and hung up the phone.

When Cameron finally arrived at the *usual table*, Christy just glanced at her watch and said, "Twenty-four minutes." He looked mildly astonished and she quickly added, "You're a wonderful man, Cameron, but you are a very poor judge of time. Since I'm your best friend, you should know that I would appreciate having you arrive when you say you're going to arrive. And when you don't it comes across as being rude and arrogant in a way that is very unlike you. If something comes up, you have my cell number. You're obviously a very important man with many people who would likely be willing to wait for you. But I don't work for you, and I'm not going to wait for you. Fair enough?"

For a moment he looked so stunned that she wondered if he would get angry or get up and leave. He finally said, "Fair enough."

"Okay," she said and quickly changed the subject, "I'm in a generous mood. You can have anything you want. It's on me." She made a dramatic sweeping motion with her arm, indicating the more than a dozen available fast-food stands surrounding the courtyard.

"Anything?" he said. "Even McDonald's?"

"Even McDonald's," she repeated.

He chuckled and helped her to her feet. "Soup sounds good to me."

"Great minds think alike," she said, and they approached the counter to find no one waiting in line.

They were soon back at the table, digging into their clam chowder, when Cameron said, "So, to what do I owe being treated to lunch? What has brought on this frivolously generous mood?"

"Thank you . . . for the money, Cameron. It was an answer to many prayers."

Christy watched him draw in a deep breath and fold his arms over his chest before he finally said, "I was terrified you would be angry with me, and we'd start last week's episode all over again. But I just felt compelled to give it to you, and I prayed that you would know it was from the heart . . . and not be angry with me."

"Well," she glanced down, "given my recent behavior, your concerns were certainly understandable. And if you must know, my first inclination was to be angry. But it only took me a minute to realize that inclination was being fueled by pride." She reached across the table and took his hand. "So, I just want to say: thank you,

Cameron—for being my friend, and for being the kind of person who helps answer prayers on the Lord's behalf."

"It works two ways, Christina. You have been the answer to my prayers more than you could possibly know."

"You keep bringing that up," she said, "but you still haven't told me how . . . exactly."

He smiled. "And one day I will . . . when the time is right."

"I'll look forward to it."

"Well then, we both have something to look forward to. In the meantime, you got any plans Saturday?"

"I have to work half a day to make up some hours, and I've got to do grocery shopping before I come home. After that, I think I'm clear, why?"

"Well, I was hoping for a Monopoly rematch, because that daughter of yours really did me in." Christy laughed. "And I could bring a video we could all watch together, and if you're really feeling adventurous, I could bring food and cook spaghetti for the whole family . . . with bottled sauce, of course. I'm not terribly clever in the kitchen."

"It sounds divine," Christy said. "I'll make dessert."

"It's a deal," he said and together they finished their soup, talking through the trivialities of their lives as if they'd been friends forever. Christy was beginning to wonder if they had been.

Cameron returned to the office and hesitated at Bertie's desk. "Hey," he said, "do I make people wait for me?"

She looked at him suspiciously over the top of her glasses. "Is this a trick question?"

"No," he chuckled, "just answer it."

"You're not going to fire me if I'm honest, are you?"

"No," he said again.

"Okay, then. Yes, you do. All the time."

Cameron sighed loudly. "So . . . would you say I am a poor judge of time?"

"Extremely," she said and added sheepishly, "I did buy you a watch last Christmas."

Cameron looked at her and shook his head. Obviously Bertie knew something that Christy knew—something he'd been totally oblivious to. He forced back a temptation to feel defensive and simply said, "Maybe I should start looking at it."

"Wouldn't hurt," Bertie said and he walked into his office.

Chapter Twelve

January eased into February while Christy found a new serenity with her life. The healing that had taken place within herself began to settle more comfortably. The children continued to be children, and life brought its daily challenges, but Christy sensed the progression of their own growth and healing. They too had come a long way in a year, and they too seemed to have settled comfortably into their new way of life. For Christy, being free of debt beyond her mortgage and a car payment that had less than a year remaining, lifted more tangible burdens from her shoulders. With money not being quite so tight, she was able to take the kids out more to do something beyond occasionally renting a video. And Cameron was often—but not always—a part of those activities. Occasionally they got together with Bea, and Christy grew to love her even more than she already had.

Christy talked to Cameron nearly every day, and saw him a few times a week. He was often late, but he usually called on his cell phone to let her know, and he always apologized. Improvement was good, she reasoned.

The first week of February was especially cold, and Christy rarely ventured outside the house or the mall, except for the drive in between, from one garage to another. The second week of February brought a moderation in the temperatures, and she enjoyed an occasional walk through the temple grounds with Cameron. She felt increasingly comfortable with their relationship. Time had only strengthened her belief that he was a good man, in spite of imperfections that he readily admitted to. And never once had he even hinted at pressing their relationship beyond being *just friends*. Christy was grateful for that boundary in light of the transition she'd been going through, and the necessary healing that had been taking place. But as time passed, she couldn't deny her inner longing that what they shared would evolve into something deeper and richer—something romantic. *Something forever.* She'd stewed and analyzed her feelings endlessly, always coming to the same conclusion. She had no control over *his* feelings, and absolutely no reason to think that his feelings for her would ever be anything more than what he indicated now. Occasionally there was something in the way he'd look at her that made her hopeful, but she was still too vulnerable to articulate her own feelings and risk putting tension into the comfortable relationship they shared. So she enjoyed each day for what it would bring, with faith enough to believe that whatever her future had in store, it would be better than the past.

* * * * *

Christy answered the store phone and heard Cameron say, "Can you meet me at the Seagull Monument in half an hour? And yes, I mean half an hour."

She glanced at the clock. "Uh . . . yeah. I think I could do that. May I ask . . . why?"

"I only have a few minutes, but there's something I need to ask you."

"Okay. I'll be there."

Christy hurried to finish what she was doing and ended up practically running to Temple Square in order to get there on time. When she arrived there was no sign of Cameron—which wasn't a surprise. But she was a few minutes early, so she sat on the edge of the fountain and glanced toward the temple spires. No matter how many times she looked at them, they were still amazing.

"Hello," Cameron said directly in front of her and she looked up to see him smiling down at her, his hands behind his back.

"Hello," she repeated. "So, I'm here. What did you want to ask me? You said you were in a hurry."

"I am actually, but . . . well, if the answer is no, that's okay. But I just . . . have to ask."

"Okay."

"Tomorrow is Valentine's Day."

"Yes," she said when he didn't go on. She'd been all too aware of the approaching holiday with its romantic implications. But she had focused her thoughts on being grateful that it wasn't *last* Valentine's Day, when she had barely begun to accept that her husband had left her for another woman.

"So, I was wondering if you might possibly consider going on a date with me."

Christy's heart quickened as her recent concerns regarding his interest in her became somewhat assuaged.

"And if you're not ready for an official date, then . . . I can live with that. And we can go out anyway . . . as friends."

"What would the difference be . . . exactly?"

Cameron chuckled. "To be quite honest, I don't know. I just thought that . . . being Valentine's Day, it would be nice to go on a date. And maybe if we go out on a date, we'll be able to figure out the difference. So, what do you think?"

"Well . . . I uh . . ."

"Either way," he said, "you get to keep the roses."

He pulled a dozen red roses from behind his back and she gasped. "Good heavens," she laughed. "They're beautiful. Thank you."

"You're welcome. Can I pick you up at seven?"

"I'll be ready," she said and he smiled, but there was still a question in his eyes. "And since it's a date," she said, "should I dress up?"

"Absolutely," he said. "In fact, it's formal." He grinned and walked away.

Christy inhaled the roses and laughed softly. Then she hurried back into the mall, straight to a store where she frequently window-shopped, admiring the beautiful dresses. She'd had her eye on a few in particular for months, wishing she could afford one of them, but knowing she'd never have any place to wear something so eye-catching. Her enthusiasm for buying a new dress waned when she examined some price tags. She had a little to spare in savings, but not *that* much. She was just wondering if she should be going to Wal-Mart to buy a dress when she caught sight of a sea-green-colored dress at the end of the rack that she'd admired many times—and it had a red sale tag. She held her breath while she looked at the size. *It would fit.* She stood in front of a mirror and held it against her, admiring the fitted bodice of rich brocade fabric, with long sleeves and buttons down the back. The skirt was slightly full, a satiny fabric that she suspected would brush the floor, even if she wore heels. Deciding she really liked it, she took a deep breath and looked at the pricetag. She squeezed her eyes shut and opened them again, certain she was seeing it wrong. She turned to the sales girl and asked, "Is this dress really only twenty-eight dollars?"

"That's right," she said, coming closer. "Marked down from eighty-nine."

"Why?"

"Well, it has this little tear in it . . . right here." She showed Christy the tear, which she knew could be easily mended in ten minutes. "Oh, and there's an additional twenty percent off our sale items today . . . for Valentine's day."

"Really?" Christy laughed.

"By the looks of those roses you're carrying, you must have a pretty special date, eh?"

"Yes, I suppose I do. And I'll take this."

Christy grabbed a sandwich and hurried back to the store with her roses and her shopping bag from one of the most elite clothing stores in the mall. Rodney smirked but said nothing and she went to the back room to eat her sandwich and find something to put the roses in.

Cameron called her for just a minute that evening to see how she was doing, and said again that he'd pick her up tomorrow at seven.

Valentine's Day was busy at the mall, and Christy continually fought to suppress the butterflies in her stomach. She couldn't deny that she'd secretly longed for weeks to have her relationship with Cameron move beyond the friendship they shared. She knew that eventually a day of reckoning would come for her and Cameron. Either their relationship would emerge into something romantic, or it wouldn't. She prayed that whatever path her life took, she would have the discernment to know what to do, and the strength to do it and do it right. One divorce was one too many.

The minute Christy got home from work, she took a shower and got into her new dress. The kids made a delightful fuss over her going out, and Charlotte helped her with her hair, curling small sections with the curling iron, and pulling it up in back to hang in somewhat of a cascade. The doorbell rang at five after seven. Christy took a deep breath while Tim ran to answer it. She could hear Cameron teasing him, and took a deep breath before she stepped into the front room, just in time to hear Lucy say, "Mom looks so good. You are just not gonna believe it."

Cameron looked up to see Christy standing in the doorway and his heart skipped a beat. He forced himself to his senses when he realized he was staring. "Oh, I believe it," he said. He held out his hand and she stepped forward to take it. "You really do look beautiful, Christina."

"Thank you," she said and nodded toward his classic black tuxedo. "So do you."

Christy tore herself away from looking at him to give the kids some final instructions. "You can watch the video when homework and chores are done, and you can stay up until ten. It may be a holiday, but there *is* school tomorrow." They each hugged her before she stepped outside with Cameron and locked the door behind her.

Christy stopped halfway up the walk when she saw a limo parked on the street. "You're kidding. You actually *own* one of those?"

"Actually, no. I borrowed it. But I do have an in with the chauffeur." He opened the door and Christy slid in to see William in the driver's seat.

"Hello, William," she said. "How good to see you."

"And you," he said.

Cameron sat beside Christy and closed the door. The car eased forward and Christy giggled like a child. "This is pretty cool, I must admit. I've never been in one of these before."

"Well, I could count on one hand the times I have. And half of those have been funerals. But this," he took her hand, "is fun."

While they chatted comfortably through the drive into the city, Christy couldn't help thinking that nothing felt any different between them. She didn't feel any change in his attitude toward her, or any less relaxed with him, given that this was an official date.

William dropped them off in front of the revolving door of the Joseph Smith Memorial Building. They went up the elevator to the top floor, and she couldn't help being thrilled to realize they would be eating in the restaurant there. She'd passed it many times when she'd come here to gaze down at Temple Square, but she'd never had the opportunity to go inside. The meal was exquisite, and Cameron was as charming and comfortable as ever. Then he asked, "So, does an official date feel different?"

"No, not really," she said, "beyond the amount of money you're spending."

He chuckled. "I can date on a budget. Next time I'll take you to a dollar movie and we'll eat at Carl's Jr."

"Only if I can have a piece of chocolate cake."

"Of course," he said. "You can't eat at Carl's Jr. without having chocolate cake."

When their meal was finished, they stepped out into the long hallway, where a fountain was gurgling pleasantly. The huge windows revealed an incredible view of the city, with Temple Square in the foreground. Christy had come here many times, but rarely at night.

"Let's sit," Cameron said, motioning to the wide marble ledge against the window.

They sat in silence for several minutes while Christy absorbed the view. Cameron looked at the floor, seeming lost in thought.

"Is something on your mind?" she asked quietly.

He glanced up briefly toward another couple admiring the view and said nothing. A few minutes later when they were alone, she asked, "So, what's on your mind?"

He chuckled tensely and she realized he was nervous, which made her nervous, but she didn't know how to ease the tension.

"I . . . uh . . . have to admit I've had a thought going around in my head for quite some time now, and I had no intention of sharing it with you . . . yet . . . tonight," he corrected. "But . . . suddenly I can't get it out of my head, and . . ."

"Okay, I'm listening," she said, but he hesitated. "Does this have anything to do with the way I was the answer to your prayers that you've always managed to evade telling me?"

"Yes, I suppose it does." He sighed and leaned his forearms on this thighs, his back to the window. "The thing is . . . those weeks between my father's death and Christmas were some of the lowest in my life. With my father gone I had to take a good, hard look at my life. And I didn't like what I saw. I had no close friends. My only immediate family member was living in sin in New York. And beyond my activity in the Church, my entire life was trying to swim upstream in a business world so full of cynics and politics and underhanded cheating that I'd begun to believe the world had little good left in it, and certainly nothing good for me. I have to admit that the pain of my father's death was kind of the straw that broke the camel's back. I looked back to the time when I'd had a wife and son, and wondered what had happened to the man who'd had a home and a purpose. The more I thought about it, the more I realized that I had become cynical and crusty, just like most of the people I work with. My father had been a great example of managing to keep his dealings straight and his every word and deed completely honest, but I began to wonder if I could fill his footsteps while I was constantly going up the down staircase, if that makes any sense."

"Yes, it does," she said gently, taking his hand.

"I must admit that my church attendance dropped significantly. I don't mean that my testimony wavered, because it's deeply ingrained in me. I think I was just . . . weary, and maybe feeling . . . unworthy. As if the state of my life was something I had brought on myself and I had lost the right to have God bless me. I did this charity game thing because it was something my father had talked about doing for years. After his death, with the holidays approaching, I thought it was a way of carrying out his last wishes, so to speak. And while it provoked some good things, I felt my cynicism increasing as I realized that the people my employees had received help from were clearly hoping to be rewarded. I began to wonder if there were any truly good Samaritans out there at all."

He sighed and looked toward Christy with eyes that seemed to see into her heart and soul. She took a deep breath as she sensed where this was headed now. He looked back toward the floor and threaded his fingers between hers. "About a week before Christmas, I hit such a low that I had trouble getting out of bed. I remember sliding to my knees by the bed, and I have no idea how long I was there, crying more than praying. I told the Lord straight out that I needed a sign. Not in the way that the sign seekers of the scriptures asked for signs; but I needed some tangible reason to press forward in every aspect of my life. I'd needed something to make me believe that mankind was good, and life was worth living." He chuckled humorlessly. "And you know, when my car broke down on Christmas Eve, I had almost been contemplating driving it off a cliff."

Christy gasped, then felt embarrassed by her reaction. She looked at him closely, hoping to see some evidence that he was partly teasing, but his face was more sober, more intense, than she'd ever seen it.

"I didn't know how I could face Christmas without my father, let alone embark on one more year of living alone and fighting single-handedly to keep the Chandler corporation honest and upstanding. When the car quit and the snow was coming down hard, I was more angry than I'd ever been in my life. I all but cursed God for throwing one more curve ball at me. Then I just sat there, feeling more despair than I'd felt when I lost my son, my wife, my father." He glanced toward her and added firmly, "When I started walking, I was thinking that maybe freezing to death would be easier than driving the car off a cliff. I think it was my fear of dying in such a state of mind that forced me to start praying." He chuckled. "And I got this image in my mind of that scene in *It's a Wonderful Life*. You know the one, where he's standing on the bridge, ready to throw himself in the water, because he believes he's worth more dead than alive. And then . . ." He focused his eyes on her. "The angel came and saved him."

Christy didn't realize she was crying until he reached up to wipe her tears. "I could never tell you, my sweet, dear friend, what your appearance in that moment meant to me. By the time William had picked me up at your house, my entire perspective had changed. You had proven to me that mankind *was* good, that life *was* worth living. You were tangible evidence that God had heard and answered my prayers, because I felt the warmth of His Spirit penetrate me as it hadn't done for years. You were my angel, a messenger from my Father in Heaven. And what was equally remarkable was the fact that *you* needed *me*. I suddenly had purpose. And I had perspective."

Christy sniffled and reached into her bag for a tissue. When it became evident he was finished, she said, "That's incredible. And all this time I thought *you* were an angel sent to help *me*. You had all the right answers, the right attitude, and the empathy I needed to help me get past my delusions and get on with my life."

Cameron smiled. "Funny how that worked out, isn't it."

Christy nodded, then, except for the running water of the fountain, a silence fell around them, which drowned out the buzz coming from the two restaurants on either side of the foyer. A little family emerged from the elevator and gathered at the window to admire the view. Christy felt grateful they'd not been interrupted during the intensity of his confession. She liked this spot and didn't want to move. After a few minutes the family moved on and they were alone again.

"Hey," he said in a tone that indicated a drastic change of subject, "can I ask you something?"

"Sure," she said easily.

"You know . . . there are times in everyone's life when big decisions come up . . . choices that could make a huge difference—things that are life altering. It can be as simple as where to live, which house to buy. And there are many personal decisions. For me, decisions like that come up in business quite regularly." Christy nodded and motioned for him to go on. "And I can't count the times that I've been grateful to have the guidance of the Spirit in such matters."

He was quiet for a minute and she said, "I agree. But you said you were going to ask me something."

His eyes became distant and his expression intense. "Have you ever just . . . known in your heart that something was right? It may or may not make sense logically, but no matter how you add it up, you just know it's right. And it's not like you had some great manifestation or burning in the bosom to know it's right, you just *know* it's right, and when you stop to think about it, you realize that you've *always* known it was right?"

Christy let his words sink in for only a moment before she felt a rush of goose bumps as it occurred to her that he'd just perfectly described the way she felt about *him*. She had no idea where he was headed with this, but it was easy to look into his eyes and say with conviction, "Yes, I know exactly what you mean."

He returned her gaze intently, as if he were searching for something, then he smiled subtly as if he had found it. He chuckled tensely but didn't move his gaze as he said, "Then what do you say we just . . . get married?"

Christy laughed and was about to scold him for teasing her about something like that, until she caught the intensity of his expression. Her laughter turned to an abrupt cough. She studied his eyes for only a moment before she stated the obvious. "You're serious."

In one succinct movement he dropped to his knees and took both her hands in his. She felt herself begin to quiver from the inside out the same moment she felt his hands trembling. A distinct sparkle in his eyes was enhanced by a glimmer of moisture. While she was attempting to accept the reality of what was happening, he tightened his hands and said in a quavering voice, "Tell me you feel it, Christina."

Christy silently replayed the preamble that had led to his proposal . . . *You just know it's right, and when you stop to think about it, you realize that you've always known it was right.* She gasped and erupted to her feet. Her heart threatened to pound right out of her chest. While she was consciously aware of her every breath, she felt more than heard him stand behind her. He took her upper arms into his hands that were still trembling. In a husky voice he spoke just behind her ear. "I had no intention of saying any such thing when I picked you up this evening. But all of a sudden I just . . . had to." When she could find no response, he added in a whisper, "Talk to me, Christina."

"How long is always?" she asked, keeping her back to him. "Are you trying to tell me that you were contemplating a proposal before William picked you up at my house on Christmas Eve?"

"I'm saying that I knew you would play a significant role in my life." His voice became more steady but no less intense. "And if I'm way off base, here . . . If you don't feel that way about me . . . and you would prefer we just remain friends, then all you have to do is say so. I'm telling you how I feel, and what I want. I'm not assuming that you feel or want the same things. And if it's just . . . too soon, then . . . we'll postpone this conversation for a while." She heard him sigh. "Hey, I realize this is pretty heavy for a first date, but . . . I guess I just couldn't hold it inside any longer. I just had to let you know how I feel."

"And how is that . . . exactly?"

He pressed his hands down her arms and back up again. "Are you trying to get me to admit that I love you?"

"Yes, actually," she said, hearing her own voice quaver.

"I love you, Christina."

She turned to face him, marveling at the raw vulnerability showing in his eyes. But it was mingled with an acute adoration that had always been there. She simply hadn't seen it for what it was. Or perhaps she'd been too frightened to acknowledge what she'd been looking at.

"Is it all right for me to admit that on our first date?" he asked, a hint of moisture still glistening in his eyes.

"But this isn't really a first date, is it," she stated, pressing a hand to his face.

He smiled a bit sheepishly. "No, I guess it's not."

"But . . . when you said that we were *just friends,* I know you meant it. You've never once made me feel like you were pushing something I wasn't ready for. I just want you to know how I appreciate that. Your patience and acceptance have helped me through some pretty rough days."

"And now that we're here," he said, "I would hope that whatever we choose to do, we will never lose the friendship we've gained. Because the trust and respect between us is a rare treasure, Christy, and I don't think that either of us can go forward in life without knowing beyond any doubt that it will always be there; that no matter what we might come up against, there will always be trust and respect."

"Of course," Christy said, then she laughed at the absurdity of what she was thinking—and saying. She looked away, feeling terribly nervous, wondering if she'd actually said something in her rambling to make him think she'd agreed to his proposal. In an effort to clarify, she quickly said, "But . . . there's so much to talk about. We would have to decide who will . . . will . . ."

"What, Christy?"

"Well . . . who will do the laundry, and pay the bills, and cook, and change the diapers. And how to discipline the children, and who will be in charge of family home evening and—"

"It's all negotiable," he said, touching her chin to make her look at him. "We can talk about all that and more, and we can go into this well prepared and communicating. That's the way it should be. The important thing is . . . if we both know . . . right here," he pressed a hand over his chest, "that this is the right thing, then the trust and respect and commitment will carry us through the laundry and dishes and . . . diapers. Did you say diapers?"

"I did." Her brow furrowed. "I mean . . . I've always felt like I wasn't done having children. I've always felt like there were a couple more . . . maybe . . . and . . . Did you want more kids? I mean . . . *if* . . . this worked out and—"

"Yes, Christina, I want more kids."

She looked into his eyes and declared, "I can't believe we're talking this way."

He chuckled close to her ear, sending a shiver down her back. "Neither can I, but . . . maybe we should give this some time and think about it."

Christy quickly searched her feelings, feelings that she now realized she had become comfortable with long ago. She asked, "Do you need to think about it, Cameron?"

"No," he said firmly. "Do you need to think about it?"

She inhaled deeply, as if to convince her head of what her heart already knew. But it was easy to say, "No, I don't need to think about it."

She heard him suck in his breath. Then he smiled. "Does that mean the answer is yes?"

"What was the question . . . exactly?"

Once again he dropped down on both knees and took her hands into his; his trembling had increased. "Will you marry me?" he asked, emotion straining his voice.

"Yes, Cameron," she said while her view of him misted over, "the answer is yes."

They laughed together. He stood and embraced her, then he looked into her eyes. "And since this isn't our first date, do you think it would be all right if I kissed you?"

She smiled. "Since we seem to be engaged, I think that would be more than all right."

He smiled. "I was hoping you'd say that."

As he bent to kiss her, Christy recalled their conversation beneath the mistletoe on Christmas day. She closed her eyes just as she heard him say in her memory: *I'm implying that I would very much like to kiss you, Christina, but not at the expense of your respect.* A quick tally of their weeks together assured her that he had certainly earned her respect—and her heart. When their lips met, the evidence she had that he was a good man met with all she felt for him, bursting into a tingle of fireworks, leaving her so filled with strength and life that she felt weak. She took hold of his shoulders in order to keep her balance, and she drew back just enough to look into his eyes. "Wow," she said, her voice hushed and dreamy.

"Yeah," he chuckled. "Wow!"

She saw his eyes turn even more wistful and asked, "What are you thinking?"

"I'm thinking that I'd like to kiss you again, and I'd like to spend the rest of my life kissing you. What are *you* thinking?"

"I'm thinking that . . . I'm terribly happy, and terribly amazed that I could be this happy, when not so many weeks ago I felt like my life was over."

"That doesn't sound so terrible."

"No," she laughed softly and touched his face, "not terrible at all. So . . . kiss me again."

He smiled and pressed his lips to hers once more with a savoring kiss that spoke volumes of innocence and anticipation. He stepped back as if to put distance between them, wearing a smile that nearly made her blush.

"Well," he said, taking both her hands in his, "it would seem we have a wedding to plan."

"Oh," she said with obvious dismay.

"You haven't changed your mind already, have you?" he asked, sitting on one of the velvet benches in the center of the corridor.

"No, but . . ." She sat beside him. "I must admit that . . . the one thing that makes me hesitate is just . . . the wedding itself. Just the thought of all the family dynamics and the fuss, and—"

"So, let's just . . . get married. We don't need anybody's permission. And the only people who *really* need to know are the children . . . and well, I know Bea can keep a secret, and she might be willing to stay with the kids while we take a honeymoon. Oh, and . . . I guess we'll have to tell our bishops." He motioned toward the windows at the end of the hall. "And the temple is right across the street."

Christy inhaled the idea, then she laughed. "I think I like that. And then what? I just . . . call my parents and tell them I'm married?"

"Sure. Or better yet, you could take me to meet them . . . as part of our honeymoon. And we can send out announcements just to let people know we're married. But we can do that later. All we really need time for now is to decide who will be doing the laundry and the dishes. However, let me say right now, straight up front, that I have an issue with changing diapers."

"Oh, yeah?" she said as if she clearly expected a challenge.

"My father told me that it took a real man to change diapers. Therefore, in an effort to prove my masculinity, I insist on changing every single diaper as long as I'm with the baby. Obviously, if I'm at work, I can't change a diaper, so you'll have to cover for me, but I can do a lot of work at home, actually and . . . Is it all right if I move in with you? Because I really hate living in that apartment and . . . Are you crying?"

Christy nodded and pressed her face to his shoulder. "What?" he asked, putting his arms around her. "I'm sorry. You can change the diapers if you want to that badly, but . . ."

Christy laughed through her tears and looked up at him. "I'm just so happy."

"Does that mean you love me, too?"

"Oh, yes, Cameron, I love you. I think I always have."

"Always? Are you trying to say you fell in love with me when I first got in your car?"

"Oh no," she insisted, "I think it was long before that. I just hadn't found you yet."

Cameron smiled. "Yeah, I know what you mean." Then he kissed her again.

"Hey," he said, taking her hand almost before the kiss was done, "come along. This date isn't over yet."

Christy laughed and followed him into the elevator. They walked out onto the street and found it a relatively pleasant evening—for February. They walked less than a block then got into a horse-drawn carriage and snuggled beneath the quilts left lying on the seat. Through their tour of the heart of the city, in time to the clopping of the horse's hooves on the street, they talked quietly about the tender feelings that had led to this event—feelings that neither of them had dared admit to. Christy marveled at all she was feeling, and she silently thanked God for sending her such a wonderful man.

William picked them up at Temple Square, only a few steps from where the carriage dropped them off. Christy rode home with Cameron's arm securely around her, and her head against his shoulder. She couldn't recall ever feeling so perfectly secure in all her life. As the car merged into the canyon, Cameron said quietly, "Hey, I think we're both pretty sure about this, but I think it would be a good idea if we both fast about it . . . just to be absolutely certain. What do you think?"

"I think that's very wise. How about starting now?"

"I'm with you," he said. "I'll bring Chinese over tomorrow late evening, and we'll decide if we've had any stupor of thought."

Christy giggled. "Sounds wonderful. The Chinese, anyway; not the stupor of thought."

He pressed a kiss into her hair and muttered, "I'm not terribly worried."

"Me neither, but . . . it's always good to make sure you're getting your answers from the top."

"Amen," he murmured and kissed her head again.

Chapter Thirteen

Cameron left Christy with one more kiss on the doorstep, then he resisted letting out a loud whoop as he headed back to the limo. His joy escaped in a bout of laughter, once he was in the front seat of the car.

"I take it you had a good evening," William said.

"The best of my life . . . so far. Hey, is that car phone any stronger than the typical cell phone?"

"I believe so."

"Would you give Bea a call and ask her if I can just stay there tonight, then I'll drive this thing back down in the morning."

A minute later he heard William saying, "Are you still up?"

"Of course she's still up," Cameron said loud enough for her to hear. "We both know she's a night owl. If she's not sick, she's still up."

He heard William laugh before he said, "This upstart nephew of yours was wondering if he can spend the night. He didn't want to come in and scare you." William listened for a minute then said, "Okay, we'll be there soon and I'll check it."

"Check what?" Cameron asked once he'd turned off the phone.

"The furnace has been acting up. Pilot goes out once in a while."

"It's a good thing she has you to take care of her," Cameron said.

"I enjoy taking care of her," William said.

Cameron found his aunt curled up on the sofa by the fireplace, reading a novel. "Hello," he said, bending to kiss her cheek.

"Hello right back," she said. "You certainly seem chipper."

"I am actually."

"Is that why you wanted to stay? Did you have something to tell me?"

"I do, actually," he said, sitting across from her and removing his tie. "But it's a secret."

"Okay, you know I can keep a secret."

"Yes, that's why I'm telling you. That, and . . . I will probably need your help."

"I knew there would be a catch," she chuckled. "So, out with it."

"Well . . . I'm making plans to elope."

"Elope?" she echoed, every bit as astonished as he'd hoped. "Are you talking about running off and marrying little Christy Hardy?"

"I am," he said, then let out a delighted laugh at the very idea. "I asked her tonight, and she said yes."

Bea laughed with him. "That's pretty hasty, isn't it?"

"In a way, yes, but . . . we both feel it's right, and we're fasting just to make sure. I've really thought about it a lot, and I think she has too, actually. I truly believe we've got the bases covered."

"Well, I think that's wonderful," she said, then her brow furrowed. "But why elope? Are you just teasing me, or—"

"No, actually. She's concerned about the fuss her family would make; I guess you know they're all real chummy with the ex-husband's family."

"Yes, I recall that now. I can understand all that . . . but . . . eloping?"

"Well, it's not like I'm going to cart her off to Vegas or something, Bea." He made a thoughtful noise. "I suppose I could; they do have a temple in Vegas, don't they. But I think we prefer our very own temple right here in town." She let out a laugh of relief and he went on. "So, we just . . . get a marriage license, some marriage recommends from our bishops, someone to stay with the kids, and we just . . . go get married and then . . . well, *then* we'll go to Vegas . . . on our way to California for a little honeymoon. And that's when I get to meet the parents."

Bea laughed again and clapped her hands together. "That is the best plan I've heard in years, my boy." She pointed a finger at him. "And I know why you need me. I can't give you a temple recommend or a marriage license, so you must need me to stay with the kids."

"Would you?"

"I'd love to," she said. "They're great kids and, well . . . they're almost related, aren't they."

"Yes, they are." He let out another delighted laugh at the thought of being able to share Christy's children. It was all just so perfectly perfect.

"Oh, and there is one other thing that occurred to me on the way home—something you could do."

"Anything," she said eagerly.

"Well, we don't need much for this kind of wedding, but I want her to have a new dress to be married in. I think she can afford it, especially considering that she doesn't have to worry about how to deal with unexpected expenses any more. But until we're actually married, I think she'd be a little proud about asking me for the money, so . . . could you take her shopping, and just encourage her to get what she wants?"

"I would love to," Bea said. "And don't you worry. I can be graciously diplomatic and assertive."

"Yes, you can," Cameron said.

"So, tell me how this all came about. The last twelve times I asked, you insisted that you were *just friends*. Fill me in. The night is young."

Cameron glanced at the clock and laughed. Nearly midnight. Then he embarked on telling her all the details of their evening, and all he was feeling. He knew he couldn't sleep anyway.

* * * * *

Christy felt certain she'd never be able to sleep. It took her a while to finally drift off, but she did so with images in her mind of Cameron's newly confessed love. She woke up feeling as if she'd emerged from a delightful dream. Her delight increased when she remembered that it was real. Cameron Chandler had asked her to marry him, and barring any forthcoming stupor of thought, she had every reason to believe that the two of them would be very happy together. She couldn't help recalling the many mornings she'd awakened following Keith's departure, with the same dreamlike sensation. But that had been a nightmare. In contrast, she felt perfect joy.

Christy filled her breakfast time with added prayer on behalf of the purpose of her fast, earnestly expressing to her Father in Heaven all of the reasons she believed that this marriage was the right choice. She asked that the Spirit would guide her feelings to know if the decision before her was right. She kept that prayer in her heart as she got the children off to school, then set out for the city. She arrived at the store early and was able to get some book work done.

Through the morning Christy frequently recalled the events of the previous evening and how they had changed her life. Butterflies would often seize her stomach, and she had to suppress a delighted giggle. In spite of her obvious excitement, she kept a prayer in her heart to know if the choice before her was right. She repeatedly asked her Father in Heaven that she would be able to discern His will through her own emotions. Later that morning a thought occurred to her that sent her heart briefly plummeting. She reminded herself that it was only a temporary setback, but it could definitely hold up their plans. And she needed to discuss it with Cameron. She called his office but they said he hadn't come in yet. She called his apartment and got the machine. She felt a little concerned until he called a short while later and told her he had spent the night at Bea's, and he'd had to return the limo.

"So, do you prefer driving the thing, or sitting in the back?" she asked.

"That depends on whether or not *you're* sitting in the back."

"Hey, there's something I need to talk to you about."

"You sound upset."

"Not really . . . but it could put a cog in our plans. I know we're not eating, but . . . could you meet me at lunchtime, anyway?"

"Sure, where?"

"How about the JS building chapel at twelve-thirty?"

"I'll be there," he said. "Oh, and . . . I love you."

Christy laughed softly. "And the same."

"Rodney is standing there."

"Very perceptive. I'll see you in a while."

Christy was seated alone in the chapel beyond the organist for about twenty minutes before Cameron showed up and sat beside her. "Sorry, something came up."

He gave her a sheepish smile and she asked, "Everything okay?"

"Oh yeah. I'm just . . . a poor judge of time. So, what's on your mind?"

"What about the sealing, Cameron?"

"What about it?"

"I'm still sealed to Keith, and—"

"And as I understand it, they generally discourage you from applying for a cancellation until you're ready to be sealed to somebody else. And because I'm still sealed to Jolene, I'll need to get clearance from the Brethren."

"But it takes time, doesn't it?"

"It can . . . especially if the ex-spouses don't want to cooperate. But do you want to know what I think?"

"Yes, of course."

"I can only speak for me, my feelings, our situation, but . . . if we know beyond any doubt that this is right for us, I think we should just get married. We can be married in the temple for time, and as soon as the approval is given, we'll be sealed. If you think I'm being selfish or impatient, Christy, say so. But I've been alone a long time, and quite frankly, I'm tired of it. I want us to be a family, to live like a family. I want to be able to see to your needs, so you can be home with your children—*our* children," he corrected and she smiled. "I don't want any more opposition to creep in and give us trouble. Well . . . we both know opposition will always be present in our lives, but we can take it on together. So, that's what I think. Maybe you should take some time and think about it."

"And maybe we should just set a date."

He smiled but said, "Maybe you should take some time and think about—"

"That's what I'm doing, Cameron. That's why I'm fasting. I'll sleep on it, okay? And, of course, I'll pray about it. And if I don't get any stupor of thought by tomorrow, we're setting a date."

He smiled and pressed her hand to his lips with a lingering kiss, while his eyes never left hers. "I love you, Christina," he said.

"And I love you . . . Cameron," she replied, pressing a hand to the side of his face.

They walked together back across the street before he left her at the door to the mall and went on down the street to his office.

Cameron came over that evening with Chinese food for the whole family. He and Christy slipped into the laundry room and closed the door to pray together before they broke their fast. When the prayer was finished, he asked quietly, "How are you feeling, so far?"

"Fine," she smiled. "And you?"

"I feel very calm . . . and at peace. No lightning bolts or anything, but I don't think that's the way it's supposed to be. I just feel at peace."

She smiled. "Yeah, me too. Like I said earlier, I'd like to sleep on what we should do about the sealing thing, but . . . I know it's right to marry you, Cameron. I know it in my head, and I feel it in my heart. And that's all I need."

He smiled and kissed her quickly before they heard Tim calling, "Where are you, Mom? I can't find the chopsticks."

They all enjoyed the Chinese food, except for Lucy, who made herself a peanut butter sandwich and ate an apple with it. "She'd shrivel up and die if it weren't for peanut butter and apples," Christy said.

"That's okay," Cameron said to Lucy. "When I was your age I didn't like Chinese food either."

Lucy gave him a smile that warmed Christy through. To think of him being a father to these children made her happier than she had ever imagined she could be after Keith had left her. She was certain Keith would not take kindly to the idea of sharing his children with a stepfather, even though it had apparently been no problem for her to share her children with Patricia. But Keith didn't seem to work according to logic these days. For that and many other reasons, she just wanted to get married and deal with the outside repercussions later. She uttered a silent prayer for the hundredth time that day, and continued praying off and on until she slept that night. She woke up and prayed again. When that calm, peaceful feeling only deepened, she knew beyond any doubt that the decisions they had made were right.

Later that morning, the phone rang about five minutes after the kids left for school. Christy glanced at the caller ID and chuckled. *Chandler Corporation.* She picked up the phone and heard Cameron say, "How about February 28th?"

Christy laughed and put a hand over her quickened heart. "You're serious."

"Hey, I told Bea we were going to elope, and she said she'd stay with the kids while we have a honeymoon. So if we're going to elope . . ." He chuckled deeply.

Christy glanced in her planner at the date, and the days following it. She had to admit, "I don't see any reason why not." She laughed. "I can't believe this is happening." He laughed as well, but said nothing. Attempting to be more logical, she said, "I just have to get a Primary substitute for the following Sunday, and make sure that the store is covered. I have vacation time coming, so I don't see a problem." It occurred to her that being married to Cameron, she would no longer need her job. But she decided to deal with that after she got back. It would take time for everything to settle.

"Okay," he said. "You see what you can do. I'll call the temple, and we'll just . . . go for it." He laughed again, a perfectly happy laugh that fully expressed her own feelings.

"Hey," he said more soberly, "we both need to keep praying and stay close to the Spirit, because neither of us wants to get into something we're not ready for. I just want you to know that any time between now and then, you can change your mind."

"I guess the same applies to you," she said. "But I already know it's right."

"Okay, but . . . if you decide it's too fast, all you have to do is say so."

"All right, but . . . I think the 28th is fine. We'll just plan on it."

Cameron laughed again. "Can I take you to lunch?"

"I was hoping you'd ask," she said and he told her he'd meet her at the store at one o'clock, since he had a meeting that he felt sure would go until after noon.

Christy arrived at work, fighting to keep the full extent of her joy from showing too obviously. She asked Rodney if he could cover the store for a week, beginning the 28th, explaining that she would be taking a much-needed vacation. He readily agreed and didn't ask any questions.

Cameron came to get her for lunch only ten minutes late. While she was finishing up something on the till, he spoke to Rodney in a typical way. "How's it going, Rod?"

"Good, and you?"

"Great, thanks."

"I'm ready," Christy said and they left the store together.

She was thrilled when he insisted they get a quick sandwich, and then go look at rings. They came to a decision quickly when it became evident they both preferred simple gold bands. Christy returned to the store barely able to hold her excitement inside. That evening, while she was helping the kids with their homework, Bea called to say, "Are you working Saturday?"

"For a few hours in the morning, why?"

"I was wondering if we could do some shopping together. I could meet you downtown when you get off."

"Shopping?" she asked with lighthearted suspicion.

Bea laughed softly. "I understand you'll be needing a wedding dress, and we haven't got a lot of time."

"I suppose I do," Christy said. She quickly tallied the money in her savings and wondered if she dared use it, then she inwardly laughed at herself, knowing that she would soon be supported by Cameron's income. "Shopping sounds wonderful. Keith is supposed to have the kids this weekend, so we ought to eat out while we're at it."

"I'll look forward to it," Bea said.

That evening Cameron came over for supper. Christy made chicken noodle soup from scratch that the kids loved, and Cameron was equally pleased. After the kids had finished and left the table, they talked quietly of their plans. They decided to wait and tell the children until the night before they would be getting married, since they didn't want them to leak the news, which could bring on contention and arguments with Keith. Christy had made the children aware that her relationship with Cameron had changed, that they were dating and cared very much for each other. She felt certain the children were all fond of him, comfortable with him, and okay with the idea of her moving on with her life. She felt they were as prepared as they could be.

On Friday evening, Cameron picked Christy up outside the mall to meet some friends of his for dinner out. "So, tell me about these people," Christy said as they drove toward the restaurant where they would meet.

"Dean and Beth Howard are their names. Dean has worked with me forever. He's about ten years my senior, I believe. He started working for my father right out of college, and quickly rose to the top. He's an amazing man, and is now the vice president; my right-hand man, so to speak. They're not members of the Church, but not for my lack of trying." He chuckled comfortably. "He's very good-natured about my nagging him to read the Book of Mormon, but then more than half of my employees are not LDS, and—"

"Really?" she said. "Right here in Salt Lake City?"

"That's right," he said. "In fact, I think that's a typical statistic. We have a lot of missionary work to do right here in the Mormon capital of the world."

"Amazing," she said.

"So, anyway. Dean and I quickly became friends when I got out of college and started working full time with my father. They've got two kids, and another on the way; they just barely found out about that. Dean and Beth helped me through some rough times. I can't say that Dean and I could ever be best friends," he smiled at her, "not the way you and I were friends. I mean, he's supportive, and fun to be with, and he'd give me the shirt off his back if I needed it, but that doesn't mean I could pour my heart out to him. Does that make sense?"

"Absolutely," she said.

"So, anyway. I haven't told Dean we're getting married, but I did want you to meet them."

"It sounds delightful," Christy said, and that's exactly what the evening turned out to be. She recalled seeing Dean at the office, and both he and his wife were kind and fun to be with. They talked and laughed freely, and it was rare that anything came up that made her realize they weren't members of the Church. It was evident they were good people with high standards, and she really liked them.

On Saturday, Christy thoroughly enjoyed her outing with Bea, and expressed her gratitude for all this woman had done for her. "It seems only right that you would become my aunt, too," she said over a late lunch.

"I couldn't be happier about having you as my niece," Bea said. "I felt something between you and Cameron the first time I saw you together."

"Really?" she said, thinking she shouldn't be surprised.

"Really," Bea repeated. "Some things are just right, and you know it in your heart."

Christy sighed to hear one more point of validation. She knew more every day that she was doing the right thing. She certainly didn't expect their life together to be problem free or without challenges. But she felt that she and Cameron had the right ingredients to work together, remain committed, and solve those problems effectively.

It took some time, but Christy finally found the perfect dress. It was appropriate for the temple, with long sleeves and no sheer lace. It was feminine and elegant, without being gaudy or overdone. Unlike the dress she'd worn for her first wedding, she wanted to be able to use this as a temple dress for years to come, and it was beautiful without being impractical.

Cameron met them in the city that evening when their shopping was finished, and he took them both out to dinner. While they discussed their plans with Bea, Christy felt the reality settling in that within days she would be married to this man. When they asked Bea if she would like to attend the ceremony, they were both surprised to hear her say, "I would like to be there, yes. But I'm going to decline. That way, no other family member who wasn't informed can feel cheated. And when the two of you are sealed, you can be surrounded by family and friends. And I will definitely be there for that."

Christy squeezed Cameron's hand and felt him smile at her. It was evident that he too appreciated Bea's insight and wisdom. And Christy had to admit that she liked the idea of having the sealing to look forward to. She knew that would be an equally important event in their lives.

The remaining days were filled with secret anticipation of an event that felt more right and good every day. Opposition crept in with Cameron and Christy both facing challenges on the work front, and a flu bug going through Christy's household. Everybody seemed to be over it two days before the wedding, but Christy began to worry about leaving the children, worrying over the possibility that they might become ill or get hurt. Cameron and Bea both assured her that they would be fine, and if something happened, Bea would certainly be able to handle it. Christy finally had to admit that she was letting unfounded fears get hold of her, and when she turned her prayers toward finding peace and trusting in the Lord to see that all was well in their absence, she felt much better.

The night before the wedding, Cameron brought pizza for the family. They ate and went about the usual evening routine of homework and chores. When it was time to gather for prayer, Cameron asked them all to sit down for a few minutes. "There's something your mother and I need to talk to you about," he said.

They all watched Cameron with eager anticipation, but she wondered if they had any idea what might be coming. Cameron glanced briefly toward her, and she sensed that he was nervous, but he'd told her earlier that if he was taking on the patriarchal role in this family, he should be the one to tell them. She gave him a nod of encouragement and he turned to face the children.

"You know," he said, "I've really enjoyed the time I've been able to spend with your family, and I've really grown to care for you—all of you." He reached for Christy's hand. "In fact, your mother and I have grown to care for each other very much, and we have decided to be married."

"I just knew it!" Lucy said, then turned to Tim. "I told you they'd get married, but you didn't believe me."

"Did too," Tim said. Lucy scowled at him, and then there was silence.

"So, what do you think?" Christy asked.

Following more silence, Lucy asked Cameron, "Are you going to live here with us?"

"I am," Cameron said.

"Tim," Christy said, "what do you think?"

He shrugged his shoulders.

"Charlotte?" Christy asked, unnerved by a lack of an enthusiasm she'd been hoping for.

"It's not up to me if the two of you get married," she said with an edge.

"Well, we're not asking your permission, sweetie," Christy said. "We've both fasted and prayed and we know that it's the right thing to do. We simply want to know how you feel about it."

"Whatever," she said, and again there was silence.

"Okay," Christy drawled, reminding herself that she couldn't expect an outpouring of feelings. At least they weren't being outwardly belligerent.

"The thing is," Cameron went on, "since we've both been married before, and we think there are some people we know that might not be real happy with us getting married, we've decided to just go ahead and do it. We're kind of eloping, and we're not going to tell anybody but you until we're already married."

"You mean, it's like a secret?" Lucy asked with a subtle disdain that was untypical of her. Christy had to wonder if, in spite of their previous acceptance of Cameron, the idea of a marriage was still difficult for the children.

"Yes, it is, actually," Cameron said.

Tim made a noise to indicate a subtle intrigue.

"So . . . when?" Charlotte asked.

"Tomorrow," Cameron said and Charlotte let out a brief sound of shock.

"Sister Hammond is going to come and stay with you, and since she's Cameron's aunt, that kind of makes her your aunt, too. We're getting married in the temple tomorrow morning, then we're going on a little vacation together. And Bea will stay right here with you while we're gone, and we'll call every day."

When nothing more was said they knelt for family prayer, as they had done a number of times with Cameron there. Christy went to tuck the kids in bed, and spoke with them each privately to see if she could better gauge how they were feeling. Tim and Lucy were equally unwilling to say much beyond their not wanting her to leave for a week. Beyond that, they both seemed relatively indifferent. Christy was a little more nervous about approaching Charlotte. But her oldest daughter said nothing.

Attempting to open a conversation, Christy said, "It could take some adjustment having him move in with us . . . but I think life will be better for all of us."

Charlotte just shrugged and Christy left her to do some reading before she went to sleep. She returned to find Cameron sitting on the couch, scratching the cat under its chin. "He likes me," Cameron said.

"I'm glad you're not allergic. We'd have a tough choice on our hands." He looked mildly alarmed and she smiled. She sat down beside him and leaned her head on his shoulder.

"Is he the only one that likes me?" Cameron asked in a severe tone that provoked Christy's emotion to the surface. "Hey," he said, touching her chin and wiping her tears, "what did they say? Be honest."

"They didn't say anything. I really believe they like you, but . . . I had really hoped for even a little bit of enthusiasm or *something*. I guess going to movies or playing board games is okay, but having you move in is *not* okay."

"You mustn't worry, Christy," he said, putting his arms around her, which didn't seem to disturb the cat. "This is pretty big stuff for them. You can't expect them to adjust overnight. I'm going to do my best to let them know I love them and prove that I'm not trying to replace their father. But it will take time for them to trust me, and that's okay."

Christy nodded and he asked, "You still want to go through with it?"

"Absolutely," she said in spite of her concerns over the children. "How about you?"

"There is absolutely nothing better I could do with my life," he said and pressed a kiss into her hair.

They talked quietly for only a short while before they concluded that they both needed to try and get some sleep. Christy kissed him goodnight at the door, in awe that within hours she would be Mrs. Cameron Chandler. She felt restless when she went to bed, and feared that she'd never sleep. But she finally drifted off before one A.M. and slept soundly until the alarm went off. Bea came over before the kids left for school, and she told each of them that she'd be there when they got home. "Now I'm going to be here most of the time, but sometimes while you're at school, I might be at my house. So I've written my number down for you, so you can call me there if I don't answer here, and you need anything."

Christy hugged each of the children as they left to catch their bus, and she promised to bring them each a surprise. They all seemed a little down and she had to wonder if her marrying Cameron simply put unknown territory before them. She prayed their hearts would soften toward this wonderful man who would be their stepfather, then she attempted to put it out of her mind.

Once alone with Bea, she went over the lists and instructions she had typed up, and told her everything she'd need to know. She gave

Bea a key to the house and hurried to finish packing. Bea was still there when Cameron arrived to pick her up—right on time. He took her bags to the car, then came back inside to get her.

When Christy announced that she was ready, Bea took each of their hands and said with conviction, "This is a joyous thing, and I want you to know that my heart is with you. Have a beautiful day, and a wonderful honeymoon, and don't you worry about a thing."

"We can't thank you enough," Christy said, embracing her tightly.

"It is a pleasure," Bea said.

"You're the best," Cameron said, embracing her as well.

"We'll call every day," Christy said.

"And you know how to reach us if there's an emergency," Cameron said.

"I know everything I need to know," Bea said. "Now hurry along or you'll be late."

Christy met Cameron's eyes as they both seemed to grasp the implication at the same time. She pressed a hand over her quivering stomach and saw Cameron do the same. Then they laughed together and headed out to the car. Neither of them had much to say through the drive into the city, and they were equally silent as they walked hand in hand toward the temple. But Christy felt perfectly at peace, and she sensed that Cameron did, too.

Christy felt as excited as a giddy school girl as the ladies in the temple helped her make certain that she looked perfect. Her whirlwind of anticipation settled into perfect joy when Cameron escorted her to the altar and knelt across from her, taking her hand into his. Their vows were spoken with perfect conviction, the only drawback being that they had yet to be sealed for eternity. But it was a day she looked forward to with a perfect brightness of hope.

When the ceremony was over, they stepped out onto the temple grounds, where a photographer that Cameron had hired met them to take some pictures. They shared a late lunch at the restaurant in the Joseph Smith Building where they had eaten the night he'd proposed to her. Christy found it difficult to believe they were actually married until Cameron smiled and said, "Guess what, Mrs. Chandler? We're officially on our honeymoon."

She smiled and said, "But we haven't even left the city yet."

"And we won't until tomorrow," he said. "I've got reservations at this great bed and breakfast; it's a restored Victorian mansion."

"Really?" Christy said and he squeezed her hand across the table.

"And tomorrow we're going to Vegas. In spite of its reputation, I've spent many days there on business and it has some great things to see that have nothing to do with gambling. If it's all right with you, I thought we could stay there a couple of days, see some sights, go to the temple. And then we can head to San Diego and I can meet my in-laws."

Christy laughed. "It sounds delightful. But you know what?"

"What?"

"Seeing that we're married, and we're on vacation, the rest is all just frosting on the cake."

"Amen," he said and reached across the table to kiss her.

Chapter Fourteen

Christy admired the view from their Las Vegas hotel room, loving the way she could see a pyramid, castle turrets, and a chilling replica of the Statue of Liberty, all from this one spot. She heard Cameron close his suitcase and knew they were ready to check out. She couldn't put off calling her parents any longer. She picked up the phone and sat on the bed to dial the number. She almost hoped they'd be out of town or something, and this could be put off. But she knew putting it off would only make it more difficult. It would be better to just see her parents and get this over with.

She was startled to hear her mother answer and interrupt her thoughts. "Hi, Mom," she said eagerly.

"Christina!" she said eagerly. "Is that you?"

"Yes, it's me."

"I haven't heard from you in a while. Are you doing all right?"

"Yes, actually. In fact, Mom, I'm doing better than I have in a long, long time." Christy saw Cameron smile from where he stood admiring the view. He turned to meet her eyes and she smiled back.

"Well that's great, but . . . obviously we have some catching up to do."

"Yes," Christy drawled. "I was hoping you didn't have any big plans this weekend. I'm in Vegas at the moment. If you'll be around, I was hoping to see you tonight and go to Church with you in the morning. Would that work for you?"

"Oh, it would be great!" her mother laughed. "What time should we expect you?"

"I'm not sure; evening sometime. Don't worry about dinner. We'll eat before we get there."

"We? Are the kids coming?"

"No, actually, but . . . I'll explain when I get there, Mom. Gotta go."

Christy hurried to get off the phone, not wanting to get into the issues long distance.

"Still think it would be better to tell her in person?" Cameron asked.

"Yes," she said, "mostly because you can be there to hold my hand, and they'll be more reasonable . . . I hope."

Christy couldn't recall the drive to San Diego ever going so quickly. She didn't know whether it was Cameron's pleasant company, or the dread of facing her parents. Either way, their arrival came much too soon. Her watch read just past eight as they pulled into the driveway of her parents' home.

"You okay?" Cameron asked.

"Ask me in twenty minutes."

"I will. But are you okay right now?"

She sighed. "Maybe I'm just blowing this all out of proportion in my head. Maybe it won't be as bad as I'm expecting."

"Maybe. Maybe not. The best way to find out is to just go in there and get it over with."

"I know," she said and he got out of the car. She uttered a silent prayer while she waited for him to walk around and open her door. When he took her hand, she noticed his palm felt a little clammy. "Are *you* okay?" she asked.

He chuckled tensely. "Ask me in twenty minutes."

"You're nervous!"

"Yes, I confess I am, a bit. This can't be any worse than what I face in business all the time, but . . . they're my in-laws."

"Yes, and once they get over the shock, they'll love you. How could they not? *I* love you."

Cameron saw her smile, but her concern was evident. She hadn't told him much about her parents beyond their being good people, active in the Church—and chummy with Keith's family. He prayed this would go well—mostly for Christy's sake. She held his hand tightly as she knocked lightly on the door and then opened it. "Mom? Dad? I'm here."

"Christina!" Cameron heard a woman call, just before he stepped inside and closed the door behind him. Christy embraced a woman near her same height and build, with mostly gray hair, wearing jeans and a T-shirt. He felt her eyes shift toward him over Christy's shoulder. "Good heavens," she said, looking more concerned than pleased. "You didn't tell me you were bringing a man."

"Well," Christy said, "I wanted to surprise you." She turned to Cameron. "Mom, this is Cameron Chandler. Cameron, my mother, Lenore Wood."

"It's truly a pleasure, Sister Wood," Cameron said, extending his hand.

She took it warmly, but her expression showed concern. "And it's nice to meet you," she said, but he wasn't sure she meant it. He told himself that she was simply taken off guard.

"Where's Dad?" Christy asked.

"Uh . . . he's just in the other room. I'll go and—"

"I'm right here," a man said as he entered the room. He was tall and thin, and Cameron saw a strong resemblance to Christy. "There's my baby," he said, embracing Christy, then he turned to Cameron with the same surprise his wife had shown.

"Cameron," Christy said, "this is my father, Melvin Wood. Dad, this is Cameron Chandler."

"Hello, Mr. Chandler," Melvin said, offering a hand.

"It's a pleasure," Cameron said.

Melvin then turned to his daughter and said, "Forgive me for being blunt, but you're vacationing with a man?"

Christy threw Cameron a cautious glance and hurried to say, "Honeymooning, actually. Cameron and I are married."

"Married?" Lenore gasped and sank into a chair.

"Oh, my," Melvin said, following too much strained silence. "Perhaps you'd better sit down and tell us what's going on."

They were all seated and Christy said, "I know this seems sudden, but the truth is that Cameron and I have known each other several weeks, and we fast became the best of friends. It only turned into something romantic recently, but we both knew beyond any doubt that we were supposed to be together. We wanted to avoid a number of . . . complications, so we just . . . got married."

"What are you saying?" Lenore asked, as if Christy was confessing a grievous sin. "You just eloped, or something?"

"That depends on your definition of eloping," Christy said. "It was somewhat hasty, but we were married in the Salt Lake Temple."

"Oh," Lenore breathed a long sigh of relief. "That's good, at least." Christy figured her mother could quit worrying about grievous sin. "But . . ."

"But, what, Mother?" Christina asked when she faltered.

"But . . . what about Keith?"

"What *about* Keith?" Christina retorted, her voice barely calm.

Lenore's voice cracked as she admitted, "I just . . . hoped that the two of you . . . would get back together . . . somehow and . . ."

Christy sighed and took her mother's hand. "Listen to me, Mom. I was wishing the same thing for a long time, but it's not going to happen. I was wasting my life away waiting for something that wasn't right any more. And do you know why it wouldn't happen? He didn't want it badly enough to ever make it work. And now that I've taken the shades from eyes and looked at this picture realistically, I know that I would not want it, either."

Lenore's eyes widened as if her daughter had just turned orange. "But . . . why?" she asked.

"Why? Mother, he left me. He cheated on me. He resents helping me support *his* children. He's become inactive in the Church. And *if* . . . just *if* . . . he decided to turn all of that around and come groveling back to me, it would take a whole lot more penitence than he would ever be willing to give before I could ever trust him again. He's selfish and dishonest. And I have no reason to believe that he would ever want to change."

Lenore turned and exchanged a harsh glance with her husband, which prompted Christina to exchange an equally severe glance with Cameron. "What?" Christy demanded.

"Honey," Melvin leaned forward and looked directly at his daughter, "why haven't you told us any of this before?"

"Because I had trouble even thinking about it, let alone talking about it. And I know how close you are to Keith's parents, and—" She stopped as she observed another long glance. "What?" she repeated.

"Honey," Melvin said again, "the story we've heard is much different."

Christina felt the color drain from her face. She was grateful for Cameron's hand tightening in hers. "I'm listening," she said.

"Well . . . I guess you should know . . . Keith's side is that . . . you were," he cleared his throat loudly, "cold . . . and distant; that you were spending more money than you made, and you wouldn't clean or cook or—"

"Okay, I get the idea!" Christina shouted. At her parents' shocked expressions, she squeezed her eyes shut and forced herself to calm down before she said something to prove Keith's lies to be true. She felt Cameron squeeze her hand and opened her eyes to look at him. She knew she would get through this simply by the perfect acceptance in his eyes that had always been there. Drawing a deep breath of courage, she turned to her parents and said, "It's simply not true. I was not a perfect wife, but neither was he a perfect husband. However, I budgeted carefully, kept the house in fair order, cooked well-balanced meals ninety percent of the time, even when I was working. I never lied to him, never spoke down to him, was never disrespectful to him. And he walked in one day and told me he'd been seeing another woman for months and he was leaving me. Simple as that. He never told me he wasn't happy and we needed to work it out. He never gave me any indication that anything was wrong. He *deceived* me. And three days after the divorce was final, he married Patricia."

Looking into her parents' dazed faces, Christy had to wonder if they believed her. She suddenly found it difficult to breathe and bolted toward the front door.

Cameron followed her and found her clutching a tree in the yard, breathing so hard he feared she'd hyperventilate.

"I'm . . . I'm sorry I dragged you through this. I had . . . no idea they were thinking that way all this time. I can't believe it. If I'd known, I'd . . . I'd . . ."

"You'd what, Christina?"

"I don't know," she sobbed and clutched onto his arms. "I just don't know."

"Christina," he said, taking her shoulders into his hands, "listen to me." She looked up at him and sniffled. "You know what they were told is not true, and I know it's not true, and—"

"How do you know?" she retorted. "How do you know I haven't just given you my distorted side of a delusional tale? How do you know you're not in for a horrible marriage with—"

"Stop that," he insisted. "I know because I have seen the honesty in your eyes since the day we met. I know because I can see the integrity in your countenance, and I can feel the sincerity of your spirit. I know because I fasted and prayed about committing my life to you, and the Lord let me know that you're a good woman, that you're everything you appear to be. I'm no fool, Christina, so listen to me when I tell you that it *does not matter* who believes what. Even your own parents. The more defensive and upset you get, the more you will give them cause to believe that what they've heard is true. Time has a way of proving the truth of someone's character, and time will prove that you're the good woman you've always been. The truth of what's past is between you and the Lord. *I'm* your family now. And we are going to go back in there and have a civil visit with your parents, and we're going to Church here tomorrow, and you're going to smile at every person who might have heard those nasty rumors, and who might be whispering, 'She's got a lot of nerve.'" He had raised his voice to mimic an old woman. "But deep inside, most of them will realize that you must not have anything to hide."

Christy reveled in his wisdom, his acceptance, his perfect love for her. She held to him tightly, gave a firm nod and wiped her tears. "That's my girl," he said just as they heard the screen door.

"Are you still here, Christy?" Melvin called from the porch.

"I'm here," she called back.

"Hey, come back in and let's talk about this. You mustn't leave like that."

Christy hugged Cameron once more and they went back in the front room to find Lenore crying quietly with a box of tissues on her lap. They all sat back down before Christy's mother said, "We had no idea, Christy. I'm so sorry."

Christy felt some relief from their apparent acceptance, but she felt she had to clarify a few points, if only to avoid any future misunderstanding. "I'm not asking you to jeopardize your relationship with lifelong friends. I'm not asking you to take sides. I'm just telling you what I should have told you months ago. Nothing more needs to be said. I just want you to know that the only thing left between me and Keith are three children, and I would only ask that they not be affected by this any more than they already have been. I want you to know that I'm happy. Cameron is a good man; he's the best thing that's ever happened to me, and I want you to get to know him and accept him as my husband, and let Keith Hardy live his own life."

Following a moment of silence beyond Lenore's sniffling, Melvin said in a lighter voice, "So, young man. Tell us about yourself."

Cameron chuckled, taken off guard by such a drastic change of course. "Well . . . I . . ."

Christy sensed his relief when she took over with an accurate explanation of his background. The conversation became more relaxed, and Christy felt immensely relived to see that her parents truly liked Cameron. But then, how could they not? They finally went to bed late, staying in the spare room that had once been Christy's bedroom. Exhausted from a long day, she quickly fell asleep, contented and at peace in Cameron's arms.

The following morning Lenore fixed Christy's favorite breakfast of bacon and French toast, then they all got ready for Church meetings, which began at eleven. They arrived early, and Christy thoroughly enjoyed introducing her new husband to many people she'd known in her youth. She especially enjoyed having him meet Keith's parents, although she had trouble holding back a little laugh in response to their horrified expressions. She wondered if they had been at all horrified when they'd learned that their son had left her for another woman. But then, they believed that she had been a horrible wife, and Keith had been justified in leaving her. The very idea was rankling, but Cameron's words came back to assuage her. *The truth of what's past is between you and the Lord.* When she was seated between Cameron and her mother, waiting for the meeting to start, she whispered to her husband, "You can bet Keith will know we're married long before we get home."

"Too bad," Cameron whispered. "I was looking forward to telling him myself."

Christy laughed softly and squeezed his hand.

After church they shared a nice dinner with Christy's parents, then Cameron and Christy washed the dishes together while Melvin and Lenore sat at the table and visited with them. They visited a short while longer before farewells were exchanged with warm feelings, and Christy felt much better leaving than she had when she'd arrived. By early evening they had arrived in Carlsbad, a nearby resort town on the beach. They stayed two nights there while Christy began to fully accept that she really was married—and truly happy.

The trip home was long but not unpleasant. They stayed another night in Vegas to break up the drive, and arrived home early afternoon. Bea was there reading, waiting for the children to return from school. They all laughed and embraced before she insisted on hearing about their adventures. The kids came running in excitedly, having seen the car in the driveway. Lucy hugged her mother, then barely gave Cameron an acknowledging glance after he'd said, "Hello." Tim followed her example and did the same. Charlotte didn't hug her mother, but she was obviously pleased to see her. She blatantly ignored Cameron. Christy was relieved to see that their subtle disdain hadn't ruffled Cameron. She focused on pulling out souvenirs and told them all they'd done, with the promise that one day they would all go to Las Vegas and Carlsbad together. The children seemed pleased with the idea, but she suspected they would prefer to leave Cameron at home.

"Have you heard from your dad?" Christy asked, wondering if he'd gotten wind of the news.

"No," Charlotte reported. "He called Saturday to tell me that he was going on a business trip, and Patricia was going with him. He'll be back the end of the week."

Christy and Cameron exchanged a humorous glance, as they both wondered if he'd not yet heard.

"Well," Cameron said, "my vacation's not over until I have to go to work in the morning. Do you guys think you could get your homework done later if we all go to a movie now?" They all eagerly agreed, and Bea joined the family for a late matinee and dinner at Chuck-a-Rama. The tension eased up some through the evening while they engaged in an activity they'd done many times with Cameron. But when he was there for breakfast the following morning, the children all seemed a bit disconcerted.

After the kids had gotten off to school, Christy rode into the city with Cameron. She dropped him off in front of his office and took his car to the mall. The morning went well while Rodney caught her up on all she'd missed and made it clear that he'd done an excellent job in her absence. He'd even hired a young man to replace Mazie, and Christy was impressed with him when he arrived mid-morning to fill his shift. With the store front covered, Christy asked Rodney if he'd come into her office for a few minutes.

"What's up?" he asked, leaning on the edge of her desk. "Oh! By the way, that Chandler guy didn't call for you once while you were gone."

"I wouldn't have expected him to," she said, then changed the subject quickly. "Hey, Rodney, how would you feel about managing the store?"

His eyes narrowed suspiciously. "What? You got a better offer elsewhere?"

"I did, actually. I think you'd make a great manager. And you've proven your abilities this last week. Of course, it's not completely up to me, but I could put in a good word for you, if you want the job."

"I'd love the job, but . . . I really don't want to see you go. What's the deal?"

"No deal, Rodney. I'm staying home with the kids from now on. I'll be doing some minimal work from home with the computer, but . . . I just get to be a mom."

"You're getting married?" he guessed excitedly.

"Already did," she said and showed him the ring on her finger. "It's signed, sealed, and delivered. I'm Christina Chandler now."

"When . . ." he stammered. "And where?"

"Last Thursday, right across the street in the temple."

"And that was your little impulsive trip?" he asked, his excitement increasing. "A honeymoon?"

"That's right," she said. He hugged her and offered congratulations. Christy laughed for no apparent reason and got back to work.

An hour after Christy returned from lunch, she got a call from Keith. "Where are you?" she asked, knowing he was still supposed to be out of state.

"I'm in Denver," he said, his voice acrid. "And I understand you had quite a vacation."

"I did, actually. And from your tone of voice, I have to assume you've been talking to your parents. Did they—"

"I cannot believe you would have the nerve to marry a man for his money and—"

"And why did you marry Patricia?" she asked, keeping her voice steady. "Was it because she's a size eight, or because she didn't have a mortgage? Your hypocrisy will get you nowhere with me. Beyond visitation arrangements, I have nothing to say to you. So, why don't you just live and let live."

"Well, if you think I'm going to keep paying child support when you've got a husband who—"

"Your obligations with helping care for *your* children have nothing to do with him."

"Well, we'll just see about that in court," he said.

"Fine," Christy said, "I'll see you there. In the meantime, you'd better mind your manners, or the judge will have a whole lot more to hear than I think you'd want him to. I'm hanging up now. Goodbye."

Christy forced her heart rate back to normal and wiped her sweating palms on her slacks before she dialed Cameron's office. He was in a meeting, but he called her back twenty minutes later. By then she had gotten past her anger and was able to calmly tell him about Keith's call.

"You handled him great," Cameron said. "So, now he knows, and we can get on with life."

"Yeah," she said, taking a deep breath. "Getting on with life sounds awfully appealing, especially knowing we can do it together."

"Amen," he said and they both got back to work.

After Christy put in her hours at the store, she met Cameron at his apartment and helped him box up the odds and ends that hadn't already been moved to her home before the wedding. They filled the trunk and back seat of the car and drove toward home while he held her hand in his. Christy didn't know what the future might bring, but as long as she had Cameron's hand in hers, she believed she could face anything. *Anything!*

Chapter Fifteen

Through the first several weeks of marriage, Christy saw evidence of the necessary adjustment in bringing two separate lives together, with their personalities, habits, and quirks. It quickly became evident that Cameron had lived alone a long time. She could see that having the children around all the time was a challenge for him to get used to, but he was always patient and kind toward them. And they settled into a quiet tolerance of him once they'd tested the waters enough to know that he would respect their relationship with their mother, and that he was not trying to replace their father. Charlotte went through a particularly belligerent stage which Cameron allowed Christy to deal with beyond his firm declaration to Charlotte that he would not tolerate her yelling at her siblings or speaking disrespectfully to her mother.

"You're *not* my father, you know," she hissed back at him. "And my life is none of your business."

Christy held her breath until Cameron countered firmly, "No, I'm not your father, Charlotte. But I am married to your mother. Her life and her happiness are my responsibility, and I will not allow you to do or say *anything* to her that is inappropriate. You are welcome to express your feelings and opinions, but not at the expense of someone else's feelings and opinions. Is that clear?"

Charlotte grumbled under her breath and stomped off to her room. Christy just smiled at her husband, grateful beyond words for his support and patience—in spite of their differences and challenges.

As more time passed she learned that he was very particular about how he wanted certain things, but beyond a couple of silly arguments they were able to communicate and compromise. She learned to adjust to certain situations that made him more comfortable, and he lightened up over issues that didn't really matter. Christy knew she had her own faults that were a challenge for him to adjust to, but they discussed those as well and worked out a compromise. Within a couple of months, Cameron had settled so fully and comfortably into their lives that it was impossible for Christy to imagine their home without him. Lucy gradually warmed up to Cameron and began calling him *Pop,* which Christy assumed was her declaration of accepting him as her other father, while differentiating him from her dad. Cameron quickly warmed to the name, and Christy often found Lucy snuggling on the couch with him while they watched TV. She hoped that Tim would follow Lucy's example, as he often did in many things, but he remained politely aloof from Cameron, more prone to siding with Charlotte's subtle disdain.

Christy reminded herself to be patient and remember that they had forever. They quickly did everything they could to get Christy's sealing canceled and other technicalities taken care of so that they could be sealed to each other, then they did their best to forget about it and let time take its course—always with the hope of eternity on the far horizon.

Christy felt an immense relief when her notice was up at the store and she was able to stay at home. Rodney called occasionally to see how she was doing, and to let her know that the store was doing just fine without her. And that was fine. She loved being home when the kids got home from school, and she was able to help Cameron with a few odds and ends that she could mostly do at home; it was just enough to keep her from getting bored. She wondered if the children had noticed how Cameron's willingness to support the family had given them back their mother, but she kept such thoughts to herself, praying that time would prove his love and commitment to them and they would come to appreciate how very blessed they were.

Cameron was required to travel occasionally for business, and Christy hated having him gone, but they both agreed that a little absence here and there had a way of making a person appreciate what they had. When Christy was put into the Relief Society presidency, working as one of Bea's counselors, she found she had plenty to keep her busy in Cameron's absence.

Cameron insisted on taking Christy out on a date once a week, and at least once a month, they shared their date with Dean and Beth. And Christy genuinely liked Beth. They found plenty to talk about and laugh over while their husbands talked business and male interests. When summer arrived, they went on a couple of outings as families, and their children had a great time together.

In August they took a two-week vacation as a family, which included some time in Las Vegas on their way to and from California. They went to Disneyland, Knotts Berry Farm, and Universal Studios, then they headed south to visit Christy's parents. Tim and Charlotte were polite to Cameron, and not opposed to laughing and having fun with him, but they continued to remain guarded and aloof beyond any surface interaction.

While they were in the area they stayed a few days in Carlsbad, just playing on the beach before they returned home. Seeing the children's joy and fascination with every aspect of the vacation, she realized that in all her years as a mother, they had never taken a real vacation. There hadn't even been a camping trip. Keith had always been too busy. She wondered now how much of his time had been related to other women in his life. The very idea made her stomach churn, but she reminded herself that Keith was behind her now. She was merely grateful to have a man in her life who took such a complete interest in the children—even if the children didn't fully appreciate it.

Following their vacation, Cameron insisted on going school shopping with Christy and the kids. By way of tradition, Christy took them one at a time and ate lunch out. Watching Cameron help the children pick out their clothes and supplies, Christy wondered once again what she had ever done without him. But she was mindful daily not to take his presence in her life for granted, and every prayer included expressions of gratitude to God for sending him into her life.

Christy's relationship with Beth deepened when her pregnancy ended with a difficult miscarriage, and Christy found the opportunity to help her through the recovery process, both physically and emotionally. Christy couldn't help but feel some degree of empathy. While she hadn't actually lost a baby, she longed to have another one of her own, but so far the opportunity was evading her. She simply prayed that when the time was right, it would happen.

During the holidays, Christy couldn't help but think of how far she and Cameron had come in a year, and celebrating their first wedding anniversary made her realize how thoroughly happy she was with her life. The children had come to comfortably accept Cameron's presence in their home, although Tim and Charlotte still maintained a relationship with him that was politely aloof. But, they were all happy and getting along, and Christy was grateful.

When Dean and Beth discovered they were expecting another baby, Christy was truly happy for them. But it deepened her own heartache in wondering if she would be able to get pregnant without medical intervention. So far, her doctor had told her to be patient and keep trying.

Over the summer months, Beth's pregnancy blossomed along with her friendship with Christy. Spending time together often helped pass time when both their husbands were away on business together, or while one of them kept busy covering for the other's absence. Following a particularly lengthy trip to New York, Cameron took Christy and the kids on a long vacation, where they basically repeated the excursion of the previous summer. And they had a glorious time.

The same day the children started back to school, Christy discovered that she was pregnant. She went into the city to get an official pregnancy test, then she went to the office and insisted that Cameron take her to lunch.

"Guess what?" she said once they were seated over a traditional bowl of soup, near the mall windows that faced the Church office building.

"The kids are in school and you are celebrating your newfound freedom," he said.

"That too," she laughed softly. "Not that I really mind having them around," she added, "but having a structured day is a good thing."

"Yes, I know," he chuckled.

"So, guess what?" she repeated.

"What?" he asked.

"I have a surprise for you."

"Obviously, but I'm still waiting."

Christy stood up and leaned over the table to whisper in his ear, "We're going to have a baby, Mr. Chandler."

He looked into her eyes, as if he wouldn't believe it if he didn't see it there. He let out a delighted laugh, then he rose to his feet and embraced her tightly. "I can't believe it," he said, sitting back down, then he laughed again.

Over lunch they speculated over the way their lives would change—for the better. He was late getting back to the office since he had to make a list of possible names, and he had to make plans for finishing rooms in the basement that would be needed with another little person in the house.

That evening at supper they told the children. Christy knew she couldn't keep it a secret when pregnancy was well-known for making her too ill to conceal it. Lucy was eager and excited. Tim reluctantly got caught up in her enthusiasm. Charlotte said nothing. Later that evening, Cameron got out an old photo album that Christy had seen a number of times. But this was the first time he had shown it to the children.

"Who is it?" Lucy asked.

"This is my son, Daniel," he said, pressing his fingers over the variety of photographs put into the album in order from his birth until his death.

"You have a son?" she asked and Tim and Charlotte moved closer.

"I do," he said. "But he was killed in an accident when he was three." They asked him many questions, which he answered easily, then he told them, "And when your mother and I are sealed in the temple, then he will be your brother."

"Cool," Tim said, obviously pleased with the idea of having a brother. Cameron tossed Christy a discreet smile. It seemed they were making progress.

While Charlotte was absent, Tim and Lucy asked questions about the sealing that Cameron answered directly the best that he could. Ironically, it was only a few days later when word came that their sealing had finally been approved. Christy felt unspeakable joy as they decided to have the ceremony September fourteenth, the end of the following week, which would give Cameron time to take care of some pending business in New York and LA. She called the temple and scheduled the sealing, then they both called family and friends to invite them to share this great event with them. Those who couldn't attend the temple were still invited to come and share a meal afterward in the Joseph Smith building. While Christy made arrangements for the event, she often stopped to ponder how very good their life together was, and she prayed that it could always be this way.

Christy was assaulted with her pregnancy-related illness right on time. But she'd done this before, even though it had been a while, and she knew how to keep her fatigue and nausea to a minimum. She quickly realized that she was much older than the last time she'd done this, but in spite of the nagging nausea, she was consumed with a tangible joy. With their sealing date on the calendar, Christy marveled at the happiness she had found with Cameron. She often found herself contemplating the event with an anticipation that even surpassed the days preceding their marriage. Just to know that he was hers, and she was his—forever—made everything good in her life that much better.

Christy was folding a pile of clean laundry when the phone rang. "Hello, my love," she heard when she answered.

"Hello," she responded cheerfully. "What's up?"

"Well, I have a change of plans, but it won't interfere with our wedding."

"Our wedding?" she laughed.

"Of course," he said. "Anyway, you know I was planning to go to New York and take care of that deal with—"

"Yes, I know," she said.

"Well, I told you about Barry."

"I don't remember."

"Well, I'm sending Dean to do the deal in New York Monday morning, because I need to go to Boston for the weekend. It's a trip I've been contemplating, but it's suddenly become urgent. Barry is a long-time business associate there, who is actually in some pretty severe financial difficulties. I've known him for years, and I need to see what I can do to help. It's kind of a personal visit, as well as business. I feel like I need to go now, and spend some time with him over the weekend, and then we can deal with the business on Monday and Tuesday. I've got a return flight Tuesday evening that will take me to L.A., so I can finish up the deal there. I'll be flying home Wednesday morning, then I should be cleared for the rest of the week, and we can celebrate. Do you think you can live without me until then?"

"Do I have a choice?" she asked, albeit lightly.

"You could come with me."

"Mmm," she said, "that sounds nice, but . . . it's not practical, and you know it."

"Yes, I know it. But it's not easy being without you."

"Well, that feeling is mutual, but we have a lot to look forward to. Bea called this morning and said she'd stay with the kids so we could have a bit of a second honeymoon next weekend. She thought it would be nice, since, as you already pointed out, we're kind of getting married again."

"I think that's a marvelous idea," he said eagerly. "I'll be counting the hours." He sighed and added, "Anyway, I'm coming home to pack and I don't have much time. I'm sorry about tonight."

"Tonight?"

"We talked about going out with Dean and Beth, and I know we could use it, but . . ."

"Hey, it's okay," she said. "I know you'll make it up to me."

"Yes, I will," he said firmly.

Christy had the laundry folded and some leftovers heated for lunch by the time Cameron came home. They ate together, then she helped him pack a few things. She felt suddenly hesitant to let him go, and had to remind herself that he would only be gone five nights. At the door he kissed her as if he might be gone a year.

"You take care of yourself," he said, lightly pressing his hand to her belly. "And take care of my baby, too."

"Oh, I will. And you take care of my baby's father." Feeling an unexplainable rush of emotion, she glanced down and tried to force it back.

"Hey," he said, touching her chin to lift her face, "what's this?" He wiped at a single tear, his brow creased with concern.

Christy shook her head, just wanting to drop it, but his expression made it clear that he wanted an answer and he wouldn't leave without one. Not wanting him to miss his flight, she hurried to say, "I . . . hesitate to say it out loud, but . . . I just think how wonderful it will be for us to be sealed, and . . . I'm almost afraid something's going to happen to make it difficult for us to get there. I'm not really . . . worried. I guess I'm just not in the mood to deal with any opposition in our lives." She took a deep breath and added firmly, "But I think the biggest problem is just these pregnancy hormones getting the better of me. I'm sure everything will be fine. Call me when you get there, and I'll see you Wednesday."

Cameron smiled. "I will." He kissed her again. "And yes, Christina, everything's going to be just fine. I promise."

After he'd left, Christy sat down and had a good cry, then she got busy doing other things and felt much better. Keeping a prayer in her heart that they would all remain safe and healthy, she went into town to do some errands and pick up the kids from school. They stayed in the city for a while and ate out before they went home to get homework and chores done. Cameron called about eight to say that he'd arrived safely in Boston, and he was staying at Barry's home. He told Christy a little more of his history with Barry, which also tied into his father, as most of his business associates did. Barry lived with his wife, Nicole, of thirty years, and the youngest of their two children had just started college on the west coast.

Christy kept busy through the weekend catching up on some Relief Society projects and visits. She was glad to see the time without Cameron going quickly. He called every morning and every evening, and e-mailed her at least once a day from the home where he was staying. The distance was lessened by his concern and love through the phone.

On Tuesday morning early, Christy felt frustrated when Charlotte told her at the last minute that she had to be at school early for a student council meeting. She hurried to get dressed, not the least bit excited that she had to take her all the way into the city, especially with pregnancy making mornings difficult. Living so far from the city definitely had its disadvantages. She made certain Tim and Lucy had what they needed in order to make their bus before she returned, then she resigned herself to the drive. If she could have planned ahead, she might have been able to accomplish some errands. As it was, the drive served no purpose beyond visiting with Charlotte. But it turned out to be a good visit, and Christy felt good about the opportunity as her daughter got out of the car.

On the drive back, Christy flipped through radio channels, searching for an inviting song. When every single station was spouting frantic news, she paused to listen. What she heard through the remainder of the drive left her grateful to be alone. She felt too shocked to speak, and too sick to know what to say if she could. Multiple commercial airliners had been hijacked by terrorists and purposely crashed into the World Trade Center Towers and the Pentagon. Innocent people were dead and many others were trapped in burning buildings. Christy groaned and wrapped an arm around her middle in an attempt to quell a deep, harsh compassion she felt for the faceless people across the nation who were personally affected by this. The implications were too horrible to ponder. The ramifications too profound to fathom.

Christy pulled into the driveway and sat for a few minutes listening, too stunned to move. Then she realized that she would get a broader perspective from the television and ran inside to turn it on. She tallied the evidence that the kids had gotten off to school and taken all they'd needed, then she flipped on the television. She quickly reminded herself that her children were safe in school, and Cameron was in Boston, many miles from the tragedy. While the horror unfolded before her eyes, Christy clutched a pillow and wept, as she felt certain every other woman in front of every other television in the nation would be doing. She absorbed the facts through a veil of disbelief, trying to comprehend how it might feel to wonder if a loved one had been on one of those planes, or in those buildings. Then it occurred to her that Cameron's sister lived in New York. She'd never met Sherry, but they had spoken on the phone a number of times, and Christy had grown to care for her. She reminded herself that Sherry lived and worked in Brooklyn, and so far the problem appeared to be centered in Manhattan. But who knew what the coming hours would bring? Then the knots inside Christy tightened when she recalled that Dean had gone to New York City to do business on Cameron's behalf. She knew that a great deal of their business was conducted in those buildings. He'd told her many times of the amazing view from the upper stories in the World Trade Center.

"Oh, help," she murmured and felt her nausea deepen. Should she call Beth? Call the office? But she found she was too numb to do anything at all as she contemplated the very idea that Cameron had asked Dean to go there on his behalf. "Oh, help," she muttered again and curled around the pillow she held, praying with all her heart and soul that Dean would be protected, that all would be well.

The ringing of the phone startled her. She picked it up to hear her mother asking if she had her TV turned on. They talked for a few minutes before she asked, "So, I assume your family is all accounted for."

Christy's heart quickened for just a moment in spite of the obvious that she'd already concluded. "Cameron is in Boston. He's supposed to fly home tonight."

"Well, that won't be possible," Lenore said, "with all the planes grounded."

"Oh, help," Christy muttered once again, more to herself, desperately wanting Cameron to be here with her. She felt an instinctive desire to see her loved ones and know they were safe.

"Well, at least he's in Boston," Lenore said. "I know he's done business in New York a great deal. We can be grateful he's not there now."

"Yes, we certainly can," Christy said, but she decided she wouldn't feel completely at ease until she talked to him. She thought again of his frequent trips to New York, and his reports of many meetings in the World Trade buildings, and felt increasingly queasy. She almost told her mother about Dean, but found she couldn't form the words.

When she hung up the phone, Christy noticed the flashing light that indicated she had a message on the machine. She knew she'd checked it before bed the previous evening, and wondered if Cameron had called while she'd been gone. She couldn't think who else might have phoned her this early. She pushed the button and heard his voice.

"Hi, it's me. Are you gone, or just busy getting ready for school? I'd try your cell phone, but if you're gone you're probably in the Bermuda Triangle. Anyway, I got done here earlier than I thought, and I got a flight to LA. I'm boarding in just a minute, so with any luck I might get done there and be home late tonight. I love you all. See you soon."

Christy started to gasp before the message was completed. The beep at the conclusion startled her back to the present and she turned toward the television, just as a list of the planes involved went up on the screen. *Boston to LA.*

"No!" she croaked and sank onto the couch. "Oh, dear God, please no." She began to shake from the inside out as the reality of what had happened to those planes was reiterated once again. *Hijacked by terrorists. Used as suicide bombers.*

Christy forced herself to her senses. "Don't jump to conclusions, Christy. Surely there were many flights out of Boston, and . . . he's fine." She grabbed the phone and quickly dialed his cell number. She'd talked to him before while he was in flight. If she could just hear his voice, then . . . "Busy circuit," she growled, then she tried again and again and again. She could well imagine the thousands of people across the nation doing exactly what she was doing, and doubted she would be able to reach him by phone for many hours yet.

"Oh, help," she murmured, then squeezed her eyes shut and prayed harder than she could ever recall praying in her life. Following her *amen* she quickly dialed Beatrice's number.

"Hello dear," she said. "Can you believe this? It's so horrible, and—"

"Cameron . . ." she began but her voice caught.

"Cameron, what?" Beatrice demanded, her voice betraying the panic Christy felt.

"He . . ." she tried again but couldn't get beyond one word.

"Is he in New York?" she asked hoarsely. "Please don't tell me he had meetings in one of those buildings."

"No, but . . ." Christy let out a sob if only to release the pressure, "he was flying from Boston to LA this morning, and . . ." She broke down and cried, unable to hold it back any longer.

"I'll be there in ten minutes," Beatrice said. "Don't you move."

Christy hung up the phone, knowing she couldn't move if she tried. The emotion rushed upon her fully. She curled up on the couch and sobbed until she felt Bea's arms come around her. She cried a few more minutes on Bea's shoulder before she felt the emotion subside into a shock that far surpassed what she'd felt when Keith had left her. Now, just as then, she felt consumed with the absolute shock that any human being would feel in being told that life on planet earth had ceased to exist, and in fact, had never existed as it had been perceived. She couldn't even fathom that something so utterly horrible could destroy all she had found with Cameron.

Bea took Christy by the shoulders and looked into her eyes. "Now, do you know for certain he was on that plane? The one that . . ."

"Not for certain, but . . . I just have this feeling that . . . he was . . . or maybe I'm just *afraid* that he was."

"Okay," Bea said, "we need to call the airline and find out." Christy nodded and turned her focus back to the horror unfolding on the television while Bea perused the phone book. Both buildings had now collapsed, and clouds of smoke and debris had swept through the canyons of New York's high-rises. Covered with ashes and soot, news people were giving reports. The horror was so incredible that Christy still felt as if she were watching some movie with fantastic special effects. But it was real, she kept reminding herself. *It was real!*

Christy grunted in frustration as Bea obviously was not finding the right number. A moment later, the news put up that list of the flights once again, directly followed by phone numbers that could be called to verify if loved ones were aboard. "Did you get that?" Christy squealed frantically.

"Yes," Bea said and was dialing the phone. She took the phone into the kitchen, but Christy heard her say, "I need to find out if my nephew was on one of those flights from Boston to LA." She repeated the message again, and gave Cameron's name, then there was a long silence before she said gravely, "Oh. Thank you."

Christy slid to the edge of her seat and turned to see Beatrice leaning in the kitchen doorway, the phone hanging limply in her hand. "Tell me!" Christy demanded.

Bea pressed a hand over her mouth, squeezed her eyes shut, and nodded firmly. While Christy was attempting to absorb the implication, Bea moved her hand and said hoarsely, "His name was on the passenger list."

Christy slumped back onto the couch, expecting herself to fall apart, expecting the pain to completely consume her. But all she could feel was shock. "I don't believe it," she muttered. "I just don't believe it. It can't be possible." Attempting to get past the shock and search her feelings, she wondered if she felt like he was alive because he was, or because she just couldn't accept the possibility of him being gone.

* * * * *

Cameron hung up the phone from leaving a message for Christy just as the final boarding was called for his flight. Standing in a short line to give his boarding pass to the attendant, he felt a sudden uneasiness. His thoughts were immediately drawn to Barry and the plight he was in. He felt like he'd done everything he could to help him without crossing lines that would either be inappropriate or wound the man's pride. But there was obviously something left undone, because he suddenly felt so drawn back to Barry's home that he couldn't have talked himself into getting on that plane. He found himself staring at the attendant while she held out her hand, waiting for him to hand her his ticket.

"Uh . . ." he said, "I forgot something, and . . . I'm just going to have to miss the flight."

She shrugged and gave him an understanding smile. "Those things happen," she said. "Sorry."

Cameron felt immensely better as he walked back through the airport, glad that he'd not checked his bag. He grabbed a quick bite to eat, since he wouldn't be having that in-flight breakfast. Then he got a cab and dozed in the back seat through the forty-minute drive to Barry's house, in spite of the annoying country music tape playing on the stereo. He paid the driver a generous tip and headed up Barry's front walk, hoping they hadn't gone somewhere. He'd said he would be home for the morning, but maybe he should have called to let him know his change of plans.

Cameron rang the doorbell and was about ready to ring it again when Barry pulled the door open, looking visibly upset. A shocked noise erupted from his throat, then he couldn't seem to speak or move. Cameron's desire to explain his appearance seemed irrelevant when something was obviously very wrong. He wondered how to ask if he'd just learned of a death in the family or something, and quickly pondered the idea that perhaps he'd felt prompted to stay to offer a different kind of support for this good man. While he was trying to come up with the right words to ask, Barry sputtered with a cracked voice, "What are you doing here? I thought you were . . . were . . . Oh, thank God!" Barry put trembling hands on Cameron's shoulders, then embraced him so tightly that it hurt.

"What?" Cameron asked, returning the embrace, then pulling back to look into Barry's eyes. "What's happened? You're shaking."

"Oh," Barry laughed and mopped his face. He picked up Cameron's bag off the porch and motioned him inside. "I'm sorry," he said, too emotional to speak. "It's. . . on the TV and . . . ." Nicole appeared and gasped before she put a hand over her mouth. She looked as if she'd been crying—more than a little.

"What?" Cameron repeated, feeling a prickly sensation run down his back that spurred a quickened heart rate.

Barry guided him toward the sofa while Nicole said, "Apparently you haven't heard. It just happened a while ago." She pointed to the television screen where he could hear a newscaster speaking in anxious tones as Nicole said, "Two different hijacked commercial airliners were crashed into the towers of the World Trade Center. It's a terrorist attack." Nicole's voice broke as she added, "One of them was the flight we thought you were on."

Cameron felt the blood rush from his head so fast that he had to grip the back of the sofa before he melted onto it. He felt himself tremble from the inside out, and his hands shook visibly as they clutched the leather sofa where he sat. He heard a noise erupt from his mouth, much like the one Barry had made when he'd opened the door. It all made sense now. His prompting, Barry's reaction to seeing him, their emotion. Yes, it all made sense—horrific, unfathomable sense.

As he began to fully absorb what he was looking at on the TV, a different reality began to settle in. He couldn't count the business meetings he'd attended in those buildings; and the faces of dozens of people he knew who worked in those towers flashed through his mind. *"Dean!"* he muttered, feeling a new terror strike him.

"What?" Barry asked.

"My vice president was in a meeting there this morning." Cameron groaned and had to put his head between his knees to keep from passing out. "Oh, please God," he murmured. "Please, don't let him die." He thought of the thousands of other people uttering the same prayer, and he wondered what might determine who survived and who didn't.

Hearing something different on the news, he sat up slowly, attempting to digest what he was seeing and hearing "Heaven help us," he murmured as the full implications settled in while he sat frozen, watching the horror unfold—the pentagon struck with a third hijacked plane; the towers collapsing on live television, before his very eyes; a fourth plane down somewhere in Pennsylvania. It was like a movie with a plot too ridiculous and too horrible to be conceived fictionally. And the very reality of what he was watching made his stomach wrench and his palms sweat. *And he had nearly gotten on that plane!* A plane that had been used as a missile of war, its passengers now completely annihilated. How clearly he recalled the faces of some of those passengers. They had all been sitting in the same area, waiting to board. He'd exchanged a few casual words with some of them. And now they were *gone!* And Dean? What about Dean? He felt a sudden rush of emotion so intense that he leapt to his feet and rushed to the bathroom without even managing to excuse himself. He locked the door and flipped on the noisy fan before he slid to the floor, his head between his knees, heaving uncontrollably. The minutes felt timeless while he wept for the nameless people who had so horrifically lost their lives this day. And equal to his grief was a gratitude too deep and rich to fully grasp. If not for changed plans, he could have been in that building this morning. Had Dean perished in his place? Had his own life been saved twice over? His gratitude deepened, along with a sense of guilt for surviving when so many others hadn't. He reminded himself not to question God's judgment, and concentrated on the gratitude for the prompting that had kept him from getting on that plane. He'd credited the uneasiness he'd felt to unfinished business in Boston. How grateful he was that he'd not rationalized away such a life-altering prompting. He thought of the lives that would be affected if he were now gone—foremost, Christina.

"Christina!" he muttered and scrambled to his feet. He hurried out of the bathroom as quickly as he'd hurried in. Barry and Nicole turned from the television. "I have to call my wife," he said, grabbing the phone. "I left a message . . . telling her I was getting on a plane . . . to L.A." He punched out the number, praying that she hadn't turned on the TV yet. He wanted her to know he was all right before she had any idea about what could have happened. He barely kept himself from cursing when he got a busy circuit. He tried calling from Barry's second line. He tried the first one again. Both of them over and over. He tried using his cell phone, Barry's cell phone.

"The circuits are all jammed," Barry reported with a calm hand on Cameron's arm. "Sit down, Cameron. You're going to hyperventilate if you're not careful."

Cameron forced himself to take a deep breath while Barry guided him to the sofa to sit between him and Nicole. "What can we do to help?" Barry asked.

"I . . . just . . . need to talk to Christy, and . . . I need to get home."

"All the planes are grounded," Nicole reported, "all across the country. Everything's so uncertain, who knows when you'd be able to get a flight?"

"Then I need to . . . rent a car . . . or buy one . . . or . . . *something*. Oh, help. I'm a mess. Forgive me, I—"

"There's no need to apologize, my friend," Barry said. "It's all more horrible than words can describe . . . and to think how close you came to . . ." Barry's voice cracked. He took hold of Cameron's hand, which made them both realize in the same instant that they were shaking.

"Honey," Nicole said, "there is Louise."

"Hey," Barry said brightly, "you can take Louise!"

"Louise?" Cameron echoed, bewildered. "Who is Louise?"

"Not who, what," Barry said and came to his feet. "Come along."

Cameron followed Barry to his garage, past the car that they'd taken back and forth to the office, to a dark green Chevy Astro van— with a *For Sale* sign in the window.

"You know," Barry said, "since Franny went off to college, we've not had this out of the garage once. It started out as a family vehicle when the kids were in high school. I've had an ad in the paper, but . . . well, it runs well except for a little glitch in the air conditioning occasionally. She's just had a tune up, and she's got a full tank of gas. It has a great stereo, both CD and cassette. I was hoping to get ten grand for her." He chuckled. "After all the deals you've made for me the last few days, I can assure you'd I'd make a great deal on her for you."

"Ten grand sounds good to me," Cameron said, feeling hope and determination assuage his grief and concern. "I can write you out a check now if you'll throw in that cooler." He pointed to a small ice chest sitting on a shelf, just the right size to keep a few cold drinks in through a long journey.

"Done!" Barry said and heartily shook his hand. "And I've got a great road atlas I'll throw in, so you don't get lost."

After trying unsuccessfully again to call Utah, and writing Barry a check, Cameron loaded his luggage into the back of his new ticket home. He took a minute to remove the few CDs that were stashed in with his laptop, so he'd have something to listen to.

As he turned to Barry, there were no words to express the enormity of what they'd shared this morning. "Hey," he said, "I can keep trying to get through to your wife; cell lines might be more difficult to use, I don't know."

"I appreciate that," Cameron said, then an idea occurred to him. "Hey, can I use your computer for five minutes?"

"E-mail!" Barry said as he perceived Cameron's idea.

"Exactly. Hopefully, she'll turn on the computer before she turns on the TV."

"Well, you can hope. But with something like this, I think she's a lot more likely to know what's going on before she hears from you."

"That's what I'm afraid of," Cameron said gravely, then he sat at the computer to send his wife a message that he prayed she would find soon.

Chapter Sixteen

An unusual noise startled Christy from her thoughts, and she looked up to see Bea sitting across from her, weeping uncontrollably. Christy quickly moved to her side and put an arm around her. The evidence of Bea's emotion began to seep past the numbness blanketing Christy, and she felt an indescribable pain beginning to smolder in the deepest part of her. Knowing she could never cope with such pain, she immediately began to pray. How could she ever forget the way Cameron had told her to do that very thing when she'd finally faced the full depth of the pain of her divorce? Once again she marveled at the peace that crept in to buffer her grief. And in her heart she knew that the Atonement would help her get through— whether he was still alive or not. A rush of emotion reminded her that it wouldn't be easy, regardless of any inner peace she might feel.

Glancing up, her eye caught the porcelain seagull that Cameron had once given her, sitting on a high shelf in the curio cabinet. She had always considered it a symbol of miracles. And if she was not blessed with the miracle of having him live through this, she knew she had the miracle of Christ's love that would bind her wounds. And she felt hope.

"It's going to be all right," she heard herself saying to Bea, amazed at how she could be so calm. As Bea's emotion began to quiet, Christy heard a snatch from a report on the TV about someone receiving an e-mail from a victim before the building had gone down. Her heart quickened at the idea, and she wondered if she was kidding herself into believing that the Spirit was pushing her toward the computer.

"What are you doing?" Bea asked, wiping at her face with a lacy handkerchief.

"I'm checking my e-mail."

"Right now?" Bea asked.

"Yes, right now," she said and waited an eternal minute while the computer connected to the Internet. Her eye immediately caught an unread message from the e-mail address of where Cameron had been staying in Boston. She could hear her heart pounding in her ears as she waited for the message to come up, then she sobbed into her hand as she read: *My Dear Christina, I felt uneasy about the deal with Barry, like something was left undone that couldn't wait, so I went back. I'm assuming you know what's happened, and I'm praying that you get this message before you figure out the connection. I didn't get on that plane, therefore I'm safe and fine, but the circuits are busy and I can't get through on the phone. I'm taking Barry's van and heading west. I'll keep trying to call. I love you, and we still have a date. Cameron.*

Bea appeared behind her and demanded, "What is it? What's wrong?"

Christy shook her head and pointed at the screen, unable to speak. It was difficult to tell if Bea was laughing or crying as she read the message. They held each other and sobbed, unable to speak, but knowing no words were needed to express the depth of their gratitude.

* * * * *

Barry and Cameron shared a brotherly embrace in the garage. "Call when you get home," Barry said. "And be careful."

"Thank you . . . for everything," Cameron said, then he climbed into Louise's front seat and backed the van out of the driveway. He was barely onto the main road when an idea occurred to him, spurred by something he'd heard on the TV a little earlier. He drove quickly back to the airport, parked the van, and hurried to the car rental counters, where the lines were long with people who all shared a common expression of shock and grief over the reasons that had caused them to be stuck in this airport, far from loved ones—just as he was.

"Okay, Lord, help me out here," he muttered under his breath, not knowing where to begin.

He took a deep breath and approached a man in his twenties, wearing a suit and tie. "Hey, where you headed?" Cameron asked.

"Denver," the man said skeptically, as if he feared that Cameron was hoping to hitch a ride with *him*—if he could get a car.

Cameron chuckled. "I'm on my way to Salt Lake City. You're welcome to ride along. I'm just trying to get there as quickly as I can. Are you interested?"

"Am I?" The man chuckled and picked up the briefcase and small suitcase at his feet. "How much do you want?"

Cameron felt startled. He hadn't expected—and wouldn't want—to be paid. "Uh . . ." he struggled for a suitable response, "no smoking or swearing, and I get to choose the radio station."

"That's it?" the man laughed again. "What's the catch?"

"No catch. I've been blessed enough to get a van to drive home. It's got five more seats that I need to fill. Maybe if we can stir up a few more people, and we can take turns driving, we can all get home faster."

"I'm in," he said and held out his hand. "Gary Reilly."

"Cameron Chandler. It's a pleasure to meet you."

"Hey," a dignified-looking man with grey hair, wearing a golf shirt, touched Cameron's arm, "did I hear you say you're headed west, with some room to spare? I'd pay anything. My wife went into the hospital last night while I was here helping our son remodel his house. I need to get to her."

"Where do you need to go?" Cameron asked, praying it wouldn't be too far out of the way. How could he turn down such a plea?

"If I could get to Kansas City, I can get a ride from there. If you're headed to Denver, it's not far off the main stretch."

"Get your bags," Cameron said, mentally calculating the square footage of space behind the back seat of the van. He was glad to have noted that the van was the extended version, which would hold more luggage.

"Oh, thank you, my boy," the man said and actually got tears in his eyes as he extended his hand.

"Not a problem," Cameron said, returning the handshake. "We're all in this together. Cameron Chandler."

"Tom Hendricksen," the man said.

While Tom and Gary chatted, Cameron perused the lines, trying to be inspired as to who could travel the same route, and might need his help the most. He asked one man who needed to go to Georgia. "Sorry, can't help you," he said. "Good luck." The next person he asked had to get to South Carolina, and he gave the same answer. He began to feel like a stuck recording as he faced people who needed to get to Houston, Minnesota, and Maine. He marveled as he spoke to people how there was not even the slightest sense of frustration or tension. He suspected that every person here was only grateful to be alive, and too full of grief for those suffering to complain.

He felt compelled toward an African-American woman near his age, looking more upset than the rest of the crowd. "Excuse me," he said, "there's a few of us headed west. I've got room for a few more. Where you headed?"

"Columbus, Ohio," she said, her eyes showing disbelief at his offer.

Cameron quickly opened the atlas tucked under his arm to double check. "Close enough," he said. "You've got a seat if you want it." He motioned toward Tom and Gary. "They're coming too," he said to assure her that they wouldn't be traveling alone.

"How much do you want?" she asked in a way that made it evident she had little, if anything, to pay him.

"My rates are pretty stiff," he said with a smirk. "You can't smoke or swear, and I choose the radio station."

She hesitated before she let out a stilted chuckle. "You're serious."

"Yes," he drawled. "What do you say?"

"I'm with you," she said and eagerly stepped out of the car rental line.

She told him her name as he walked her over to Tom and Gary, and he introduced them. "This is Kaniesha Brannon," he said. Both men shook her hand and he left them to chat while he rounded up two more passengers: a man going to Indianapolis, and a woman headed for St. Louis. He introduced Victor and Anne to the others, then they all followed him out to where he'd left the van.

"Meet Louise," he said to everybody. "I bought her from a friend a couple of hours ago. He said her name is Louise."

"Hello, Louise," they all said in haphazard unison. Victor actually kissed the hood with a loud smooch, declaring loudly, "Louise, my love, I'm eternally grateful." This made the others chuckle, and Cameron was grateful for the light spirit among the group that helped counterbalance the subtle shock showing in all their eyes. He couldn't go more than a few minutes without remembering that the United States of America was under terrorist attack, on American soil, with an unimaginable death toll. He felt certain that the deep sense of security felt by every American had been deeply shaken, and would not easily—if ever—be recovered.

* * * * *

Once Christy and Bea had recovered from the shock of believing they'd lost Cameron, and the subsequent shock of realizing they hadn't, they sat together on the couch, watching the horror unfold. Christy kept nibbling on crackers and cheese to keep her stomach settled, intermittently crying over the reality unfolding before her eyes. Bea kept handing her tissues from the box she held on her lap, and they both contributed regularly to the pile of used tissues accumulating on the coffee table.

When the phone rang they both gasped, making it evident how tense they'd become. Christy answered it to hear a man's voice say, "Mrs. Chandler?"

"Yes."

"This is Barry . . . in Boston; your husband's been staying with me."

"Yes?" she said eagerly. "I got his e-mail a while ago."

"Oh good," he sighed loudly. "He was frantic when he couldn't get hold of you, and I told him I'd keep trying."

"So, he's really okay?" she asked, wiping away a new string of tears.

"He really is," Barry said, and she could hear emotion in his voice, as well. He told her what had happened, and how Cameron was on his way home in the van that Barry had just sold him. She thanked him for calling, and for being such a good friend to Cameron. The emotion they'd just shared through a brief phone call made her feel as if they were good friends, as well.

A minute after she hung up the phone, it rang again. "Hello?" she said eagerly, her heart pounding.

"Oh, Christina," she heard Cameron say, and she couldn't hold back more tears.

"Cameron," she cried, "you really are all right."

"I really am," he said, "relatively speaking. I'm alive and well, and I'm grateful, but I'm pretty shaky."

"Yeah," she managed to say, "me too."

"Did you get the—"

"I got the e-mail," she said, "and Barry called a few minutes ago, but . . . I got your phone message earlier after I'd already seen what had happened, and . . . I thought you were . . ." She couldn't go on.

"I'm so sorry, Christy. I was so afraid that's what would happen, but . . . I couldn't get through, and . . ."

"It's okay," she said and attempted to table her emotion. "You're alive and I'm more grateful than you could possibly imagine."

"Oh, I think I can imagine," he said.

"So," she said after a minute of emotional silence, "Barry told me you're driving home."

"Yeah, we just stopped to get some burgers and we're heading out."

"We?"

"Well," he chuckled, "I went back to the airport and found some passengers who were as desperate to get home as I was. We've figured out a route that pretty much goes straight west and takes in all their stops."

"Do you know how long it will take?" she asked, wanting to just hold him in her arms.

"Not exactly," he said. "That atlas says it takes about forty-five hours to drive from Boston to Salt Lake. We're planning to take turns driving so we can keep going and save time, but we'll have to make stops, and I think we're going to need at least one night in a motel to get by safely."

"Of course," she said. "Just as long as I know you're coming . . ."

"I think we'd better postpone our date. With the planes grounded . . . and so much uncertainty. I'm not sure when I can get there . . . and we want family there, and . . ."

"I know. You're right," she said. "It will give us something to look forward to. I'll call the temple."

Following another long moment of silence, he said, "Christina." His voice turned grave. "Dean had meetings in that building today—meetings I should have been at."

"I know," she said, emotion breaking her voice again.

"Have you talked to Beth? Do you know if—"

"I haven't," she said. "I still haven't adjusted to knowing that you're alive. I was afraid of upsetting her more, but I'll call her."

"I pray to God he made it out of there. I can't even imagine how . . ." His words trailed off.

"I know," she said. "You don't have to say it."

Following a minute of quiet sniffling, while they both fought to control their emotions, he said, "I know Sherry and Jeff must be fine, and I don't know if you can even get through to New York, but . . . will you try to call . . . and just make sure?"

"Of course."

"They both live and work in Brooklyn, but . . . I'll just feel better when I know they're all right."

"Of course. I'll keep trying until I get them."

"Thank you. I'll keep checking in."

"Can you keep your cell phone charged, or—"

"Yes, I've got the car adaptor with me, so you can call me any time."

Through tears she couldn't hold back, Christy said, "Thank you for being alive . . . for listening to that prompting . . . for being the kind of man who gets those kinds of promptings."

"Well," he swallowed hard, "obviously it wasn't my time to go."

"For that I am truly grateful."

"As we both are. I just pray that it wasn't Dean's time to go."

Christy agreed and reluctantly got off the phone. She took a minute to sustain her emotion before she dialed Beth's number. She only got the machine, and said after the beep, "Beth, it's Christy. I don't know what to say. Have you heard anything? Are you all right? Please call me. I'm here for you."

She hung up the phone and dialed the office to talk to Bertie. She told Christy that a few employees had been in New York, but they were all accounted for except Dean. He had been in a meeting at the World Trade Center that had started early that morning. Christy made her promise to call if she heard anything.

Christy then called Sherry's number in New York, but she got a busy circuit. She sent a quick e-mail and hoped they might respond soon. As Cameron had said, they'd feel better just to know his sister and her boyfriend were all right.

Bea made some sandwiches that they ate in front of the TV. Christy felt compelled to watch, perhaps feeling that she might eventually be able to believe that what she was seeing had really happened. She kept hoping for some positive message to counteract the shock and horror. Speculations over the plane downed in Pennsylvania struck her deeply as logic seemed to say it had been headed for another target, another icon of American power. Stories of heroism began to filter through. The president's words were full of strength and comfort, as were those of the mayor of New York. But she could well imagine them crying off camera, just as she imagined many of these news reporters were also crying. How could they not? Christy felt an intense empathy for those who had lost loved ones, or those who didn't know. When she thought of how close Cameron had come to getting on that plane, she wept uncontrollably for several minutes, gradually returning to a state of shock with intermittent tears.

They turned off the TV for a while so Bea could make some calls, and Christy forced herself to lie down. She put in the CD that Cameron had given her soon after they'd met. Closing her eyes to absorb the tranquil music of *Jonathon Livingston Seagull,* she felt another layer of hope blanket her. The horror and uncertainty would not easily relent, but given the present reality, hope was no small thing.

When Bea had finished her calls for Relief Society, she reported to Christy that every woman she had talked to was upset and in tears. She felt certain that to some degree, every American was grieving, whether they had lost someone or not. This was not just a matter of lost lives, but an attack on the very network of security and peace that America represented. While her heart ached for the countless people more directly affected by this, she found herself, every few minutes, thanking God for preserving her husband's life. And each time she added a plea on behalf of Dean and those who loved him.

When the children came home from school, she hugged them each tightly. Just to know that she had them close to her, and they were well, seemed an incredible blessing on such a day. They had heard some of the news in school, but not much. Christy sat them down and told them what had happened, and how close Cameron had come to getting on that plane. They all showed varying degrees of emotion, which she considered a good sign as far as their acceptance of Cameron went. She told them about Dean, then they all knelt to pray together. When the prayer was done, Christy found herself talking to the children about her gratitude for the gospel, and the peace she could find, even in such a situation. They asked questions, and she tearfully bore her testimony of the Atonement, and of their Father in Heaven's love.

"Hey," Charlotte asked, "doesn't Cameron's sister live in New York?"

"Yes, honey. But Sherry and Jeff live in Brooklyn, and it's across the bridge from Manhattan. I'm sure they're fine, but I'll keep trying to get hold of them so we can know for sure. We should remember them in our prayers as well."

Seeing that the children were still upset, she suggested they pray again. Christy prayed aloud for God to comfort all those who had lost loved ones, and those whose loved ones were missing. She prayed for the rescue workers, that they would be comforted and protected. She prayed for the leaders of the nation and throughout the world, that they would be guided and inspired in the decisions before them. She prayed that Dean would be all right, and that his family would be comforted. She prayed for Jeff and Sherry. And then she expressed gratitude for Cameron's safety, for his means to travel home, and for having the gospel in their lives, and the peace it afforded them. After the amen was spoken, Christy suddenly felt exhausted. She laid down on the couch while Bea got the children busy in the kitchen, helping her fix some supper. But after they'd eaten and homework was done, they were all in front of the television, watching history unfold as the dust began to settle—quite literally.

* * * * *

Through the first several hours of the drive, the occupants of the van were all silently riveted to the news they were hearing on the radio. They stopped at a convenience store to gas up and use the restrooms. Cameron got some ice for the cooler, and everyone stocked up on snacks, drinks, and some sandwiches.

Victor drove when they set out again, and Cameron sat in the seat across from him. When the news began to get repetitive, Cameron said, "We seem to be hearing the same thing over and over. How about if we just check in on the news once in a while?"

"Good idea," two of them said together and the others made noises of agreement.

While Cameron was wondering where to start some conversation, Victor said, "So, Cameron, tell us why you're in such a hurry to get home. Not that I blame you; I'm just curious."

"Well, I'm sort of supposed to be getting married Friday, but I'm afraid it will have to be postponed."

"I thought you were already married," Gary said.

Cameron chuckled. "I am, but . . ."

"You're renewing vows," Keniesha guessed.

"Not exactly," Cameron said, "you see, we . . ."

"Oh no," Victor groaned. "Didn't you say you were heading to Salt Lake? Don't tell me you're one of those Mormons, and you're getting married to *another* wife."

Cameron laughed. "No, Victor, don't worry. I *am* a Mormon, actually. But I only have one wife, and that's the way it's going to stay."

Victor heaved a dramatic sigh that made the group chuckle. "You had me worried there for a minute."

"Well, if you must know, plural marriage has not been a part of Mormonism for more than a hundred years," Cameron said. "I always find it funny that such an issue is what we're best known for."

"So the polygamists we're hearing about on TV aren't Mormons?"

"Whatever they claim to be, they're certainly not members in good standing of the church that *I* belong to, which is actually The Church of Jesus Christ of Latter-day Saints; Mormon is kind of a nickname."

"I just learned something new," Gary said.

"Yeah, me too," Tom added.

"So, what's this sort-of-getting-married thing?"

Cameron had to smile. He had a captive audience, asking golden questions. Maybe this wouldn't prove to be so bad, after all—at least for the six occupants of Louise.

"It's kind of a long story," Cameron said, "but we do seem to have time to kill."

"I'm all ears," Victor said.

"Make it a good story," Tom said. "I think we could use one."

"I hope it has a happy ending," Kaniesha said with a ring of cynicism.

"Oh, it does, actually," Cameron said. "Now that I didn't get on that plane."

"What plane?" two of them asked in unison, their voices sounding shocked.

"Are you saying what it sounds like?" Victor asked.

Cameron glanced back briefly to absorb the looks on the faces of his traveling companions. While they had all been frustrated with *not* being able to fly, they had obviously picked up on the irony. "I was handing over my boarding pass when I had this feeling that the business I'd come to Boston to do wasn't finished. I took a cab to the friend's home where I'd been staying. By then, the plane was . . ." He couldn't finish.

"That's incredible," Gary said with a tone of reverence.

Following a long minute of silence, Anne said from the back seat, "We're still waiting for that story."

"Okay," Cameron said, "the thing is . . . my wife and I have both been married before; both divorced." He went on to explain the basic concepts of temple marriage, and how the sealing was a part of eternal marriage. He told them how the prior sealings needed to be canceled before they could be sealed to someone else, and that it was a time-consuming process, especially when dealing with difficult ex-spouses. "So," he finished by saying, "my wife and I were married a year ago last February, but we're supposed to be sealed on Friday. We have family coming to share the event, and we're taking a little second honeymoon. But as I said, it will have to be postponed."

"And you really believe that you'll be together forever?" Tom asked.

Cameron glanced toward him briefly and said with conviction, "I know we will."

When a long moment of silence followed, Cameron wondered if his conviction had impressed any of them, or if they simply thought he was crazy.

Cameron turned on the radio again when the conversation became tense. They listened for nearly an hour to hear the new developments. They made a rest stop and listened some more, until again it became old news. Cameron flipped off the radio and asked, "How about if we listen to a CD for some variety?"

"You did say you got to choose the music," Gary said, then they all joked about the stiff rates. Cameron glanced at the few CDs he had, and grabbed the soundtrack to *The Jazz Singer* by Neil Diamond. He felt surprised as the music began, and he became pierced by an intense combination of patriotism and heartache. He'd heard the song a thousand times, and had always loved it, but never had the lyrics touched him so deeply as now.

> *Far, we've been traveling far*
> *Without a home, but not without a star*
> *Free, only want to be free*
> *We huddle close and hang on to a dream . . .*
> *Home, it seems so far away*
> *We're traveling light today*
> *In the eye of a storm . . .*
> *Every time that flag's unfurled*
> *They're coming to America . . .*
> *Freedom's light burning warm*

Realizing the conversation around him had become completely still, Cameron glanced around to see varied expressions of emotion, even a few discreet tears. When the next song began, a voice from the back called softly, "Could you play that one again?" Amid noises of agreement from the others, Cameron began track one again. While the CD played through, the group remained mostly silent. Cameron suspected that, like himself, they all had a great deal to think about.

Several songs into the CD, an upbeat love song began that seemed to lift the mood. A few measures into it, Tom said, "Hey, did you hear that? Start that over. I think we have a theme song."

Cameron began the track again, and they all laughed to hear: *Hey, my Louise, if I take you home . . .* By the time the song ended, some of them were trying to sing along, even though they didn't know any of the lyrics beyond: *Hey, my Louise.*

When the CD ended, they listened to the radio again for a while to hear the updates. While the events of the day often felt dreamlike and surreal, hearing the news was a stark reminder that it had really happened. He wondered about Dean, as he did every few minutes, and knots tightened in his stomach. He wondered about Sherry, praying that she had been safe in Brooklyn when all of this had happened. And again he was struck with deep gratitude to be alive and well. But his gratitude was tainted by an underlying guilt. *Why him?* Why had he been spared when so many others were gone? The thought brought tears and he pressed a hand over his eyes, grateful that Tom was driving.

Cameron was startled when Gary lightly slapped his shoulder and muttered quietly, "You okay, buddy?"

Cameron forced a chuckle, but his emotion was evident and he had to admit, "No, I don't think I am."

"That's understandable," Anne said with compassion. "I'm not sure any of us are okay. I mean . . . I just keep thinking: I don't have any loved ones that were anywhere near those buildings . . . or on those planes. But I still feel sick to my stomach. I think about it and I . . . can't believe it's real."

"I can relate to that," Tom said. "I keep asking myself: how could this happen here? Will we ever feel completely safe again?"

"For that matter, were we ever really safe?" Gary asked. "Or have we just been complacent? In denial?"

"That's a good point," Victor said. "Maybe we've all just been taking our peace and security for granted."

"We probably have," Tom said. "One thing's for sure—none of us will ever be the same. Whether we lost a loved one in this or not, we all lost something."

"Amen," Cameron muttered, amazed at the shock and disbelief he felt over the very idea of something like this happening. Then he thought of Dean . . . and Dean's family. And he couldn't hold back the tears.

"Hey," Gary said quietly, touching his arm, "is there somebody you know who . . ."

He didn't finish but Cameron nodded. Everyone became completely still, since they'd obviously overheard. Cameron sensed their expectancy and he forced back his emotion enough to say, "A man I work with, a friend . . . He was supposed to be in one of those buildings this morning . . . in a meeting."

"Good heavens," Anne gasped, then her voice broke. "You just can't think too hard about that. You just can't."

Another tense silence settled over the group until Victor said, "I think we need to talk about something else. We've all got plenty of time to let this sink in. I don't know about you, but if I try to take it in too fast, I'm gonna lose my mind."

Cameron heard a couple of noises of agreement before Tom said, "Well, we all know why Cameron here has to get home. What about the rest of you? Victor, where were you headed when you got grounded?"

"Well, I was actually on my way to Europe to spend some time with an old friend who works in France. We've been planing the trip for months; he was going to take some time off, and we were going to do some sightseeing. But I think I'd do well to stick close to home until the dust settles."

"Interesting choice of words," Kaniesha said, and they all turned briefly toward her, realizing this was the first time she'd spoken in hours. Cameron sensed an air of cynicism in her voice, just as he had earlier, and he wondered what her story might be. He felt drawn to this woman, who was the quietest among the group. Instinctively he felt like there was something he could do to help her, if only he knew what. She would be the first to get off, since her stop was the closest. He could only pray that he'd figure it out before the chance was lost.

Chapter Seventeen

"You got a family?" Tom asked Victor in an obvious attempt to keep the conversation steered from horrors they could do nothing about.

"I'm divorced," Victor said. "Have been for years. But I got three great kids. I see them regularly. I'm glad to know they're safe at home with their mother; she's a great mom. So, what about you, Tom? Where are you headed?"

"Well," Tom said, "I was in Boston helping my son remodel his house. I got a call that my wife went into the hospital last night, and I was trying to get home to her."

"And where is home?" Anne asked.

"I live just south of Kansas City," he said.

"And what's wrong with your wife?" she added. "Do you know?"

"She's been diabetic for years, and once in a while it just gets the better of her. I'm sure she'll be fine, but she needs me to be with her, and . . ." His words trailed off and Cameron sensed he was struggling with emotion. He felt that all of these people, no matter how serious or trivial their change in plans, had been struck with the disruption of life as a result of this horrific tragedy. Emotions were close to the surface for good reason.

As the conversation continued, they learned that Anne was widowed with grown children, and she had been in Boston on business as head of marketing for a sales firm. Gary had been flying home from New York, where he'd attended a meeting in the World Trade Center the day before. His plane was barely in the air before it landed in Boston after the emergency had commenced. He'd been married three years, and had a six-month-old baby boy.

Kaniesha was the last to speak, and only with much prodding. She had just attended her grandmother's funeral in Boston, and was anxious to get home to a twelve-year-old daughter. Beyond that she said nothing about herself, but again Cameron sensed some underlying pain in her life.

Following a stop for gas and food, the radio was turned on again only minutes before President Bush addressed the nation. Cameron listened, feeling a deep mixture of emotion—the same emotions he sensed from his traveling companions. He felt hope, strength, and firm resolve from their leader, but he was especially touched when the president said: *Tonight I ask for your prayers for all those who grieve, for the children whose worlds have been shattered, for all whose sense of safety and security has been threatened. And I pray they will be comforted by a power greater than any of us, spoken through the ages in Psalm 23: "Even though I walk through the valley of the shadow of death, I fear no evil for you are with me."* . . . *None of us will ever forget this day, yet we go forward to defend freedom and all that is good and just in our world. Thank you. Good night and God bless America.*

After listening to some commentary on the address, Cameron said, "Wow. That's amazing."

"What?" Tom asked, flipping off the radio. "I mean . . . it is, but . . . I was just wondering about your view."

"To hear our president speak so openly about prayer and God is just so . . . comforting. It makes me feel better."

Some of the others made noises of agreement that were stifled when Kaniesha said, "How could God let something like that happen? Why does He let so many horrible things happen in this world? How can you even believe in God when we live in such a world?"

Through a taut silence, Cameron knew he had to respond. He had no idea of the beliefs of anyone else who was with them, beyond their apparent agreement with the statement he'd just made. But he knew his own beliefs, and he knew this was one of those moments in life that demanded his bearing witness of the truth. He was glad to be sitting in the middle seat, across from Kaniesha as he turned and looked directly at her in the dusky evening light.

"No one can say for certain," he said gently, "why horrible and difficult things happen in this world. But I do know that this world was created for the purpose of testing those of us who live here. We all came to this world with our free agency, and with opposing forces of good and evil all around us."

"But . . . couldn't God have prevented this?" Kaniesha asked. "Couldn't he have stopped it? How could he let so many innocent people die . . . in such a horrible way?"

"I could never pretend to second guess an omnipotent God," Cameron said. "But I believe God is bound by certain laws. While His love for each and every one of us is constant and unconditional, He must allow us to make our own choices. I believe His sorrow this day is great. I believe He is mindful of each and every person affected by this, and I believe that if we, as a nation, and the world, turn to Him, in our own ways, He will comfort those who sorrow. He will guide us through. But the bottom line for me is this: in spite of anything that might happen in this life, no matter how difficult it may be, there is peace in knowing that the Son of God atoned for our sorrows, and provided a way for us to be with Him beyond this life. As we live for those blessings, we can find peace."

Cameron felt his words run out and became acutely aware of the silence surrounding him. Kaniesha said nothing more, but he sensed more hope than doubt from her. The silence was finally broken by Tom saying, "Amen." More voices echoed him, but Cameron wasn't certain whose they were.

* * * * *

Christy reached for the phone to once again try calling Beth. She almost tried Sherry again, but realizing it was two hours later in New York, she decided to try again in the morning. Through several tries to Beth's house, she'd gotten nothing but a machine. She dialed the number again and gasped softly to hear Beth answer.

"Hi, it's Christy. I've been trying to reach you. Are you—"

"Oh, Christy," she cried. "I haven't heard from him. I can't even begin to think . . . what to do . . . where to start. I can't get through to anybody who can tell me anything. It's all so crazy and . . ." She broke down, and Christy attempted to be rational on her behalf. But it was difficult when she knew all too well how Beth felt. Except that

Christy knew now her husband was safe and well. And Beth had no reason to believe the same.

"Where are the kids?" Christy asked.

"They're with a neighbor; they've been there for hours. I need to bring them home, but I don't want them to see me this upset, and . . ."

"Are you alone?"

"Yes, but . . . my mom is driving from Reno. She'll be here later tonight. She headed out as soon as it happened this morning and after I told her Dean was there."

"Okay," Christy tried to think straight, "I'm on my way over. It'll take me about half an hour. Tell your neighbor I'll come and get the kids when I get there, and I'll stay until your mom comes."

"You really don't have to—"

"I need to be with you, Beth. I'll be there soon." She gave Beth her cell number and added, "Once I'm out of the canyon, you can call if you need an ear to listen. I mean it."

Beth sounded slightly more calm as she got off the phone. Christy hurried to explain the situation to Bea and the children. Bea offered to just spend the night and see that everything was fine. Christy hugged them all and hurried to be with her friend.

Once inside Beth's front door, the woman literally crumbled in Christy's arms. Christy eased her to the couch and sat close beside her, just letting her cry. When she'd calmed down somewhat, Christy said, "Okay now, we're not giving up hope until there is no reason to have hope. A lot of people got out of those buildings. But communications are obviously not up to capacity, and it's probably a mess at those hospitals. We're just going to keep praying, okay?"

"Okay," Beth said.

"How are you feeling?" she asked, motioning toward her well-rounded belly.

"I've forced myself to keep eating," she said. "I think I'm okay." She rubbed her belly tenderly and Christy couldn't think too hard about the possibility of this baby's father never coming home. She pressed a hand briefly over her own belly, grateful that her baby's father was on his way here, safe and sound.

"Will you go get the kids, then?" Beth asked.

"I will," she said. "Are you going to be okay?"

"Yes, I think so."

"Hey, it's okay for your kids to know you're upset. They're probably upset, too."

"I hadn't looked at it that way."

"I'll be right back," Christy said and quickly went to the specified home across the street to get Dean and Beth's children. The neighbor offered to help in any way possible, and told Christy the children had been given a good supper. Christy walked back with them, then urged them to sit on the porch with her, where they talked for a few minutes. They were well aware of the situation, and obviously concerned, but they were full of hope that their father would be all right. She explained that their mother was very upset, and that they could help their mother feel better by being strong. They eagerly agreed and Christy took them inside. She kept her distance while Beth talked with her children and they all cried together.

"Christy?" Beth called to her, where she was straightening up the kitchen.

"Yes," Christy answered as she moved into the family room where they were sitting close together on the couch. "You said something about praying. I confess . . . it's not something I know much about. Could you . . ."

"I'd be happy to," Christy said, and she motioned for them to kneel on the floor and hold hands in a circle. She bowed her head and offered a prayer much like the one she'd spoken with her own children, including her gratitude for Cameron's safety. She prayed that Dean would be safe, and that his family would be given an outpouring of comfort and strength, whatever the outcome might be. She expressed gratitude for their many blessings, and for the friendship they shared, then she closed with an amen.

When the prayer was done, she looked up to see Beth gazing at her with startled eyes. Before Christy could question her, she asked, "What about Cameron?"

Christy almost felt guilty for her own knowledge that her husband was safe, under the circumstances. She simply said, "He was supposed to be on one of those planes." Beth put a hand over her mouth. "I had every reason to believe that he was, but . . . he had a feeling that his business wasn't done . . . and he went back."

Beth sighed deeply and tears slid down her face. Her voice was warm with compassion and hope as she said, "God was with him, then."

Christy nodded. "It wasn't his time to go."

Beth's eyes narrowed slightly and she asked, "What do you mean?"

"Well . . . we've already heard on the news so many little incidents of people . . . getting stuck in traffic . . . deciding not to go there for odd reasons . . . being at home sick. I firmly believe that every good person has a time when they're meant to leave this world, and if it's not their time, God maneuvers them out of harm's way, somehow. It doesn't make losing someone any easier, but recognizing God's hand in the situation can bring some measure of peace."

Christy almost expected Beth to argue or hurl back a cynical statement. With the possibility that her husband could be dead—and Cameron was not—it would have been understandable for this woman to feel angry and confused. But Beth simply said, "I never thought about it that way, but . . . it makes sense."

Christy helped Beth get the children calmed down and in bed, then she heated up some leftovers for the two of them. As they sat to eat in the quiet house, Beth said, "I'm ashamed to admit that I've thought about God more this day than I have in twenty years. I grew up with a basic belief in God, but religion was never a part of our lives. Funny how I look at all of this, and I wonder how such a thing could happen. And I imagine that it would be easy to get angry with God; and many people probably are, but . . ."

"But you're not?" Christy asked.

Beth shook her head. "I just keep thinking that . . . even the most basic belief in God gives me the hope that I could actually get through losing him." Her chin quivered and she looked down. "And I've found myself praying that if he is gone, that he went quickly . . . and didn't suffer . . . and I've felt comfort to think of him being beyond the horrors of this life. When I think of all those people on the planes . . . and of the impact point in those buildings . . . I just think how at least it was over quickly. They didn't suffer." Her emotion became stronger. "And I pray Dean didn't suffer."

"And maybe he's all right, Beth. Either way, we'll get through."

Beth nodded and wiped at her tears, then she forced herself to eat the food in front of her. As soon as she'd eaten, she turned on the TV and they sat close together, tightly squeezing each other's hands, hanging on every little update of information, and disbelieving the repeated footage of the buildings exploding and crumbling.

"You know," Beth said, relatively calm, "I think if I watch it enough, I might start to actually believe that what I'm seeing is real."

"Yeah, me too," Christy said. "I've asked myself a few times if I've got some kind of sick mind to keep watching images of that plane going in, over and over. But I think you're right. I think we're just trying to accept it as reality."

They both became enthralled by scattered reports of heroism, and a rising determination and patriotism that was as stirring as the tragedy was sorrowful. Hearing many reports of *God Bless America* being sung and spoken by the nation's leaders, they cried for different reasons. Beth leaned her head on Christy's shoulder and muttered, "It would seem I'm not the only one realizing a need to turn to God."

Christy drifted to sleep on Beth's couch, and woke up once to see that she was dozing in the recliner nearby, with the television still on. She fell back to sleep and woke up when she heard something going on. She sat up to see Beth embracing her mother, while they both wept. The three women talked for a short while before Christy went home. Beth offered her the guest room for the rest of the night, but Christy felt rested enough to get home, and wanted to be with her family.

* * * * *

As it became fully dark, the little group in the van devised a plan to take shifts, with one person driving no longer than two hours, and another sitting across from him with the assignment of keeping the driver awake with the radio or conversation. Victor had had the insight to purchase earplugs during one of their stops, saying he'd done this kind of traveling before. This allowed those who needed sleep to be able to do so more easily, while the driver could stay awake.

Cameron slept for a few hours, then started driving about three. He contemplated the events of the day, ending with the testimony he'd born to Kaniesha—and the others. He recalled that there were a few copies of the Book of Mormon in his luggage, since he always traveled with them. He couldn't help hoping that he might have the opportunity to appropriately put them into the right hands. Such an endeavor could certainly make the trip more than worthwhile.

About quarter to five, Cameron had to admit that he was getting too heady to be safe. While Anne was driving he fell quickly to sleep, with a prayer in his heart for Dean, for Sherry and Jeff, and for every other person in the world who shared his grief and worry.

* * * * *

Once at home, Christy tiptoed into every bedroom, gently touching the heads of her children and crying silent tears. How grateful she was to know they were safe, and she could only pray that their futures would be secure—and free. She could not deny that America was on the brink of war, and it was not likely to be brief. She attempted to comprehend the changed world her children might grow up in, but it was a thought she couldn't even entertain at the moment. *One day at a time,* she told herself and concentrated on the moment.

Christy peeked in on Bea and found her sleeping soundly. She checked the doors and lights and crawled into her own bed, crying herself to sleep as she grieved for a friend, a nation, and for herself in almost losing the man who held her heart. "Oh, thank you, God," she muttered into her pillow, and her next awareness was the phone ringing. She quickly surmised that it was very early morning, according to the hazy light in the room. She grabbed the phone and attempted a coherent, "Hello?"

"Christy!" Beth said on the other end. "He's okay!"

Christy immediately started to cry, unable to even ask how she knew.

"He called . . . from a hospital," Beth reported, her voice somewhere between frantic and joyful. "He started down the stairs as soon as it happened, and he was about a block away when the first building fell. He said he's bruised up a bit from some debris, and he inhaled a lot of smoke and stuff . . . but he sounded fine . . . and he's flying home as soon as the airports open, and Oh! I can't believe it. I'm so grateful; *so* grateful!"

"Me too," Christy said. "Thank you for calling. When we get our husbands home, we're going to have to celebrate."

"Yes," she said, "we are."

Christy hung up the phone and laid back on her pillow, silently expressing gratitude for Dean's safety. She drifted back to sleep and was awakened by the alarm as it turned on the radio. She felt the sensation of emerging from a bad dream, and a relief in knowing that it hadn't been real. Hearing commentary on yesterday's events instead of the usual morning music, she felt silent tears slide into her hair. It *was* real. It *had* happened. But she still couldn't believe it. She just couldn't believe it!

She had just reached over to turn off the radio when she realized Tim was standing in the doorway. "You okay?" she asked and he rushed to jump onto the bed beside her. "What is it?" she asked when he said nothing.

"Mom?" he asked. "If Cameron had died, would you have had to go back to work?"

Christy felt a rush of gratitude. In his childlike perception, Tim had obviously grown to appreciate the blessings Cameron had brought into their lives—if only superficially. She attempted to answer him honestly and without emotion. "No, honey, I wouldn't, because we have something that is called life insurance, and if Cameron were to die, we would have plenty of money to provide for our needs."

Tim thought about that a minute before he nodded and said, "I'm glad he's coming back anyway, 'cause I'd miss him if he never came back."

Once again, Christy fought back her tears and said, "I'm glad he's coming back too."

With that Tim bounded out of the room to get ready for school. Christy forced herself out of bed, once again recounting all she had to be grateful for.

* * * * *

Cameron awakened to sunlight and a report that Kaniesha had spoken to her sister on a cell phone, and she would be meeting her in just a few minutes. They had arrived in Columbus, Ohio.

"Why didn't your sister go to the funeral in Boston?" Anne asked Kaniesha.

"She's got a couple of tiny children, and just couldn't leave. That made me the family delegate from this city, I guess. My sister watched my daughter, so it worked out fine."

Cameron sensed that Kaniesha's spirits had lifted a little this morning, but he felt a bit panicked to realize she would be leaving soon; he'd felt like there was something she needed that he had to offer. He hoped that perhaps he already had done that in the words he'd shared, but he really didn't think so. He uttered a quick prayer when he heard her say to Gary, who was sitting in the driver's seat, "The station's right up there, past that stop light. She should be there by now, and you people can have a rest stop."

As they pulled up next to the gas pump, Tom insisted on paying for gas this time and pulled out his credit card. Cameron said to Kaniesha, "I'll help you get your bag."

He opened the back of the van and she pointed to the one that was hers. "Hey," he said, purposely keeping his hand on her suitcase, "are you going to be okay?"

"Sure," she said with a forced smile, "why?"

"Forgive me if I'm being presumptuous, but . . . I just sense something isn't right; something more than what happened yesterday, and . . . I wonder if there might be something I can do to help."

She glanced down and he could see that she was fighting tears. "There's nothing anyone can do," she said. "Nothing will ever bring the people I love back from the dead; they're gone forever, and that's something I'm just going to have to learn to live with. I guess thinking of all those innocent people dying just brings it too close to home."

"You mentioned your grandmother, but . . ."

"My mother and son were killed in a car accident more than a year ago, and I just cannot . . ." Her emotion got the better of her while Cameron's heart pounded audibly.

"Kaniesha," he said, knowing now why he'd felt prompted to talk to her, "I lost my son the same way several years ago. I lost my mother when I was twelve, and my father died of cancer less than a year ago."

She gave him a penetrating gaze and asked in a voice more hopeful than cynical, "And you still find peace through your belief in God?"

"Absolutely. That is where the ultimate peace can be found, my friend."

A different kind of tears appeared in her eyes before she said, "Now that it's time to go, I wish we could talk, and—"

"Hang on," he said and set her suitcase on the ground behind the van before he dug into his own. He reached into one of the outside pockets and pulled out the little blue hardbound book. It was one of the copies he'd prepared for handy access when traveling. His picture and testimony were inside the front cover, along with a card that offered a free video from the Church, and a number to call that would allow missionaries a possible opportunity to deliver that video. He had a tape flag attached to the verses in Moroni he had under-lined—the verses that issued the challenge of learning the truth of the Book of Mormon.

"Here," he said, handing her the book after he'd quickly jotted his phone number on the same page where his testimony was written. "I know we don't have much time, but if you try and set aside any preju-dices you might have about God, or Mormons, or religion, and just read this with an open mind and an open heart, I promise you that it will change your life. Start with these verses I have marked here," he pointed them out, "then start at the beginning, read all of the intro-ductions and stuff first. If you have questions, you can call the number on this card, and someone will come to visit with you and answer them."

Kaniesha smiled and looked at the book, then up at him. "I'll read it. Thank you. And thanks for the ride. That trip to Boston broke me. I was standing in that car rental line, praying that my credit card would clear, but doubting it would. I'd maxed it out to get the plane ticket for the funeral."

"Do you need a loan, or—"

"No, no," she said. "We're fine. I just can't afford to be traveling at the moment. But thank you . . . for everything. I wish there was some way I could repay you or—"

"Just read the book; that's thanks enough."

She reached into her bag and handed him a business card. "Keep in touch," she said and walked away with her suitcase in one hand, and the Book of Mormon in the other. Cameron offered a little prayer in her behalf. She waved as she drove away with her sister, and he hurried into the store to use the restroom and grab something to eat before they headed out again.

Cameron sat in the front passenger seat while Gary continued to drive, insisting that he was wide awake for the moment. They listened to the news for a while to hear any updates, but most of what they heard were personal commentary and experiences. Some of what Cameron heard lifted his spirits with hope and patriotism, and some of it made him ache too deeply to comprehend.

Cameron was startled to hear his cell phone ring. He grabbed it and turned down the radio.

"Cameron," he heard Christy say, and that alone soothed his aching heart.

"Good morning, my love," he said. "Is everything okay there?"

"Yes, we're fine."

He had to ask the question most prominent on his mind. "Have you talked to Beth? Do you know if—"

"I went over there last night," she said. "It's been rough, but . . ." her voice broke and he feared the worst. But she said firmly, "Dean's all right, Cameron."

"Oh, thank you, Lord," he breathed, then had to put a hand over his mouth to hold back a spontaneous sob.

"Is your friend all right?" Tom asked.

Cameron turned toward him and said, "Yes, he's all right."

They all cheered and he could hear Christy laughing. "It sounds like you've got a lot of support at that end."

"Yes, actually, I do. Tell me what happened."

"He called Beth really early this morning," she said. "He was in one of the hospitals with some minor injuries, and some trouble breathing, but he's fine."

Cameron knew from the report that Dean must have been pretty close to the collapse of those buildings. He couldn't even comprehend what he must have witnessed. He forced his voice past his emotion and said, "Oh, I'm so grateful. Have you heard from Sherry yet?"

"I haven't. I'll try again as soon as we get off. I've e-mailed them, and I finally got through once last night, but they just had the machine on. I left a message, but you know how they are. Even in the best of times, they're so busy that it takes days to get a call back."

"I know," Cameron said, wishing his sister would have the sensitivity to think that they might be worried, and call to let them know she was okay. He reminded himself not to panic and focused on his conversation with his wife. She told him more of her visit with Beth, and what Dean had told his wife on the phone. She updated him on Bea and the children, and the difficult time she'd been having with all that had happened, admitting that she'd been prone to crying a great deal, and she'd had trouble sleeping.

"Yeah, me too," he said, not wanting to get too specific with other ears listening so closely. He told Christy where they were, then got off the phone, the image of being reunited with her clear in his mind. And once again, he silently thanked God for sparing his life, and he expressed a heartfelt gratitude to know that Dean was safe and well. They were truly blessed.

Chapter Eighteen

Christy was grateful for Bea's presence while the children were getting ready for school. She helped answer their questions and assuage their fears. They were thrilled to learn that Dean was all right, but Charlotte especially kept asking about Sherry, and Christy had nothing to tell her. They asked about Cameron with an eagerness that implied their growing affection for him; perhaps nearly losing him had made a difference. She told them they could all talk to him for a few minutes after school.

Once the children were off, Bea said, "If it's all right with you, I'm going to run home and get a few things and hang out here for a while longer."

Christy sighed with relief. "I would love it. I just . . . don't feel like being alone."

"Well, me neither," Bea said, and she was back in less than an hour.

Later in the morning while they were watching the ongoing television coverage together, Christy caught her breath to see Cameron's picture appear on the screen during a local section of the news broadcast. It was a picture she recognized from once seeing it in the newspaper. She grabbed Bea's hand as she heard the newscaster state, "Prominent Utah businessman and philanthropist, Bruce Cameron Chandler, a resident of Salt Lake, came within minutes of stepping onto United flight 175 from Boston to Los Angeles, which was crashed into the World Trade Center in New York City, early yesterday morning. A friend reported that Mr. Chandler just felt like his business in Boston wasn't finished and he needed to stay. He is now driving west with a vehicle acquired from a business associate, anxious to be reunited with his wife, Christina."

Christy let out a little laugh, and the newscast quickly went on to something else. Later that day, she received calls from two television stations and three newspapers, wanting to verify the story and ask some questions. She kept the calls brief and refused a personal interview, but hearing them discuss the situation helped deepen her conviction of how very blessed they had been. Once again, she sat down and cried, consumed with a combination of gratitude and grief.

Christy tried several times to call Sherry and Jeff in New York. She kept getting the machine, and left three different messages, wishing they would consider their relatives and just take a minute to let them know they were okay. Christy spoke to Beth on the phone a few times through the day. They shared common emotions in their gratitude and relief, and in the grief and empathy they felt on behalf of others. Throughout the day Christy phoned her parents and siblings, just to make certain all was well with them and their families. She repeated Cameron's story to each relative, feeling they should know, while each time she marveled over the miracle. They were truly blessed, indeed!

* * * * *

"Nothing personal," Victor said, groaning as he stretched, "but this road it getting awfully tedious."

"Boy, you can say that again," Gary added.

"This road is getting awfully tedious," Anne said and they all chuckled.

Listening to the radio off and on, and visiting in between, they were all impressed with the tremendous acts of heroism through this crisis, and the astounding sense of nationwide patriotism. They even heard the Mormon Tabernacle Choir singing "The Star Spangled Banner"—on a popular music station. The DJ claimed, "We don't usually do the Mo-Tab Choir, but it seems appropriate."

"Hey, that's your choir," Victor said to Cameron.

"Yes, indeed," Cameron said proudly.

Hearing the national anthem moved them to embark on a discussion of how their patriotism had been stirred. They were all certainly glad to be Americans, but it was evident they shared a unanimous awakening to just how blessed they were to live in such a country, and how grateful they were for the spirit and determination that would surely see their country—and the world—through this crisis.

"Well," Tom commented, "those terrorists simply don't understand what they're up against. I bet they didn't count on the spirit of Americans; we're not a people to be defeated by something like this. If anything, I think that patriotic spirit has been rallied into a determination that will make us triumphant in ridding the world of such evil."

"Well, this is the promised land," Cameron said.

"I've never heard it put quite that way," Tom said, "but it certainly fits."

Cameron smiled with secret delight as he went on to say, "That term is used frequently in a book I've read several times. It's actually a record of ancient America, documenting the civilizations that came here from the old world, who are the ancestors of the Native Americans."

"Really?" Tom said. "I've never heard of such a record."

"Well, because it's written in scriptural form, and was translated through a religious leader, many people doubt its authenticity. But I've studied it extensively, and I'm absolutely certain of its truth."

Tom looked interested, albeit slightly dubious. And while the conversation was basically between the two of them, he sensed the others were listening. He pressed on while he had a captive audience.

"Anyway, about 600 B.C., these people leave Jerusalem, build a ship, and are guided to this land. God tells them that it is a land of promise with a great purpose, and as long as its inhabitants are righteous, it will be protected. Of course, many centuries later, it was the freedom of religion incorporated into the establishment of this country that made it possible for this record to come forth along with the restoration of the full gospel of Jesus Christ."

Cameron went on to explain how the Church had been taken from the earth, and then restored. Then he told how the light of Christ existed inside every human being, and they made the choice of whether they honored that light by the way they lived, or drove it away. He then added, "It's my personal belief that when we feel that warmth inside we call patriotism, it is directly connected to that light of Christ. Because this is the promised land, those of us who respect and honor it are touched with that spirit. Good people across this land will be stirred to recall that this land was founded on the motto, 'In God we Trust.' It seems logical to me that when the president of our nation admonished the country to pray, and the majority of them rose to the challenge, that God has poured out those blessings already, and He will continue to do so. It makes sense that this burst of patriotism, this deep determination to rise above this, is one way God is pouring out his blessings upon us, and laying the groundwork for us to rise above this horrible evil. And look at all the outpouring of heroism, of generosity, and all the stories we're hearing of people who *didn't* die, who could have."

"Like you," Gary said quietly.

"Yeah," Cameron swallowed carefully, "like me." He sighed and concluded by saying, "Forgive me for being so vehement, but I really feel that God is the source of this rallying of hearts to patriotism, and it is His endorsement of the individual human spirit that prompts them to hope and faith and determination." Cameron heard the words come back to him and felt certain he was being guided by the Spirit. The concept made perfect sense, and he found that he actually felt a little better.

"No need for apology," Tom said. "It's a theory I've never heard before—exactly that way, at least. But it makes sense to me."

"So, what is this book?" Victor asked.

"It's called the Book of Mormon," Cameron said, fully expecting a negative response from someone as he recalled his missionary experiences.

"I've heard of that," Anne said. "Quite frankly, what I've heard isn't good."

"I could echo that," Victor said, but at least they both seemed to respect Cameron's views, rather than scoffing at them.

"I've heard a number of the rumors myself," Cameron said. "But it's been my experience that any person who will overlook any prejudice or hearsay, and read the book with sincere intent will come to see it differently."

"Seems fair," Victor said, then the conversation drifted elsewhere and Cameron could only hope that some positive seeds had been planted.

That afternoon they arrived in Indianapolis, where Victor was left at his home, which was only a few minutes from a main freeway interchange. They were soon on the road again, taking turns driving as their minimal sleep the previous night began to catch up with them. Cameron napped for a couple of hours, then took the wheel. Christy called after the kids got home from school. He talked to each of them for a few minutes—even Charlotte—and felt touched to hear their expressions of relief that he was okay. He spoke with Bea for a minute as well. It was good to hear her voice, but he was dismayed to realize that, as of yet, there had been no word from Sherry. He tried to push it to the back of his mind, certain she was just busy—and somewhat insensitive—which was typical.

Cameron was still driving that evening when they arrived in St. Louis, where Anne was met at a gas station by a friend who picked her up. She thanked Cameron for the ride, then added, "And thanks for the things you said. You've given me some food for thought that I think has actually helped. I wish you the best."

"And you," he said as they exchanged a firm handshake.

"It's getting roomier," Gary said, stretching out on the backseat to rest as they started out again, with Tom at the wheel.

A while later when it was getting dark, Cameron said, "I don't know about you, but I think we ought to get a room and get a good night's sleep, or we're never going to make it. It's amazing how exhausting it can be to sit in a vehicle."

"I second that motion," Tom said. "My old bones are not liking this at all."

"Well, my young bones aren't too happy about it either," Gary called from the backseat.

They stopped in Columbia, Missouri, and got a room that Gary insisted on paying for. It was relatively spacious, with two full beds, and they had a rollaway brought in, so they could each have their own sleeping space. Cameron knew that he and Tom could have afforded to get their own rooms, and there were plenty available, but he felt somehow better in the company of his new friends, and he suspected they felt the same way.

Once checked into their room, they went out and shared a good meal, which Tom insisted on paying for, but Cameron pledged to pay for breakfast before they set out in the morning. Back at the room, they each had lengthy phone conversations with loved ones. Tom reported that his wife was doing well, and their daughters were with her, but he would sure be glad to see her. Gary spoke quietly with his wife, and Cameron sensed some concern, but he said nothing and Cameron didn't want to pry.

Before settling down for the night, Cameron sat in bed, by habit, and read from the Book of Mormon. Tom read from a novel he'd been carrying with him, and Gary had some business magazines. They had all agreed that they needed some time to unwind, but the TV in the room was broken, which Cameron figured could be a blessing in disguise.

Perusing the Book of Mormon, Cameron was mindful of some things he'd heard throughout the newscasts, regarding these terrorists who were responsible, which spurred him to look in the index for certain references. He read some scattered verses about the promised land, and Captain Moroni's vigilance in preserving the freedom of the people, words which somehow reminded him of the president's recent stance, and the idea gave him warm chills. Then Cameron came across some verses in Ether, chapter eight, that prompted him to mutter aloud, "That's incredible!"

"Are you going to share?" Tom asked, startling Cameron to recall that he wasn't alone.

"Well, it's kind of a long story," Cameron said. "And I don't know if it can compete with that book you're reading, but—"

"I can read this any time," Tom said.

"And I've already read these stupid magazines once," Gary said, tossing them aside.

"Is that the book you were telling us about earlier?" Tom asked.

"The very same," Cameron said, and once again he felt a secret delight.

He gave a brief explanation of the division of the Nephites and Lamanites, and their wars through the generations. He explained the concept of secret combinations, and he also shared the concept that these records had been kept by prophets down through the generations, and they had been abridged by a man named Mormon, who was also a prophet.

"Hence, it is called the Book of Mormon," Gary said from where he leaned against the headboard of his bed. Cameron couldn't tell if his interest was only for the sake of easing some boredom, but he took the comment at face value.

"Precisely," Cameron said and went on. "Now, forgive all the explanations, but it does have a point that I think you'll appreciate, given the present circumstances."

"I'm enjoying it, actually," Tom said, and Gary gave a nonchalant wave of his hand to indicate that he should go on.

Cameron explained briefly how the Bible is a book that we cherish, because it has so many powerful stories and principles that aid us, even in this present day. They both agreed readily, so Cameron knew they had Christian backgrounds. He explained that the Book of Mormon was also written by ancient prophets for the people of our day, so that we could learn from these people's experiences. He told them of the relationship of Mormon and Moroni, and how the latter had completed the abridgement. He told them that frequently the abridgers would pause in the narrative to interject prophetic commentary, as if to say, 'This is how it applies to you.'

"Are you with me so far?" Cameron asked, and was pleased to see that he was holding their interest, despite their obvious fatigue.

"Indeed," Tom said earnestly.

"I'm waiting for the punch line," Gary said. "Whatever it is that you just read got you very excited; and if you've read it several times, I'm curious as to what could surprise you."

"Well," Cameron said, feeling chilled, "the last time I read this part, America hadn't been attacked by a secret organization, attempting to overthrow our freedom."

"Okay, so read us that part," Tom said.

Cameron cleared his throat and found the verses that had touched him. "Okay," he said, "this is Moroni's commentary in the middle of a story." He began with verse twenty-two, and read, "'And whatsoever nation shall uphold such secret combinations, to get power and gain, until they shall spread over the nation . . .'"

"Like Afghanistan," Gary interjected.

"Exactly," Cameron said excitedly before he continued to read, going back a little, "'. . . until they shall spread over the nation, behold they shall be destroyed; for the Lord will not suffer that the blood of his saints, which shall be shed by them, shall always cry unto him from the ground for vengeance upon them and yet he avenge them not.'"

"Incredible!" Tom muttered.

"That's what I said. Now moving down a little, it says," and he read from verse twenty-four, "'. . . when ye shall see these things come among you that ye shall awake to a sense of your awful situation, because of this secret combination which shall be among you; or woe be unto it, because of the blood of them who have been slain; for they cry from the dust for vengeance upon it, and also upon those who built it up.'"

"That gives me chills," Gary said.

"It does indeed," Tom added. "Is there more?"

"A little," Cameron said and went on to verse twenty-five. "'For it cometh to pass that whoso buildeth it up seeketh to overthrow the freedom of all lands, nations, and countries.'" Cameron looked at the words on the page and shook his head, feeling his already unshakable testimony of this book deepen immensely. "The thing that amazes me," he said to his new friends, "is that . . . well, all through the book, the people it's written about refer to the places they live as lands and cities. But nations and countries are not terms they used. I feel as if this is literally written for us . . . now."

"It certainly applies," Tom said. "I must admit that I'd like to read that book."

Cameron smiled. "I just happen to have another copy or two with me. But I think I'd better give it to you in the morning. You look tired."

Gary yawned. "I think we're all done in."

"Yes," Tom yawned as well, "and I'm only hours away from my sweetheart."

Cameron glimpsed something dark in Gary's eyes before he turned over to go to sleep. Cameron reread those verses once more, then he reached for the light. Following a lengthy prayer in the dark, he slept soundly until Tom nudged him awake. "I'm getting awfully anxious. I'll drive and you can rest some more if you like."

"I'll be ready in twenty minutes," Cameron said and took a quick shower, noting that Gary and Tom had already showered and shaved.

While Cameron was closing up his suitcase, he pulled out a copy of the Book of Mormon and handed it to Tom. "It's all yours. Enjoy."

"I believe I will. Thank you."

They ate a hearty breakfast and headed west once more, with Tom driving. Tom was met in Kansas City by one of his married daughters, who was obviously very glad to see him. Her eyes filled with tears as she thanked Cameron and Gary for bringing her father home, then she gave them a Ziploc bag with homemade cookies, and two large sack lunches with some exquisite-looking sandwiches, vegetables, and chips.

Tom exchanged a firm handshake with Cameron and Gary, and Cameron quickly added this man's name and phone number to the list of the others who had been dropped off previously.

"Okay," Gary said, as they set out again, "this is going to be a long day. I figure we should get to Denver late this evening, and I think you should just plan on spending the night at my house tonight. If you're going that last stretch alone, you need your sleep."

Cameron had to agree. "Thank you. I think I will."

Not far into the drive, they pulled out the sandwiches Tom's daughter had brought. Gary helped Cameron situate his so that he could eat while he drove. "Now, that is a sandwich," Gary commented after the first bite, while he examined the slices of turkey, ham, and two kinds of cheese, along with lettuce, tomato and sprouts, all piled on heavy wheat bread.

"It certainly is," Cameron said, thoroughly enjoying every bite, especially after all the pre-packaged sandwiches and fast food they'd been eating along the way.

They listened to the radio most of the afternoon until it began to get old, and Gary turned it off. Cameron sensed that he was upset for some reason, and he ventured to ask, "You okay?"

"Relatively speaking," Gary said.

A minute later Cameron asked, "Want to talk about it?"

Gary turned toward him, seeming surprised, then he said, "You know, I've listened to a lot of things you've said these last couple of days, and most of it's made sense. I have to admit that I never imagined that Mormons would be like you. What little I've heard about them was . . . well it was nothing like you."

"I think that was a compliment," Cameron chuckled.

"Yes, actually, it was. But I have something I'd like to ask you. Of everything you've said, there's one thing I can't get out of my mind."

"What's that?" Cameron asked when he hesitated.

A hardness that Cameron had seen many times rose into Gary's eyes as he asked, "Do you really believe in eternal marriage?"

Cameron gazed at him for as long as he could manage before he needed to look back at the road, saying with conviction, "Absolutely, as long as it's performed by the proper authority."

"And you believe that your church has that . . . authority?"

"I know they do."

"And other churches?"

"There are many good churches in this world, and there is much truth to be found there. I feel that any belief in God that makes people pray and focus on living righteously and helping others is a wonderful thing. But I also know that only one church has the full truth that was restored to the earth once the freedom of religion was established in this land, which made it possible."

Gary shook his head and laughed softly. "That all makes so much sense."

"Yeah," Cameron said. "Is that a problem?"

"The only problem is that . . . I have to wonder why this would come up now . . . in this way, when . . ." His voice broke and he turned away, clearing his throat loudly.

"When what?" Cameron asked.

Gary looked down and swallowed carefully. "My wife has cancer," he said and Cameron blew out a long breath. "She might make it. She might not. I grew up believing in God, but I never gave it a lot of thought . . . until this came up. Some people have told me they believe in life after death, and that we would be together eventually no matter when one or the other of us left here. But I haven't found anything to back that up. I've talked to a couple of clergymen who have, quite frankly, given me answers that are elusive, answers that make no sense. I actually prayed that I could find the answer, which is the first time I've prayed at all since I was a child. But if I had to believe that what I feel for Amy would end with death, I don't know if I could cope. And thinking about the thousands of people out there who have lost their loved ones so tragically, I wonder how *they* can cope." He turned directly to Cameron and added, "It might sound strange, but . . . I'm beginning to think that my getting stranded in that airport was the answer to that prayer."

Cameron shrugged his shoulders and laughed softly. "Maybe. Whether we had crossed paths or not, the Lord would have found a way to get the message to you."

"Really?" he asked skeptically. "How so?"

Cameron laughed again. "We have approximately sixty thousand missionaries, all over the United States, and the world. I'd wager that a couple of them would show up at your door eventually. As it is, I'll make a call as soon as I get home, and they'll probably be there next week—only if you want me to, of course. They can answer your every question."

Gary gave an emotional smile as he said, "I'd like that. And I'd like one of those books, too."

"I just happen to have one more on hand," Cameron said. "But those missionaries always carry a few spares."

"Like you."

"Well, yeah. We're all missionaries, in a way. It's just like . . . well, when you've tasted chocolate, and you know it's incredible, you want everyone in the world to taste chocolate, so they can know for themselves that it's incredible. Because you can't explain how chocolate tastes, and some people might have heard that chocolate is nasty. But when you know it's great stuff, you just want to pass it out everywhere you go."

Gary chuckled and a few minutes later they pulled into a service station for a rest stop. When they got back in the van, Cameron handed him the Book of Mormon, and a Hershey bar that he'd just bought. "Enjoy," he said and Gary chuckled again. He perused the book quietly for a while, then he took a turn driving and asked Cameron some questions. The conversation became so enjoyable that Cameron was amazed to realize they'd arrived in Denver. While Gary drove toward his home, through the darkened streets of the city, Cameron called Christy on his cell phone and gave her an update. He felt sick to hear that there was still no word from Sherry. His fear on her behalf was something he couldn't even acknowledge, so he pushed it out of his mind.

"I'll see you tomorrow," he said. "And I'll call when I'm getting close."

"I'll be counting the hours," she said. "Oh, by the way, our date is rescheduled for the twenty-eighth, and I've already let everybody know."

Cameron savored the hope he felt in that statement. "I'll be looking forward to it," he said.

"So, I take it your wedding thing got postponed," Gary said after Cameron had hung up the phone.

"Yes, she just told me it's been rescheduled for two weeks from tomorrow."

"And you say you'll have family and friends there?"

"That's right. Some of them won't be able to go into the temple, because you have to be a member of the Church in good standing, and I have many friends who are not members. But we're having a dinner together afterward to celebrate." He turned to Gary and said, "Maybe you should come, my newest friend. And bring your wife."

Gary smiled. "It sounds nice, but . . . we'll have to see if she's up to it."

When they arrived at Gary's home, Cameron stood discreetly in the doorway while Gary held his wife and they both cried. How could he not anticipate a similar reunion with Christina tomorrow? When their greetings were completed, Gary introduced him to Amy, and their little son, Braden, who was just beginning to crawl. Amy was a pretty girl, with a simple beauty that shone through her pale countenance. She wore a scarf tied around her head, with no hint of hair beneath it. She served them a lovely meal, and left to put the baby to bed before they were finished eating. When she returned to the table, Gary said, "Cameron here has told me some things that I think would interest you." He turned to Cameron and said, "Tell her about the temple thing." His voice broke when he said it, and Cameron noticed how his hand tightened over Amy's.

Cameron leaned his forearms on the table and told her his own story, and how he and Christina would be sealed in a couple of weeks, and how, because of the ordinance, their marriage would go beyond death. Amy's eyes brightened, but she was obviously tired. Cameron offered to help Gary with the dishes. Amy thanked Cameron for bringing her husband home and went off to bed. When the dishes were finished, Gary made sure Cameron had everything he needed and they turned in for the night. Cameron lay in Gary's guest room and marveled at the poignant joy he had found through this good man and his wife. He prayed that they would be together a long while in this life—and forever in the life to come. Then he fell asleep with thoughts of Christina, counting the hours until he could see her tomorrow.

Cameron left early after sharing a breakfast of fruit and bagels with Gary and Braden. Amy was still sleeping. Gary gave him a hearty embrace before he set out, and they promised to keep in touch.

The remainder of the drive was long and difficult for Cameron. Without the buffer of companionship, the experiences of the past few days assaulted his mind and emotions. He felt again his fear on Dean's behalf, and the subsequent relief of knowing he was safe. He felt ongoing concern for his sister, and an incomparable relief for being alive and returning to his family. As he contemplated his brush with mortality, he cried long and hard. And his emotions deepened to a tangible ache as he considered the thousands who hadn't survived, and all those who loved them. The uncertainty of the nation's future, and the role it would play in this fight against terrorism left him uneasy, but there was comfort in the passages of the Book of Mormon that made much of what was happening feel chillingly familiar. There was added comfort in the evidence of the nation turning to God for much-needed help and comfort.

While intermittently searching through radio stations, he was able to hear the majority of a memorial service being broadcast from Washington, D.C. He was touched by the prayers of many different religious leaders, and was moved to tears while listening to the president's powerful speech, again with many references to God. A little later he was able to pick up a memorial service being broadcast from Temple Square. He thought how good it was to hear the prophet's calm voice in the midst of such madness, and he was touched to hear the choir's songs of peace and patriotism.

Cameron was surprised to realize that he was actually in Utah. He'd lost count of the states he'd driven through, but he did know he'd driven nearly 2,400 miles. When he was less than an hour from home, he called Christy to tell her he was almost there.

"Now we can start counting minutes," he said. "And no man will ever be happier to see his wife than I will be."

"I love you, Cameron," she said with a catch in her voice. "And I'm so grateful that you're coming home."

"So am I," he said.

Chapter Nineteen

Christy hung up the phone and cried. It seemed she had cried more in the last three days than she had in her entire life. She had tried to convince herself that her emotions were enhanced by overactive pregnancy hormones, but she had witnessed the worst national tragedy on American soil since the Civil War, and she had almost lost her husband.

Realizing he would be here soon, she hurried to tidy up the house and make herself look presentable. For three long days she had anticipated Cameron's return, a reunion unmatched by any other with the irony of what could have been.

Her heart quickened when she caught sight of the green van pulling into the driveway, and she knew that it was him. She couldn't imagine his exhaustion after driving 2,400 miles in three days, nor could she ever comprehend his own feelings about his close brush with mortality—feelings undoubtedly shared by thousands of people who had narrowly escaped becoming part of the unspeakable carnage.

Christy stepped out onto the porch just as Cameron got out of the van. He left the door open and moved across the lawn to meet her. Time seemed to slow and then stop as he swept her into his arms, and together they wept. He held her tightly against him while he buried his face in her hair, then he took her face in his hands and kissed her lips, her eyelids, her wet cheeks, then her lips again.

"Oh, I love you," he murmured.

"I love you," she cried and he kissed her again.

When their tears turned to laughter, he hugged her again, then he held her hand as he returned to the van to close the door and get his luggage. His bags were barely set down inside the front door when he pulled her into his arms again and kissed her as if they'd been separated for years. With all that had happened—and could have happened—it felt like years.

Feeling weak and light-headed, Christy eased him to the couch where they sat close together. "There's so much I want to say," he said, "and I don't know where to begin."

"It will take some time to catch up," she said. "But that's the beauty of being with you. We have time to catch up."

"Yes, we do," he said, looking into her eyes.

Christy met his gaze and knew there was something she needed to tell him—before he asked. And she could almost feel the question already forming in his eyes. "Cameron," she said, holding his hands a little tighter, "there's something I have to tell you." He sucked in his breath and she wondered if he sensed what was coming. "I only found out last night after you'd called, and I thought it would be better to tell you after you got here."

Christy glanced down, but not before Cameron saw fresh tears in her eyes. His heart rate quickened with dread as the only possibility for her distress stormed into his mind. "What?" he demanded in a whisper.

Christy swallowed hard and met his eyes. "Jeff finally called." She bit her lip. "Sherry's missing, Cameron."

Cameron leaned back and pressed a hand over his mouth. He didn't know where to start to ask for details, and was relieved when she went on. "All Jeff knows for certain is that she said she was meeting a friend for brunch in . . . Manhattan."

"Oh, dear God," he muttered and pressed his head into his hands.

"This friend worked in one of the towers, and Sherry occasionally went to her office. But Jeff knew no more than that. He hasn't been home because he's been out looking for her. He kept hoping she'd turn up in one of the hospitals, but . . . she's still missing."

"In other words," he croaked, "she's . . ." He wrapped his arms up over his head and groaned.

"We don't know for certain, Cameron," she said. "There's still a chance that . . ."

"That what?" he shouted. "Don't you think that every single person who loves someone who is missing is hoping there's a chance that they are just in a hospital somewhere with amnesia and no identification? It's been days, Christina. If she's been missing that long there's only one logical explanation. She's beneath a million tons of rubble with nearly five thousand other people, who were either crushed or incinerated, and . . . Oh, God, help me!" he howled and curled up on the couch, feeling as if the fist of terrorism had reached right down his throat and torn his heart out.

Christy held him while he cried, his head buried in her lap. He felt his grief slip into a numb blanket that seemed to buffer—if only temporarily—the reality that his sister was gone. Even if logic didn't defy the possibility of a miracle, in his heart he could only pray that she had gone quickly, that she wasn't trapped and suffering through these past days while an impossible rescue effort worked unceasingly.

"I wish I knew what to say," Christy whispered, gently pushing her fingers through his hair.

"Just don't let go," he said, tightening his arms around her. "Don't ever let go."

"Never," she murmured and bent to kiss his face.

"I'm the only one left," he said. "I have no immediate family left in this world."

Christy recalled a conversation between them soon after they were married, when she had felt misunderstood by her parents. She told him now what he'd told her then: "I'm your family, Cameron. And you mustn't forget that families are forever."

He looked up at her and sighed deeply. "Yes, and that brings me great comfort when I think of my parents . . . and my son. But the reality of Sherry's life is just . . ." His words were broken by emotion.

"I know it's hard, Cameron. And I can't say I know how you feel. But I do know the Lord will carry you through this. You're the one who taught me the full extent of peace that can come through the Atonement. And that's what you have to hold onto now."

Again he tightened his arms around her. There were no words to express what her presence in his life meant now. If he'd had to face this in the frame of mind he'd been in prior to meeting her, he felt certain it would have undone him completely. But she was here, giving him the love he needed, and telling him the things he needed to hear.

"Hey," she said, "the kids will be home any minute. If you need to be alone, I can tell them you're resting, and—"

"No, it's okay," he said and sat up. "I need to see the kids." He showed Christy a sad smile. "They're my family."

Christy returned the smile and touched his face.

"Do they know?" he asked.

"Yes, I told them this morning. Charlotte has asked about Sherry hourly since this happened. She doesn't even know her, but it's as if she just . . . feels something."

Cameron nodded his head and forced back a new threat of tears. A few minutes later the children came in and Cameron laughed, then cried, as Lucy and Tim ran simultaneously into his arms before he could even stand up. They clung to him, expressing their love in a way he'd never dared hope for. He was momentarily speechless when they drew back, and Lucy admitted tearfully, "I'm so glad you didn't die. Because we love you . . . and we need you."

Cameron glanced at Christy to see his own emotion mirrored in her eyes. He hugged them again and said, "I'm glad too. Because I love and need you, too—all of you." He looked up at Charlotte standing above him. Tim and Lucy moved back and he wondered if she would overcome her usual teenage standoffishness. Her lip quivered as she said with a distinct air of maturity, "I'm so sorry about your sister, but I'm so grateful that you're all right."

Cameron stood up and she hugged him tightly, crying against his shoulder. "It's going to be all right, Charlotte," he said, pressing a hand over her head. "It's hard, but there are two things that are going to get me through." She looked up at him as Tim and Lucy moved close again. "I have the gospel. And I have you; you're my family now. And everything's going to be okay."

They all hugged again, then Christy suggested they kneel together and pray. She offered the prayer at Cameron's request, since he'd become too emotional to speak. She expressed gratitude for Cameron's safe return, and that they could be together as a family. She also offered gratitude for Dean's safety. She prayed for the rescue workers, the leaders of the nation, and especially for those who were grieving for the loss of loved ones. She prayed specifically for Cameron's heart to be touched with peace through this loss of his sister, and that all those who loved and cared for Sherry would be comforted as well.

Cameron knew he needed to call Jeff before it got too late in New York. He prayed for strength and wisdom and dialed the number. The machine answered, but as soon as Cameron started to talk, Jeff picked up the phone.

"Sorry," he said, "there are some people I just can't talk to right now."

"I understand," Cameron said. "I just got home a few hours ago, and Christy told me. I can't believe it, and I'm sure you are—"

"There's not much to say," Jeff said, and the despair was evident in his voice. "Christy told me what happened to you. I'm glad you're all right."

"Thank you. Me too, but . . ."

Jeff began to cry, and Cameron cried as well. They talked for nearly an hour, vacillating between fear and grief, and the sharing of good memories. Like Cameron, Jeff hoped that if Sherry truly was gone, she had not suffered. Cameron knew Jeff well enough not to try offering comfort of any religious nature, so he just listened and offered empathy. But he did say as he was hanging up, "You're in our every prayer."

"Thanks," Jeff said, and they promised to talk every day.

Following his telephone conversation with Jeff, Cameron felt it was a good distraction to unpack his luggage, if only to find the souvenirs he'd purchased for everyone in Boston. He'd anticipated coming home from an ordinary business trip, and he always brought little surprises. The family appreciated his gifts, but he was gratified by the added warmth in their eyes that let him know his safe return meant more than any gift he could give them. He suggested they order pizza for dinner, even though it meant giving the driver an extra big tip to bring it all the way to their home. Then they sat together while Christy showed him bits and pieces of news that she'd video-taped through the last few days—things that Cameron had heard, but not seen, through his journey. While some of the news footage was difficult to watch, some of it enhanced the feelings of hope and patriotism he'd felt through the journey. And all of it helped him begin to digest what had happened.

While the family ate pizza and drank root beer, they talked about the events of the past few days. They each took a turn sharing their feelings, and Cameron marveled at the insight of the children. He was also amazed by their courage, and by their testimonies of the gospel that put their fears and concerns into perspective. He realized that he could learn a great deal by listening to them.

*****

Cameron had trouble sleeping that night as the possibilities of what his sister's final hours on this earth had been like haunted him. He prayed, he got up and read the scriptures, he prayed some more, and finally felt compelled to take something mild to help him relax. He prayed himself to sleep and woke late. Sharing Saturday brunch with his family seemed such an exquisite luxury. He wondered if he would ever look at life the same way.

That afternoon, Christy went with him to visit Dean and Beth. Dean had stayed with a business associate in New York once he'd been released from the hospital. He'd finally been able to get a flight home the day before. The four of them shared common feelings in having narrowly avoided death, but for Dean it had been much more traumatic. He spoke of the sounds that wouldn't leave his mind: hearing the building fall, sharing the fear of people around him, choking in the cloud of smoke, ash, and debris that had threatened to suffocate him. And he admitted tearfully that there were some things he'd seen that he couldn't even repeat—the kinds of things that men who had been to war would have nightmares about decades later. Beth told them he'd already met once with a psychologist, and he felt certain that more counseling would be needed to get beyond these experiences that had changed his life.

"I'll never be free of it," Dean admitted. "Just like everyone else who witnessed it firsthand, the change is too deep to ever go away. But I have to learn to cope, and not let it undo my life." Then he added, "But there were so many that didn't make it. And I wonder . . . why I did."

Cameron appreciated Dean's insight and courage, and admitted in an emotion-filled voice, "I've wondered that myself."

"I just . . . had this feeling that I needed to leave the building," Dean said, his voice trembling. "What makes one man get such a feeling, and another not?"

Cameron exchanged a glance with Christy. They both knew this was not the time to get into discussions of religion or deep spiritual matters. But he felt certain that when emotions settled somewhat, they would be able to explain the workings of the Holy Ghost to these people, and they would likely very much appreciate its purpose and meaning. For now, Cameron was too caught up in his own grief to say anything more than, "Or maybe some men ignore such feelings."

Dean took a sharp breath, as if that in itself held some meaning for him. Cameron saw him reach for Beth's hand at the same time he felt Christy's hand tighten in his. He couldn't begin to articulate the gratitude he felt that he and Dean had been spared, that they were together with their wives. But he felt a contrasting sorrow for the thousands who were not so lucky—Jeff among them. While Jeff and Sherry had chosen to not be married—a choice Cameron certainly didn't agree with—he couldn't credit this man with loving Sherry any less than Cameron loved Christina. The gospel had never been a part of Jeff's life, a fact that made Cameron ache for him all the more. How could any human being cope with such loss, such grief, without the underlying peace of the gospel?

On the drive home from Dean and Beth's, Cameron's mind replayed the events of the last five days. While images of those buildings crumbling into rubble assaulted his memory over and over, he could only imagine where exactly his sister might have been, and how she had actually died. He thought of the reason for the attack, the hatred and evil that made no sense, and he felt a tangible rage seethe from the deepest part of him. Unconsciously he pressed a hand over his chest, aware of a burning there that was intensified by his sharp breathing.

"Are you okay?" he heard Christy say.

"No, I don't think I am," he muttered and pulled the car off to the side of the road.

He groaned and pressed his head to the steering wheel. "What is it?" she asked, putting a hand on his shoulder.

"How could they do something so . . . so . . . *abhorrent* . . . so . . . *barbaric?* It makes me want to just . . . ooh!" he snarled and got out of the car, grateful that they were on the canyon road where little or no traffic would pass by. Christy got out and leaned against the car, watching and listening while he paced back and forth, ranting and screaming about the atrocity of such a thing happening in *this* country and tearing *his* life apart. He finally stopped to face Christy silently, not certain if he'd run out of energy, or if he'd come to the conclusion that such anger would do nothing but eat him alive from the inside out.

Christy reached out and touched his face. With perfect compassion in her eyes, and the echo of his own grief in her voice, she said gently, "There are so many thousands of people who feel the way you feel right now. For every person lost, there are dozens who knew them and loved them. And it's so difficult to make sense of something that makes no sense. But justice will be satisfied, Cameron. The leaders of this nation, and many throughout the world have pledged to rid the world of this evil. We don't know the outcome. We know it will likely be a long, hard road. But it is a righteous endeavor, and God will be with those who are fighting to defend peace and freedom. As individuals, we can do little beyond putting our trust in those leaders, and praying that they will be strengthened and guided. We can live our lives as spiritually and patriotically as we are capable, knowing that whether in this life or the next, justice *will* prevail."

Cameron nodded and squeezed his eyes shut, feeling hot tears sear through his lashes. Christy kissed his face and added, "There's nothing I can tell you that will erase your anger or confusion, and I can't say I know completely how you feel, because I didn't love her the way you do. But I love you, and for a while I thought you were gone. And I do know that being angry is part of grieving. We've both grieved before and survived. We'll do it again, and we'll do it together."

Cameron nodded again and they got back in the car, with Christy driving. As they pulled into the driveway, he couldn't find the motivation to even get out of the car. Christy just sat beside him, simply offering the silent support he needed.

"I just can't believe it," he finally said. "I can't believe it's happened. I can't believe it's real. I can't believe she's gone. Sometimes I . . . think about the things I've heard on the radio, and seen on TV, and I think my mind processes it as if it were a movie. Are we so programmed in this day and age, when we've seen so many incredible images through the technology of film-making, that when we see something like that, because we've only seen it on the television screen, our brain perceives it as . . . something fictional?"

"It certainly makes sense," Christy said. "In fact, I think you've pretty much described something I've felt but couldn't put into words. I think you're right."

"And it's like . . . when you hear . . . real people being interviewed who saw it, even Dean . . . who was there . . . They talk and a part of me is just . . . wanting to say, 'Stop pulling my leg. This has got to be some fantastic gimmick or something, because it just *can't* be real.'" He sighed and ran a hand through his hair. "But it is real, isn't it?"

"I'm afraid it is."

"You know, Christina, I can't count the meetings I've attended in those buildings, the meals I've eaten there. And I keep thinking about all the people I've encountered there, some whose names I never knew. But there were many with whom I was well acquainted. And I wonder . . . Who made it? Who didn't? How long will it take to find out?" He shook his head. "How long will it be before I stop trying to convince myself that it actually happened?"

"You just have to take one day at a time, Cameron. In this case, I think it's good to not think too much about the big picture. When it comes to such grief, I think it's a blessing that we can't comprehend it all at once; we'd never be able to withstand it. You know, right after Keith left me, and I was falling apart . . ." He turned to look at her. "I felt all the same emotions you're feeling now, and I'm sure you did the same when you lost your son, and your dad, and when Jolene left. I couldn't believe it. I refused to accept it. I was angry. But I remember Bea telling me more than once not to worry too much about next month, or next year, or even tomorrow. I just had to make myself get up in the morning, take a shower, take life one hour at a time. And that's how I got through. One day I realized that I had come to believe it was real, and I could go on." She reached for his hand and added, "And you had a lot to do with that . . . with helping me go on."

Cameron marveled at her wisdom, her compassion, her strength. He leaned over to kiss her and felt the one thing that he knew could get him through: *hope.*

The following day, at the request of the Prophet, sacrament meeting took the form of a prayer and memorial service out of respect for the recent tragedy,. Cameron's thoughts were so focused on his sister that he had trouble keeping his emotions under control. But Christy kept her hand in his, and little Lucy snuggled close to his side, silently expressing her gratitude that he was alive and well. He reminded himself to stay focused on his gratitude, and to remember that above all, he was grateful for the Atonement that gave him the hope of being able to get through this.

Cameron forced himself to go back to work on Monday. He met Dean in the downstairs lobby, which was typical, and they got on the elevator together, briefly discussing how difficult—but necessary—it was to force themselves through the motions of normalcy, during this time when everything seemed anything but normal. When they stepped off the elevator, a cheer went up as they were met by the majority of employees they worked with directly, and the lobby was decorated with yellow ribbons, interspersed with patriotic decorations that had obviously been resurrected from the Independence Day decor. Cameron was caught off guard, and emotions that were never far from the surface threatened to erupt. A glance at Dean told him that he was struggling to keep it together even more so. Bertie apparently picked up on the problem when she hushed the small crowd and said, "We all know this has been tough for you, and it's going to be a challenge to get through for a while. We just want you to know that we're all grateful you're both safe, and our prayers are with you." A more reverent applause sounded to echo her words, and Cameron said, "Thank you—all of you. We appreciate your love and support . . . and your keeping it all together for us while we were gone. You might have to keep it up for a while, because I'm not sure we're all here just yet. But give us time. We'll get through this."

They both went into Cameron's office and simultaneously went for a box of tissues. "We're pathetic," Cameron said, grabbing it first and then passing it to Dean. "We're like a couple of old spinsters watching a sappy movie."

"Well," Dean said with a sniffle, "I heard somebody say that crying was healthy, that it made you stronger."

Cameron chuckled. "Boy, we're gonna be strong."

While Cameron attempted to focus on the business at hand, he was grateful for Dean's perfect empathy for his ongoing grief and inner shakiness over all that had occurred. The people they worked with were more gracious and kind than usual, which only seemed to serve as a deeper reminder of the circumstances. The words of concern and the pitying glances Cameron received made it evident that everyone had heard about his missing sister. He caught Bertie crying at her desk and asked what was wrong.

"Oh, I don't know," she muttered and blew her nose. "I wasn't affected personally by this, other than almost losing you and Dean. But . . . I just can't stop thinking about it. I just can't get over it. I know I'm not alone; many people feel this way, but . . ."

Cameron squatted beside the older woman's chair and took her hand. "Hey," he said, "grieving is something we just have to go through when we lose something—anything. And whether or not you lost someone in this atrocity, we've *all* lost something. Don't get down on yourself for feeling this way. Just go ahead and let yourself grieve, and hey . . . we'll just stock up on tissues and cry together."

She smiled through her tears and Cameron returned to his office, but the words of comfort he'd given Bertie came back to him. Thinking them through again, he realized he knew grief well. As Christy had reminded him a couple of days ago, he'd felt grief's companionship many times in his life. And he had to admit that he was actually grateful for the losses he'd suffered that helped him understand what was taking place within himself now. He didn't have to wonder if he was crazy, or if he'd get through it. He just had to recognize the familiarity of what he felt, and know that with time, the shock, the anger, the disbelief, and the sorrow would all gracefully merge into peace. He thought of the good that could come out of adversity, and he could easily see that nationally, much good had already come in contrast to this horrible tragedy. And he needed to remember all the struggles of the past he'd learned and gained strength from—strength that would get him through this present process of grieving.

The grief always struck him keenly when he made his daily call to Jeff, to see how he was doing. A week beyond the day America had gone to its knees, it became fully evident that Sherry would not come back. While it was difficult to find closure under such circumstances, they all had to accept that her body might *never* be found. When Cameron suggested to Jeff that they have a memorial service, he warmed quickly to the idea, but admitted, "You know as well as anyone that I know nothing about religion. I know Sherry had some problems with it, but I know deep down she believed in God and respected Him. She would want the service to be . . . well, you know. I'm assuming you know, because I'm not sure I do, so . . . would you arrange it? I know it's a lot to ask, but—"

"It's not a lot to ask, Jeff. She's my sister. I would be happy to arrange it. Let me see when we can get a flight out, and we'll take care of it."

Jeff gave a humorless chuckle and said, "You'd actually fly out here?"

"Yes, I actually would." Cameron chuckled in return. "I'd rather fly than drive. Besides, it's my patriotic duty to fly, according to the President. I may not be able to personally take on these terrorists, but I can fly."

Cameron spoke with Christy and Bea, and arrangements were quickly made for the three of them to fly to New York. The children would be able to stay with ward members who had children their ages. They were okay with the situation beyond their concerns about air travel. Cameron assured them that taking a plane was never safer than now, because of the heightened security. He also told them that they had prayed about the decision to go, and they felt peace in knowing that they would be all right. He told them that the Lord would not have saved his life last week, only to have him die this week.

During the flight, Cameron sensed a different mood altogether among the passengers. There was more reaching out among them, even beyond the persons sitting on either side. There were more group-level discussions, with people sharing not only their fears and concerns, but also their hope and determination. Cameron saw quiet courage in the faces of many people, inspired by the passengers who had diverted more tragedy by taking one of the hijacked flights down in a field in Pennsylvania.

Cameron had done a great deal of traveling in his life, and in the process he'd encountered many people. But he'd never experienced the poignancy and underlying unity that he felt during this particular flight. He could feel the changes everywhere he turned, and he was deeply grateful to see evidence that many of those changes were for the better.

Chapter Twenty

When the plane landed safely in New York, every passenger cheered and applauded. The relief at safe arrival was evident. And many offered heartfelt gratitude to the flight attendants and pilots, whose eyes reflected that their thoughts were no doubt with those other flight attendants and pilots who had been heinously murdered for a purpose that none of them understood.

Jeff met them at the airport, looking even worse than he had sounded over the phone. Driving away from the airport, Cameron thought of the times he'd told Christy he'd like to take her to New York, to share with her the love he had for many aspects of this city. Under different circumstances, he would have taken her to the Statue of Liberty, Central Park, and Times Square. And most ironic of all, he recalled specifically wanting to take her to Wall Street, and to the twin towers, to show her the view from the top of the world, to share with her these places where he had conducted so many hours of business, and where he had shared so many memories with his father. As it was, he had no desire to go anywhere near Manhattan. He had no desire to see with his own eyes what he could barely tolerate seeing on television. A part of him simply wasn't prepared to fully accept that 220 stories of concrete and steel had been diminished to rubble.

Jeff drove them back to the apartment where he had lived with Sherry. He apologized for the state of the apartment, but admitted he'd done nothing but barely exist since September eleventh. Cameron immediately got out the phone book and made some calls to locate the closest LDS bishop, while Bea and Christy dug right in to help clean up the apartment, with Jeff guiding them on what needed to go where. Cameron also pitched in when his calls had been made. When the kitchen was presentable, Bea dug into the cupboards and freezer and started to cook some supper. They were barely finished eating when the bishop arrived at the door with one of his counselors and the elders' quorum president. They offered genuine compassion, and a willingness to do anything they could. Before they left, the Relief Society president arrived with one of her counselors. A service was planned for Saturday morning, with practically nothing for them to do except show up. Cameron's only concern was Jeff's request that he speak at the service. In his heart he knew it was the right thing to do; he knew that he could express the proper love and respect for Sherry, and he could give the gospel message and perspective that needed to be shared at such a time. But at the same time he felt unequal to the task, considering his own emotional state. He could only pray that the Spirit would guide him.

After the Church representatives left, Jeff brought out his address book, as well as Sherry's, and a list was made of the calls that needed to be made. Using the two phone lines in the apartment, Cameron and Jeff divided the list and called every friend and colleague of Sherry's that they knew of. Some coworkers offered to spread the news through Sherry's office, and they promised to be there.

When it became too late to make phone calls, Cameron talked quietly with Jeff about the financial situation. He made an adequate income, but he was concerned about being able to stay in the same place without Sherry's income to contribute to the rent and utilities. He did say that she'd had some decent life insurance, and he was her beneficiary, just as she had been his. It would help, but until he had a death certificate, he could not collect it. He had heard that certificates would be issued soon, which was a relief, but it could still take time.

The following day, Christy and Bea worked together on kitchen duty and deeper cleaning. Jeff admitted that he felt somehow comforted by the restored order and cleanliness of his surroundings. It was also obvious that Jeff hadn't been eating well, as evidenced by his intense appreciation of the meals they put before him. While the women kept busy with the house, Jeff asked Cameron if he would help him sort through some of Sherry's things. "I know you'll only be here a few days. It has to be done, but I can't do it alone, and . . ." He broke down as he had several times since their arrival, and Cameron told him he'd be happy to help him, and they could cry together—which they did.

Most of Sherry's clothes and nonpersonal things were put into boxes and bags that Jeff said he would donate to charity when he felt ready to let them go. When it came to more personal things—letters, photographs, keepsakes—Cameron and Jeff divided them appropriately as mementos of a woman they had both loved. Looking at a number of Sherry's things laid out on the floor, Jeff said, "I wish . . . we had something to bury . . . something to put a gravestone on . . . a place I could go to . . ."

He broke down once again and Cameron said, "Why couldn't we? If a casket and grave sight would help, then let's do it. She's my sister, and I would be honored to pay the expenses. When you collect the life insurance, you can use it to meet your financial needs. But I think having a casket—even if it's empty—might help us have more closure. And if they . . ." He paused, not wanting to sound insensitive, but he felt compelled to verbalize something they couldn't ignore. "If they actually find . . . some remains, we'll have the casket brought up and put her in it."

Jeff was too overcome to speak, but Cameron sensed his approval of the idea. That afternoon they made quick arrangements for a casket, purchased a burial plot, and ordered a headstone that wouldn't be delivered for some weeks, but at least it was taken care of. While the two of them were driving back to the apartment together, Jeff shared some of the realities of his days of searching for Sherry. Cameron listened compassionately, although he felt a little queasy hearing about the many papers Jeff had filled out concerning Sherry's physical characteristics in order to help rescue workers identify her remains, if any were found. He'd given them dental records and her toothbrush, as well as hair from her hairbrush to be used for DNA matching. Cameron had trouble sleeping again that night. He was deeply troubled with the very idea of such methods of identification being necessary.

Prior to the service, Cameron stood with Jeff and his aunt in a receiving line. He was pleasantly surprised to hear one person after another, for over an hour, tell him what a good woman his sister was.

He heard stories of the encouragement, support, and service she had given to others; how her vivacious personality and innate positive attitude had affected lives for the better. He felt deeply comforted to realize that, in spite of her not living some of the values she had been raised with, she had still applied many Christian principles by her code of giving and serving. For the first time since news had come that she was missing, he imagined her being with his parents, and something warm inside him encouraged him to believe that it was likely true.

As the service began, the bishop—a man who had not even known Sherry—expressed genuine compassion and hope for these people. Beautiful musical numbers were given, along with a eulogy written by a close friend. Cameron felt nervous when it was his turn to speak. He put his hands on both sides of the podium and willed back his emotion with one last, quick prayer that he would be able to speak from the heart, that the Spirit would guide him to put the notes he'd written into words that would touch hearts and offer comfort. He cleared his throat and began with a voice that trembled only slightly. "I come before you at a time of great sorrow and with the prayer that I will be able to express the thoughts of my heart in a way that they may comfort *your* hearts. Never in my wildest imaginings could I have believed that my sister would die as a casualty of war . . . on American soil, far from any military base; a war unlike any other that has ever faced us, or our forefathers, as a people. I have lost loved ones before. In fact, I am now the only remaining member of my immediate family. I recognize the grief I feel, but there is a confusion and heartache at its core that is terribly unfamiliar. I have seen accidents and disease take those I love, but such things just happen. They are often nobody's fault. But this . . . this seems so thoroughly senseless."

Cameron fought to control the emotion creeping into his words, and he swallowed carefully. He focused on the notes he'd scribbled in the middle of the night and attempted to gather his thoughts before he continued. "As a nation comprised of individual Americans, we will never be the same, singularly or collectively. The wounds of hatred and evil are fresh in our hearts and souls, and while wounds may heal, the scars are deeply impressed upon us, and will forever serve as a reminder of what we have lost. As individuals, our losses may vary. As a country, we have lost a sense of security that can never be completely recovered. But with that lost sense of security, we have also lost complacency. We no longer take for granted the freedom and abundance that we as Americans enjoy. For those of us who lost colleagues and loved ones, the wounds go deeper and are more personal. But the very manner of their death has an element of ambiguity—there is no body to touch, and the casket we close and put beneath the ground contains only pieces of our own memories, and items that are no longer significant to this woman who has passed into a world where the tangible objects of our comforts and success mean nothing. Those of us who remain behind grieve, but it is not for Sherry that we should grieve. I testify to you that she is in a better place. Her life goes on, and she will have the opportunity to make choices, and to progress within the boundaries of that world beyond the veil of death. We grieve because we will miss her; we will often wonder how her life might have unfolded had she been able to live it to its fullest. But I feel confident that she crossed to the other side with a huge multitude who shared the horror of whatever their final minutes or hours might have entailed, a horror that has been soothed by the light that met them as they were freed from this earthly existence."

Cameron went on to briefly explain aspects of the plan of salvation, as far as they related to death and what lay beyond it. He bore testimony of the resurrection of the Savior, and stated with conviction his knowledge that peace could be found only through Him who had long ago paid the price for our grief and sorrow.

Glancing over his notes once more, he went on to say, "The news broadcasts of the last week and a half have brought the reality of unspeakable horrors, but they have also brought us countless tales of heroism, and newfound evidences of patriotism for those of us in this generation who were not here to witness our last world war. We have seen much evidence of the good that can come from adversity. We have witnessed and felt the outpouring of love and compassion from a God who has heard our prayers, and answered them through the spirit of patriotism and determination in the heart of every wounded American. As individuals, we have a choice. We can allow this tragedy, and the loss of one we cared for so deeply, to defeat us and break our spirits. Or we can take hold of that patriotism, that determination, that *hope* that we've been blessed with, and we can put one foot in front of the other and press forward as individuals, as family and friends, as communities, and as a nation. We should not let this thwart or destroy our dreams and the great places we will take our lives. But we most certainly should be looking at our lives differently. That's the way Sherry would want it. We should be hugging our children a little tighter. We should be more appreciative of our every friend and loved one. We should evaluate our priorities and perhaps make some adjustments. We should be more focused on living the way the God who created us would have us live. We should serve each other, give to each other, and band together in every big and little way to defend freedom, to overcome prejudice and evil, and to make this country, and this world, a better place. If we don't do this, then the lives lost—including our own sweet Sherry—will have been lost in vain."

Once again he struggled with his emotions as he shared his love for his sister. He bore testimony of his knowledge of a just and loving Father in Heaven who will carry us through if we only turn to Him with humility. And once again he bore witness of life after death, and of the divine sacrifice of the Savior. He concluded in the Savior's name and heard a chorus of amens, spoken with conviction, from a group of people that he knew were predominantly not religious.

Engulfed with an enormity of emotion, Christy sat watching her husband speak at the pulpit, and then return to his seat. The vicarious grief she had felt on behalf of the thousands of people affected by this disaster had become more personalized in the grief she felt for her husband's sister, a woman she had never officially met, but certainly felt that she knew. But the emotional roller coaster she'd ridden since the morning of September eleventh had been buffered by the blanket of gratitude surrounding her. Contemplating how far she had come in the past two years, she felt in awe of this man that God had sent into her life. His strength, his wisdom, even his vulnerability, filled her life more completely than she had ever imagined possible in marriage. But his greatest asset, in her opinion, was his deeply rooted testimony of the gospel, which spurred his integrity, his compassion, and his insight. She felt him meet her eyes from where he sat next to the bishop on the stand in the chapel. They shared a sad smile, and she knew that, somehow, they were going to be all right.

Following the service, the local Relief Society provided a beautiful meal for all who had attended the funeral. Cameron was not surprised, but was deeply comforted by this manifestation of love from complete strangers. He heard many positive comments from Sherry's friends and colleagues about the service and the meal, and he noticed a number of people conversing with the bishop. He couldn't help hoping that this experience may have planted some seeds among people who were in need of the comfort the gospel could bring them.

The flight home was very similar to their flight to New York, and it became evident that people were not going to quickly recover from all that had happened. But for Cameron, he felt more peace in the closure he'd found with his sister's death. And now there was nothing for them to do but move forward.

Once they had returned home and settled back into a routine as far as it was possible, Cameron tried to focus on their sealing in the temple. He called each of the people who had traveled with him from Boston and invited them to the luncheon they would have afterward at the Joseph Smith Memorial Building. He knew it wasn't feasible for any of them to travel this far for such a thing when they really didn't know each other that well, but it gave him an excuse to call them, and he had a good visit with most of them. He was thrilled to learn that Kaniesha was reading the Book of Mormon, and she asked him some questions. And Tom had been contacted by the local missionaries following his call for the free video. He had committed to nothing, but Cameron had good reason to hope that these people's lives might be changed for the better.

He was unable to reach Gary, and he felt concerned, wondering if his wife was back in the hospital. He left more than one message on the machine, and stuck a note in the mail. He'd simply have to keep trying, if only to let this new friend know of his concern, and see if there was anything he could do to help.

Little more than two weeks beyond the day that had shaken the world, Cameron stood in his office, hands in his pockets, looking out the window toward the street below. The images that had robbed him of sleep and peace of mind had lessened in intensity. But he often found himself pondering the losses. At *ground zero* they had barely begun to remove the tons of rubble that had become a hideous grave-yard. While the numbers were still not certain, there were thousands of lives lost, and each of those lives represented many, many more who would be affected by each loss. He recalled reading a report of the bloodiest days in American history. Pearl Harbor had taken 2,388 lives, and it far exceeded anything that had occurred since, including the Oklahoma City bombing, and attacks on American embassies in other countries. The Battle of Antietam in the Civil War had initially claimed about 4,700 lives from both sides, and 3,000 of the wounded later died. And now, just starting into the twenty-first century, America had witnessed an event with casualties nearing those of the bloodiest battle of the Civil War. And while this enemy was ambiguous, unlike any enemy America had ever countered before, the battle lines were very clear. It was a fight between good and evil. God willing, good would prevail.

On a more personal level, Cameron had gotten past the denial, the anger and rage, and he'd adjusted to the reality that his sister was gone. But he felt certain that, like every other American, and many others around the world, he was forever changed. He would never again look at a high-rise, or a jet plane, or the American flag in the same way. He felt grateful for his own second chance at life, and for his friend and colleague being spared. He felt grateful to be living in a nation willing to fight for freedom and peace, just as Captain Moroni and so many other heroes from the past had done. He felt grateful for the evidence that this great nation had turned to God at a time when they needed Him most. Evidence that the nation's new motto had become 'God Bless America' stirred him deeply. He felt more grateful than ever before to have the gospel in his life, to have a living prophet, and to have the Book of Mormon that made this horrible nonsense almost make sense. In spite of all that had happened, and all that had been lost, he could come up with a very long list of what was good in his life—Christy and the children ranking close to the top. But still, there was a heaviness in his heart that he hoped would not ever leave him completely. He never again wanted to take his freedom, his life, his American citizenship for granted. He hoped that the complacency that he and every other American had unwittingly been guilty of would become forever extinct. And he could only pray and hold onto the hope that the years ahead would not bring more heartache too close to home.

When the sorrow threatened to overcome him, Cameron lifted his eyes toward the Angel Moroni atop the temple spire that he could barely see from this angle. Tomorrow he would go to the temple with his sweet wife. That, in itself, represented every reason he had to feel peace and hope. Yes, he concluded in the deepest part of his soul, good *would* prevail.

* * * * *

Kneeling at the altar of the temple, Christy put her hand into Cameron's and looked into his eyes. She recognized a recently familiar sadness there, but the peace beneath his sorrow shone brilliantly—a peace that she shared and understood, in spite of the happenings in a difficult world. The words of the ceremony, and the very reality of being here, surrounded by family and friends, within temple walls and all they represented, put the fears and horrors of the world into perfect perspective. Of course there would be uncertainty and difficulty. But the peace of the gospel, and the Atonement and Resurrection of Jesus Christ put a constant, bright star of hope against the black sky of adversity. And Christy knew that all would be well.

Following the ceremony, everyone met in a room on the top floor of the Joseph Smith Memorial Building, at the other end of the hall from where Cameron had first proposed marriage to Christy. They were met there by family and friends who were unable to attend the temple, many of whom were not members. But Dean and Beth, and many others, had a deep respect for Cameron and Christy's beliefs, and what this day represented for them. Barry and Nicole had even flown from Boston to be there, managing to work in a business trip with the occasion. Seeing them, Cameron marveled at how tragedy could deepen the bonds of friendship. For nearly half an hour they mingled and visited with friends and loved ones, accepting many congratulations. They were nearly ready to be seated and begin the meal when Christy nudged Cameron with her elbow and whispered, "Do you know those people?"

He turned toward the door to see Gary and Amy Reilly, holding hands. Gary wore a suit and tie, and Amy a soft floral dress with a lovely white hat. "Good heavens," Cameron murmured and rushed across the room, pulling Christy along.

Gary smiled when he saw him coming. They met with laughter and a hearty embrace. "I can't believe it," Cameron said. "You came all this way . . . for lunch?"

Gary chuckled and Cameron said to Christy, "Honey, this is Gary Reilly, from Denver, and his wife, Amy."

"Oh, of course," Christy said, shaking each of their hands. "I'm so glad you could come."

"This is my wife, Christina," Cameron said, putting his arm around her.

"Your *forever* wife, now," Gary said. "Right?"

"Right," Cameron said, looking briefly into Christy's eyes. Then he turned to Gary. "I wasn't sure if you got my message. I couldn't reach you, and—"

"Amy's been staying some with her mother, and I've been working hard," Gary explained. He exchanged a glance with his wife that spoke volumes of how they cared for each other. "And at the moment," he added, turning back to Cameron, "the prognosis is good."

"That's great," Cameron said.

"And we didn't just come for lunch," Gary said, "although that certainly helped motivate us."

"Really?" Cameron said, guiding them toward a table where they could be seated.

"Actually, we got here yesterday, and we've spent hours at Temple Square. It's amazing, you know."

"Yes," Cameron said with a chuckle, "I know. The temple gets more beautiful every time you look at it. There's just something about forty years of pioneer craftsmanship."

"Yes, that certainly is impressive," Gary said, "but I don't think it's nearly as impressive as what it represents . . . and what's possible there." He glanced again at his wife, then looked at Cameron with moisture glistening in his eyes. Taking hold of Cameron's hand in a firm grip, he said quietly, "I would never say that what those terrorists did was a good thing. It was unspeakably horrible. But I can never say that I'm not grateful for what it brought into my life. Being rescued from that car rental line in Boston was the best thing that happened to me . . . to us. And I just wanted to be able to look you in the eye and thank you . . . for all you've shared with me that helped me make sense of so many things that never made sense before."

Cameron's voice broke as he replied, "I was just the messenger."

"Well, the message you brought was hope, my friend. And in a world gone mad, there's no message greater than that."

"Amen," Cameron said and embraced his new friend.

Their tears turned to laughter as they parted, then the two men each turned to embrace their wives.

"I love you, Christina Chandler," Cameron whispered in her ear. He drew back and smiled at her. "Thanks for rescuing *me* from that blizzard on Christmas Eve."

"Hey," she said and kissed him quickly, "I was just the messenger."

This book is dedicated to the heroes, the victims,
and every person in the free world whose lives were changed
by the events of September 11, 2001. May you have hope.

* * *

*Wherefore, whoso believeth in God might
with surety hope for a better world . . .*
—ETHER 12:4

About the Author

Anita Stansfield has been writing for more than twenty years, and her best-selling novels have captivated and moved hundreds of thousands of readers with their deeply romantic stories and focus on important contemporary issues. Her interest in creating romantic fiction began in high school, and her work has appeared in national publications. *Someone to Hold* is her nineteenth novel to be published by Covenant.

Anita lives with her husband, Vince, and their five children and two cats in Alpine, Utah.

NEVER
LOOK BACK

Sydney stared resentfully at the legal pad that the bishop had put in front of her. Bishop Middleton continued to distribute the tablets, then addressed the group. "I'm going outside to take care of the livestock. While I'm gone there will be no talking." This comment he directed specifically toward Sydney. "When I'm done I expect to see those pads filled." He moved to the door and put his coat on, then stuck his head back into the living room. "And don't worry about anyone seeing what you write. I'll keep what you tell me strictly confidential." With those words, he opened the front door and walked out into the snow.

Sydney resisted for a few seconds, but as everyone else picked up their legal pads, she scowled and grabbed hers too.

<u>Legal Pad #1</u>

My name is Sydney Cochran, and I am being forced to write this. It is a complete waste of time since I know that putting my miserable life into words can't possibly make any difference. We should be concentrating on the crimes that have been committed and the obviously guilty party, but since I'm outnumbered, I'll play along.

I was born and raised in Eureka, Georgia, a town of about 30,000 people right on the Alabama state line, situated between a U.S. Army base and one of the most popular bass fishing lakes in the southeastern United States. I am thirty-one years old and the only messed-up member of my otherwise perfect family. My father teaches European history at Auburn University and is on the Columbus stake high council. My mother is an accomplished homemaker. My two older sisters graduated from college, married in the temple, and then did their parts toward multiplying and replenishing the earth.

I was different from the very start. My sisters are named Rebecca and Rachel and after having them, my parents thought their family was complete. Then, four years after Rachel's birth, my father was chosen to fill a highly coveted professorship in Auburn's history department. To celebrate, my parents took a two-week trip to

Australia, where I was conceived. Still giddy from my father's professional success and the opportunity to travel, they named me Sydney and called me their little souvenir. However, the novelty of having a baby wore off quickly.

My father's new job included arduous social obligations, and while my sisters were old enough to behave like perfect little ladies, I didn't fit very well into the polite, academic world. My mother still shudders when she tells of lectures I disrupted and concerts ruined by my presence. After I broke a rare Native American artifact at the home of a colleague, I stayed with Grandma Lovell whenever my parents hosted a dinner, attended a seminar, or traveled to a convention. So, for as long as I can remember, I've had my own room at Grandma's.

The Lovells are Baptists, but Mother joined the Church shortly after her marriage to my father. I doubt Grandma was happy about her daughter embracing my father's religion, but she didn't let that affect her relationship with us. Grandma is not a hugging, snugly type of person, but I never questioned her feelings for me. At her house I could watch any television show, regardless of its educational value, my clothes didn't have to match unless we were going into town, she cooked what I liked to eat, and bedtime was negotiable.

The only obligation intrinsic with spending the night at Grandma's was that in the morning I had to pay visits to her immediate neighbors. She would pull my hair into a tight ponytail before I made my rounds and give me instructions like, "Be sure to tell Miss Mayme that her roses are looking particularly lovely this year" or "If Miss Glida Mae is wearing a new dress, say it's very becoming."

Grandma lives in a settled community, and when I was young I thought her neighbors were ancient. From my current, more mature perspective, I realize that they were just middle-aged then. Now they are ancient.

I would begin my morning with Miss Glida Mae Magnanney, who lives in a pink house to the right. Miss Glida Mae has always been partial to floor-length gowns and has large, butterscotch-colored, sausage curls that frame her pudgy face. She claims to have been in several films during the 1940s and whenever I watched an old movie I studied the credits carefully, but never saw her name. I liked to visit her first because she didn't have air-conditioning and by ten o'clock her house was stifling. She usually offered me candy, and her general kookiness was entertaining to a point, but I tried to escape before I started to sweat.

From Miss Glida Mae's I would walk across the street to spend some time with the Warrens. They are devout Auburn fans, and I felt an obligation to like them since my father worked for their favorite university. They painted their garbage cans orange and blue, and had a custom War Eagle license plate. It was even reported that Mr. Warren wore Auburn underwear, although I never witnessed this personally. His wife, Miss Thelma, made fresh cookies every day and always sent some home with me in a foil-wrapped packet.

To their immediate right was a couple from Vermont named Howart. Miss Glida Mae told me that when the Howarts moved to Eureka, the neighborhood welcomed them enthusiastically with casseroles and frequent visits. Then Mrs. Howart informed a delegation from the Baptist Church, who had stopped by to invite them to Sunday services, that they didn't socialize and would prefer to be left alone. I tried to get Grandma to confirm this, but every time I broached the subject, she would just shake her head and mutter under her breath. In spite of their rumored unfriendliness, Grandma insisted that I go by the Howarts' each morning, which only took a few minutes since they rarely answered the doorbell and never let me inside.

I saved my visit to the Camps on the left side of Grandma for last. Miss Mayme Camp was an energetic housekeeper, and if I arrived too early, I would be drafted into helping with chores. However, if I got there after the house was clean and Miss Mayme was safely on the phone, Mr. Camp would be free to take me out back for a two-man game of baseball.

Miss Mayme was concerned about my soul because of my mother's odd determination to raise her children in the Mormon faith. Therefore she often invited me to stay for dinner so she could teach me New Testament scripture verses and Protestant hymns. Every summer she arranged for me to attend Vacation Bible School with the Baptists and could usually convince Grandma to bring me to the semiannual revivals. At these meetings, traveling evangelists predicted awful fates for those who had not been saved, sinners confessed all, and an occasional devil had to be cast out. They were more exciting than anything I'd seen on television, and I looked forward to them almost as much as Christmas.

When I was ten I convinced Grandma to take me by the local YMCA during their boys' baseball registration. I assured her that my parents wouldn't mind me trying out. To their credit, my mother and father attended my games, sitting uncomfortably in the stands. I'm sure they hoped I would outgrow my roughneck ways, but I didn't. I played soccer, basketball, and softball all the way through my junior year in high school.

I always made my parents drop me off at Grandma's after a particularly painful defeat or stunning victory. The Howarts stayed safely in the walls of their quiet home, but when the other neighbors saw us arrive, they found an excuse to come over. If my team lost, Mr. Warren would call the officials names and Grandma would fix biscuits and gravy to comfort me. If we won, Mr. Camp made me describe every play, and Grandma would make a banana pudding to celebrate.

By the end of tenth grade, my GPA was adequate and my athletic ability had me within reach of several college scholarships. My parents no longer complained about attending games and even started a scrapbook for newspaper clippings. Then Craig Cochran entered my life.

There are two wards in Eureka, and right after my sixteenth birthday the boundaries were redrawn, which moved my family from the second to the first ward. Church was not my highest priority, and I didn't really care about the change until that first Sunday. From my slouched, bored position in the back of the chapel, I noticed the Cochran family before we finished the opening song.

Brother Cochran was the weatherman for Channel 8 in Columbus. Every responsible Georgian watches the weather religiously to keep informed about hurricanes blowing up from the Gulf, hot and cold air colliding to create tornadoes any month of the year, rare paralyzing snowstorms, and life-threatening heat indexes. My parents were loyal viewers of Channel 8, so Brother Cochran was like a family friend. My eyes skimmed over Sister Cochran and studied their three sons.

I never thought much about boys except in terms of how fast they could run or how far they could throw a ball, but the Cochran's oldest son was cute enough to make me forget my batting average. He was tall with black hair, bright blue eyes, and a sunburned nose. After a few discreet inquiries I learned that his name was Craig, and his parents were moving permanently into their vacation home on Lake Eureka so that Sister Cochran could have the inspiration of nature to write children's books about a family of chipmunks.

For the first time in my life, I was actually anxious to attend youth activities, and my parents attributed this change of heart to their fervent prayers. In July Craig left on his mission and I watched until his address was posted on the bulletin board. I rewrote my first letter to him at least seven times before I mailed it, and then I waited to see if he would respond. He wrote me back in less than a week and said he had enjoyed my letter and asked me to write again soon.

With that encouragement, I mailed him letters weekly for the next two years. I sent him jokes, misprints from the paper, Halloween candy at Easter, and tacky cards of every variety. I was so obsessed with Craig that I didn't have time for sports or studying. When my senior year began, the school counselor told me that with my grades, the chances of me getting a scholarship, even to a small college, were slim to none. But who cared about college, anyway?

Craig Cochran came home at the end of May, and by that point there was some question as to whether or not I would even graduate. I went to the airport the night he flew in and kept telling myself that no human being could live up to my expectations, but I was wrong. Craig was breathtakingly perfect and hugged me along with his family and friends, then asked if I would come to the stake center where he was going to be released. After the trip to Columbus he insisted that I accompany him to an open house in his honor. Throughout the evening he kept me close to his side, sometimes even taking my hand in his, clearly defining our relationship to other guests.

He attended my graduation and then for the next few weeks he called me every day. He took me hiking and fishing and out to dinner at the waterside resorts around Lake Eureka. My parents were mildly alarmed by the relationship and advised us not to get too serious. Craig's father was in Columbus most of the time, and his mother was too busy writing about chipmunks to notice that he was dating me exclusively.

Craig got a letter in July saying that he had been accepted at BYU for the fall term, and my father took us all out for dinner to celebrate. Afterward Craig and I drove to the lake. Then, as we looked out at the lights of Eureka, he asked me to marry him. I knew I was very young, but I felt so wise. I said yes and, in spite of my parents' strong objections, we were married in August in the Atlanta Temple.

For the first few months of our marriage we were both busy getting settled into our new lives in Provo. I had never been west of the Mississippi, had never seen a real mountain or streets named after four-digit numbers. By the time I learned my way around, I was pregnant.

I don't know exactly when Craig's discontentment began. Later he told me that he realized he had made a terrible mistake almost instantly. At first he tried to talk to his parents, who told him no marriage was perfect and that over the years he would learn to be content.

Our oldest son, Ryan, was born the next fall, and Trent came along less than two years later. Craig was gone a lot, either at the library studying or attending extra classes or lectures. He wasn't very romantic, but I blamed it on his schedule and fatigue. I threw myself into motherhood, and the boys kept me too busy to worry about Craig or our relationship.

Craig graduated from BYU and was accepted into the medical program at the University of Utah. When his parents came for graduation they bought us a small house near the campus in Salt Lake, and I thought I would die of happiness. I had a brilliant, handsome husband, two beautiful boys, and a home of my own. I stayed up late at night to watch *Home and Garden* on TV and used the ideas I saw to decorate our house.

Craig took a nights-and-weekends job at the hospital in addition to his classes and was rarely home. We would go for days without even seeing him and he missed church often, but since he was working hard for our future, I tried not to complain about his long hours. Sarah was born the year Ryan started kindergarten, and as Craig's residency drew to a close, he was offered several jobs but accepted a position at Lakeside Hospital in Eureka so we could go home.

During the Christmas break that year we returned to Georgia for the first time since our marriage. Both families were pleased about our plans to move and offered to help us prepare. The Cochrans took us on tours of countless neighborhoods looking for a house, but Craig's parents didn't like anything that was available and finally insisted that we build. They bought a lot for us near them, then we met with the developer and chose a floor plan. The developer said that construction would begin as soon as the weather permitted.

After the holidays we went back to Utah for Craig to complete his residency. By the time school ended for the summer there were decisions to be made about our new house on almost a daily basis. To speed things up, Craig suggested that the kids and I move in with his parents for a few weeks so I could work with the contractors while he sold our house in Salt Lake.

When the house was finished, Craig's mother helped me decorate it, insisting on all new furniture. We closed on August 15, and Craig started his job at Lakeside Hospital the next day. When he came home for dinner that first night, neither of us knew what to say. It had been months, maybe years, since we had eaten a regular family dinner together. I felt the awkwardness but was sure that after we got used to each other again things would be fine.

I also thought that once we were back home Craig would start coming to church, but he didn't. Every week he had a new excuse and finally I just stopped asking. Then shortly after Christmas I came in from the grocery store and found Craig sitting alone in the living room. He said the kids were with a neighbor and he had something important to discuss with me.

I thought maybe he didn't like his job or the new house or living in Eureka. Instead Craig told me he wanted a divorce. He said he was desperately unhappy in our marriage. It was not my fault, he assured me. We were just not right for each other. He had tried to "tough it out" but he had recently met someone else. She was a nurse at the hospital, and while their relationship could still be classified as a close friendship, he wanted to make a clean break with me so that he would be free if marriage became a consideration at some point in the future. Therefore, he had rented an apartment near the hospital and planned to move out that very night.

I cried and begged and pleaded and promised to change anything, but he was firm in his decision. I called his parents to come over and talk him out of it, and he sat in silence while they told him all the reasons he shouldn't throw our marriage away. Then the bishop arrived. After listening to my tearful narrative, he said that there was no need to rush into anything. He recommended that Craig stay at his parents' house for a few days and then we could talk again.

Finally Craig sat forward and addressed us all. "It's not a matter of trying harder. I don't love Sydney and I never did. When I could stay away from home a lot I was able to deal with it. But now . . . " He waved around the brand-new, beautifully furnished room. "Sydney can have the house. I'll agree to whatever alimony and child support she needs. I'm not trying to ruin her life; I just want a chance at happiness."

What was there left to say? His parents told me he would come to his senses. The bishop told me if I prayed and read my scriptures, things would work out. Craig told me the name of his attorney and recommended that I get one of my own. I dragged my feet for several days hoping that Craig would realize his mistake. I thought he'd miss the clothes I kept washed and folded in his drawers, the nutritious meals I put on the table, the children, and the well-ordered life we had built together. I thought he'd come back, but he didn't.

During our marriage, Craig never had much time for the children, and probably didn't even know what grade they were in. But after he left us he called them every night, bought them gifts, stopped by their schools and introduced himself to their teachers, and occasionally even suffered through lunchroom food with them. His message was clear. He loved the children. The only member of the family he wanted a divorce from was me.

The day the papers were delivered was unquestionably the worst of my life. Up until then, it had all been like a nightmare that I just had to work my way through. The words, typed neatly on fresh white paper, made it terribly real.

As promised, he was giving me the house and the van we had recently purchased. He offered a generous monthly living allowance and half of our meager savings. All he asked in return was a liberal custody agreement. I had read articles about divorce, urging that children not be used as pawns, and couldn't imagine any reasonable parent doing such a thing. But when I realized that Craig was really going to break his covenants and promises to me, I wanted revenge. And since the children were all that mattered to him, they became my only weapon.

I found myself a lawyer and told her to demand everything Craig had offered and in return give him the minimum visitation rights allowed by law. The new papers gave Craig the third Saturday each month, Christmas Day from noon until six and three weeks in the summer. His lawyer called the proposal absurd, but I held firm. If Craig got a divorce, it would be on my terms. I never expected him to accept, but finally he did.

My parents had moved to Columbus, but they visited me frequently. My sisters came, too, offering words of comfort and support. But everything they said sounded like different variations of the basic idea that I had somehow ruined my marriage. If I had been a better wife, Craig wouldn't have looked to someone else and now I had to live with the consequences.

On the day we met at my lawyer's office to sign the final papers, I knew I looked haggard and defeated. Craig, on the other hand, looked better than he had in years. He had gained a few pounds, he seemed rested, and his nose was sunburned. I could have easily killed him.

I left the lawyer's office feeling utterly worthless, so I turned toward the one place where I had always found acceptance and solace. Grandma met me on the back porch and led me to the kitchen table. While she rolled out buttermilk biscuits, Miss Mayme and Mr. Camp came in. Miss Mayme said that she was morally opposed to divorce but would continue to pray for us anyway. Mr. Camp sat beside me and patted my hand awkwardly.

Miss Glida Mae arrived at this point and told me that after Humphrey Bogart had divorced her she thought she had no reason to live, but in time she had gotten over him just as I would with Craig. Miss Mayme told Mr. Camp to escort the actress home so she could take another dose of her medication. As they left, they passed the Warrens, dropping by to offer their support.

When Mr. Camp returned, we sat around the table and discussed my future. I was determined not to accept anything from Craig. Not the house, not alimony, not even child support. To this end, Grandma suggested I move in with her. I didn't want to be more of a burden than absolutely necessary, so I agreed on the condition that she would let me buy the groceries, pay the utilities, and handle the housework.

Mr. Warren said that even though living with Grandma would save me money, in order to buy groceries and pay the power bill I still needed a source of income. I told them that I had no special skills but wanted flexible hours so I could be home when the kids were. This was a tall order and everyone was quiet for a few minutes. Then Mr. Camp said the clubs on Lake Eureka were always advertising for wait-resses, and he had heard that they earned good tips.

Miss Mayme was horrified at the idea of me working in an establishment that sold alcohol, but Mr. Camp pointed out that I would be *serving* the beverages, not *drinking* them. A newspaper was located and calls were made. A quick investigation determined that the best hourly wage and greatest tip potential was available at a large, new dinner club called The Lure. I could work mostly during the hours when the children were asleep, and I couldn't help but smile at the public humiliation Craig would suffer when it was known that his ex-wife was working at a club to support his children.

The Lure offered a training course to interested applicants for a fee of $120, and this amount would be refunded to anyone who was actually hired. All the neighbors thought this was a very good deal and encouraged me to sign up immediately. Since I had exactly $23 in my purse, I nodded and silently abandoned the idea.

The old folks began formulating a plan for moving our possessions to Grandma's. Mr. Warren offered the use of his pickup truck and Miss Thelma said she'd call her son to provide additional manpower. I left my children in Grandma's care and led the way to Craig's house with Mr. Warren and Mr. Camp following close behind me in the pickup. Mr. Warren's son met us there and I showed them the things that needed to be transferred. When we left with the last load, I put my keys to the house and the van on the kitchen counter without a note of explanation. Then I climbed into the truck and sat between Mr. Warren and Mr. Camp on the drive back to Grandma's. I knew Craig would hate it that his children were living in my grandmother's old neighborhood, leaving their schools and making friends all over again.

I informed the new principals that allowing Craig access to the children during school hours violated our custody arrangement, so he couldn't meet with teachers or eat in the cafeteria. Even though Craig had never been a particularly good father, I knew that the kids loved him and I regretted the necessity of my actions. But the whole mess was his fault and I hoped that someday they would understand. If I redoubled my efforts and became the "perfect mother" surely I could compensate for Craig's absence from their lives.

When Craig finally found us at Grandma's house, I made him stand on the front porch, pointing out that he wasn't scheduled for a visit until a week from Saturday at eight in the morning. He started to argue, but I reminded him that this was the life he had chosen, since he had been so unhappy married to me. His eyes held mine for a few seconds, then he turned and walked away in defeat.

I have always been active in the Church, but after Craig left me I found going to my meetings difficult. I felt like such a failure and was uncomfortable around the ward members. Ironically, Craig's decision to end our marriage was followed closely by a new interest in religion and he started attending regularly. There was no way I was going to sit in the same chapel with him and our children like one big happy broken family, so I quit going to church altogether.

Our move to Grandma's house placed us in the second ward boundaries, and although I hated to inflict more change on my children, I thought it might be easier to adjust to my divorced status in a ward where I wouldn't have to worry about seeing Craig. So I asked that our records be transferred to the second ward. But the next Sunday as I dressed for church, I thought about going through the whole story with a new bishop and started feeling ill. Then I imagined the reunion with members of the second ward, who had known me since I was a little girl. They had been my Primary teachers and Young Women advisors. They had taught me to follow the pathway to lasting joy and to choose the right. I couldn't face them now that my life was irretrievably ruined. So each Sunday I took Grandma to the Baptist Church and dropped my children off at the second ward chapel, then went back to sit alone in the empty house until it was time to pick them up.

Shortly after our move to Grandma's, I found an envelope addressed to me in the mailbox. There was no postage or return address, so I knew that one of the neighbors had put it there. Inside I found six crisp twenty-dollar bills and an application for The Lure's waitressing course. The next day I enrolled in the class and a month later had a job at the biggest dinner club on Lake Eureka.